Adela Rimbon

The

BARBARA CARTLAND

Collection

The
BARBARA CARTLAND
Collection

Volume 1

Two Hearts in Hungary
A Theatre of Love
Too Precious to Lose

CHANCELLOR
PRESS

Two Hearts in Hungary first published in Great Britain
in 1991 by Mandarin Paperbacks
A Theatre of Love first published in Great Britain
in 1991 by Mandarin Paperbacks
Too Precious to Lose first published in Great Britain
in 1991 by Mandarin Paperbacks

This collected volume first published in Great Britain
in 1992 by Chancellor Press
an imprint of
Reed International Books Limited
Michelin House
81 Fulham Road
London SW3 6RB

ISBN 1 85152 209 3

Printed in Great Britain by The Bath Press

CONTENTS

ABOUT THE AUTHOR

Barbara Cartland, the world's most famous romantic novelist, who is also an historian, playwright, lecturer, political speaker and television personality, has now written over 540 books and sold over 600 million copies all over the world.

She has also had many historical works published and has written four autobiographies as well as the biographies of her mother and that of her brother, Ronald Cartland, who was the first Member of Parliament to be killed in the last war. This book has a preface by Sir Winston Churchill and has just been published with an introduction by the late Sir Arthur Bryant.

"Love at the Helm" a novel written with the help and inspiration of the late Earl Mountbatten of Burma, Great Uncle of His Royal Highness The Prince of Wales, is being sold for the Mountbatten Memorial Trust.

She has broken the world record for the last sixteen years by writing an average of twenty-three books a year. In the Guinness Book of Records she is listed as the world's top-selling author.

Miss Cartland in 1978 sang an Album of Love Songs with the Royal Philharmonic Orchestra.

In private life Barbara Cartland, who is a Dame of Grace of the Order of St. John of Jerusalem, Chairman of the St. John Council in Hertfordshire and Deputy President of the St. John Ambulance Brigade, has fought for better conditions and salaries for Midwives and Nurses.

She championed the cause for the Elderly in 1956 invoking a Government Enquiry into the "Housing Conditions of Old People".

In 1962 she had the Law of England changed so that Local Authorities had to provide camps for their own Gypsies. This has meant that since then thousands and thousands of Gypsy children have been able to go to School which they had never been able to do in the past, as their caravans were moved every twenty-four hours by the Police.

There are now fourteen camps in Hertfordshire and Barbara Cartland has her own Romany Gypsy Camp called Barbaraville by the Gypsies.

Her designs "Decorating with Love" are being sold all over the U.S.A. and the National Home Fashions League made her in 1981 "Woman of Achievement".

Barbara Cartland's book "Getting Older, Growing Younger" has been published in Great Britain and the U.S.A. and her fifth Cookery Book, "The Romance of Food" is now being used by the House of Commons.

In 1984 she received at Kennedy Airport, America's Bishop Wright Air Industry Award for her contribution to the development of aviation. In 1931 she and two R.A.F. Officers thought of, and carried the first aeroplane-towed glider air-mail.

During the War she was Chief Lady Welfare Officer in Bedfordshire looking after 20,000 Service men and women. She thought of having a pool of Wedding Dresses at the War Office so a Service Bride could hire a gown for the day.

She bought 1,000 secondhand gowns without coupons for the A.T.S., the W.A.A.F.s and the W.R.E.N.S. In 1945 Barbara Cartland received the Certificate of Merit from Eastern Command.

In 1964 Barbara Cartland founded the National Association for Health of which she is the President, as a front for all the Health Stores and for any product made as alternative medicine.

This has now a £650,000,000 turnover a year, with one-third going in export.

In January 1988 she received "La Medaille de Vermeil de la Ville de Paris", (the Gold Medal of Paris). This is the highest award to be given by the City of Paris for ACHIEVEMENT – 25 million books sold in France.

In March 1988 Barbara Cartland was asked by the Indian Government to open their Health Resort outside Delhi. This is almost the largest Health Resort in the world.

Barbara Cartland was made a Dame of the Order of the British Empire in the 1991 New Year's Honours List, by Her Majesty The Queen for her contribution to literature and also for her years of work for the community.

Two Hearts in Hungary

AUTHOR'S NOTE

When I visited Budapest at Easter in 1987 I found it one of the most beautiful cities in Europe.

At the same time, everything was very different from when the Empress Elisabeth of Austria found it the joy and delight of her heart.

During the Revolution, as is inevitable, much of the inside of the Palace had been gutted, but it has now become a Museum.

The Karolyi Palace was pulled down in 1933 and a great number of the old houses have been lost.

Although there appears to be no poverty, I was aware of the constrictions that being behind the Iron Curtain imposes on the Hungarians, who have always loved to be free.

As I was driving along beside the Danube with exquisitely beautiful views on each side of the road I asked:

"Where are the horses? It seems extraordinary to come to Hungary and not see horses!"

"You are now in the Holiday Area," I was informed, "and you have just left the City, which is the Business Area. The next area is Agricultural and after that, a long way away, you will be able to see some of our horses."

I can imagine nothing could be more frustrating to an Hungarian, when horses have always been as much a part of his life as his family.

When I left Hungary my passport was inspected three times at the Airport by soldiers wearing large pistols at their belts.

I can only assume that they were ensuring that I was not a Hungarian trying to escape!

Chapter One

Lady Aletha Ling ran into the house, across the hall and into the Breakfast Room.

She knew she was late, but it had been such a wonderful morning.

She had therefore ridden for longer than she intended.

As she entered the room her father the Duke of Buclington looked up and she said quickly:

"I am so sorry to be late, Papa. Do forgive me, but it was so lovely in the sunshine that I forgot the time."

Her father smiled and Aletha saw with relief that he was not annoyed.

In fact he looked very pleased and she wondered what was the reason.

She helped herself from the side-table on which stood a row of entrée dishes.

They contained fish, sausages, kidneys, eggs and fresh mushrooms.

Then as she sat down at the table her father said:

"I have received some very good news!"

"Good news, Papa? From whom?"

"As it happens from the Empress of Austria!"

Aletha put down her fork and exclaimed:

"Do you mean she has accepted your invitation?"

"She has," the Duke said with satisfaction. "Her Majesty is coming here for a week before she goes to Cottesbrook Park in Northamptonshire."

Aletha gave an exclamation before she said:

"So she is going to hunt with the Pytchley."

"She is," the Duke said, "and undoubtedly Earl Spencer will be delighted!"

Aletha was remembering that two years ago the Empress Elizabeth had rented Easton Neston at Towcester.

She had wanted to hunt with the famous Bicester and the Duke of Grafton's hounds.

To say she caused a sensation was to put it mildly.

The English had not believed the stories of her horsemanship, thinking that anyone as beautiful as the Empress would only be a 'Park-Rider'.

In fact it was whispered that the two picked horsemen, Colonel Hunt and Captain Bay Middleton, who were instructed to give Elizabeth a lead, were not very pleased about the assignment.

"What is an Empress to me?" Captain Middleton asked the Duke. "I will do it, but I would rather be on my own."

He took back his words the moment he met the Empress.

Himself one of the best riders in England, he recognised her brilliance on a horse besides her incomparable beauty as a woman.

He had fallen deeply in love.

Young though she was at the time, Aletha had the idea that her father also had lost his heart to the irresistible Empress.

The Duke too was an outstanding rider.

After the Empress had returned to Austria she had invited him to stay with her.

He had returned admiring her even more than he had done when she was in England.

Aletha guessed that he had been very anxious that his invitation to Ling Park should be accepted.

The tension of waiting had certainly made him somewhat disagreeable these last weeks.

But now at last the reply had arrived.

"I am so glad for you, Papa," Aletha said, "and it will be very exciting for me to meet the Empress."

Two years ago she had only been sixteen.

She had therefore not been asked to any of the parties which were given for the Empress.

Nor had she been able to go out hunting with her father.

She had in fact been at School the whole time the Empress was in England.

When Aletha returned to Ling for Christmas everybody, including the Duke, was still talking about her.

She could understand that the Empress had become his ideal woman.

He had been very lonely after her mother died.

Aletha suspected there were quite a number of women only too willing to try to make him happy.

But he had busied himself with his estates, his horses and, of course, his daughter.

There was no doubt that the Duke loved Aletha and he hated being parted from her.

He had sent her to a Finishing School simply because it was the right thing to do.

Only now, when she was to make her debut this Season, was she able to be with him day after day, as they both wanted.

The Duke had his own pack of hounds.

Aletha as she ate her breakfast, guessed that he was thinking what were the best days' hunting they would be able to give their distinguished guest.

Then suddenly the Duke put down the letter he had been holding in his hand and said:

"I know what I must do! I cannot imagine why I did not think of it before!"

"What is that, Papa?" Aletha asked.

"When she stayed at Easton Neston the Empress brought her entire stable from Hungary."

"I had no idea of that, Papa."

"We want more horses – of course we want more horses," the Duke said, "and I will buy them in Hungary."

Aletha's eyes lit up.

"That is what I have always wanted you to have, Papa," she cried. "Besides the Empress loves Hungary more than any place in the world, and the horses she rides come from there."

"She may *ride* them," the Duke said, "but we are going to *hunt* them, and I am determined to have the very best."

"But of course," Aletha agreed.

She knew her father"s stable was already full of superb horses and his racing-stable was outstanding.

At the same time, there was always room for more.

She herself had always longed to ride the fiery, swift Hungarian horses that had captured the imagination of Europe.

"If you are going to Hungary, then of course, Papa, you must take me with you," Aletha said.

The Duke sighed.

13

"I wish I could do that," he said, "but you know I have to leave next week for Denmark."

Aletha gave a cry.

"I had forgotten that! Oh Papa, must you go?"

"How can I refuse?" the Duke asked. "I am to represent Her Majesty, and she was talking to me about it only two days ago."

"It would be much more fun to go to Hungary!" Aletha said.

"I agree with you," her father replied. "But it is impossible, so Heywood will have to go for me."

James Heywood was the Duke's Manager.

But in a rather different relationship than was usual for men in that position.

To begin with he was a gentleman.

Secondly, he had been outstandingly brilliant as an amateur rider, winning a great number of races on his own horses.

Unfortunately, he had lost almost all his money through bad speculation.

He was therefore forced to work for his living rather than just enjoy himself by riding.

It was the Duke's father who had realised Heywood"s capabilities and had employed him nearly twenty years ago.

James Heywood was getting on to be an elderly man, but his eye for a horse was still as keen as it had ever been.

The Duke, who was always extremely busy, had trusted him to buy most of the horses he possessed.

"Yes, Heywood must certainly go," he said as if he was thinking aloud. "We shall want eight or ten outstanding horses besides those we already possess."

"I suppose we shall have time to train them to the English countryside, Aletha questioned, "and to acclimatise them by the Autumn?"

Her father smiled.

"Shall I say we will do our damndest!" he replied. "I shall look forward to the Empress's delight when she sees what we have provided for her."

There was a look in her father's eyes when he spoke of the Empress which Aletha recognised.

She wished now as she had wished before that he could find somebody to take the place of her mother.

She knew that she personally would feel jealous because she wanted him to herself but she longed for him to be happy.

The Duke was still a very handsome and attractive man.

He had married young and his son, who was now twenty-three, had been born the following year.

Because his wife was not strong there was a gap of five years before Aletha arrived.

The Duke had not yet reached his fiftieth birthday.

As he was extremely athletic he had the figure of a young man, even though there were a few grey hairs at his temples.

"It will be lovely for Papa to have the Empress here," Aletha told herself unselfishly.

However she could not help thinking it very sad that she and her father could not go to Hungary together.

It would certainly have been an adventure and one she would have greatly enjoyed.

She understood however that he could not refuse to do what the Queen required of him.

After that the Season would be in full swing.

There would be a thousand Social events in which the Duke would be involved.

Also as a débutante she was to have a Ball in London and be presented at Buckingham Palace.

"I must get in touch with Heywood at once," the Duke was saying. "Is he here or is he at Newmarket?"

Aletha thought for a moment.

"I am almost sure he is here, Papa. I saw him two days ago, and I know he is going to Newmarket next week."

"Then I will send for him – send for him immediately!" the Duke said. "What are we waiting for?"

He rang the gold bell which stood on the table beside his elbow.

The door was opened.

As was traditional, the servants were not in the room during breakfast.

Bellew the Butler appeared almost instantly and the Duke said: "Send a groom as quickly as you can for Mr. Heywood!"

"Very good, Your Grace!"

He responded to the urgency in the Duke's voice by moving from the room more quickly than he usually did.

As he left the Duke said:

15

"I am just wondering if we should have the 'Queen's Suite' redecorated?"

"I think it is unnecessary, Papa," Aletha replied. "You had it done two years ago for Princess Alexandra, and also the rooms occupied by the Prince of Wales. They have hardly been used since."

"I suppose not," the Duke agreed, "and we both know that all the Empress will be interested in is our stables."

He spoke complacently.

They were both aware that the stables at Ling were outstanding and the envy of every other Landowner in the County.

"This will certainly delight our huntsmen," the Duke went on. "They have been rather downcast recently by being overshadowed by the Bicester, and they will certainly be piqued that this year the Empress has chosen the Pytchley."

"That will give them an excellent reason for polishing themselves up," Aletha said, "and I will need a new riding-habit!"

"I suppose from Busvine, the most expensive Tailor in London!" the Duke smiled.

"Of course and you, Papa, will need some new boots from Maxwell."

"I hate new boots!" the Duke complained. "My old ones are very comfortable."

"They are not smart enough," Aletha insisted.

She got up from the table as she spoke and kissed her father's cheek.

"I am so glad for your sake, Papa, that the Empress is coming. I know it will make you happy, and all the smart gentlemen in London who give themselves airs will be green with envy!"

The Duke laughed.

"You flatter me! You know as well as I do, my dearest, that the Empress is coming for the horses – not for me!"

"Now you are being mock-modest, Papa," Aletha teased, "and it is well-known that the Empress loves handsome men! A little bird told me that when you were in Vienna she danced with you every night, and many more times than she danced with anybody else."

"I cannot imagine from where you get all this nonsensical gossip!" the Duke complained.

But he was obviously pleased with himself.

Aletha thought it would be impossible for any woman not to find him attractive.

Later in the day the Duke told Aletha what instructions he had given to Mr. Heywood.

As he did so she was regretting even more that her father could not go to Hungary and take her there with him.

She had read about the beauty of Budapest and the wonders of the Steppes where the horses galloped.

She had also heard of magnificent Palaces built by the Hungarian aristocrats.

They, she had been told, were the most handsome and attractive men in Europe.

If this was true she could understand why the Empress preferred the Hungarians to the rather prosaic and stolid Austrians.

In fact, everyone knew she was very unhappy in Austria and only felt free and unrestrained when she was in Hungary.

The magnetism of the country drew her.

But there were also stories of handsome, hard-riding men.

They told her in words that were poetical and as beautiful as the country itself how much they loved her.

Aletha was very innocent.

She had not yet learnt of the *affaires de coeur* which were common in London amongst the Marlborough House set following the example of The Prince of Wales.

She had always been interested in the stories of the Empress of Austria and her overwhelming beauty.

She had therefore learnt a great deal about her simply by listening to her father's guests.

Of course the servants also talked incessantly about the Empress after she had visited England.

The gossip of the Servants' Hall was something Aletha's mother, if she had been alive, would have disapproved of her daughter hearing.

In 1874 the Empress had visited the Duke of Rutland at Belvoir Castle and hunted for the first time on English soil.

One of the housemaids from the Castle was now employed at Ling.

Emily, for that was the girl's name, talked of nothing but the beauty of the Empress and Aletha learned a great deal from her.

Also, although he did not mean it, from her father.

"The Queen, accompanied by John Brown," she heard him say

17

to one of their guests, "called at Ventnor where the Empress had taken a house."

"I hear she was there," the Earl replied, "because her daughter was ill, and sea-bathing was thought to be good for her."

"That is right," the Duke agreed. "But I am told that John Brown, of all people, was dazzled by the Empress's beauty!"

There was a great deal of laughter at this.

Aletha knew it was because John Brown was a rather dour Scottish gillie who was attached to Queen Victoria.

Because he was Her Majesty's favourite he was often rude to the Courtiers and Statesmen in a way they resented.

When the laughter subsided the Duke's guest said:

"John Brown may have been bowled over, but little Valeria was terrified of the Queen. In fact, she said: 'I have never seen such a fat lady!'

There was more laughter, but Aletha, listening to the conversation was interested only in what was said about the beautiful Empress.

There was a great deal more gossip when she came to England again two years ago.

Then, needless to say, everybody talked about her association with Captain Bay Middleton, and the fact that the Empress was always in high spirits and quite untiring.

She had attended every Steeple-Chase in the neighbourhood, and after one competition had awarded a silver cup.

It was then that people began to speculate as to whether it was the hunt or the man with whom she was hunting that made her seem more beautiful than she had been before.

Aletha had met Captain Middleton with her father.

She could therefore understand why the Empress admired him so much.

He was thirty, tall, good-looking with red-brown hair and a dark complexion.

He was called "Bay" after the famous horse of that name which had won the Derby in 1836.

Bay Middleton had been invited to Godollo for the hunting and so was Aletha's father.

Aletha had prayed at the time that one day she might go with him.

Now the Empress was actually coming to Ling!

She knew nothing could be more thrilling for her father, herself and everybody in the house and on the estate.

There was no doubt that Mr. Heywood was excited when he heard the news.

"I was going to talk to Your Grace," he said to the Duke, "about some horses that are coming up for sale at Tattersall's this week. But if we are to buy Hungarian bloodstock, it will be unnecessary."

"Why do we not have both?" the Duke asked. "And if you leave for Hungary at the same time as I go to Denmark, there will still be time to have them in perfect trim by the time the Empress arrives."

"You know there is nothing I would enjoy more, Your Grace, than spending your money!" Mr. Heywood remarked.

The Duke laughed.

News of the Empress's proposed visit in the Autumn ran like wildfire through the house, the estate, the villages and the County.

The following days there were endless callers.

They had really come just to ask if it was true that the Empress intended to stay at Ling.

"It is quite true," Aletha said over and over again.

She waited to see the surprise, excitement and expression of envy which sprang to the callers' eyes.

Despite her assurance that nothing needed doing to the Suite the Empress would occupy, her father had already given orders that some improvements should be made.

The gold leaf on the ceilings and dados was to be touched up.

"How long are you going to be in Denmark, Papa?" Aletha asked when he began to arrange for his things to be packed.

His medals and decorations also had to be taken from the safe.

"I am afraid it will be at least two weeks, my dearest," he answered, "I wish I could take you with me."

"I wish you could," Aletha said. "It will be very dull here without you."

"Your Cousin Jane is coming to stay," the Duke replied.

Aletha made a little grimace but she did not say anything.

Cousin Jane was over sixty and slightly deaf.

She lived only a few miles away, and was only too willing to come to Ling to chaperon Aletha whenever she was asked to do so.

At the same time, she was undoubtedly a bore.

Aletha knew that her father was careful not to have Cousin Jane to stay when he was at home.

However, there was one consolation.

She could escape from listening to Cousin Jane's constant complaints about her health by going riding.

Aletha had once suggested another and younger relative should chaperon her, but found she was a very bad horsewoman.

She became very resentful if those who were riding with her went ahead, leaving her behind.

It was not the same as having her father there to ride with her.

Whenever he was at home there were amusing people turning up to see him day after day.

There were also Point-to-Points and Steeple-Chases which took place in the vicinity.

"Do not be away too long, Papa!" she begged.

"Not one minute more than I have to," the Duke replied. "Much as I like the Danes, I find the ceremonial visits and the endless speeches that go with them extremely boring!"

"Surely the Queen could find somebody else to send in your place?" Aletha suggested crossly.

The Duke's eyes twinkled.

"Her Majesty likes to be represented by someone who looks the part!"

Aletha laughed.

"Which you certainly do, Papa! In fact, I suspect that as usual you will leave behind you a great number of broken hearts, and this time it will be Danish ones!"

"I cannot think where you get these ideas!" her father replied.

At the same time she knew he rather enjoyed the compliment.

The day before the Duke left, Mr. Heywood arrived for a last word about the horses, before he too left the next morning for Hungary on his mission for the Duke.

They talked about them all the afternoon.

Finally Mr. Heywood stayed for dinner, sending a groom to his house so that he could change into his evening-clothes.

When Aletha came down wearing one of the pretty new gowns which had been bought for her début in London he said:

"You will undoubtedly, Lady Aletha, be the Belle of every Ball you attend, just as I remember your mother being many years ago!"

"I shall never be as lovely as Mama," Aletha answered, "but I will certainly do my best not to disgrace Papa as his only daughter."

"You will never do that!" Mr. Heywood replied.

He spoke with a sincerity she liked.

She knew he admired her, and it was somehow very consoling.

She was always afraid she would not live up to the reputation of the beautiful Lings who all down the centuries had been acclaimed for their beauty.

They had been painted by every famous artist of their time.

In the Van Dyck Gallery at Ling there were portraits to which she bore a recognisable resemblance.

Also to those by Gainsborough, Sir Joshua Reynolds and Romney which hung in the Drawing-Rooms or on the stairs.

"I am certainly up against some very stiff competition!" Aletha thought.

Yet she knew that if Mr. Heywood admired her she need not be as nervous as she had been two or three years ago.

Then she had gone through what she always referred to as her 'Ugly stage'.

She was very conscious that her father's friends had said:

"Oh, is this Aletha? I always expected she would look like her mother who I thought was one of the loveliest people I had ever seen."

They had not meant to be unkind.

At the same time, Aletha had prayed every night that she would grow more beautiful.

Then, almost like a miracle, her prayers had been answered.

Now she could definitely see, when she looked in her mirror, a distinct resemblance to her mother and to the other beautiful Duchesses.

But she was still apprehensive.

Later in the evening, when Mr. Heywood had gone, Aletha said to her father:

"I hope, Papa, Mr. Heywood is right, and when I appear in London people will admire me."

"What you mean by 'people' is men!" the Duke said. "I can assure you, my darling, that you are very lovely now, and will be even more so as you grow older."

"Do you really . . mean that . . Papa?"

"I do," the Duke answered, "and I am already looking round to find you a husband."

Aletha stiffened and stared at him in astonishment.

"A . . h . . husband?" she stammered.

21

"Of course," the Duke said. "If your mother was here I know she would be as anxious as I am that you should make a brilliant marriage, and with somebody we would welcome as a son-in-law."

Aletha was silent for a moment.

Then she said in a small voice:

"I think . . Papa, I would . . rather find . . my own husband."

The Duke shook his head.

"That is impossible!"

"But . . why?" Aletha asked.

"Because in Royal and noble families like ours marriages are always arranged discreetly but definitely."

He paused before he added:

"As my only daughter I shall be very particular as to whom you will marry, and determined it will be somebody who will, in common parlance, 'fit in'."

"But, Papa, suppose I do not . . love him?"

"Love usually comes after marriage and I promise you, my precious daughter, I will find you a man with whom I am quite certain you will fall in love."

"B . . but . . suppose," Aletha said in a small voice, "he does not . . fall in love with me and only . . wants me because I am . . your daughter?"

Her father made a little gesture with his hand.

"That, I am afraid, is inevitable. A man, if he is an aristocrat, of course hopes he will fall in love in the same way as I fell in love with your mother."

It was as if he was looking back in time before he went on:

"But he usually accepts what the French call a 'mariage de convenance' simply because 'blue blood' should be matched with 'blue blood' especially if his bride is beautiful enough to carry on the line in the way that is should be."

Aletha was silent.

Then she said:

"I think that sounds very cold-blooded, and rather like being a piece of goods on the counter of a shop."

"It is not really like that," her father said a little sharply. "I promise you, my dearest, I will not make you marry anyone you do not like."

22

"I want to . . love someone," Aletha said softly, "and I want him to . . love me for . . myself."

"A great many men will love you for yourself, but when it is a question of marriage, I think I am far more likely to choose the right man to ensure your future happiness than anyone you could choose for yourself at your age."

"What do you mean by that?" Aletha asked.

"I mean," the Duke replied, "that a young girl is easily deceived by a man who has the 'gift of the gab' as it is called."

He thought before he went on:

"Honeyed words do not always come easily from somebody who is self-controlled and has been brought up not to 'wear his heart on his sleeve'!"

"What you are inferring," Aletha said slowly, "is that I might be carried away by what a man says to me and not by what he is feeling."

"There are men who can be very glib," the Duke said cynically, "especially when it is a question of money and rank."

Aletha was silent.

She knew that any man in England, whoever he was, would consider it a privilege to be the son-in-law of the Duke of Buclington.

She was the Duke's only daughter.

While the major part of his fortune would go to her brother, who at the moment was in India as *Aide-de-Camp* to the Viceroy, some of it would be hers.

She had also been left a considerable sum of money by her mother.

Her father had not put this into words.

She was, however, intelligent enough to realise there would be fortune-hunters in London who would consider it a great triumph if they could marry her.

It would not be for herself, but, as he had said as her father's daughter.

"We have not really had a chance to talk of this before," her father was saying, "but I had intended to do so before we go to London."

He paused a moment and then went on:

"My dearest, you have to be sensible and leave things in my hands. You have trusted me since you were a child, and I cannot believe that you will not do so now."

23

"I love you, Papa, and of course I trust you," Aletha said. "But I want to fall in love as you fell in love with Mama, and she with you."

"That is something that happens only once in a million years!" the Duke replied. "When I walked into the room and saw your mother, there seemed to be a dazzling light about her, and I knew that I had found the girl – whoever she might be and from wherever she came - that I wanted as my wife!"

"And Mama said," Aletha replied, "that when she saw you she knew you were the man of her dreams."

"We were very, very happy," the Duke said.

There was a pain in his voice that was always there when he spoke of his wife.

"I too want to feel like that," Aletha said quickly. "I want to meet the . . Prince of my . . Dreams!"

"Then you must just pray that is what you will do," the Duke replied.

She knew as he spoke that he did not believe it was possible.

As he said, what had happened to her mother and him was something that might happen once in a million years.

The Duke rose to his feet.

"If I am to leave so early I think I should go to bed. Do not worry about anything, my precious, and we will talk about this when I come home and before we leave for London."

He put his arm around her before he added:

"Enjoy yourself with the horses. I promise I will make up to you for the two weeks of boredom as soon as I return."

"I shall miss you . . Papa."

"As I shall miss you."

The Duke walked up the stairs with his arm round her shoulders.

When they reached her bedroom door he kissed her affectionately.

As he went down the passage to his own room the Duke was mulling over in his mind the young men he had seen recently at Court.

It was not easy to choose one who seemed to be suitable as a husband for his daughter.

There always seemed to be a flaw.

Something which told him instinctively that they would be unfaithful within twelve months of the Wedding Ceremony.

"I will find somebody," he thought confidently as he got into
bed.

Aletha having undressed, pulled back the curtains and was looking
out of the window.

There was a full moon and the stars filled the sky.

It was still cold at nights, but the moonlight on the lake glimmered
like silver.

The daffodils were just beginning to make a carpet of gold beneath
the old oak trees.

Usually Aletha was very moved by the beauty of her home and
everything about it.

Tonight, however, she was looking out with unseeing eyes.

She was thinking of leaving everything she loved and which was
familiar of going away with a strange man to a strange house.

There would be strange servants instead of those who had known
her since she was born.

There would be strange relatives who would doubtless disapprove
of many of the things she did.

Perhaps the man she married would not ride as well as her father
did, or for that matter, as well as she rode herself.

"How can I bear it?" she asked. "And yet I want love the . . love
which will make everything . . even a cottage seem . . wonderful
because . . he is there."

She found herself thinking of the Empress Elizabeth.

Because of the beauty, so many men loved her and, if gossip was
true, there were some she loved in return.

Aletha knew she wanted something very different for herself.

She wanted marriage in which the outside world did not
matter.

A marriage where the only thing that counted was her love for
her husband and his love for her.

She looked at the moon.

"Am I asking the impossible?" she enquired. "Must I really be
content with 'second best'?"

She knew that love after marriage would never be the same as
marrying the man of her dreams.

Would horses, however magnificent, however swift, however
exciting, be the same as love?

She wished that this topic of conversation had not arisen the night before her father was to leave for Denmark.

She wanted to go on talking to him.

She wanted to try to make him understand that while she was perhaps asking the impossible.

She must nevertheless strive to find it.

She suddenly had a terrifying feeling.

Suppose, almost before she could realise what was happening, she found herself the wife of some strange man with whom she had very little in common?

"I cannot bear it!" she said aloud.

She thought that if that should happen she would run away.

Her father was going to Denmark.

Perhaps in Denmark he would find her a husband?

A foreigner, a man whose language was different and about whose national customs she knew nothing.

She felt a sudden panic sweep over her.

It was almost as if she had been sailing on a smooth sea which had suddenly become tempestuous.

"I must escape!" she thought.

Then she told herself she must be sensible, talk to her father and explain to him how she felt.

Because he loved her he would understand.

She had an impulse to run to his room; to tell him now what she was feeling.

She wanted to know that he understood, as he had understood when as a child she was frightened of the dark.

Then again she told herself that would be a very selfish thing to do.

He had to leave so early in the morning to cross the North Sea to Denmark.

"Why does he have to go now – at this moment?" she asked angrily.

Instead they could have been setting off together from Tilbury to Ostend and travelling from there by train to Budapest.

Together they could have inspected the Hungarian horses.

They would have ridden side by side in the strange, wild country, which was the joy and delight of the Empress.

"If we were there it would be easy to talk to Papa about love," Aletha told herself.

26

But it was Mr. Heywood who was going to Hungary instead of them.

It would be he who would have all the fun of selecting the finest horses.

It was something she knew she would enjoy more than anything she had ever done, especially if she could be with her father.

She could imagine how excited they would be at finding really superb animals which were exactly what they wanted.

It was exasperating to think that everything had gone wrong.

She turned from the window.

It was no use wishing for the moon.

She had to stay at home and worry about the future.

It was certainly something she could not talk about to Cousin Jane.

Impulsively she turned again to the window to look up at the stars.

"Let me . . find a man I will . . love . . and who will . . love . . me."

It was half a wish and half a prayer, and she felt as if it flew up into the sky.

Perhaps, she thought, there really was a "man in the moon" who was listening to her.

Then as she put up her hand to draw the curtains and shut out the night, she had an idea.

It was so extraordinary, so incredible, that for a moment she was still.

Then something strong and defiant rose like a flame within her.

It seemed to seep through her body and into her brain.

She looked up once again at the moon as if that was from where the idea had come.

"I will . . do it," she said softly, "but you will . . have to . . help me!"

Chapter Two

Aletha had very little time in which to carry out what she planned to do.

In fact she took two or three hours to pack her clothes which she had seldom done herself.

She had also to decide how she could obtain enough ready money with which to travel.

As was to be expected, she had only a small amount of cash in her handbag mainly to use in Church.

It was also there in case she had to tip somebody unexpectedly when she was out riding.

She knew however she would need quite a considerable sum for the journey she had in mind.

There was only one solution and that was the jewellery which she had inherited from her mother.

Because she loved it she had been allowed to wear some of the pieces since she left School.

So she kept a number of the brooches and bracelets in the drawer of her dressing-table.

The tiaras, the necklaces and the ear-rings were all in the safe.

These she could not obtain without alerting the Butler.

He would undoubtedly think it very strange that she should want jewellery in the middle of the night.

She therefore looked through the brooches she had inherited.

This was a diamond crescent brooch which had been too big for her at her age to wear.

She knew the stones were good and therefore it was valuable.

She put it into her handbag.

Then she remembered somewhat belatedly that she would need her passport.

She had one of her own because soon after her mother died her father had thought it would be a good idea for them to have a change of environment.

He had taken her to France to stay with the *Comte* de Soisson who was an ardent race-horse owner like himself.

Before leaving the Duke had anticipated that he might have to return to England at the request of The Queen.

He had therefore arranged for Aletha to have her own passport instead of just being included on his.

It was a letter signed by the Marquess of Salisbury who was Secretary of State for Foreign Affairs.

It was fortunate there was no way of identifying the holder except that she was in possession of the passport herself.

For Aletha had already decided that once she was on foreign soil she would use a false name.

It was unlikely when she had reached Hungary that her passport would be looked at except by officials.

Then she thought of what she was intending to do . . she knew it was outrageous. It might also be dangerous.

When her father learned of it he would undoubtedly be infuriated.

At the same time, she told herself, unless she was unlucky, she would be able to return home before he did.

Then there would be no reason why he should suspect that she had not been staying with one of her friends.

Cousin Jane had arrived at six o'clock that evening and had fortunately gone straight to bed.

Consequently her father had asked Mr. Heywood to dinner, so that they could go on talking about horses.

Aletha was delighted that they had all escaped from a boring meal with Cousin Jane mouthing banalities or else discussing her health.

It was in fact her health that had solved Aletha's problem.

Her Lady's-maid had come to Aletha to say:

"I am afraid, M'Lady, my mistress isn't well. She's got a very bad cold and as it's infectious I've put her straight to bed."

"That was very sensible of you," Aletha replied. "I certainly have no wish to catch a cold at the moment."

"She'll be better in a day or so," the maid said confidently, "and Her Ladyship always likes staying at Ling."

29

Aletha gave a sigh of relief.

Now she knew she could put her plan into operation.

When she finished packing she sat down and wrote a note to Cousin Jane.

She said that as she was ill she was going to visit some friends for a few days.

She also left a letter for her father just in case he should return before she did.

Because she loved him she told him the truth.

He would be angry, but at the same time with any luck his anger would have abated by the time she did return.

She looked at the clock.

She had finished everything she had to do, and should now rest.

She planned to leave as soon as she dared after her father had gone.

It was four miles to the Railway Station and she knew he was leaving at six o'clock.

She also knew from their conversation at dinner that Mr. Heywood had arranged to travel to London with her father on the same early train.

He would reach London in time to catch the Steamer to Copenhagen which left shortly before mid-day.

If he missed it there would be a delay of two days.

That would certainly upset the programme that had been planned for him in Denmark.

Because Aletha was so excited and at the same time nervous of what she was doing she was unable to sleep.

She lit a candle every hour to see the time.

When it was six o'clock she heard her father walking down the corridor towards the stairs.

She could also hear the footsteps of his Valet and of the footmen carrying down his luggage.

He had been very insistent that she should not see him off.

"I want you to sleep until your usual hour, my dearest," he said, "and also, if I am honest, I am rather disagreeable first thing in the morning, and I do not want you to think of me like that when I am away."

"I could never think of you in any way except with love," Aletha assured him, "and that you are the most wonderful man in the world!"

Her father kissed her.

"You are a good girl," he said, "and I am very proud of you. I am quite certain Heywood is right and you will take London by storm."

"I hope so, Papa," Aletha replied.

Now as she heard him leaving she wondered if he would be so angry with her.

If so he might refuse to allow her to make her début.

Then she knew that if he did so it would cause a scandal.

So she was quite certain that when she did return her escapade would be hushed up and nobody told about it.

"I will get back before Papa in any case," she decided, "and I am sure I can swear Mr. Heywood to secrecy."

When she knew her father had left the house she got up and dressed.

She was taking a considerable amount of luggage including her hunting-boots and riding-habits.

Besides of course her pretty new gowns and her smart bonnets.

There was just a chance that she might meet some of the exciting Hungarian aristocrats.

If so she was determined to look her best.

At a quarter past six she went from her bedroom dressed in a travelling-cloak.

To her rather plain bonnet she had fixed a veil which had belonged to her mother.

Only married women wore a veil and she thought it would be an effective disguise.

She did not intend to reveal herself to Mr. Heywood until fully committed to the journey.

Meanwhile she would appear to be an older woman who could be travelling alone.

This was actually a hazard.

When Aletha had come back from France without her father she had been escorted by an elderly lady's maid and a Courier.

It was he who arranged everything for her.

He was there as a protection from the moment she left the French Château until she was back at Ling.

But she was determined that nothing, however difficult, would prevent her from reaching Hungary.

As she came down the stairs two night-footmen were still on duty.

They and two other footmen who had been there to see her father off, looked at her in surprise.

She ordered two of them to collect the luggage from her bedroom.

Another was told to run to the stables and say she required a carriage to take her to the Station.

"Because we were so preoccupied last night with His Grace," she said, "I forgot to tell anyone that I too am leaving this morning to stay with friends."

She knew this would be repeated throughout the house when it was discovered she had gone.

The carriage came round to the front door surprisingly quickly.

The Duke always became extremely irritable if he had to wait when he wished to go anywhere.

The grooms were therefore used to saddling a horse or putting a pair between the shafts in what was record time.

Aletha's luggage was piled into the carriage.

Only as the footman opened the door for her did he ask:

"Be ye goin' alone, M'Lady?"

"It is such a short distance," Aletha replied with a smile, "that it was not worth my taking a maid with me."

The footman shut the door and they drove off.

As she reached the Station she expected to have a long wait until the next train came in.

In fact, it was only fifteen minutes before one appeared.

The Porter, who knew who she was, found her an empty First Class compartment, and put a label on the window marked 'RESERVED'.

As the train moved off Aletha thought with satisfaction that she was safely over the first hurdle.

Now she had to be very sensible when she reached London.

She had time to plan exactly what she should do.

The train steamed past fields green with the young crops and woods where the trees that were just coming into leaf.

By the time they reached the suburbs Aletha had everything planned in her mind.

She knew she could not afford to make any mistakes or miss the ship that was sailing from Tilbury at one o'clock.

A Porter found her a Hackney Carriage and having tipped him before he shut the door Aletha said:

"Tell the driver to go to the nearest Pawnbroker's. It must not be too far out of our way because I have to catch a Steamer at Tilbury."

The Porter looked at her in surprise.

Then he said rather familiarly:

"Come wivout yer money, 'ave ye?"

"Yes, I have," Aletha replied. "I was stupid enough to leave it on my dressing-table, so unless I am to miss the ship to Ostend, I have to pawn my brooch!"

The Porter grinned.

"That"ll teach yer t'be a bit more careful next time, Ma'am!"

"It certainly will," Aletha agreed.

The Porter gave the instructions to the Cabby who appeared to understand.

He whipped up his horse and they drove off.

When they stopped at the Pawnbroker's Aletha was relieved to see that it had a respectable-looking-shop-window.

It was in a comparatively quiet street.

She got out of the carriage.

Feeling nervous, although she did not show it, she was pleased to see that the shop was empty of customers.

An elderly man with a large hooked nose was behind the counter.

"Good-day," she said.

Holding out her diamond brooch she went on:

"I would like to pawn this for a very short time because I unfortunately left my money at home and have to catch a Steamer to Ostend."

It was the excuse the Porter had put into her mind.

"When'll you be back?" the man asked in a somewhat aggressive tone.

"In ten days," Aletha said firmly. "I promise you I have no wish to lose my beautiful brooch, but I cannot travel with no money in my purse."

The man turned the brooch over in his hand, examining it very closely.

Then he said:

"I'll give you £70, an' I wants £100 back when ye redeems it."

Knowing the value of her mother's diamonds Aletha knew she was being cheated, but she was not prepared to argue about it.

33

"I will accept that," she said, "as long as you promise me that you will not sell it in the meantime. It belonged to my mother, and I could not bear to part with it for long."

The old man looked at her penetratingly as if he was questioning whether or not she was speaking the truth.

Then unexpectedly he smiled.

"I believe ye," he said, "but another time don't be so careless! Young ladies o' your age shouldn't be patronising Pawnbrokers."

"It is something I have certainly never done before," Aletha said, "and thank you very much for helping me, but it is very important that I catch this particular ship."

The Pawnbroker opened a drawer which appeared to be full of money and counted out £70 very carefully.

He handed it to Aletha and she put it away in her handbag.

"If you're alone," he said in a fatherly manner, "you keep a tight 'old on that there 'andbag o' yours. There be thieves an' pick-pockets as'll 'ave it off ye."

"I will do that," Aletha answered.

"There be plenty o' thieves, I 'ears, on the ships," the Pawnbroker went on, "an' if they don't take it off a pretty girl at cards, they'll take it wiv kisses!"

The way he spoke made Aletha shiver.

He gave her a ticket by which she could redeem her brooch.

She put this too into her handbag which she tucked tightly under her arm.

Then she held out her hand.

"Thank you very much," she said, "I will remember your advice."

"You do that," he said, "an' if you ask me, you"re too young t'be travellin' alone."

Aletha smiled at him.

But when she got back into the carriage she knew he was right.

She might encounter quite a lot of trouble until she gained the protection of Mr. Heywood.

She knew however that it would be a terrible mistake for him to see her before they were in the train from Ostend.

It was an express which would take them first to Vienna.

She had heard him discussing the journey with her father, although she had not listened very attentively at the time.

It had not occurred to her then that she might do anything so outrageous as to join him.

When the idea had come to her last night she had felt it was something she had to do.

Why should she stay at home and listen to Cousin Jane croaking over her illnesses?

She should have been travelling with her father to Hungary to buy the horses with which to delight the Empress.

She could not accompany him, but why not Mr. Heywood?

The moment she began to think about it everything seemed to fall into place like a Jig-saw puzzle.

She had to be sure that Mr. Heywood could not make her return home like a piece of unwanted luggage.

It would be impossible once they were in the train on their way to Austria.

They arrived at the Dock and she saw the Steamer waiting.

It was getting on towards one o'clock and there were quite a number of people going up the gang-way.

Mercifully there was no sign of Mr. Heywood and she hoped that he had already embarked.

Then she felt with a sudden panic that she might at the last moment find there was no accommodation for her.

She pulled her veil down over her face.

Because of what the Pawnbroker had said, she put on a pair of spectacles that her father had used when he had visited Switzerland one year.

He had bought them out there and when he got back to England he explained:

"The sun was so brilliant on the snow that it hurt my eyes. The Swiss Ambassador suggested I should wear these slightly tinted spectacles."

Aletha had not thought of them again until she was just leaving the house.

Then she remembered the spectacles were in a drawer in a chest which contained dog-leads and riding gloves.

She had slipped them into her handbag before she ran down the steps to get into the carriage.

She felt now as if they protected her from the world.

Also if Mr. Heywood did happen to see her he would be most unlikely to recognise her.

She thought the Cabby looked at her in surprise.

She certainly appeared somewhat different from the way she had when he had picked her up.

She found a porter to carry her luggage and went ahead of him up the gangway.

Having travelled with her father she knew that not having a reservation meant she had to go to the purser's office.

There were several people ahead of her.

When finally it was her turn she asked if it was possible to book a cabin.

To her relief there was one available.

She knew this was because the cabins were expensive and the majority of travellers were not prepared to spend extra money on them.

A steward brought her luggage into the cabin she had been allotted.

When he shut the door Aletha thought with relief that she was now safe until they reached Ostend.

Having crossed the Channel to France with her father, she knew she was a good sailor.

Although the sea was slightly "choppy" with the wind churning the waves into "white horses" she did not feel in the least seasick.

Only when the Steamer was out of sight of the coast did she think with delight that she had taken her second hurdle in style.

"I have been clever," she told herself. "At the same time, I must not be seen by Mr. Heywood when we reach Ostend."

She guessed like most men, he would want to walk around the deck and enjoy the sea breeze.

The Courier had booked them the best cabin aboard the Steamer in which she had travelled with her father.

He had however "pooh-poohed" the idea of staying in it.

"I hate being shut up," he had said firmly.

He walked around the deck almost the entire time they had taken to cross from Dover to Calais.

As Aletha was hiding, she wanted to stay in her cabin for as long as possible.

Only when one of the stewards suggested he should take her luggage ashore did she come out.

Keeping her head low she hurried down the gangway to walk the short distance to where the train for Vienna was waiting.

As she did not have a ticket she had to buy it before she went aboard.

In a way it was a blessing because it ensured that Mr. Heywood would have already taken his seat.

He would certainly not be looking particularly for anybody he might recognise.

The First Class fare with a Sleeper was expensive.

Aletha thought it was a good thing she had been sensible enough to have plenty of money for the journey.

She knew of course that Mr. Heywood would have to pay for her return.

At the same time in case anything went wrong she might have to look after herself.

It would be frightening to be in a foreign land and penniless.

At least she had her ticket.

The Porter discovered in which carriage her Sleeper was located and carried her luggage into it.

Aletha could speak French fluently.

She enquired from him how long it would be before the train stopped so that the passengers could eat at a Station Restaurant.

The Porter replied with all the information she required.

She realised that despite her spectacles and the veil which covered her face, he was looking at her with an undoubted look of admiration in his eyes.

"I must be careful," she told herself.

She certainly had no wish to be involved with any of the male passengers other than Mr. Heywood.

Ten minutes after she had boarded the train it began to move out of Ostend.

She had taken the third hurdle.

Now at least she felt safe from being sent home ignominiously.

The next difficulty would be to find Mr. Heywood.

There had been a great deal of talk in the newspapers about the introduction of coaches with corridors.

It would mean that the passengers could move from one compartment and from one coach to another.

Her father had disapproved of the idea.

"Men could frighten attractive women by knocking on their doors and entering their compartments."

He paused a moment and then went on in a hard voice:

37

"It would also make it easier for thieves to rob a traveller when he was asleep."

"I saw in one newspaper," Aletha had replied, "that it might mean that a train that was going a long distance could have a Restaurant Car, and the passengers could walk down the corridors to it."

"Then one would have to eat while being shaken about by the movement of the train," her father replied, "which is something that women, at any rate, would dislike."

At the moment, however, Aletha thought it would have made it much easier for her to find Mr. Heywood.

As it was, she would have to wait until the train arrived at the Station where they would disembark to have a meal.

She took off her bonnet and settled herself comfortably in her carriage.

At least she had one to herself.

She thought how uncomfortable it would have been if she had to travel with other people.

It would mean sitting up all night, instead of being able to lie down.

She had read in the newspapers how comfortable Queen Victoria's private carriage was in which she travelled in France.

Her Majesty's Sitting Room was connected with her bedroom and a luggage room in which her maid slept on a sofa.

Aletha thought that if she had been with her father perhaps they would have been able to have a private coach.

It would have been very exciting.

"Nevertheless," she told herself, "I am on my way, and now I shall see the Hungarian horses that thrill the Empress, and will certainly please her when she comes to stay at Ling."

Because she was interested in the land through which they were passing she sat looking out of the window.

She was quite surprised when she found the time had passed more quickly than she expected.

In fact, it was nearly six o'clock - the time at which the train was expected to stop.

She thought it would be a mistake not to wear her veil and spectacles until she found Mr. Heywood.

She therefore dressed herself carefully as she had been when she came aboard.

When she looked in the small mirror she thought that even her father would have found difficulty in recognising her.

With a great deal of smoke and even more noise the train steamed into a Station and came to a halt.

There were numerous people on the platform, so some of them were boarding the train, others meeting travellers from it.

There were also porters and trucks containing the Mail and a great deal of luggage.

Aletha waited a few minutes before she opened her carriage door.

She made sure that the steward in charge of her coach understood that she was leaving her possessions while she had dinner.

She thanked him in her excellent Parisian French when he told her he would take care of them.

Then she walked to the Restaurant.

It appeared to her when she first entered that every table was taken.

She could see no sign of Mr. Heywood.

She thought helplessly that she might have to return to the train without having anything to eat.

Then a man who was sitting at a table near to the door said to her in French:

"There is a seat here, *Madame*."

With a quick glance Aletha realised that beside the man who had spoken to her there was an elderly couple.

They looked, she thought, as if they might be Austrian.

A little reluctantly, still hoping she would see Mr. Heywood, she sat down in the empty seat.

"It is always difficult to find a place," the man said who had spoken to her before, "unless one jumps out of the train almost before it stops."

"I should have thought they might have enough places for everybody!" Aletha replied.

She spoke in a cold voice.

She felt by the way the stranger was smiling at her that he was not deceived by her disguise.

Because he was polite and there seemed no point in being rude, she allowed him to suggest what was palatable on the menu.

She knew a Frenchman would advise her better than anybody else.

She refused however when he asked if she would share his bottle of wine with him.

"No, thank you," she said firmly.

"You are making a mistake," he said. "You must know that in places like this it would be dangerous to drink the water."

He paused and smiled at her before continuing:

"What I have ordered comes from a famous Vineyard and is quite excellent!"

Because it seemed stupid to refuse, Aletha accepted a glass.

The food was not long in coming.

Yet while she was still eating, the elderly couple, having consumed little but drunk two huge mugs of beer, returned to the train.

"Now we can talk," the Frenchman said. "Tell me about yourself, because I can see, *Mademoiselle*, that despite those disfiguring spectacles you are very pretty!"

Aletha stiffened.

She was about to reply that she was not a *Mademoiselle*.

Then she realised that although she had thought of everything else, she had not remembered she should be wearing a wedding-ring.

The idea had not occurred to her when she had taken off her gloves to eat.

But the Frenchman had not missed the ringless fourth finger of her left hand.

As she did not reply he bent a little nearer to her.

"Tell me about yourself," he said, "and may I say I find you very fascinating and intriguing."

"I am just a traveller, *Monsieur*," Aletha replied, "and as time is getting on I am anxious to get back to the train."

"It will not move for at least another twenty minutes," he replied, "and I want to know a great deal about you, and also you must tell me which coach you are in."

There was something in the way he spoke that made Aletha look at him sharply.

He put his hand out and took hers.

"I have not a Sleeper," he said. "I was unfortunately too late to obtain one, so why should you not be generous and share yours with me?"

Aletha tried to take her hand away but he held onto it.

"We could both be very happy," he said softly, "on what is otherwise a very tedious and uneventful journey."

"The answer is 'No', *Monsieur* definitely 'No!'" Aletha said.

She meant to speak in a firm, crushing voice but instead she only sounded very young and rather frightened.

The Frenchman's fingers tightened on hers.

"I will make you very happy," he said, "and when we are alone I will tell you how beautiful you are, and how thrilled I am to have found you!"

There was a determination in his voice which frightened Aletha.

It flashed through her mind that if she went back to her carriage he would follow her.

She might be unable to prevent him from entering her compartment.

Then she knew she would be at his mercy.

There would be nothing she could do about it.

She thought quickly that the only thing she could do was to appeal to the steward.

But the Frenchman might even be able to prevent her from doing that.

She felt her heart thumping in her breast, and a sense of panic swept over her.

The waiter came up for the bill, but the Frenchman did not loosen his hold on her hand.

He pulled two notes out of his pocket and gave them to the waiter.

"I would prefer to pay for myself!" Aletha said.

"I cannot allow you to do that," the Frenchman insisted.

She struggled to free her hand but he still held it captive.

He took the change from the waiter, put it into his pocket and rose to his feet still holding on to her fingers.

She sat still looking up at him and now she was really frightened.

The people in the Restaurant were moving towards the train.

In a few minutes she would have to go back to her compartment.

The Frenchman began to pull her to her feet.

She tried to resist him but it was hopeless.

Then as he moved towards the door still holding her prisoner, she saw coming from the very back of the Restaurant a figure she recognised.

The Frenchman, dragging her as if she was a reluctant mule, had almost reached the door.

He had to wait for several people to pass and as he did so Aletha saw Mr. Heywood coming nearer.

With a sudden twist of her hand she moved sharply away from the door.

It took the Frenchman by surprise.

She pushed past the passengers queueing up to go through the door and threw herself against Mr. Heywood.

"I have . . found . . you! I have . . found you!" she cried.

Mr. Heywood stared at her in sheer astonishment before he exclaimed:

"Lady Aletha! What on earth are you doing here?"

"I am on . . the train," she answered, "and . . looking . . for . . you."

It was then, before she could say any more, that the Frenchman was beside her.

He took her by the arm, obviously having no idea that she had been speaking to Mr. Heywood.

"Come along," he said, "there is no escape, so do not run away from me again."

"Go away and leave me alone!" Aletha demanded.

She was conscious as she spoke that Mr. Heywood was taller and looked very much stronger than the Frenchman who was not a big man.

She took Mr. Heywood's arm.

As if he realised what was happening he said in English:

"Who is this fellow? Is he bothering you?"

"Send him . . away! Please . . send him . . away!" Aletha begged.

There was however no need for Mr. Heywood to say anything.

The Frenchman obviously understood what Aletha had said and realised he was defeated.

He turned and pushing his way through the crowd disappeared through the Restaurant door.

Aletha gave a sigh of relief.

"I . . I was . . frightened," she said in a small voice.

"Do you mean you are here alone?" Mr. Heywood asked. "I cannot understand . . '

"I wanted to . . come to Hungary with . . you as Papa cannot

.. take me," Aletha said, "and I .. had no .. trouble until .. that Frenchman .. talked to me."

"You must be crazy to do anything so outrageous!" Mr. Heywood said. "Have you a compartment to yourself?"

"I have .. a Sleeper."

She realised he was frowning and in fact looked extremely angry.

By this time they had reached the door of the Restaurant.

The passengers were all hurrying onto the train, some of the doors had been slammed shut.

"Where is your compartment?" Mr. Heywood asked.

Aletha went towards it and he said:

"I will come and see you at the next stop. You are not to get out until I do so! Then I want a full explanation of what is going on!"

He stopped speaking a moment before he went on:

"I think, Lady Aletha, your father would be very angry if he knew you were here."

"I .. I know that," Aletha agreed, "but I did so want to .. come with .. you and buy .. the Hungarian horses for .. the Empress."

"I have to think how I can send you back with somebody to protect you," Mr. Heywood said grimly.

"I will not go!" Aletha retorted. "And I have a splendid idea which I will tell you about when you have .. time to .. listen."

She knew by the expression on Mr. Heywood's face that this was not the right moment to appeal to him to help her.

By this time they had reached her compartment.

To her relief the steward was standing beside it.

He was waiting to lock the door when she was inside.

She looked up at Mr. Heywood.

"I shall be quite .. safe until you .. find me at the next .. stop," she assured him.

Mr. Heywood did not answer.

Instead, in what she realised was quite fluent French, but with a decided English accent, he told the steward that no one was to approach her compartment.

Then he tipped the man so generously that he was overcome by what he had received.

Without saying any more to Aletha Mr. Heywood turned and walked away towards his own compartment.

It was, she saw somewhat ironically, in the next coach to her own.

"*Bon nuit Madame!*" the steward said as he closed the door.

The bed had been made up while Aletha was in the Restaurant.

She sat down on it feeling for the moment apprehensive that Mr. Heywood was so angry.

Then she told herself it was what she might have expected, but there was nothing he could do.

He could either take her home immediately which would mean he could not buy the horses her father wanted.

Or else he would have to carry out the plan she had thought out so carefully.

As she undressed she thought how lucky she had been to find him.

She had never anticipated that anybody would behave as the Frenchman had done.

Now as she thought about it, she could imagine it would be quite a clever way of getting a comfortable compartment without having to pay for it.

Perhaps, besides finding a pretty woman amusing, he was also a thief.

If she had been obliged to endure his presence, he might have taken her money and what jewellery she had with her.

She could understand why Mr. Heywood was horrified at the idea of her travelling alone.

"All the same, I am here," she thought triumphantly, "and it will be impossible for Mr. Heywood to send me back!"

She undressed and got into bed.

The vibration of the wheels soon soothed her to sleep.

When Aletha awoke it was morning.

She remembered the train would stop for breakfast and she had to be dressed by the time Mr. Heywood came to collect her.

She pulled up the blind.

The countryside through which they were passing was very beautiful.

There were high hills in the distance, forests and broad shining rivers.

She wished she knew exactly where she was, and, what was more important, when they would reach Vienna.

She dressed herself, but now she removed her mother's veil from her bonnet.

She put the coloured spectacles away in one of her boxes.

The sun was shining and she thought she would not need the heavy cloak in which she had travelled yesterday.

Instead she unpacked a short jacket which was trimmed with fur.

She knew, although she could see little of herself in the mirror, that she looked very smart.

She only hoped that Mr. Heywood would admire her as he had done before.

He might then not be so angry as he had been last night.

Her gown, which was in the very latest fashion, was draped in the front and caught at the back into what was a very small bustle.

She knew that any woman on the Station would be aware that she was wearing a model which had originally come from Paris.

Then as the train came slowly into the Station, she was still afraid.

Perhaps Mr. Heywood would be too angry at her escapade to think of anything but that she was her father's daughter.

She should have been properly and correctly chaperoned, besides having a lady's-maid and a Courier with her.

Chapter Three

Mr. Heywood collected Aletha from her compartment.

They walked side by side and in silence towards the Restaurant.

When he had ordered coffee and two dishes of fresh fish, he said:

'Now, Lady Aletha, I want the truth, and the whole truth, as to why you are here."

"The truth is quite simple," Aletha replied. "If Papa had not had to go to Denmark I would have come with him to Hungary."

She smiled at him tentatively before she went on:

"Instead of which I was left with Cousin Jane who, as usual, was ill, and I could not bear to miss all the fun."

"Your father had no idea of what you were doing, I presume?" Mr. Heywood said in an uncompromising manner.

"No, of course not. I waited until he had left the house, then took the next train to London and joined the ship at Tilbury."

Mr. Heywood tightened his lips.

"And you did not make yourself known to me for the simple reason that you knew I would have sent you back."

"Of course," Aletha agreed. "And now I do beg of you to make the best of the situation."

"Do you really think I can do that?" he asked in an irritated voice. "You know as well as I do that you have to be chaperoned, and God knows where we will find one in Vienna, or anywhere else!"

"There will be no need for a chaperon," Aletha said quietly.

Mr. Heywood stared at her.

"What do you mean by that? You must be aware that as a débutante it could ruin your reputation for ever if it was known where you were at this moment."

"No one is going to know that 'Lady Aletha Ling' is here, unless you tell them."

She spoke defiantly and as Mr. Heywood stared at her she explained:

"You will be interested to know that I am in fact 'Miss Aletha Link' and your granddaughter!"

There was a stupefied silence, then unexpectedly Mr. Heywood laughed.

"I do not believe it!" he said. "I cannot be hearing this!"

"You must see," Aletha said, "that it is a very plausible explanation for my presence, and who is to know in Hungary whether you have a granddaughter or not? Certainly no one will think of me as Papa's daughter."

"Did you really think up this ridiculous Fairy Tale yourself?" Mr. Heywood asked.

"It is not as ridiculous as you might think," Aletha answered defiantly. "You have been asked by the Duke of Buclington to buy him some horses. Who is to care whether you arrive with a wife, a daughter, or a granddaughter?"

She realised as she spoke that Mr. Heywood's eyes were twinkling.

She suddenly had the idea that despite his age he was so good looking that he would not expect to be asked to be somebody's grandparent.

As if he knew what she was thinking, he said:

"You are certainly original, Lady Aletha!"

"*Aletha*," Aletha corrected him. "'Lady' Aletha will cease to exist as soon as we cross the frontier into Austria and then into Hungary."

"In other words," Mr. Heywood said, "you are using your own Passport."

"That is true," Aletha replied, "but if you think that dangerous, I am quite certain I can alter my name from 'Ling' to 'Link', and change the word 'Lady' into 'Miss'."

"I think that would be a mistake," Mr. Heywood said, "and we can only hope that the frontier officials will not be so impressed by you that they talk about your visit."

Aletha heard what he said with a lift of her heart.

She knew that he had accepted the position she had contrived for herself.

47

There was in fact, little else he could do.

She leaned across the table which fortunately they had to themselves.

"Please let me enjoy myself with the horses," she said. "I cannot believe you will have to go to parties or spend much time with the owners."

While her father treated Mr. Heywood as a Gentleman, to foreigners he would only be a man the Duke of Buclington employed.

They would not expect to entertain him themselves, or invite him to meet their womenfolk.

"That is true," Mr. Heywood said to her surprise.

She was aware that once again he knew what she was thinking.

"At the same time," he went on, "you may find it slightly uncomfortable to be just my granddaughter and meet on equal terms people who will treat you very differently from what you are accustomed to.

"I am not interested in anything but the horses," Aletha replied, "and I want to visit Hungary more than any other place in the world!"

"I only hope you are not disappointed!" Mr. Heywood remarked dryly. "And do not forget that there will be a 'Day of Reckoning' when you return home."

"I am hoping to do that before Papa returns," Aletha said.

"And if you do not?" Mr. Heywood enquired.

"Then he will naturally be very angry," Aletha admitted. "At the same time, I am sure he will not want anyone to know of my escapade because if it was talked about it would certainly be damaging to my reputation."

Mr. Heywood laughed again.

"You are incorrigible!" he said. "But you have obviously thought out every detail. Quite frankly, I cannot think how I can send you home without coming with you myself."

"Without the horses?" Aletha exclaimed. "Think how upset Papa would be if he could not produce them as a surprise for the Empress!"

Mr. Heywood was silent as he continued to eat his breakfast.

Aletha knew that she had won her battle, or rather jumped her fourth hurdle.

She was very elated with herself.

When they were back on the train Mr. Heywood came to her compartment where the steward had put away the bed.

They sat down on the cushioned seat and he told Aletha about the next stop where they would have luncheon.

There was so much more she wanted to ask him.

"How long are we staying in Vienna?" she enquired.

"Only one night," Mr. Heywood said. "Your father wanted me to see the Direktor of the Spanish Riding School who uses a number of Hungarian horses as well as the Lippizaners."

"Oh, I do want to see them!" Aletha exclaimed.

"I think that would be a mistake," Mr. Heywood said. "The Direktor knows your father well, and if he saw you he would undoubtedly mention you in the letter which he will write to His Grace telling him how pleased he was to help me."

Aletha sighed.

"It seems such a wonderful chance."

"I know," Mr. Heywood agreed. "At the same time, unless you are going to make things worse than they are already, you have to let me decide what is best for you."

Aletha smiled at him.

"All right, you win! And thank you for being much nicer about this than I deserve."

"I am only horrified," Mr. Heywood said, "that you have got your-self into a situation which may have far-reaching consequences."

"You mean I may not be allowed to be a conventional débutante!" Aletha said. "In that case, I shall just have to work in the stables at Ling and with the race-horses at Newmarket and everybody can forget about me."

"I think that is very unlikely," Mr. Heywood said. "Now please, Lady Aletha, while we are travelling, remember you are a very beautiful young woman, and Hungarian men are very romantic and impressionable."

"That is what I have always heard," Aletha said.

"Then you must concentrate on the horses and not listen to anything that is said to you."

"Now you are being unkind," Aletha complained. "Of course I want the men I meet to think I am beautiful. I have always been so afraid that, in comparison to Mama, no one would even look at me."

"Your mother was the most beautiful person I have ever seen,"

Mr. Heywood said, "and I am sure she would be horrified at the way you are behaving now."

The way he spoke made Aletha glance at him in surprise.

Then impulsively, without thinking, she enquired:

"Were you in love with Mama?"

Mr. Heywood started.

"That is a question you should not ask me," he began.

Then he smiled.

"I think every man who came in contact with your mother loved her," he admitted. "She was not only beautiful, but she was so charming, so kind, and so very understanding. Everybody told her their troubles."

"Including me," Aletha said. "It would be much more exciting to make my début in London if Mama were with me instead of Grandmama."

She paused before she added in a low voice:

"She is always very disagreeable when her rheumatism hurts her."

"I am sure it will be much more enjoyable than you anticipate," Mr. Heywood said. "But you must understand for your mother's sake, as well as your father's, I have to protect you from getting into unpleasant situations such as you encountered last night."

"I never expected a perfect stranger to behave like that!" Aletha exclaimed. "If as he intended, he had forced his way into my compartment, he might have . . tried to . . kiss . . me, and that . . would have . . been . . horrible!"

Mr. Heywood thought he would have done a great deal more than that.

But he had no intention of enlightening Aletha as to what might have happened.

"Forget him!" he said sharply. "It is something that will not occur again. But you understand that you must keep beside me, and not do things on your own."

"Very well, Grandpapa!" Aletha said mischievously.

They arrived in Vienna late in the evening and drove to a new Hotel.

Aletha learnt it had been opened only two years ago.

It was certainly very impressive.

When Mr. Heywood changed the single room he had booked for a very luxurious Suite she was delighted.

The Sacher Hotel had already a reputation not only for being the smartest Hotel in Vienna, but also for having the best food.

Aletha was hungry because she had not found what they were offered at the last stop very palatable.

When they went downstairs to the impressive Dining-Room she looked around her with delight.

She had only stayed in Hotels once before on her journey to France with her father.

Now she thought the tables with their lighted candles and the waiters scurrying about serving the well-dressed and elegant diners were very exciting.

She appreciated that Mr. Heywood in his evening-clothes looked almost as smart as her father would have done.

She had put on a very pretty gown which she had never worn before.

They chose their dinner with care from a long and elaborate menu and Mr. Heywood ordered a bottle of wine.

"I suppose you are going to tell me that you are old enough to drink wine?" he remarked.

"Of course I am!" Aletha replied. "I am grown up, and anyway, Mama always allowed me to have a little champagne at Christmas and on birthdays."

"I find it difficult to think of you as a grown-up young lady," Mr. Heywood commented. "I saw you first as a tiny baby, and you grew into an attractive little girl . ."

"Then I went through a very plain period," Aletha said honestly. "I used to pray every night that I would be as beautiful as Mama."

"I am not going to tell you that your prayers were answered," Mr. Heywood said. "I will leave all those compliments to the young men with whom you will dance when you get to London."

As he spoke Aletha remembered that one of them would be chosen by her father to be her husband.

The idea made her shudder.

She told herself that whatever Mr. Heywood or anyone else might say, she would enjoy this journey.

She was on her own.

She was not overshadowed by some strange man who had

51

asked her to marry him just because she fitted in with his Family Tree.

As if Mr. Heywood wanted her to enjoy herself he described to her what the world had been like when he was a young man.

He said that her mother had taken first London by storm when she was a débutante.

Later she captured the hearts of everybody at Ling when she had married Aletha's father.

"Why did you never marry?" Aletha asked him towards the end of dinner.

She knew as she spoke that many women must have found him attractive.

As he did not answer, she added:

"Was it because of Mama?"

"Partly," Mr. Heywood admitted, "but when I was enjoying myself in London, I had no wish to tie myself down."

"All you wanted to do, according to Papa, was to win races. And that is what you did do!"

"I won quite a number on some exceptional horses," he said. "Then, as I expect you know, the crash came."

"How could you lose all your money?"

"Very easily," he replied, "but I do not want to talk about it."

"No, of course not," Aletha said sympathetically. "Go on with what you were telling me."

"It was then your grandfather offered me the job of looking after his Racing Stud, and when he died, I continued to be employed by your father."

Without his saying so, Aletha was aware that although he enjoyed his position, it hurt his pride to work for someone else rather than being his own master.

"I am sure Mama understood how you felt," she said aloud.

"Your mother was always charming to me and," as I have already admitted, it would have been impossible for any man not to love her. At the same time, she was only aware of one man – your father."

"And Papa thought only of her," Aletha replied.

She paused before she added:

"That is why I am glad he likes being with the Empress."

"Of course," Mr. Heywood said, "and you and I have to find him such superb horses that they eclipse anything the Empress owns herself."

Aletha clapped her hands.

"That is exactly what we will do."

They left the Dining-Room.

When they reached their Sitting-Room Mr. Heywood said he was going first thing in the morning to see the Direktor of the Spanish Riding School.

"You are to stay here," he commanded, "and not go out until I return!"

"I want to see something of Vienna before we leave," Aletha said.

"I am sure we will have time after luncheon," Mr. Heywood replied. "Our train does not leave for Budapest until ten o'clock."

"Promise you will hurry back, otherwise I shall feel so frustrated at being cooped up in the Hotel that I shall fly out of the window!" Aletha threatened.

"I promise I will not be long," Mr. Heywood laughed. "Good-night, Aletha!"

It was the first time he had used her name without her title.

Aletha smiled before she said:

"You are the nicest, and quite the handsomest grandfather anyone could wish for!"

"Now you are flattering me!" Mr. Heywood said. "And I am suspicious that you are trying in some underhand manner to get your own way about something."

Aletha laughed.

She thought as she went to her bedroom that at least she had succeeded in making him agree to everything she had suggested.

It was annoying for Aletha in the morning when she was up and dressed but had to stay in the Suite.

It was in the corner of the Hotel and she could look out of the windows, in two directions.

She could see clearly the people moving about in the streets.

Carriages drove by, and the sunshine made everything seem as if it had turned to gold.

She thought if she listened she would hear the music of Johann Strauss.

Small boys were continually whistling.

How could she be in Vienna and not hear the music which had electrified London as well as everywhere else?

She knew that soon she would be dancing to one of the famous Waltzes.

Once again she thought it might be with a man whom her father had already chosen for her as a husband.

Her eyes darkened.

"How can I make Papa understand that I will marry no one until I fall in love?" she asked.

There was no answer to this question.

Because once again her thoughts were depressed and dismal, she gave a cry of delight when Mr. Heywood appeared.

She ran across the room towards him.

"You have found out what you wanted?"

"The Direktor has given me a letter," Mr. Heywood replied, "to the man in Budapest who looks after the Royal Stables."

"Do you think he will know where we will find the best and the most magnificent horses?" Aletha asked.

"I am sure of it!" Mr. Heywood replied. "And now as you have been so good, we will drive in an open carriage through the streets of Vienna before we have luncheon."

Aletha had her bonnet ready.

As they went downstairs she felt as if her feet had wings.

There was a smart carriage drawn by two white horses waiting for them outside the Hotel.

They set off with Aletha enjoying everything she saw.

The high buildings, the fountains, the bridges over the river, and finally the great Cathedral which was known as the 'Stephansdom'.

"Please can I go inside?" she asked Mr. Heywood.

"Of course," he answered.

He told the coachman to stop and they walked into the wonderful old building in which the Viennese had worshipped for centuries.

Inside there was the scent of incense.

Aletha felt strongly the vibrations of faith.

Candles were flickering in every Chapel and in front of the images which stood against every pillar.

She felt the atmosphere was different from anything she had felt in any other Church.

Dropping to her knees she meant to pray for her father.

Instead she found herself praying fervently that she would find what she was seeking.

That she would be married for herself and not because she was her father's daughter.

She went on praying with a fervency which came from her very soul.

Suddenly she knew in some strange way she could not explain that her prayers had been heard.

It was almost as if somebody, perhaps her mother, was telling her that all would be well.

She must not be pushed into a loveless marriage.

If she married it would not be to some stranger who was not the 'Prince of her Dreams'.

When she rose to her feet she went up to the nearest image and putting a coin into the box in front of it lit a candle.

Her mother had told her when she was quite small that if one lit a candle it carried the prayer she made up into Heaven for as long as the candle remained alight.

Aletha chose the longest and most expensive candle.

Mr. Heywood was waiting for her at the end of the aisle.

When she joined him she had no idea that her face was radiant with a light that seemed to come from within herself.

Without thinking, just as she might have done with her father, she slipped her hand into his.

He led her out of the Stephansdom and into the street.

They returned to the Hotel in the carriage which was waiting outside.

The train which carried them from Vienna to Budapest was not as comfortable as the one in which they had travelled from Ostend.

Mr. Heywood arranged that they had adjacent compartments.

When he tipped the attendant heavily he became very attentive.

He made sure their beds were made up as comfortably as possible when they were having dinner.

This was at a Station they reached two hours after the train had started.

The food was not exciting. At the same time, it was edible.

After the excellent luncheon they had enjoyed at the Sacher Aletha was not hungry.

She had also before they left had a slice of the famous Sacher cake.

It was made from a secret recipe known only to the Hotel.

It had been invented by one of the young Sacher sons when he was only sixteen.

Aletha thought it was the most delicious cake she had ever tasted.

Their dinner therefore was not really important and their real interest was the horses.

"What shall we do if we cannot find the ones you really want?" Aletha asked.

"There is no fear of that," Mr. Heywood replied. "I am only afraid our task will be difficult because we shall want to buy hundreds rather than the eight or ten His Grace requires."

"If we tried them all out," Aletha remarked, "we would still be riding in Hungary when the Hunting Season begins!"

Mr. Heywood laughed.

"That is certainly a thought, and one which would certainly not please your father!"

"And it is so important," Aletha said, "that we get home before he does!"

"I hope for your sake we do!" Mr. Heywood replied.

They reached Budapest the next morning.

The moment she stepped from the Station, Aletha was entranced by the beauty of the City.

She thought that no place she had ever seen before had such a fairylike quality about it.

Even the City"s Eastern Railway Station named the Keleri Pu which was extremely magnificent had something magical about it.

"Actually," Mr. Heywood told her, "Keleri Pu is one of the grandest Stations in Europe."

"It seems strange," Aletha said, "that people should exert themselves to build such enormous Stations. Perhaps it is because they are so impressed by trains."

"Of course they are," Mr. Heywood agreed. "And quite rightly. Think of the time it would have taken if we had had to come all this way from England by carriage!"

Aletha laughed.

"That is true!" she replied.

Then as they drove away from the Station she could only look at the great towers and Palaces.

There were also the houses which had an almost Morrish appearance.

The Churches were a mixture of Gothic and Baroque with Renaissance monuments and riches.

They drove up a winding road rising higher and higher.

"Where are we going?" Aletha asked.

"Before we even unpack," Mr. Heywood answered. "we are going to the Royal Palace to see the man to whom the Direktor of the Spanish Riding School gave me an introduction."

He pointed to where above there was an enormous building.

"It is certainly impressive!" Aletha remarked.

She could see a great many pillars and a huge dome silhouetted against the sky.

"Is there any chance of the Empress being here now?" Aletha asked hopefully.

Mr. Heywood shook his head and she was disappointed.

When they reached the Palace she was extremely impressed with the huge terrace outside it.

There was a beautifully carved fountain and an enormous equestrian statue.

Mr. Heywood told her it was of Prince Eugene of Savoy.

He had fought the Turks at the end of the 17th Century.

He looked very dashing on his plunging horse.

Aletha thought he was just how she expected a Hungarian to look.

From the terrace there was a panorama of the City with the Danube dividing it.

It was so lovely that Aletha did not mind when Mr. Heywood said:

"I suggest that you sit here while I go inside and see if I can find the gentleman I wish to consult."

As she did not answer he said:

"You will be quite safe in the carriage."

There were sentries on either side of the door through which he disappeared.

Aletha sat looking in the opposite direction.

She thought that no view from any Palace could be more beautiful.

Then because she wanted to see it from the balustrade itself, she got out of the carriage.

She walked first to the beautiful fountain.

Its water was pouring iridescent over rocks and statues into a stone basin beneath it.

Then as she reached the balustrade to look down at the boats moving slowly on the Danube she said involuntarily:

"Could anything be more beautiful?"

"That is what I was thinking!" a voice said.

She started, then saw that standing beside her was a young man.

He was handsome, and there was something so dashing and different about him that made her sure he was Hungarian.

He spoke in English, but with just a faint accent.

As she looked up at him he said:

"I thought for a moment you must be one of the Sylphs from the Danube whom I have often been told about but have never seen."

Aletha laughed.

"That is what I would like to be," she said. "But surely no Palace could have a more wonderful view than this, and no Palace could be more impressive!"

"We are very proud of our Palaces," the young man replied, "and even more so of our horses!"

"They are what I have really come to see," Aletha told him.

"But you will not find them in Budapest," the Hungarian said.

"No, I know," Aletha answered, "and my . . my . . grandfather is inside the Palace now, finding out where we must go to see the finest of them."

"Why are you so interested?" the young man asked.

Because he was inquisitive Aletha remembered that she should not be talking to a stranger.

It might be indiscreet anyway to tell him too much, and perhaps a different story from what Mr. Heywood was telling.

Instead of answering, she looked down at the river below.

A boat, its sails unfurled, was moving majestically down the River.

"If I am too curious you must forgive me," the Hungarian said, "but you must understand it is a surprise to find a Sylph who is English standing outside the Palace and saying she is looking for Hungarian horses."

It sounded so ridiculous that Aletha could not help laughing.

"It just happens to be true!" she said.

"Then I only hope you will not be disappointed," the Hungarian replied.

"I am quite sure that will not happen," Aletha answered.

She was about to say something more, when there was the sound of horses' hoofs and the turning of wheels.

The next moment a carriage appeared and swept up to the front of the Palace.

It was a very smart vehicle with a coachman and footman wearing an elaborate livery.

The bridles and accoutrements of the horses were all of gleaming silver.

Seated in the carriage was a woman holding a small sunshade over her head.

The Hungarian had turned round as the carriage approached.

Aletha did so too and was able to have a quick glance at the occupant of the carriage.

She was exceedingly smart, and also very beautiful.

She had dark flashing eyes.

The ostrich feathers on her bonnet fluttered in the breeze as she looked towards the Hungarian.

She raised an elegantly gloved hand in his direction.

It was a call for him to attend to her, and he bowed in response.

Then he said to Aletha:

"I hope one day I may have the pleasure of seeing you again. In the meantime, I know you will enjoy the horses of my country."

"I am sure I shall," Aletha replied.

He walked away and she felt sure he was very athletic and would certainly be a good rider.

As he reached the lady's carriage the footman jumped down to open the door for him.

He stepped into it to sit beside the lady with the sunshade.

She gave him her hand and he kissed it.

As he did so Aletha turned away, feeling she was somehow prying on something which did not concern her.

As the horses drove away she deliberately stared down at the boats on the river.

She did not turn round until the sound of the horses' hoofs could no longer be heard.

She had only to wait a little longer before Mr. Heywood returned.

He looked surprised when he saw she was not in the carriage.

He walked to where she was standing.

"Has he been able to help you?" Aletha asked eagerly as he joined her.

"I have exactly the information I wanted," he replied, "with an introduction to the man who is my *vis-a-vis* in each of the places we shall visit."

"That is splendid!" Aletha said excitedly. "Where are we going?"

"First of all," he said, "we are going to the Castle of Baron Otto von Sicardsburg."

Aletha raised her eye-brows.

"He sounds German."

"He is. He married a Hungarian Princess and is a very wealthy man."

"His horses are good?"

"I am assured they are superb," Mr. Heywood said "and fortunately for us, as we have so little time, the Baron's Castle is not far from the Palace of the Estérházys who also have some of the finest horses in the whole of Hungary."

Aletha smiled.

"Shall we go there at once?"

"As quickly as the train will carry us!" Mr. Heywood replied.

As they drove away from the Palace he said:

"I suppose you know you have broken all the rules in walking about in the precincts of the Palace without permission?"

"I never thought of it!" Aletha exclaimed.

"I wonder no one reproved you for the offence," Mr. Heywood remarked.

Aletha thought there had been no reproof from the Hungarian.

'In fact he had looked at her with an expression of admiration which she had never seen before in any man's eyes.

He was certainly very good-looking and exactly what she thought a Hungarian gentleman – or was it aristocrat? – would look like.

It somehow seemed appropriate that he should be accompanied by a beautiful woman and driven away in a smart carriage drawn by superb horses.

"If I was breaking the rules," she thought, "I am not surprised he came and spoke to me, since of course he was curious as to why I was there."

She thought she would like to remember him because he had admired her and likened her to a Sylph.

The conversation she had with him was however certainly not something she would relate to Mr. Heywood.

Chapter Four

The train carried them from Budapest to Györ which was in the Province of Sopron.

They got out at Györ which was a fascinating old town with houses of every period, and some beautiful Churches.

Mr. Heywood hired a carriage which was to take them to the Castle there which was where the Baron Otto von Sicardsburg lived.

Aletha thought it was very exciting to be in the country.

She looked eagerly around her and naturally at the horses.

She saw quite a number of them in the fields, or turned out to grass.

She thought they were different from any horses her father possessed, and was sure they were just as spirited as they were reputed to be.

The Castle was some way out of Györ, but Mr. Heywood told her they were going in the right direction for their next call.

This was the Palace of Prince Jözwel Estérházy.

"Tell me first about the Baron," she pleaded, "or I shall get the two families muddled."

"Prince Estérházy would not be complimented," Mr. Heywood said. "He is one of the most important aristocrats in Hungary and is very proud of his heritage."

"And the Baron?" Aletha prompted.

"From what I gather from my informant in the Palace," Mr. Heywood said, "he is not very well liked, but that might just be national prejudice."

"I would much rather be with a Hungarian in Hungary," Aletha smiled.

"So would I," Mr. Heywood agreed. "I find the Germans difficult, especially when it comes to business."

"Then let us hope we shall not have to stay with him for long."

Aletha was however impressed as they drove up the long drive after passing through some enormous gates and saw the Castle ahead of them.

It was quite different from an English Castle and yet it had an unmistakable charm.

It was obviously very old with arched windows which made it picturesque.

As they had gone uphill to reach it there was a magnificent view over the countryside.

Aletha was certain it had been a fortress of defence in ancient times when Hungary was continually at war.

It had three large square turrets with flat tops which was unusual, but when they entered the court-yard the later additions were elaborate and Baroque.

Mr. Heywood got out of the carriage to explain to the servant who answered the door why he had come.

The carriage was then instructed to drive to the back of the Castle where the stables were located.

Separate from them was a house which was of a very different period from the Castle itself.

It was here that Mr. Heywood presented his Letter of Introduction.

He and Aletha were immediately taken into a Sitting-Room where a middle-aged man greeted them.

His name was Hamoir Kovaks and he informed them in faltering English that he was in charge of the Baron's horses.

Mr. Heywood discovered that he talked French far more fluently.

They conversed in that language while consuming glasses of Tokay which Aletha tasted for the first time.

She had always associated it with the romance of Hungary and thought it was delicious.

By the time Mr. Heywood had explained to Mr. Kovaks exactly what he required it was too late to see the horses that evening.

Instead they were shown to their bedrooms where they changed for dinner and came down to find Mrs. Kovaks waiting for them.

She was a pleasant, rather stout woman who when she had been young must have been very pretty.

But she was obviously of a class that was accustomed to being subservient to the nobility and was shy of foreign guests.

It made conversation difficult and Aletha was glad when they retired to bed.

The next morning both she and Mr. Heywood were up very early and hurried to the stables before breakfast.

The actual stables were not in any way as good as those at Ling, but the horses were everything that Aletha expected them to be.

After a quick inspection they had breakfast, then with Mr. Kovaks to guide them rode into the open countryside.

Grooms followed, each leading horses, so that they could change mounts whenever they pleased.

It was thrilling for Aletha.

Yet when they turned for home she had the feeling, without his saying anything, that Mr. Heywood was a little disappointed.

This was confirmed when as they walked back to the house he said to her in a low voice:

"Good, but not good enough!"

"Do you think we shall find something better?" Aletha asked.

"I am sure we shall," he answered. "At the same time there are more being brought here for us to try."

When they went back after luncheon there were about twenty fresh horses in the stable-yard.

As Aletha walked towards them eagerly a man came from the direction of the Castle.

At one glance she realised that it was the Baron.

He certainly looked German, but he was younger than she had expected and in a way good-looking.

He was very tall, over six foot, and he walked with an unmistakable swagger.

He greeted Mr. Heywood in a condescending manner.

"I hear you have come from the Duke of Buclington," he said, "and of course I shall be pleased to sell His Grace any horses that take your fancy."

As he spoke he looked at Aletha for the first time, and his eyes widened.

"Who is this?" he enquired.

"My granddaughter is travelling with me," Mr. Heywood explained in a somewhat repressed tone.

"Then she must certainly be mounted on one of my best horses!" the Baron said. "And I will accompany you on your ride in case

Kovaks, you are not describing the best points of my animals accurately."

It sounded almost rude, but Mr. Kovaks merely bowed his head and said deprecatingly, and with what seemed almost unnecessary humility;

"I do my best, Master!"

"So I should hope," the Baron retorted.

He looked at Aletha.

"I will go to change," he said, "then I shall see with my own eyes if the way you ride is as beautiful as you look."

He was obviously paying her a compliment.

At the same time there was something familiar in his voice which made Aletha raise her chin.

The Baron did not take long to change.

When he came back he made a terrible fuss as to which horse he should ride.

Then he complained that the girths were not tight enough or the stirrups were too short.

He was showing off his authority, and Aletha thought he was just the sort of man her father would dislike.

Finally on the Baron's instructions she and Mr. Heywood accompanied him while the grooms came behind with fresh horses.

Mr. Kovaks was left in the court-yard.

They rode over much the same ground they had covered earlier in the morning.

Then the Baron drew in his horse and suggested that Mr. Heywood should change to one of the other animals.

"There are some jumps over there," he said pointing in the direction of them, "which I would like to see you take, and I am sure you will not be disappointed in the horse you are riding."

Mr. Heywood dismounted and Aletha said to the Baron:

"May I jump them with my grandfather?"

"No," the Baron said firmly. "The jumps are high for a woman."

Aletha was about to argue, then thought it would be a mistake.

As soon as Mr. Heywood had ridden away the Baron drew his horses nearer to hers and said:

"And now, Pretty Lady, tell me about yourself."

He spoke in an ingratiating tone which made her nervous.

She touched her horse with her whip to make him move forward.

The Baron followed her and he said:

"You ride superbly, and you are very lovely! There are a lot of things I want to talk to you about."

He spoke good English but with a decided German accent.

"I am listening, Baron," Aletha said coldly.

She did not look at him as she was watching Mr. Heywood riding towards the first jump.

He took it brilliantly and went on to the next.

"My wife is away," the Baron was saying, "and I find it very lonely in the Castle, which I want to show you. You will enjoy seeing it."

"I am sure it is very interesting," Aletha said, "but as we are here for such a short visit I doubt if my grandfather will have time."

"As it is your grandfather who is buying the horses and not you," the Baron said, "I will take you round this afternoon."

Aletha opened her lips to protest.

Then she thought it would be dangerous to antagonise the Baron.

She decided she would ask Mr. Heywood to say she was indispensable to his judgement as to which horses he required.

"What is your name?" the Baron asked.

"Aletha," she replied without thinking.

"A lovely name," he said. "As lovely as your eyes, and of course your lips."

He had drawn nearer to her, and as he spoke he put out his gloved hand and laid it on hers.

"We are going to know each other very much better than we do at the moment," he said softly.

Again Aletha urged her horse from him.

Then on an impulse she rode at the jump Mr. Heywood had just taken.

She heard the Baron give a shout as she went, but she pretended not to hear.

Her horse took the jump with some inches to spare and she felt her heart beating with delight that she had been able to do it.

Mr. Heywood had disappeared into the distance over the third jump and she followed him.

She took the second in style but her horse nearly fell at the third.

She managed however to keep him on his feet and to remain seated.

She found Mr. Heywood just ahead of her.

She rode up to him and he asked:

"Why did you follow me? These jumps are difficult for you on a horse you have never ridden before."

"I am here, safe and sound!" Aletha said blithely. "As a matter of fact I am running away from the Baron."

"What has he been saying to you?" Mr. Heywood asked.

"He was just paying me a lot of tiresome compliments," Aletha said evasively.

Mr. Heywood turned back the way they had come, but avoided the jumps.

"The whole trouble," he said, "is that you should not be here on this journey, and certainly not without a chaperon."

"I am perfectly all right, as long as I am with you," Aletha said soothingly.

She felt she had made a mistake in telling him that the Baron had been familiar.

He might make up his mind to buy what horses were available here, then return home immediately.

"What do you intend to buy?" she asked to change the subject. "I thought the horse you are riding took the first fence magnificently!"

"They certainly are outstanding," Mr. Heywood replied. "But I expect the Baron, knowing your father is a rich man, will ask an exorbitant sum."

When they reached the Baron he was all smiles.

"I have never seen the horses jump better!" he said. "But of course, they had exceptionally good riders."

He was looking at Aletha as he spoke, but she was careful not to meet his eyes.

They tried two or three other horses, then when they returned to the stables the Baron insisted they should have luncheon with him at the Castle.

There was nothing Mr. Heywood could do but accept the invitation.

He knew it would be extremely embarrassing for Kovaks if he refused.

The Castle was undeniably impressive with enormous rooms with arched ceilings.

There were huge stone fireplaces in which a whole trunk of a tree could be burnt when it was cold.

The Banqueting Hall could have seated fifty people with ease.

Aletha felt as if they were like peas rattling in a pod, while the servants in elaborate liveries served them on silver plate.

The furniture however was heavy and not attractive.

The pictures that hung on the walls were not particularly interesting.

When they left the Dining-Room they moved into a Salon.

It was large and elaborately furnished but not in good taste.

The Baron left them for a moment and when he came back he said:

"As I am alone here and greatly enjoy your company, I have given orders for your things to be moved from Kovaks so that you will be my guests tonight."

He was obviously speaking to Aletha and she saw Mr. Heywood's lips tighten.

He could hardly refuse to accept the Baron's invitation and said:

"You are very gracious. At the same time, you will understand that we have to leave you early tomorrow to visit Prince Józsel Estérházy's Stud."

"You will find nothing there that I cannot supply," the Baron said sharply.

"I am afraid the arrangements are already made," Mr. Heywood said, "but I would like to buy for His Grace four of the horses we rode today."

"I am sure the Duke will need more than that!" the Baron retorted.

"It is actually a question of price," Mr. Heywood said.

Because it was something in which she was not interested, Aletha rose from her chair and walked across the room to the window.

The panoramic view was breathtaking.

At the same time, she was uneasily conscious that while the Baron was talking to Mr. Heywood and obviously haggling over the price, his eyes were on her.

She could almost feel them boring into her back.

She wished ardently that they could leave this afternoon.

Then she told herself she was being needlessly apprehensive.

As long as Mr. Heywood was there, what could the Baron do other than pay her exaggerated compliments?

They returned to the stables.

The Baron insisted that there were a number more horses Mr. Heywood should try before he finally made up his mind.

He tried to persuade Aletha that she had ridden enough for one day.

He would like, he said, to show her the gardens of the Castle and later the Castle itself.

She however made it clear that her only interest was in riding.

As Mr. Heywood backed her up, the Baron's stratagems to get her alone were defeated.

Finally they went upstairs to dress for dinner.

The Baron showed them their rooms with a triumphant air, as if he expected them to be very impressed.

The rooms were large and furnished in Germanic taste which had a typical pomposity about it.

The Baron first showed Aletha into her room, then took Mr. Heywood a little further down the corridor to his.

A maid was waiting for Aletha and her luggage had been unpacked.

A bath was brought to her room, and when she was dressed she was wondering if Mr. Heywood would call for her when there was a knock on the door.

The maid opened it.

He came in speaking slowly so that the maid understood.

He told her he wished to speak to his granddaughter alone.

She went out closing the door behind her, and Mr. Heywood walked towards Aletha.

She was standing, having just risen from the stool in front of the dressing-table.

"I am sorry about this," Mr. Heywood said in a low voice.

"You mean our having to stay in the Castle?"

"I mean having that German making eyes at you!"

"I am glad we are leaving here tomorrow," Aletha said, "and please, do not leave me alone with him."

There was a note of fear in her voice.

"I will take good care of that," Mr. Heywood said, "but you understand that you must lock your door and make certain there is no other access to your bedroom."

Aletha looked at him in astonishment.

"You do not mean . . you cannot imagine . . he . . ?"

"I would not trust him as far as I could see him!" Mr. Heywood said.

"But . . I never thought . . I never imagined that a . . a gentleman would . ."

"I know, I know," Mr. Heywood said quietly, "but, as you are aware, you should not have come here without a chaperon."

"I have you," Aletha said.

"As he thinks I am nothing more than a Senior Servant," Mr. Heywood said, "I would not put it past him to drug my milk or have one of his servants give me a crack on the head!"

Aletha gave a little cry of horror.

"Now you are frightening me, and suppose somehow he comes to my room and tries to . . kiss me?"

"I have an idea — if you will agree."

She looked up at him and he said:

"When you come up to bed, undress. Then as soon as your maid has left you, come to me. I am just two doors further down the passage. I will make sure that no one can break in, and we will exchange rooms."

Aletha clasped her hands together.

"That is clever of you, but suppose he sees us doing that?"

"I have ascertained that he sleeps a little way away in the huge Master Suite which obviously inflates his ego."

"Then that is what we will do," Aletha said. "And please make sure that when he finds I am not here, he does not come to your room."

"If he manages to get in here thinking he will find me, I shall knock him down!" Mr. Heywood said. "I may be getting old, but I can still deal with bounders like him!"

There was a grim note in his voice which made Aletha say:

"Thank you, thank you, for being so wonderful! I am sorry to be such a nuisance."

Unexpectedly Mr. Heywood smiled.

"It is the penalty for being beautiful," he said, "and I hope you are taking the lessons that this journey is teaching you, to heart."

"In future," Aletha said, "I shall encase myself in armour-plating and carry a stiletto!"

Mr. Heywood laughed.

"At least you have a sense of humour!" he said. "Now come along, let us face the music and look out for the pitfalls."

They walked down the stairs and when they entered the Salon the Baron was waiting for them.

Aletha had to admit that he looked his best in evening-clothes although she avoided his eyes.

He, however, gave her his arm to take her into dinner and it was something she could hardly refuse.

As they left the Salon he put his hand over hers and she felt the pressure of his fingers.

"You are driving me crazy!" he said in a low voice which only she could hear.

She did not answer, but looked straight ahead, carrying herself stiffly.

When they reached the Dining-Room the plates on which they were served were gold.

Magnificent goblets studded with precious stones ornamented the table.

The food was excellent, but rather heavy.

The Baron deliberately talked only to Aletha, ignoring Mr. Heywood as if he was not there.

He was quite perturbed that Aletha answered him in mono-syllables.

He talked of his importance in Hungary, the advice he had given to the Emperor, and the house he was redecorating and restoring in Budapest.

Everything he said was egotistic and affected.

Aletha thought it would be impossible to find anyone more conceited or more pleased with himself.

They returned to the Salon.

She was just about to say she was tired and would like to go to bed when the Butler came into the room to say:

"*Herr* Kovaks wishes to speak to Mr. Heywood, Herr Baron."

"Perhaps it could wait until tomorrow," Mr. Heywood suggested.

"Herr Kovaks is in the hall, *Mein Herr* and says it is very important," the Butler replied.

Mr. Heywood knew enough Hungarian to understand, and reluctantly he got to his feet.

Aletha also rose.

"I know you will understand," she said to the Baron, "but I am very tired, and I would like now to go to bed."

"Of course you shall do that," the Baron agreed, "but first I have a small present for you which I will show you while your grandfather is talking to *Herr* Kovaks."

He went to a table on which there was a small package.

There was nothing Mr. Heywood could do but follow the Butler out of the room.

As the door shut behind him the Baron said:

"You are very beautiful, Aletha, and this is the first of many presents I hope to give you."

"It is kind of you," Aletha answered, "but I . . I do . . not really . . want a present."

"Open it!" the Baron ordered.

She undid the ribbon and removed the tissue paper from a long thin velvet box.

She opened it and, to her astonishment, inside was a narrow bracelet set with diamonds.

She stared at it and the Baron said:

"Now you understand how much I want you, and I will tell you later how much you attract me."

Aletha gave a little gasp and shut the velvet box.

She replaced it on the table saying:

"Thank you, but you will understand that if my mother was alive she would not . . allow me to accept such an . . expensive gift from a man . . especially one who is a comparative stranger."

The Baron merely smiled.

"I will not be a stranger for long, and I have a great deal more than a bracelet to offer you, my pretty one!"

He was very close to her and Aletha felt his arm go round her waist.

Quickly she extricated herself.

Before he could prevent her she ran across the room and reached the door.

"Goodnight, *Herr* Baron," she said and went out into the Hall.

Mr. Heywood was in conversation with Mr. Kovaks.

Aletha was certain it was the Baron who had arranged that Mr. Heywood was forced to leave them alone.

He looked at her enquiringly as she hurried past him in the direction of the staircase.

"I am . . going to bed . . Grandpapa," she said.

He knew by the inflection in her voice that something unpleasant had occurred.

He took a step forward as if he would go with her, then changed his mind.

He continued to talk to Mr. Kovaks until the Baron came to join them.

In her bedroom the maid helped Aletha undress.

She put on her nightgown.

Before she got into bed she saw that her negligee which was very pretty, was lying on a chair.

Beneath the chair were the soft heel-less slippers which would make no sound as she walked down the corridor.

She told the maid she wished to be called early.

When the woman had gone she got out of bed to listen at the door.

She could hear voices and knew that Mr. Heywood and the Baron were coming upstairs together.

They were talking about horses.

She listened as they passed by.

Then as she looked down she realised there was no key in the lock.

She knew then that Mr. Heywood had been right in guessing what the Baron intended.

She thought how horrible it would be if he touched her and if his lips tried to take possession of hers.

She was thankful that Mr. Heywood had warned her what might happen.

Otherwise she would never have had the slightest idea that anyone who was supposed to be a Nobleman would behave so disgracefully.

Especially towards a guest in his own house.

She found it difficult to wait until everything was quiet before she went to Mr. Heywood's room.

He would have been provided with one of the footmen as his Valet.

Aletha knew she must be sure he was alone before she went to his room.

She was also afraid she might encounter the Night-footman, who would be quenching some of the sconces after everybody had retired to bed.

The minutes seemed to pass by like hours.

At last she heard two men talking in low voices as they passed her door.

She thought they would be the man who had valeted Mr. Heywood and also the Baron's Valet.

As soon as she could hear them no longer, she very cautiously opened the door and peeped out.

As she expected the lights in the corridor had been dimmed.

The candles of every second sconce were extinguished.

She shut the door behind her and moving like a startled fawn ran down the corridor.

The door to Mr. Heywood's room was ajar, and as she rushed in he was standing waiting for her.

A long dark robe which he was wearing made him look very tall and, she thought, very protective.

She ran to his side saying as she reached him:

"There is . . no key in . . my door!"

"It is what I might have expected," Mr. Heywood said angrily. "Well, there is a key here and I have made sure there is no other way into this room. Lock the door as soon as I have left."

"S . . suppose he . . does somehow get in?" Aletha insisted in a frightened voice.

"If he does, scream! I shall be listening for you," Mr. Heywood replied.

He smiled at her.

"I am used to sleeping with one eye open when I am attending to sick horses."

"Then I will scream very loudly!" Aletha promised.

Mr. Heywood put his hand on her shoulder.

"Do not worry," he said. "I will deal with the Baron, and we will leave first thing tomorrow morning."

"Thank you . . thank . . you!" Aletha said, "I hope Papa never learns about this . . but if he does . . I know he . . will be very grateful . . to you."

Mr. Heywood was walking towards the door.

"Lock yourself in as soon as I am outside," he said softly.

Aletha did as she was told.

TWO HEARTS IN HUNGARY

Then she got into the big bed which was the same size as the one she had been allotted.

Because she was frightened she did not blow out the candles.

She merely lay with her eyes shut, saying a prayer of gratitude because Mr. Heywood was so kind.

The Baron was repulsive!

This was certainly something she had not expected to find in Hungary.

The Hungarian she had met by the balustrade outside the Palace had been very different.

He had paid her compliments, but they had not revolted her in the way the Baron's had.

He had certainly looked at her with admiration when he called her a 'Sylph'.

But he had not seemed in any way over-familiar or frightening.

"I wonder if I shall ever see him again?" she asked herself wistfully.

Even if she never did, she had a feeling that his looks and his charm had somehow set a standard.

It would be by that she would judge other men in the future.

The men she was to meet in London, and the man who was to be her husband!

Chapter Five

Aletha had breakfast in her bedroom which she knew must have been arranged by Mr. Heywood.

Everything was packed.

When she came downstairs she found him waiting for her in the hall.

He did not speak, he merely guided her through the front door.

Outside there was a travelling-carriage drawn by four horses.

She guessed that Mr. Heywood had arranged this with Hamoir Kovaks.

She suspected it had nothing to do with the Baron.

She got into the carriage, Mr. Heywood tipped the servants and followed her.

She realised it was not yet half-past eight and there was no sign of the Baron.

Only when they were down the drive could she no longer repress her curiosity and asked:

"What . . happened? Did you . . have a scene with . . him last . . night?"

Mr. Heywood sat back comfortably against the padded seat.

"It was a good thing," he said, "that you obeyed me. As I expected he came to your room and was very surprised to find me there."

"What happened?" Aletha asked breathlessly.

Mr. Heywood smiled.

"I wanted to knock him down and teach him not to behave in such a way again, but I thought it would be a mistake in case he talked about you, and somehow the story got back to England."

"Then . . what did you do?" Aletha asked.

She could not help feeling a little disappointed that the Baron had not got his just desserts.

At the same time she realised that Mr. Heywood was a much older man.

He might have been hurt if they had struck each other.

Mr. Heywood's eyes were twinkling as he said:

"I pretended to be asleep when the Baron came in! I woke up with a start when I saw him peering at me in surprise."

"I should think he was astonished!" Aletha murmured.

"I had left two candles burning," Mr. Heywood went on, "and when I saw him I exclaimed:'

"'Forgive me, *Herr* Baron, I fell asleep and forgot to blow out the candles. How clever of you to realise that was what I had done, and I can only apologise profusely for my carelessness!'"

Aletha laughed.

"That must have taken him aback!"

"It certainly did," Mr. Heywood said, and after a moment he remarked:

"'See it does not happen again!'"

He walked towards the door and then, as if he could not prevent himself from asking the question, he enquired:

"'Why has your granddaughter changed her room?'"

"What was your answer to that? Aletha enquired.

"I said, staring at him pointedly:

'She was frightened when she found there was no key in the lock. It must have been overlooked. But she had promised His Grace the Duke before we left England that she would always lock her door in Hotels and also houses in foreign countries. She would not wish him to think she had disobeyed his instructions!'"

Aletha laughed.

"What did the Baron say to that?"

"He murmured something," Mr. Heywood replied, "then went from the room."

He paused before he added:

"I made quite sure he went to his own apartments, and I left my door ajar all night so that I could hear if you were in any trouble."

"Oh, thank you . . thank . . you!" Aletha exclaimed.

"You have been so clever! As he is such a . . horrid man, I wish you could have taught him a lesson! But it is much more diplomatic for us to leave without there being any unpleasantness."

"That is what I thought," Mr. Heywood agreed, "and you do see

77

that in future you must make quite sure there is a key in your door and lock it."

"I am sure this sort of thing would not happen in England!" Aletha said innocently.

There was a somewhat cynical twist to Mr. Heywood's lips but he did not disillusion her.

Instead he started to talk about the Palace they were going to visit.

"It will take us some time to get there," he said, "so we will have luncheon on the way and arrive early in the afternoon."

"Tell me more about Estérházys," Aletha pleaded.

"The Palace was built in the 18th century," Mr. Heywood replied, "by Miklós Estérházy and it was called 'Magnificent' by his contemporaries."

"I am longing to see it," Aletha murmured.

"It was under his patronage," Mr. Heywood went on, "that it acquired European fame and his home became a 'Hungarian Versailles'."

"How did he do that?" Aletha asked.

"Not only was the Palace beautiful, but imaginative festivities took place there and were attended by the Empress Maria-Theresa. But even that did not satisfy Estérázy.

"What else did he want?" Aletha asked.

"First he had his own Opera House built, and employed Franz Joseph Haydn as Conductor to his private Orchestra."

"How wonderful!"

"Then he added a Puppet Theatre, and every kind of entertainment which brought all the famous people in the world to Fertōd."

"I cannot wait to see it!" Aletha exclaimed.

"I doubt if it will be as sensational now as it was then," Mr. Heywood said, "and do not forget that we are concerned only with their horses."

"I will not forget that!"

She realised that Mr. Heywood was hesitating over something else he was about to say to her.

She waited a little apprehensiveiy, wondering what it could be.

"You have come with me," Mr. Heywood began, "and you have also chosen to be my granddaughter. You must therefore not be surprised if you are treated differently from the way to which you are accustomed."

"Of course I understand that," Aletha said.

"I have always been told that the Hungarians are very conscious of their own importance," Mr. Heywood went on. "I do not want you to feel insulted when you are treated as I will be – as a paid servant in your father's employment."

"I understand that," Aletha said, "but if people had any intelligence, or should I say, sensitivity, they would be aware the moment they met you that you are a gentleman, and I, if nothing else, am born a Lady."

She spoke fiercely, but Mr. Heywood merely laughed.

"People treat one another as what they believe them to be, rather than what they appear to be but you may be quite certain the horses will not be class-conscious!"

They both laughed and Aletha settled down to enjoy the beauty of the countryside.

There were mountains, twisting rivers and fields filled with wild flowers.

It made them appear like an Oriental carpet of brilliant colours and indescribable beauty.

They had luncheon in a small village where the women were wearing national dress.

The food was plain but good.

Aletha began to forget the Baron and to enjoy the enchanted land she had always believed Hungary to be.

The peasants looked happy and sang as they worked.

"Of course the Empress loves being here," she said, "and as the Hungarians love beauty it is not surprising that they love her!"

"*Adore* her is the right word," Mr. Heywood corrected. "She comes here whenever she can escape from the protocol and dullness of the Court in Vienna."

"We must make her very happy when she comes to Ling," Aletha said softly.

"I am sure we will find exactly the horses we want at the Palace of the Estérházys," Mr. Heywood said confidently.

"Did you buy any of the Baron"s horses?" Aletha asked.

"I bought two just to make Kovaks feel that he has not been a failure," Mr. Heywood replied.

"That was kind of you."

They reached Fertōd early in the afternoon.

As soon as Aletha saw the huge wrought-iron gates, then the exquisite Palace, she knew it was even more wonderful than she had expected.

The Palace had a square tower surmounting it which was characteristic of Hungarian architecture.

There were oval-shaped windows and the brilliant carvings above each one were unique.

The statues on the roof and the pillars which supported the portico were all reminiscent of Louis XVI.

As he had done before, Mr. Heywood left her in the carriage while he presented his credentials inside the building.

Aletha was entranced by the beautifully laid out garden with three fountains and many statues.

There was colour everywhere – the flowers, the shrubs, the trees all appeared to be in blossom.

The sunshine made everything dance in front of her eyes.

It was as if she was watching a Ballet taking place in some magical theatre.

As she looked back at the house she saw a man coming out through the front door and supposed it was Mr. Heywood.

Then to her astonishment she saw it was the Hungarian who had spoken to her on the Terrace of the Royal Palace in Budapest.

He was obviously going riding and carried a whip in his hand.

His high top-hat was set at a jaunty angle on his dark head.

He looked casually at the carriage with its four horses before he saw Aletha.

For a moment he was still as if in astonishment.

Then he walked towards her.

"Is it possible that it is you?" he asked. "Or am I dreaming?"

He was speaking in English and she replied:

"I told you I was looking for horses."

"Then you have come to see mine – or rather – my father's."

"I naturally had no idea they were yours!"

He looked at the empty seat beside her and asked:

"Surely you are not alone?"

"No, my grandfather is inside the Palace, explaining to somebody why we are here."

"This is the most surprising and delightful thing that has

80

ever happened!" the Hungarian said. "Suppose we start by your introducing yourself to me?"

For a moment Aletha forgot who she was pretending to be and said:

"I am Aletha Li –!"

She quickly amended it to 'Link' having very nearly betrayed herself.

The Hungarian bowed.

"I am delighted to meet you, Miss Link," he said, his eyes twinkling, "and I am Miklós Estérházy, eldest son of Prince Józsel."

"I know I should curtsy," Aletha remarked, "but it is rather difficult while I am sitting down!"

Prince Miklós laughed and opened the door of the carriage.

"Let us go to find your grandfather," he suggested, "and discover what is being arranged."

Aletha had the idea she ought to wait in case, as had happened at the Castle, they were driven to another house.

But the temptation to go inside the Palace was too great.

She stepped out of the carriage, Prince Miklós putting out his hand to help her.

They walked inside and she saw at once that the interior was as beautiful as the outside.

The French influence was obvious and made everything look graceful rather than ponderous as it had been at the Baron's Castle.

They walked through the hall in which a number of footmen were in attendance and quite a long way down a passage.

"I think your grandfather will be with Héviz," Prince Miklós said, "who looks after our horses. He will doubtless be telling him how marvellous they are before he even has a chance to see them!"

As he spoke he opened a door.

They went into what Aletha thought was either a Secretary's room or an Estate Office.

There were maps all over the walls and a number of tin despatch boxes piled at one side.

The Prince was not mistaken.

Mr. Heywood was sitting in front of a desk where a man was talking in broken English and gesticulating with his hands.

Both men rose as they entered and Aletha said quickly to Mr. Heywood:

"I forgot to tell you, Grandpapa, that I spoke to Prince Miklós when I was waiting for you outside the Royal Palace."

She smiled at him as she went on:

"Of course I had no idea who he was, or that I would meet him here."

Mr. Heywood held out his hand.

"I am honoured to meet Your Highness!"

"And I am delighted that your desire for horses has brought you to Fertōd!"

He looked at the other man and added:

"I am sure, Héviz, you have already sold him a dozen before he has even seen them!"

"I hope so, Your Highness," was the reply.

"As I am going to the stables," the Prince said, "I suggest you and your granddaughter come with me."

"That is exactly what we would like to do, Your Highness," Mr. Heywood replied. "But I think first I must discuss where we are to stay, and must pay the carriage I hired to bring us here."

"If I had known, I would have met you at the Station," the Prince replied.

"Actually we came from the Castle at Györ," Mr. Heywood informed him.

"From Baron von Sicardsburg:" the Prince enquired. "He boasts a lot, but I can assure you, his horses in no way compare with ours. Is that not true, Héviz?"

"It certainly is, your Highness!"

"He is a . . horrid man!" Aletha said impulsively. "I am sorry we bought . . anything from . . him."

Prince Miklós gave her a sharp glance.

"You are quite right in what you say," he replied, "and you should have nothing to do with him."

"I hope . . never to . . see him . . again," Aletha murmured.

Then she thought she was being indiscreet and looked towards the door.

"Do let us go to the stables," she begged.

The Prince turned to Mr. Heywood.

"You and your granddaughter must of course stay here," he said. "Is your name the same as hers?"

"No, Your Highness. My name is Heywood – Aletha"s mother was – my daughter."

He spoke in a way which told Aletha that he disliked having to tell a lie.

Because it also embarrassed her, she moved quickly towards the door.

The Prince was just in time to open it for her.

They walked ahead down the passage followed by Mr. Heywood and *Herr* Héviz.

When they reached the hall the Prince gave orders to the footmen to bring their luggage inside.

While Mr. Heywood was paying the coachman the Prince took Aletha down a corridor.

"We can reach the stables quicker this way," he said, "and you can see a little of my home while we do so, although there is a great deal more I want to show you."

"I have already heard how magnificent it is," Aletha said, "and I would have been very upset if I had to go home without seeing the Music Room."

"So you also like music," the Prince said.

His voice deepened as he added:

"I have thought about you so much since I left Budapest. Have you thought of me?"

It was a question she had not expected and the colour came into Aletha's cheeks.

She knew she ought to say that she had forgotten him completely, but the lie would not come to her lips.

"You have!" the Prince said triumphantly when she did not answer. "I could not believe it was not on the order of the gods that we were brought together on the terrace of the Royal Palace."

"My g . . grandfather said I had done . . wrong in getting . . out of the carriage," Aletha said.

"I think you flew out of it," the Prince answered, "and because you are not human, no one saw you except me!"

Aletha laughed.

"I am quite prepared to believe everything is magical which happens in Hungary!"

"You like my country?"

"It is so beautiful that I can understand why the Empress loves it and longs to come here."

"So you have heard about our Empress!"

"Yes, of course, and that is why Papa . ."

She bit back the words just in time.

She was going to say: "That is why Papa is buying horses for her to ride when she comes to stay."

Instead, tumbling over her words she finished:

" . . my g . . grandfather is buying Hungarian horses for the Duke of Buclington."

"I had supposed they were for himself!" the Prince exclaimed.

"That is what he would like them to be," Aletha said, "for he was, when he was young, one of the best amateur riders in England, but he lost all his money."

"And are you saying that the Duke of Buclington now employs him?" the Prince enquired.

"Yes, that's right," Aletha said.

There was a little pause and because she was aware of what the Prince was thinking she said:

"I believe, Your Highness had offered us the hospitality of your home under a false impression. If you wish to change your mind, my grandfather and I will of course, understand."

"I have no intention of changing my mind," the Prince said quickly. "I only thought that your grandfather looked very much an English gentleman."

"That is exactly what he is!" Aletha said sharply.

The Prince looked at her and she saw that he was smiling and his eyes were twinkling.

"Now you are accusing me," he said, "of a crime I have not committed. In fact, your grandfather looks so handsome with all the qualities we admire in an Englishman, that I could not believe he was not rich as well."

Aletha had the feeling he was getting out of a rather uncomfortable situation very cleverly.

Because she had no wish to quarrel with him she smiled and said:

"I do feel that we are imposing on you, and I have already been told how proud and autocratic the Hungarian nobility are."

The Prince laughed.

"Now you are definitely trying to put me down a peg or two!" the Prince replied. "Please, my beautiful Sylph, do not be unkind to me!"

He spoke so beguilingly that Aletha felt she could say no more.

A moment later they were joined by Mr. Heywood and the Hungarian.

The stables certainly deserved the same description as the Palace – 'Magnificent'.

They were very different in every way from those which were owned by the Baron.

As they went from stall to stall, Aletha had eyes only for the horses and she knew they had found exactly what her father wanted.

Each horse seemed to be superior to the last.

When they had inspected at least two dozen she looked at Mr. Heywood and said:

"Shall we make an offer for them all?"

"You will do nothing of the sort!" the Prince remarked before Mr. Heywood could reply. "These horses are all far too precious for us to part with them, and how can you be so cruel as to suggest that I should walk rather than ride?"

"I know our arrival has kept you from riding," Aletha said, "but if we change very quickly, could we please ride with you?"

"How long will you take to change?" the Prince asked.

"Two minutes!" Aletha replied and he laughed.

"I will allow you eight more," he said, "and after that we will go off without you!"

Aletha gave a little cry of horror and it was *Herr* Héviz who said:

"I will take you to your room. I am sure one of the maids will have unpacked for you."

They went back to the Palace and *Herr* Héviz had difficulty in keeping up with Aletha.

She almost ran down the corridor and up the very impressive staircase.

A footman had alerted the Housekeeper.

Aletha was taken to a very magnificent bedroom.

She was sure she would not have been given it if the Prince had not thought Mr. Heywood was buying the horses for himself.

However she had no time to think about that.

She started to change into one of her attractive riding-habits.

She put the hat with its gauze veil on her head without even looking in the mirror.

85

Then she ran back the way she had come without waiting for anybody to guide her.

When she reached the stables it was to find that Mr. Heywood was already mounted on a very fine chestnut.

He was walking it round the cobbled yard.

There was a black stallion waiting to be saddled for the Prince and another horse beside it which Aletha knew was for her to ride.

It was a grey and was outstanding in every particular.

As she reached the Prince he said with a smile:

"I said you were a Sylph and only a Sylph could have flown so quickly."

"I am sure I have a minute to spare!" Aletha said breathlessly.

"You know I would have waited for you," he answered quietly.

She thought he would cup his hands to help her into the saddle.

Instead he held her on each side of her small waist and lifted her.

Because he was so close she felt a strange little tremor go through her that she did not understand.

Then he adjusted the skirt of her habit over the stirrup.

As he finished he looked up to say:

"I know I will not be disappointed when I see you ride, but if I am – I shall want to shoot myself!"

"Now you are being over-dramatic and very Hungarian!" Aletha said without thinking.

Only when his laughter rang out did she wonder if she had been rude.

Herr Héviz did not go with them.

The Prince led Aletha and Mr. Heywood out of the stable-yard and into some well-kept paddocks.

They passed through them.

Then Aletha found what she had always heard of – the wide unhedged wild grassland which appeared to go on into an indefinite horizon.

The horses needed no encouragement to go as fast as they wanted.

As they galloped over the grass, butterflies hovering over the flowers and rose in front of them, and the song-birds swept away overhead.

To Aletha it was like riding into a Paradise she had always known existed, but had never expected to find.

As she raced forward, her eyes dazzled by the sunshine, she was aware of the Prince riding beside her.

He looked very much a part of his horse.

Only when they had galloped for over a mile did they instinctively draw in their horses together.

"That was wonderful!" Aletha exclaimed. "Even more wonderful than my dreams!"

"That is what I thought when I first saw you!" the Prince replied.

She looked at him in surprise.

It was impossible to reply for at that moment Mr. Heywood, who had been a little way behind them, drew in his horse.

"I can only say, Your Highness," he said to the Prince, "that your reputation where your horses are concerned is fully justified."

He paused a moment and then went on:

"It is impossible to find words with which to express their excellence and superiority."

Listening, Aletha agreed with every word.

"That is what I wanted you to say," the Prince replied, "but let me make clear, so there is no mistake, that the horses you are riding are not for sale!"

"I rather suspected that!" Mr. Heywood said ruefully.

"We have however a great many others which I know will please you," the Prince said. "Tomorrow you will ride those which can, if you wish, travel to England."

Aletha longed to say that, however expensive it might be, she wanted to own the horse she was riding.

But she knew it would be a mistake to interfere.

So she said nothing and they turned for home.

As they rode back the Prince took them by a slightly different route.

Because it was now late in the afternoon they passed peasants returning home from their work in the fields.

They were singing as they went.

Aletha thought the girls' voices as they mingled with the baritone of the men, were very lovely.

The Prince saw the rapt expression on her face and said:

"I knew this was what you would enjoy, and having come to Hungary you will, I know, want to hear our gypsy music."

"Yes, of course," Aletha said. "Is it possible?"

"Nothing is impossible where you are concerned," he said, "and I will arrange for you to hear the gypsies tomorrow night. In fact, we will have a party."

Aletha's eyes lit up and she said:

"That is very kind of you, but we have not yet met your mother or your father."

"My mother is dead," the Prince replied, "but my father, like myself, enjoys a party, particularly if it is given for somebody very special."

Aletha wanted to say she was quite sure Prince József would not think that either she or Mr. Heywood were very special.

However she kept silent.

Later, after they had gone up to dress for dinner, Mr. Heywood came to her room to take her downstairs.

She was not alone – the maid was still there.

"I hope you are enjoying yourself," he said.

She was wearing one of the beautiful gowns that had been bought for her in London because she was to be a débutante.

It was white and the material was draped in the front over a skirt of silver lame which clung closely to her figure.

At the back there was a bustle of white and silver ribbons.

They began as a huge bow and ended with the ends of the ribbons trailing behind her.

With every movement she made she glittered like moonlight on water.

She had known as she put it on that it would remind the Prince that he thought she was a Sylph.

She had not expected to wear any jewellery in Hungary while pretending to be Mr. Heywood's granddaughter.

But she had taken some of her mother's with her in case she needed more money.

She therefore could not resist putting a small collet of diamonds round her neck.

Then she added a brooch shaped like a star between her breasts.

Mr. Heywood was looking at her admiringly as the maid left the room.

"I suppose you realise," Aletha said in a low voice, "that we are not entitled to these bedrooms, nor, I think, should we be eating in the Dining-Room."

Mr. Heywood looked puzzled.

"Prince Miklós thought you were buying horses for yourself," Aletha explained.

"Ah, now I understand," Mr. Heywood said. "I thought we were being treated differently from the way we were at first received at the Castle!"

Aletha knew that the Baron would not have offered her a diamond bracelet if he had been aware of her true identity.

Nor, she thought, would he have dared, if he had known she was her father's daughter, to enter her bedroom.

She waited for Mr. Heywood to reply seeing that he was thinking it over before he spoke.

Then he smiled.

"Well, we may as well make hay while the sun shines!" he said. "Perhaps tomorrow night we shall find ourselves moved out of the best rooms of the Palace into a pig-sty!"

"It will not be as bad as that," Aletha laughed, "but I shall not mind if I have to spend the night with the horse I was riding this afternoon!"

"I thought you liked that one," Mr. Heywood said, "but the Prince made it quite clear they were not for sale."

"If you ask me," Aletha said, "I think it was rather sharp practice to try and tempt us with something that was out of reach!"

Mr. Heywood laughed.

"Do not say that to His Highness or we shall definitely find ourselves sleeping in less comfortable beds!"

He walked across the room and Aletha was aware that he glanced at the lock on the door.

The key showed prominently as he opened it.

He did not say anything.

Aletha wanted to tell him she was absolutely sure there would be no need for her to lock her door tonight.

The Prince had said some flattering things.

Yet her instinct told her that he would never insult her in the way the Baron had done.

She did not know how she knew this, but she did know it.

She was convinced that what he felt for her was something very different.

At the same time he was Hungarian, and she had been warned that Hungarians were romantic.

She had also read and she was sure it was in a book she was not supposed to read, that they were very ardent and passionate lovers.

She was not certain exactly what that implied, but it was why the Baron had wanted to come to her bedroom.

It made her shudder even to think of it.

"He was not romantic," she thought, "just bestial, and it is degrading to think that he might have touched me!"

Prince Miklós was different.

There was something about him that reminded her of the Knights of Chivalry she had read about when she was a child.

When she thought of it, he might be like her Dream Lover.

Then she told herself she was being imaginative and quite ridiculous.

Because the Prince thought she was pretty, he had paid her compliments.

He would have complimented in the same way any woman who took his fancy.

To take him seriously would be a great mistake.

Then it suddenly struck Aletha that perhaps he was being so familiar because her grandfather was a paid servant of the Duke.

She would therefore not be a Lady, but of a lower class.

She felt as if a cold hand gripped her heart.

With an effort she made herself remember that she was in Hungary only for a few days.

Once they had bought the horses they would go home.

She would never see Prince Miklós again.

"It would be a great mistake to think too much about him," she told herself, as they walked down the stairs.

The Prince was waiting for them in a very beautiful Salon where they were to meet before dinner.

As she and Mr. Heywood entered the room he moved from the fireplace at the end of it.

He had been talking to several other people and came towards them.

He looked so smart, so dashing and so outstandingly handsome in his evening-clothes that Aletha felt a very strange feeling within her breast.

As he reached her she knew that for no apparent reason she was blushing.

The Prince took her hand.

"Need I tell you that you look exactly as if you had stepped from one of the fountains," he said. "And now, I want to introduce you to my father."

As Aletha made a very graceful curtsy to Prince József she realised he was an older edition of his son.

His second son Nikolas also resembled him.

However his daughter Misina was attractive in a very different way.

Aletha was to learn later that she resembled her mother who had been a Romanian Princess.

All the Estérházys were extremely pleasant to Aletha and Mr. Heywood.

The conversation at dinner was witty and so amusing and they all seemed to be laughing.

The food was outstanding and they drank Tokay and French champagne.

They ate off Sèvres china.

Aletha thought it was infinitely preferable to the flamboyant gold plate with which the Baron had entertained them.

"What did you think of the Castle at which you stayed last night?" Prince József asked Aletha.

"I was very impressed by the outside of it," she replied truthfully, "but the inside is pompous and in no way compares with Your Highness's lovely Palace."

The Prince laughed.

"That is what I thought the only time I was there."

"And what did you think of the Baron?" Prince Nikolas enquired.

The way he spoke made Aletha realise that he had already heard from his brother that she disliked the Baron.

She therefore said demurely:

"I thought he was very like his Castle!"

They all laughed, and Prince József said:

"That was a very diplomatic answer, Miss Link. It is always a mistake to make enemies, unless one is obliged to do so."

"You can say that, Papa," Misina exclaimed, "for the simple

91

reason that people are too afraid to oppose you, and therefore you have no enemies."

"I should be more flattered," the Prince replied, "if you told me they loved me for myself."

"I think that is impossible," Misina replied, "and it applies to all of us."

"What do you mean by that?" the Prince enquired.

"Because the Estérházys have a kind of aura about us. That is what people see and think of first," his sister answered. "They are not really concerned with US as real people."

Aletha knew she had put into words exactly what she was thinking herself.

She said before anybody else could speak:

"I think if people are intelligent and sensible they seek what is real and true, apart from the trappings. I want to be liked just for myself and not for any other reason!"

As she spoke she saw Mr. Heywood glance at her.

She realised she had been talking as Lady Aletha Ling and not as 'Miss Link'.

"Of course," she added quickly, "there is no comparison between all of you here with this wonderful Palace behind you, and an ordinary person like myself."

It was rather a lame cover-up.

At the same time, she felt nobody would realise she had 'made a gaffe'.

Just like the French, the Estérházys loved an argument.

They were all discussing whether position title and wealth prevented those who had it from being human.

"Can you imagine," Misina asked scornfully, "that anybody thinks the Pope or the Emperor are just 'ordinary' men?

"To me a woman is a woman whether she is the Empress or a peasant!" Prince Nikolas said.

He spoke very positively.

His family were aware that he was head-over-heels in love with the Empress Elizabeth.

"Frankly I think Misina is right," her father said finally. "If everybody was to be the same, the whole structure of society would collapse!"

"And a good thing too!" Prince Nikolas said.

Aletha noticed that Prince Miklós said nothing.

After dinner Misina played the piano brilliantly.

Aletha was able to listen to some of the beautiful Hungarian music, as well as melodies by Johann Strauss.

She was unaware that she swayed a little to the melody of 'The Blue Danube'.

Prince Miklós was watching her and the expression in his eyes made her feel shy.

Finally when they went up to bed he escorted her to the foot of the stairs.

Mr. Heywood was having a last word with Prince Józsel and he said in a low voice which only she could hear:

"It makes me so happy to have you here! In your shimmering gown you not only seem part of the fountains but also of my home."

"You . . you are flattering me," Aletha said lightly.

"I am serious," he replied, "and I shall lie awake counting the hours until tomorrow!"

Her eyes met his and she found it very difficult to look away.

Then as she went up the stairs beside Mr. Heywood she told herself again that she must not take him seriously.

He was just being romantic, and how could anyone be anything else when they were in Hungary?

Chapter Six

As Aletha dressed for dinner she thought it had been the most exciting day she had ever spent.

They had started riding the new horses which had been brought to the stables immediately after breakfast.

They were not as impressive as those which the Prince wished to keep.

At the same time, a lot of them were young and had tremendous possibilities.

Aletha knew from the look on Mr. Heywood's face that he was more than delighted with what the Prince had produced.

It seemed inevitable, Aletha thought, that she should ride beside the Prince.

Mr. Heywood went off on his own, taking jumps unexpectedly so as to test the horse he was on.

Occasionally he would gallop off only to return looking more pleased than he had before he started.

"It is hopeless," Aletha said to Prince Miklós during the afternoon. "My grandfather obviously finds it impossible to choose which are the best."

The Prince laughed.

"I assure you we are only too willing to sell those we do not want for ourselves."

"That is the whole point," Aletha replied. "You are being greedy!"

"I am also greedy about other things besides horses."

He was looking at her as he spoke with the expression in his eyes she had begun to expect.

Every time she was aware of it she felt a little tremor in her breast.

She knew that being with him was not only interesting, but also thrilling.

"When I go home," she thought, "I shall never see him again, so it is no use feeling like this!"

But she could not suppress what she was feeling.

Nor could she stop herself from knowing that her heart turned over when he paid her a compliment.

"You are too good to be true!" he said. "Ever since I met you I find it hard to believe you are real."

"My father once said that if you prick a King he bleeds, and that makes sure he is a human being."

She expected the Prince to give her some witty answer.

Instead he looked away from her.

When she glanced at him in surprise she knew instinctively that he wished to say that he wanted to kiss her.

The idea did not shock her.

Nor did she feel disgusted, as she had when the Baron had spoken of her lips.

"Perhaps it would be very exciting to be kissed by a Hungarian in Hungary," she thought, "and certainly very romantic!"

Then as she glanced at the Prince she knew he was reading her thoughts.

For a moment they just looked at each other.

"I suppose you know," he said, "you are torturing me unbearably! The sooner you go back to England the better!"

He spoke so violently that she stared at him in astonishment.

Without speaking another word he turned his horse and started to gallop back towards the Palace.

After a few seconds she started to follow him.

He rode ahead until they reached the entrance to the stables.

Then he waited.

She rode up beside him and he said:

"Forgive me! Sometimes you torture me beyond endurance!"

She looked at him in bewilderment.

As if he realised she had no idea what he was talking about he said gently:

"Forget me! I want you to enjoy yourself and I suspect your grandfather will soon make up his mind. Then you will be leaving Hungary behind."

"But I will have . . your horses to remind me of . . your wonderful . . country," Aletha replied.

She wanted to say: "to remind me of you".

But she knew that was something which was far too intimate.

As if once again he knew what she was thinking he put out his hand.

After a moment's pause she gave him hers.

She had pulled off her glove.

As their bare skin touched she felt something like a streak of lightning run through her.

Then as the Prince took off his hat and bent to kiss her hand, she knew that she loved him.

It was something she had never meant to do; something she had never expected.

Yet as her love surged through her, she knew this was what she had always longed to feel for the man of her dreams.

Of course that was what he was!

She wondered how she could not have been aware of it when he had spoken to her on the terrace of the Royal Palace.

"I love . . you! I . . love you!" she wanted to say.

As she felt the hard pressure of his lips on the softness of her skin her fingers trembled.

He was aware of it and he raised his head to look at her.

To her surprise there was not the glow of admiration in his eyes but an unaccountable look of pain.

It was something she did not understand.

The Prince released her hand, put his hat back on his head and rode ahead of her into the stables.

She followed him feeling bewildered.

Mr. Heywood was talking to *Herr* Héviz.

Aletha knew they were discussing the price of a dozen horses that were being led round them by a groom.

She slipped from her horse's back without any assistance and walked away from the stables towards the Palace.

She hoped, because she could not help herself, that Prince Miklós would follow her.

But she knew that when he dismounted he had joined Mr. Heywood.

As she went up to her bedroom to change, she tried to puzzle out why he had behaved in such a strange manner.

She thought she knew the answer, but did not want to admit it to herself.

In fact her whole being shied away from what she suspected was the truth.

As if to soothe her feelings she told herself that of course the dashing and romantic Hungarians were unpredictable.

How could they be anything else?

She did not change and go downstairs.

She thought that doubtless the ladies of the party would be congregated in one of the beautiful Drawing-Rooms.

She felt she could not bear to make light conversation.

Every nerve in her body was pulsating towards the Prince.

She therefore took off her habit, undressed and got into bed.

"I will call you in plenty of time for your bath, *Fräulein*," the maid promised.

She dropped her a curtsy before she left the room.

Aletha knew that if she was staying there as her father's daughter it would have been a much deeper one.

The House-keeper would also have curtsied instead of just inclining her head.

She did not particularly wish for such obsequiousness.

At the same time it told her what she already knew.

There was a great difference between being a Duke's daughter and the grandchild of a man who could not afford to buy his own horses.

She had only to meet the Prince's father and the other members of his family to know how excessively proud they were.

Aletha had to admit that in a way her father was the same.

Yet perhaps it was not so obvious in England as it was in Hungary.

As they had ridden past the peasants coming back from the fields, all the women had curtsied to the Prince.

The men had swept their hats from their heads and bowed deeply.

They had also smiled at him with affection.

It was an affection tinged with respect that made him seem almost god-like.

"I suppose it is very childish of me to love him," Aletha thought as she took her bath. "I expect really I am just infatuated with his glamour and the Fairy Tale background of the Palace."

She thought it was exactly the right setting for the Prince of her Dreams, if that was what he was.

She had learned there were 126 rooms in the Palace.

Prince Józsel was continually speaking of how much more magnificent it had been when first erected by his ancestor.

The Opera House had been burned down and never rebuilt.

Aletha tried to laugh at herself for being as impressed as the Prince expected her to be.

"I could tell him that Ling, in its own way, is just as grand," she thought, "and actually the building itself is older!"

Then she laughed at herself again for being so childish.

She got out of her bath.

The maid helped her to dress in what she thought was the prettiest gown she had brought with her.

It was white and embroidered all over with tiny diamanté.

It made her look as if she was a flower sparkled with tiny drops of dew.

The impression was accentuated by the white flowers with diamanté on their petals which ornamented her neck.

Diamanté also glittered on the small bustle at the back where there were flowers caught in the folds of chiffon.

Tonight Aletha wore no jewellery.

The same flowers, that were something like white orchids, were arranged at the back of her head. When she went into the Salon before dinner she thought Prince Miklós drew in his breath.

A number of other men who had been invited to dinner stared at her with undisguised admiration.

"Now I know why the Estérházy Palace looks more beautiful than it ever has in the past!" one of them said to her.

She smiled at the compliment and felt her heart give a leap as she realised that the Prince was looking angry.

She knew he was jealous.

She thought how wonderful it would be if he should love her as she loved him.

Then she told herself it was too much to ask.

How could she expect that she would fall in love with the first really handsome man she had ever met?

How could she expect him to feel the same about her?

"Hungarians are romantic!" she kept repeating to herself. "Romantic!"

That meant, she knew, they would make love to every pretty woman they met, but she would not mean anything in their life.

Of course they would flit from flower to flower!

They would always be hoping they would find a more beautiful one the next day than they had found the day before.

"I have to be sensible about this," she murmured.

At the same time she enjoyed every moment of the dinner.

She found that nearly every man at the table was raising his glass to her in a toast.

The other young women were looking at her sourly.

She had already learnt that in London débutantes were not of any great importance.

Except for one moment when they were presented at Buckingham Palace.

They attended the Balls to which they were invited because their fathers were distinguished men.

But they were over-shadowed by the sophisticated married Beauties, who were acclaimed not only by Society, but by the public, and singled out by the Prince of Wales.

"This is my glorious hour," Aletha told herself, "so I had better make the most of it."

As the Prince had promised, she found they were to have a Gypsy Orchestra in the huge, magnificent white and gold Ball-Room.

It was here Haydn had conducted the first performance of his 'Farewell Symphony'.

It was the most beautiful Ball-Room Aletha had ever imagined.

The flowers that decorated it were all white, which complemented her gown.

The long windows were open to the splendid gardens outside.

Lights were hidden in the fountains which illuminated the water they flung towards the diamond-studded sky.

The Gypsy Orchestra was exactly what she had expected it would be.

The Gypsy women were dressed in their brilliantly-coloured costumes.

The women wore huge ear-rings and a profusion of bracelets on their arms.

Their headdresses of red ribbons were ornamented with gold and precious stones.

They sparkled and glittered with every movement they made.

The music started with the clash of cymbals, the bell-like ring of Tambourines.

Then the volume lifted the wild joyous music of a Gypsy dance up to the sky.

Amongst the guests some of the young girls and men moved hand-in-hand in a traditional Gypsy dance in the centre of the room.

Then the music changed and became sweeter and more tender.

The Prince put his arm around Aletha and drew her onto the floor.

Everybody began to dance and the music became compelling and romantic.

After a little time the wildness came back into the Gypsy instruments.

Those who were dancing moved quicker and quicker.

Aletha had found herself dancing with various other men, but now once again she was with the Prince.

He drew her closer to him.

To her surprise she found she could follow his steps exactly, even though she had never learnt them.

Quicker and quicker the rhythm rose, and quicker and quicker they moved.

Then as the dance grew even wilder she felt as if he carried her into the air.

Their feet were not moving on the ground, rather they flew like birds.

It was exciting and exhilarating and, when finally the music stopped, Aletha was breathless.

She also felt as if she was tumbling down from a great height back to reality.

Prince Miklós still had his arm around her.

As she looked up at him her breasts were moving tempestuously beneath the soft chiffon of her gown.

She thought there was a fire in his eyes, but told herself it was only a reflection of the light.

The guests were applauding the music which had carried them away.

Aletha thought they danced with their hearts and not their feet.

The Prince was drawing her from the Ball-Room into the garden.

She took a deep breath of the night air, as if somehow it could soothe the tumult within her.

The Prince put her arm through his and they walked past the fountains and over the soft green lawn.

They reached some bushes covered in blossom.

They passed through them and surprisingly there was a glass-house shining amongst the trees.

The Prince opened the door.

As they entered Aletha saw that the whole place was filled with orchids.

They were white, purple, green, pink and every other colour.

In some unusual manner they were lit from the floor.

They were so lovely that Aletha stood looking at them as if spellbound.

The Prince shut the door.

Then he said:

"This is the right place for you! I thought perhaps you could dissolve into the flowers you resemble. Then I would never lose you!"

Slowly, because she was a little shy, Aletha turned her head to look at him.

She thought as she did so that no man could look more handsome or so magnificent.

His evening-clothes fitted tightly to his slim, athletic body.

He wore one large pearl in the centre of his white shirt.

Aletha knew that if it were a more formal occasion and Royalty had been present, his coat would have been covered with decorations.

Her eyes met his, and they just stood looking at each other.

At last he said:

"You are so incredibly lovely, so beautiful, that you will always be in my heart!"

Aletha was about to reply that he would always be in hers when he added:

"I have brought you here tonight to say goodbye to you."

"Goodbye?" Aletha repeated. "I .. I did not .. know that we were .. leaving .. tomorrow!"

"It is not you who are leaving," the Prince replied, "it is I!"

Aletha could only look at him wide-eyed.

Then he said harshly:

"I am crucifying myself and I cannot stand being tortured any longer!"

"I .. I do not .. understand!" Aletha stammered.

"I know that," the Prince replied. "I know every thought in

101

your exquisite head, every breath you breathe, every beat of your heart!"

The way he spoke made Aletha quiver with the feelings he aroused in her.

Instinctively she put her hand to her breast to quell the tumult within it.

"I love you!" the Prince said. "I love you, as I have never loved a woman before. That is why, Heart of my Heart, I have to go away."

"But . . why . . why?" Aletha asked. "I do not . . understand!"

"Of course not," he said. "You are so unspoilt, so utterly desirable. I want to take you in my arms and carry you with me to my house in the mountains where we would be alone with no one to disturb us."

Aletha felt her whole body tremble with a strange excitement.

There was a fire in the Prince's eyes she had never seen before.

"Once we were there, my lovely one," he said, "I would teach you about love – not the cold love that an Englishman would give you, but the wild, burning, irresistible love of Hungary!"

Because the way he spoke was so compelling, Aletha instinctively took a step towards him.

To her surprise, he moved away from her.

"Do not come near me!" he said harshly. "I dare not touch you! If I do, I will make you mine! Then you could never escape and I would never let you go again."

"You . . you love . . me?" Aletha stammered as if it was the only thing she understood in all he was saying.

"I love you!" the Prince said, "I love you wildly, uncontrollably, irrevocably. But, my sweet, my precious, there is nothing I can do about it."

"W . . why? Why . . not?"

"The answer, quite simply, is that you are like these flowers, pure and unspoilt. How could I damage anything so beautiful, so perfect?"

Aletha continued to stare at him.

Then as the starlight touched her hair he turned away as if he could not bear to look at her.

"I do not think I ought to put it into words," he said, "but it would be unfair to leave you wondering."

"Please .. tell me .. please explain .. what you are .. saying," Aletha said piteously.

"I have told you I love you," the Prince said, "and I believe you love me a little."

Aletha made a little murmur and he went on:

"I can imagine nothing nearer to Heaven than to take your love and make it a part of mine, which it is already."

He made a sound which was one of pain as he added;

"But it is something I dare not do."

"Why not .. please .. tell me .. why not."

"Because my precious, beautiful little English girl, you are a lady. If you were not, if you were just the relative of an ordinary man who bought and sold horses like Héviz, I would take you away with me, and I think, my beloved, we would be very happy together."

Aletha did not make a sound.

She was beginning to understand what he was saying, and she felt as if her whole body was turning to stone.

The Prince made a gesture with his hand.

"That way is barred, and because of my family, I cannot make you my wife."

The words had been said and to Aletha they seemed to ring out.

She wondered why the orchids did not fall to the floor and the glass that covered them smash and scatter into pieces.

"You have seen my father," the Prince was saying, "and you are imaginative enough to know that it would break his heart if, as the eldest son, I took as my wife anyone who was not the equal of our blood."

Aletha did not move.

She only felt very cold, as if the blood had drained away from her body and her life had gone with it.

"From the first moment I saw you," the Prince said, "I knew you were something special, something different from anyone I had met before. As you stood at the balustrade outside the Royal Palace, it was as if you were surrounded with a white light, and I thought no one could be more lovely!"

The Prince put his hands over his eyes for a moment as he said:

"I could not sleep for thinking about you. The following days and nights you were always with me until I believed I was haunted."

He paused for a moment before he said, and his voice was raw:

"Then you came back, and for one moment I was wildly, ecstatically happy, just because you were there."

His voice deepened as he said:

"Nothing else seemed to matter. I merely waited for the moment when I could hold you in my arms and kiss you until we could no longer think of anything but each other."

Aletha knew that was what she wanted too.

Yet she could not speak as the Prince continued:

"There is no need for me to say that you ride better than any woman I have ever known. You even equal the Empress herself – but that is immaterial."

He stared at her before he said:

"It is not what you do, what you say, or even what you think. It is something Divine within yourself which I searched for, dreamt of, but thought I would never find."

Aletha knew that was what she felt about him.

She wanted to cry out and beg him not to destroy anything so perfect as their love.

But the words would not come to her lips and he continued:

"If I made you my wife, which I want more than my own salvation, it would be impossible for me to make you happy because though we would be in Heaven while we were together, we would have to live in the world as it is."

He drew in his breath before he went on:

"My family would never forgive me for making what to them would be a *mesalliance*. It would hurt you not once, but a thousand times a day to know what they were saying, what they would do, and what they would think."

He paused a moment and then went on:

"It would be impossible for me to protect you, and gradually, like water dripping onto a stone, it would destroy our love."

He drew himself up and seemed to grow taller as he said:

"That is why, my darling, I am going away tomorrow, and after that we shall never see each other again."

There was a despair in his voice that made Aletha want to reach out her arms towards him.

She wanted to tell him that he need not suffer; that she could sweep away his unhappiness.

As she was trying to find the right words he said:

"Goodbye, my lovely Sylph. I pray God will protect you and that one day you will find a man who will love you as I do, and who would take his own life rather than hurt you in any way."

He looked at her for a moment.

Then he went down on one knee and raising the hem of her gown kissed it.

Aletha looked at him in astonishment.

As he rose she said in a voice that hardly sounded like her own:

"Miklós .. wait .. I have something to .. tell you ..!"

Even as she spoke he was gone.

He had opened the door of the glasshouse and disappeared into the shadows outside before the sentence was finished.

Aletha stared after him.

It was then she put up her hands to cover her eyes.

Could this really have happened?

Could she really have heard Prince Miklós tell her that he loved her?

At the same time, he would not marry her.

"I must .. tell him," she thought, "I must .. tell him he is .. mistaken and that his .. family would .. accept me .. and we can be together .. and we can be .. happy."

She took a step towards the open door.

Suddenly a pride she had not known she possessed made her stand still again.

If he was so intuitive, if he really, as he said, could read her thoughts, her feelings, and understand the beating of her heart, why did he not know the truth?

Why was he not aware that her blood was as blue as his own?

Why did he not guess that her family were as important in England as the Estérhazys were in Hungary?

He should have known, he should have known intuitively, that she was not what she pretended to be.

How long she stood surrounded by the orchids with the stars shining through the glass above her head Aletha had no idea.

When at last she realised she must go back to the Palace, she moved slowly, as if in a dream.

It was then she told herself that her dream had ended.

The Man of her Dreams had failed her.

"If he were really so closely attuned to me, he would have known that I am I, and my Family Tree is not of the least consequence."

105

She reached a side door of the Palace and slipped upstairs.

The Gypsy Orchestra was still playing in the Ball-Room.

There was still the sound of voices and laughter.

Aletha went to her bedroom.

She did not ring for the maid who she knew would be waiting to help her.

Instead, slowly, with stiff fingers that did not seem like her own, she took off the beautiful white gown.

The dew-drops were still glistening on the flowers.

She removed the flowers from her hair and let it fall over her shoulders.

It seemed to take her a long time to undress and get into bed.

Only when she had blown out the candle and was in darkness did she hide her face in her pillow.

It was then the tears began to fall.

They were tears of despair, not only because she had lost Miklós and her heart.

He had also destroyed her dream.

Chapter Seven

Aletha cried despondently until she was exhausted.

Then she lay awake thinking that her Castle of Dreams had fallen in ruins about her.

Never again would she dream of a man who would love her for herself.

It was exactly the reverse of what she had expected to happen.

In England her father had been convinced she would be married because she was the daughter of a Duke.

In Hungary, the Prince thought she was not good enough for his family, and his love was not strong enough to fight them single-handed.

Like a child who has been hurt, she wanted to go home.

She wanted to leave Hungary now, at this very moment.

She wanted to find herself at Ling with all that was familiar about her.

Hungary had given her feelings she had never expected.

She knew it was the passion that comes with love and is part of love.

When it touched the soul it was Divine.

"I must leave," she thought, "whatever Mr. Heywood says."

He was quick-brained, and he would doubtless by now have decided which of the horses he wanted.

It would merely be a question of price and arranging for them to be safely transported to England.

"I will tell him that we must leave as soon as he is awake," she told herself.

It was still dark outside, but the stars were fading.

She pulled back the curtains.

Then she stood at the window waiting for the first fingers of the dawn to appear on the horizon.

When they did she knew it was still too early to approach Mr. Heywood.

"I will go riding," she decided.

She would ride for the last time in Hungary.

After that, she would try to forget the wild gallops before the wild emotions that the Prince had aroused in her.

She told herself despairingly that she would never feel them again.

Her marriage would be conventional.

Because she no longer cared, she would accept the husband her father chose for her.

It was bitter to know that she only had to tell Prince Miklós who she really was, and everything would be changed.

But however persuasive he might be, she knew she would never trust his love; never believe it was what he felt for her.

"If he had been one of the peasants we saw yesterday coming back from the fields," she told herself. "I would marry him and be happy in a cottage, loving him and our children."

This again was all part of her imagination.

As unreal as the romance of Hungary and, in a way, the Palace itself.

It was too beautiful, too perfect, too dream-like to be substantial enough on which to build a future without true love.

The love which, as the Prince had said, was irresistible.

But it was not not irresistible enough for him to sacrifice his pride, and the pride in his family.

"I must . . leave," she cried and started to dress.

She felt she could not be confined at the moment within the walls of the Palace.

The Prince was too near her.

Perhaps by the time she returned from her ride he would have left as he had said he intended to do.

Then she would never see him again and she prayed that she would forget him.

She put on a thin blouse and her riding-skirt.

Then, she picked up her jacket and hesitated.

Yesterday had been hot and she had the idea that today would be hotter still.

In which case, if she intended to ride hard and fast, she would not need more than her blouse to cover her.

There would be nobody to see her.

She pinned her hair tightly at the back of her head, and did not wear a hat.

When she was ready she left her room very quietly so that no one would hear.

She moved along the corridor to where there was a secondary staircase.

She knew there would be a footman on duty in the hall.

As she went she glanced in a mirror and thought her face was very pale.

Her eyes seemed enormous and she knew the darkness in them was due to the pain she was suffering.

It made her feel as if there were a hundred arrows piercing her heart.

She found her way without any difficulty to the door through which the Prince had taken her the first day she arrived to the stables.

By the time she reached them the sun was shining and turning everything to gold.

It was far too early for *Herr* Héviz to be about. She found a stable-boy who had been on duty during the night.

She told him she wanted to ride *Nyul* the grey she had ridden the first afternoon.

By the time *Nyul* was saddled another groom had appeared and asked if he should accompany her.

She understood enough Hungarian to tell him she was only going a little way and wished to be on her own.

She thought he looked surprised, but he was young and did not expostulate as *Herr* Héviz would have done.

She rode out of the stables on the superb grey.

She forced herself to think of nothing except the horse she was riding.

"Now I can forget everything except you," she told *Nyul*.

She rode through the paddocks and out through the way they had been before to reach the meadowland.

The rising sun had already brought out the butterflies and they were fluttering over the flowers.

Just as they had done before they rose in front of her like an elusive cloud.

The birds, disturbed by her approach, soared up into the sky.

Nyul was fresh, and Aletha gave him his head.

He sprang forward and she was riding as swiftly as the flight of a bird.

On and on they went until Aletha felt as if the hard lump of misery within her breast softened a little.

Now the sunshine was dazzling her eyes.

She thought that the beauty all around her was some consolation for the darkness within her heart.

She rode on further and further deep in her thoughts.

Suddenly in the distance she saw coming towards her two men on horseback.

She thought it an intrusion that they should be encroaching on her.

For the moment she was in a world in which she was completely alone.

She was just about to turn round and go back the way she had come.

Then she realised there was something familiar about the two riders.

As she stared in their direction she knew with a sensation of shock that one was the Baron.

He was riding a very large stallion which she remembered as being the best in his stables.

The groom beside him also rode a horse that was larger than the average.

There was no doubt it was the man she had no wish ever to see again.

Then she was aware that the Baron had recognised her.

The two horsemen were still some distance away, but she saw him bringing down his whip sharply on the stallion.

He spoke to his groom who also swept forward, at the same time moving out from beside him.

It was then Aletha's intuition told her that she was in danger.

Almost as if she heard the order the Baron gave, she knew he intended to come up on one side of her and the groom on the other.

Then she would be helpless and at their mercy.

Without wasting any more time she turned *Nyul*'s head for home.

As she did so, she realised she had come much further than she had intended.

The Palace was not in sight and she was no longer at the point where the Prince had turned to take them back by a different route.

She galloped for some distance, then looked back.

The Baron was far nearer to her than he had been before.

He was bending over his horse and riding almost jockey-style to overtake.

She was aware then that her sense of danger was not mistaken.

She shuddered to think what might happen if she became a captive of the Baron.

It might be a long time before Mr. Heywood or anyone in the Palace had any idea to where she had been taken.

"Help me .. oh, God .. help me!" she prayed as she heard the Baron's horse thundering along behind her.

Nyul was certainly doing his best.

At the same time, they had already ridden a long way at full gallop before Aletha had become aware of the Baron.

Now Aletha was riding faster than she had ever done in her whole life.

Yet she knew the Baron was gaining on her.

She thought as she tried to go faster still that she would rather die than be in his power.

Prince Miklós had also spent a sleepless night.

When he had left Aletha among the orchids in the glasshouse he had walked blindly across the garden.

He wanted to get away from the music and the sound of laughter.

He knew that what he was doing would break his heart and haunt him for ever.

But he had been brought up to know how great his heritage was.

It had been drummed into him that he must dedicate his whole life to being as fine and brave as his ancestors had been.

His father had said to him when he was a small boy that whatever sacrifices he had to make he must accept them willingly.

He must not fail those who had preceded him and those who would follow.

Miklós had not quite understood at the time.

He had however learnt as he grew older that his duty to his family was more important than his own desires.

At School he had worked not for himself.

By being as clever and intelligent as his father he would not fail the family when it was his turn to be the reigning Prince.

Of course there had been women in his life.

From the moment he was old enough they pursued him, tried to seduce him and make themselves indispensable.

They captured his body and he found them fascinating.

But some critical part of his brain told him they were not good enough for the position he had to offer.

His mother had been of Royal Blood and had loved her husband and her family more than anything in the world.

For Miklós she was the standard by which he judged every woman who was offered to him as a wife.

He always found them lacking.

He knew now that he would never love anyone as he loved Aletha.

From the first moment they had met he had known they were already part of one another.

As he had told her, he had seen her enveloped with a Divine light.

When she came to the Palace, he could read her thoughts and sense her feelings.

He knew that she was the woman who had been meant for him by God.

Even the Sacrament of Matrimony would not bind them any closer than they were already.

But his brain told him that marriage with a woman whose grandfather was a paid servant of the Duke of Buclington was impossible.

The ancestor after whom he was named had built the Palace.

Ever since then the Estérházys had encouraged the greatest Musicians, Artists and the finest brains of the country to come to Fertōd.

They had all served the family in one way or another.

'Served' was the operative word.

Franz Joseph Haydn might have been the greatest Musician of his age, but there could have been no question of his marrying an Estérházy.

The same applied to the Artists, the Architects, the Poets and the Writers.

All of them were welcome, but only to 'serve' the family in their various ways, certainly not become a part of it.

Perhaps the women who bore the name of Estérházy were even more proud and more implacable than the men.

Prince Miklōs knew there was not one of them, including his sister Misina, who would accept Aletha as her equal.

How could he find tranquillity or happiness in the Palace in those circumstances?

He had to live there: it was part of his Kingdom.

He had to minister to those who bore his name, in the same way as his ancestors had done.

They had built up a kingdom within a Kingdom.

They all, Miklōs thought, bowed to the Emperor but privately they considered themselves superior to an Austrian.

When finally Prince Miklós walked back to the Palace the music was silent and the guests had departed.

The lights had been extinguished in most of the windows.

He went to his bedroom to pull back the curtains from the windows.

He felt he must have more air to carry on breathing.

He did not undress, but just pulled off his evening-coat.

Then he sat with his head in his hands and suffered as he had never suffered before in the whole of his life.

When dawn came he knew he had to get away so that there would be no chance of seeing Aletha again.

Even to think of seeing her made the blood throb in his temples.

Every instinct in his body told him to carry her away to his house in the mountains and make her his.

They would be happy, deliriously, wonderfully blissfully happy.

But there was always tomorrow.

Tomorrow and the years that came after it.

Years when eventually he would have to leave her and she would never forgive him.

He rang the bell for his Valet and when the man came, told him to pack.

Because he had no wish to see anyone and have to make explanations or answer questions, he ordered breakfast in his room.

Having bathed and changed his clothes he stood at the window.

He looked out blindly over the flower-filled garden.

Beyond was the meadowland where he had galloped with Aletha.

It was separated from the gardens by a brick wall that surrounded the whole Palace.

Then he was aware there were three horses in the far distance.

At that range they were little larger than dots.

They seemed to be moving towards the Palace.

He watched them only vaguely, immersed in his own unhappiness.

Suddenly he saw, although he could hardly believe his eyes, that the leading horse was *Nyul* and Aletha was riding him.

He watched her as she rode leaning forward, straining every nerve to make the grey go faster.

Because he thought it strange he looked past her.

She was being followed by two men.

With a sense of shock he realised that one of them was Baron Otto von Sicardsburg.

He definitely recognised him.

Also the big black stallion of which he was told the Baron continually boasted.

It was then he knew almost as if she had called out to him that Aletha was frightened.

He knew her fear was for what the Baron obviously intended.

He wanted to curse him.

At the same time, he wanted to assure Aletha that whatever happened he would save and protect her.

There was no doubt now that the Baron was gaining and was in fact only a few lengths behind her.

In front of them there was no opening into the Palace garden only the brick wall.

Then as Miklós realised what he had meant to do, he felt as if he was facing a firing-squad.

Aletha was conscious of the fact that the Baron was close behind her.

She had reached the Palace, but did not turn in the direction that would lead her towards the stables.

To do so meant that she would have to pull *Nyul* in and the Baron would certainly overtake her.

She was sure he intended to snatch at her reins.

She would be powerless to stop herself from being led away beside the black stallion, back to the Baron's Castle.

"Save . . me! Save . . me!" she cried in her heart.

Then as the brick wall loomed ahead she knew what she must do.

She had never jumped on *Nyul*.

Anyway the wall was too high and too solid to risk anything so dangerous.

But it was her only hope.

She spoke to *Nyul*, feeling he would understand.

As she gathered him for the jump, he leapt into the air carrying her into the sky almost as if he had wings.

It would have been impossible, she knew, for any ordinary horse to manage such a jump.

Incredibly, Aletha was to think afterwards, it must have been with the help of God and His Angels that *Nyul* cleared it with just an inch to spare.

The horse landed, again by good fortune, in a flower-bed.

He staggered, nearly fell, but then regained his balance.

He was sweating and for the moment completely exhausted.

Aletha kept her seat but was almost unconscious with the effort.

She shut her eyes and her head drooped on her breast.

Her hair had come loose with the speed at which she had ridden.

It fell over her shoulders in a gold cloud.

She had released the reins and was holding onto the saddle.

She felt the whole world was slipping away from her.

Then strong arms were lifting her down from the saddle.

A voice which seemed to come from far away was saying:

"My darling! My sweet! How could you have done anything so dangerous? I thought you were going to kill yourself!"

She could not answer, but could only lie limp in Prince Miklós's arms.

Her head was resting on his shoulder.

He went down on one knee to hold her close against him.

The strength of his arms told her she was safe.

As he looked down at her pale face, her closed eyes and her hair, something broke within him.

Wildly, passionately he kissed her forehead, her eyes, her cheeks and her lips.

He drew her back to life, and it was the only way he could express his joy that she was not dead.

To Aletha it was as if she had stepped from a Hell of fear into a Heaven of happiness.

It was impossible to open her eyes.

She still felt as if she had drifted a long way into oblivion.

At the same time, she could feel his kisses.

As he held her lips captive, something flickered within her heart and she knew it was life itself.

"I love you! I love you!" Miklós was saying. "And I thought I had lost you!"

Because there was a note of agony in his voice, Aletha opened her eyes.

His face was very near to hers.

When she saw his expression she knew how frightened he had been that she would be killed.

"I . . I am . . alive," she wanted to say.

But her lips could not part before he was kissing her again.

Then very gently he stood up and drew her to her feet.

"I am going to carry you into the house," he said.

As if he could not help himself he kissed her again.

Now her whole being responded and she thought that lightning flashed in her breast.

There were little flames riding up her throat and touching her lips.

Miklós's voice was deep and very moving as he said:

"You are mine! Mine completely, and I know now I cannot live without you! How soon will you marry me, my darling?"

She stared at him.

"Are you . . really asking me . . to . . marry you?" she whispered.

They were the first words she had spoken since *Nyul* had jumped over the wall.

"You will marry me," Miklós answered, "if I have to fight the whole world to make you my wife!"

It was so wonderful to hear the words she had longed to hear him say that Aletha shut her eyes again.

He picked her up in his arms and started to carry her towards the Palace.

Only when they had gone a little way did Aletha say in a voice he could hardly hear:

"Do you . . really love me . . enough to . . make me your . . w . . wife?"

"No one and nothing is of any importance except you!" Miklós replied.

His lips touched her forehead before he went on:

"It will not be easy, but I love and worship you, and we will pray that nothing else will ever be of any consequence."

"Nothing . . will . . be," Aletha murmured.

They reached a side door of the Palace and Miklós took her inside.

Aletha was suddenly conscious of her hair falling about her shoulders.

"I . . I do not . . want to be . . seen," she whispered.

Miklós smiled.

He put her down but kept his arm around her.

He opened the door of a room that was not far from where they had come in.

It was one of the many small but beautiful Sitting-Rooms on the Ground Floor of the Palace.

All the pictures were by French Artists, such as Bucher, Fragonard and Greuze.

The furniture was also French.

"This is a room for love," he said as he shut the door, "and I am going to tell you, my darling, how much I love you!"

He picked her up again in his arms.

Sitting down on the sofa he cradled her against him as if she was a child.

Then he was kissing her passionately, demandingly, and possessively.

Once again they were flying in the sky and it was impossible to believe there was the world beneath them.

It was a long time later and, although they had not spoken, Aletha felt as if they had said a thousand things to each other.

There was no need for explanations.

No need for anything but love.

"How can you make me feel like this?" Miklós exclaimed.

"Like .. what?" Aletha asked for the sheer joy of hearing him say it.

"It is something I have never felt before. But then, I have never loved anyone as I love you!"

"Could .. anything be more .. wonderful?" Aletha said. "And I .. was so .. unhappy last .. night."

"You are not to think about it any more," Miklós ordered. "I was mad, crazy, to think that we could ever be without each other!"

The fire was once again back in his eyes as he said:

"You are mine, and I will kill any other man who tries to touch you!"

"I .. I think the .. Baron intended to take me prisoner," Aletha said.

"To escape him you might have killed yourself!"

There was a note of horror in Miklós's voice that was very moving.

"But .. I am alive .. and .. I am here."

"You are, my precious, and now we are going to be married immediately!"

He put her down as he spoke and rose to his feet.

"I do not intend to waste any more time," he said. "We will go and tell my father that you are to be my wife and there is nothing he or anyone else can say or do to prevent us from being married at once!"

Aletha stared at him in surprise.

Then as he was kissing her again it was impossible to tell him the words that trembled on her lips.

As he set her free she had a sudden glimpse of herself in a gold-framed mirror.

She was horrified at the untidiness of her appearance.

"Let me first go and change," she said quickly, "and then I have something to tell you."

Miklós glanced at the clock.

"They will have finished breakfast," he said, "and my father will be alone, dealing with his correspondence."

He stopped to look at her lovingly before he went on:

"But hurry, otherwise he may become involved with other

members of the family before we can tell him what we are planning to do."

Aletha had no wish for anyone to see her as she looked at this moment.

She therefore allowed Miklós to take her up a side staircase.

He left her at her bedroom door.

"I will come back for you, my Lovely One, in ten minutes," he said, "so hurry! I am afraid of being away from you even for a minute!"

"I will .. still be .. here," Aletha promised with a smile.

She knew he wanted to kiss her again and she quickly went into her bedroom.

She rang for the maid.

By the time she arrived Aletha had already washed and taken off her riding-skirt and blouse.

She put on one of her prettiest gowns and had just finished arranging her hair when there was a knock on the door.

She knew it was Miklós.

She could not help running across the room.

It was with the greatest difficulty that she did not throw herself into his arms.

"I am .. ready!" she said breathlessly.

"You look very lovely!" he answered. "I am determined that we shall be married tonight, or at the very latest tomorrow!"

She wanted to tell him why it was impossible.

Then she saw a servant coming down the passage.

She was silent as Miklós took her down the stairs.

They went across the hall and down another corridor which led them to his father's Study.

Aletha knew it was a very impressive room.

She thought if she did not have a secret which would surprise them all she would have been nervous.

Instead with her hand in Miklós's she felt as if her heart and the whole world was singing.

He loved her!

He loved her enough to marry her whoever she might be.

He opened the door of the Study.

As they went in Aletha felt a stab of disappointment as she saw that the Prince was not alone.

Standing beside him at the window was another man.

Then as the two men turned round Aletha gave a gasp.

It was her father who stood there.

He looked tall and very distinguished.

"Papa!"

Her voice rang out as she ran towards him.

She flung herself against him.

"You are .. here! How is it .. possible? Why have .. you come?"

The words seemed to fall over themselves as her father put his arms round her.

Then he said:

"The King of Denmark was ill and therefore all the festivities were cancelled. So I returned home to find my daughter had been very naughty and had run away!"

Aletha drew in her breath.

"Were you .. very .. angry?" she asked in a small voice.

"Very," the Duke replied, "if I had not been aware that John Heywood would take great care of you. But I did not expect to find that in buying my horses for me, he had also taken on the role of your grandfather."

His eyes were twinkling as he spoke and Aletha knew he was not really angry with her.

It was then she looked at Miklós and saw his astonishment.

She put out her hand towards him.

"This was the .. secret I .. wanted to .. tell you," she said.

She thought for a moment that perhaps he would be angry because she had deceived him.

Then he answered.

"Can it really be true that you are the daughter of the Duke?"

"It is really true," the Duke said before Aletha could reply, "and I have been apologising to the Prince because my daughter has been deceiving you all!"

"Of course I understand," Prince Józsel said, "that in the circumstances, it was the only way that Lady Aletha could travel if she had no proper chaperon."

"Well, I will look after her now," the Duke said.

He spoke as if he thought he must gloss over anything that might affect Aletha's reputation.

"At least, Your Highness, I shall now have the pleasure of seeing your horses for myself."

120

"And of course, riding them," Prince Józsel added.

Aletha drew herself from her father's arms.

"Now that you are here, Papa," she said, "there is something more important than even the horses, and Miklós will tell you what it is."

The Duke held out his hand to Prince Miklós.

"I guessed that was who you were," he said, "and I am delighted to have the pleasure of meeting you."

"As Aletha has just said, Your Grace," Miklós replied, "I have something very important to say and that is that I wish to marry your daughter!"

Aletha stood looking at the view.

She thought nothing could be more beautiful or more compelling.

The mountain on which she stood was high above the valley in which a river was glinting in the sunshine.

There was meadowland on either side of it.

Beyond another range of mountains as high as the one on which she was standing at the moment.

Miklós's house, which was his own private retreat, was small, but exquisite.

It had every possible comfort.

They had arrived late last night, and this morning she had awoken to think he must have taken her up to Heaven itself.

"Have you been awake for long?" she asked when she opened her eyes. She looked very lovely with her fair hair falling over her shoulders.

"I found it hard to sleep," Miklós said in his deep voice, "when you were beside me and at last we were alone."

He was touching her body and a flame began to flicker in her heart.

"I thought all the festivities and good wishes would never end!" he went on. "I wanted you like this, where no one could disturb us and I could tell you how much I love you from first thing in the morning and all through the night."

Aletha laughed.

"Oh, darling, no one . . wanted it . . more than I did . . but I had no idea it would be so beautiful or that I could be . . so happy!"

121

It had been impossible for Prince Józsel and the Duke to allow them to be married as quickly as Miklós wanted.

First they had gone to England where he had met most of the Ling relatives, all of whom found him charming.

They made such a fuss of him that Aletha was half-afraid he would find somebody he loved more than her.

When they were alone she expressed her doubts.

But Miklós kissed her so demandingly that he made it very clear how much he wanted her.

He told her a thousand times how frustrating it was for them not to be married, as he had wanted, immediately.

Then at last, with what the Duke called 'indecent haste' they were married in the Chapel at Ling.

Crowds of their relations had filled the great house and all the neighbours' houses as well.

After a few days Honeymoon in England they had come back to Hungary.

Prince Józsel had no intention of not celebrating their marriage at the Palace.

All the rooms were packed to bursting.

The wedding festivities included Gypsy music, besides a formal Ball with the best Orchestra from Vienna.

Johann Strauss had even come himself to conduct it.

As Aletha said – could anybody ask for more?

"All I want is you to myself!" Miklós had complained.

At last they had escaped.

This morning Aletha had her first chance of seeing in the daylight how fantastic the view was from Miklós's house.

As he put his arm round her waist she said:

"Now I know I have reached Paradise."

"That is how I want you to feel, my precious darling. When I built this house I thought it was the right setting for me. Now I know it is the right setting for you. You are not a Sylph, you are an Angel – my Angel! Who will always belong to me!"

His lips were on hers.

He kissed her until she felt as if they were touching the sun and its light was burning through them.

"I love you . . oh, Miklos . . I love,' you she whispered.

"As I love you!" he said. "And I want to tell you how much, but you are standing precariously on top of a precipice, so I suggest we go back into the house."

She saw by the fire in his eyes what he intended and exclaimed:

"But darling . . we have only just got up!"

"What does it matter?" he asked. "When one is in love, time stands still, and I only know that I love you, I want you, and you are mine!"

Aletha laughed.

She let him take her back to the house.

They went back into the beautiful room with a view over the valley.

It was where they had slept the previous night.

As Miklós shut the door Aletha put out her arms towards him.

He crushed her against him and she said:

"Darling . . darling . . I love . . you! But I am . . sure there is a lot . . more for me to . . see outside."

"There is tomorrow and the rest of our lives in which to see it," Miklos answered. "At the moment, there is only love."

He carried her to the bed.

Then he was kissing her wildly, passionately demandingly.

She knew this was the love she had prayed for and nothing else mattered.

Position, wealth, even beauty itself, could not be compared to the wonder of what they felt for each other.

Then as Miklos made her his she could hear the music that was the beat of their hearts.

The sunlight was seeping through them like leaping flames of fire.

The light which came from God and was . . Divine enveloped them.

Then there was nothing either in Heaven or Earth but Love.

A Theatre of Love

AUTHOR'S NOTE

It seems extraordinary that there is no book written about the many attractive and fascinating private theatres which existed in the last two centuries over the world.

There is still one to be seen in the Winter Palace in Leningrad and Prince Ysvolsov's Private Theatre is exactly as I described it in this book.

The Esterhazys' Palace in Hungary, not only had a Puppet Theatre, but also an Opera House. This unfortunately was burnt down and never rebuilt.

In big houses in England there were Christmas Traditions that were carried out by every generation.

Most of them had the present giving which I have written about here and I remember my Grandmother always gave every woman they employed in the house and on the Estate, enough red flannel to make a petticoat.

I used to think that perhaps some of them would have liked to have another colour.

Bell-ringers I remember coming to my Great-Uncle's house where we spent Christmas and I was fascinated by the beautiful tunes they extracted from their bells.

'God Rest Ye Merry, Gentlemen' is one of the oldest English carols known.

It was sung in the open air like the first great Christmas Carol in Judea and the tune was a particular favourite of the strolling bands of minstrels.

Children sang it going from door to door in the hope of receiving a small coin, an orange or a mincepie.

Chapter One

The Duke of Moorminster arrived back in England in a bad temper.

It had been a very tiring trip to Holland where he had been at the request of the Queen and the Prime Minister.

If there was one thing he found boring it was the speeches made by Statesmen who looked like Burgomasters.

Also those made by Bergomasters who looked exactly like the portraits of their ancestors in the Rijksmuseum.

He wondered as he listened if anything eventually evolved from such long-winded platitudes.

However, by what he considered extreme good luck, he was able to leave Holland a day earlier than he expected.

He therefore, through the British Embassy, cabled to London to alert his staff.

He knew, if nothing else, he would have a good dinner on his return.

Fate was however against him as the ship leaving from Rotterdam was delayed and the voyage was extremely rough.

The Duke was a good sailor, but it was raining and far too cold to go out on deck.

He was therefore confined to a cabin which he thought scornfully was too small for a rabbit-hutch.

It was some consolation when he stepped ashore at London Dock to find his own carriage drawn by two of his well-bred horses waiting for him.

Also his Secretary was there to see to the luggage.

Having greeted Mr. Watson, he drove off intent only on reaching his house in Grosvenor Square and having a hot bath.

It was far later than he had intended and he was therefore hungry.

Even the glass of champagne which his Butler had ready for him and some *pâté de foie gras* sandwiches did not entirely change his mood.

When he went up to his room he was frowning.

The footman who was there to valet him until his own Valet arrived with his luggage, looked at him apprehensively.

Mr. Watson had left the more urgent of the letters awaiting the Duke on his chest-of-drawers.

There were only a few of them.

The Duke knew that there would be a large pile downstairs in his Study.

He had no intention of reading them until tomorrow.

He looked at those on his chest-of-drawers and saw there was one in a blue envelope.

He recognised the hand-writing, as Watson had done and had therefore not opened it.

The Duke put the other letters aside and slitting open the envelope drew out a note from Fiona Faversham.

He knew before he even read it that it was a letter to welcome him home.

She had, of course, expected that he would receive it tomorrow.

Lady Faversham was now so much a part of his life that he wondered sometimes why she troubled to write to him.

While he was away in Holland he had received a letter from her almost every day.

It seemed unnecessary now for her to write welcoming him home.

She undoubtedly expected him to be with her tomorrow evening.

Then when he read the endearments with which she started her letter he knew the reason.

It was all too obvious for him to question it.

Fiona wished to marry him.

It was in fact assumed by most of their friends that that was what he would eventually do.

Nearly thirty-four, the Duke was well aware that his whole family thought it was time he produced an heir.

They continually hinted that it was in fact his duty.

They were prepared to welcome Fiona with open arms.

She was one of the most beautiful women in England and they all believed he was infatuated with her.

She was also the daughter of the Duke of Cumbria.

The only stumbling-block in all this was that the Duke himself had no wish to be married.

If he had to be, he preferred to choose his wife irrespective of anybody else's ideas.

He certainly did not wish to be pressured up the aisle by people who, he thought, should mind their own business.

That included his whole family.

He carried out his duties as he was expected to do where it concerned the innumerable Uncles, Aunts, and an amazing number of Cousins.

But he disliked their presuming on their relationship or interfering in his private life.

It was true he found Fiona Faversham very attractive. When she had burst on London when her days of mourning were over he had found it impossible to resist her.

She had been married when she was not quite eighteen to Lord Faversham.

He not only came from one of the oldest families in England, but was at the time extremely wealthy.

He was also a very attractive man.

Someone had remarked that he had enjoyed more love-affairs than most people had hot dinners.

He had fallen wildly in love with Fiona.

He had swept her off her feet and beguiled her family into believing he would 'turn over a new leaf'.

Human nature being what it is, he did nothing of the sort.

After a honeymoon visiting all the romantic places in Europe he had returned to England with his Bride.

He had then taken up his life from where it had left off.

The trouble was that Eric Faversham could not resist a pretty face.

"It really means nothing, darling," he had said to Fiona.

She had caught him out spending the night with a woman whose beauty embellished the pages of the magazines and newspapers.

"But you have been unfaithful to me!" Fiona had protested plaintively.

"I love you, and I promise you that what I felt for Isobel was no more important than drinking a glass of champagne!"

Unfortunately as the years passed the "glasses of champagne" multiplied.

Fiona was asserting that she could stand no more of it when Eric Faversham was killed.

He was taking part in a Steeple-Chase in which all the riders had wined and dined too well.

Because some idiotic member of the party had dared them to do so, they had ridden after dinner.

They wore their evening-clothes with one eye covered with a black patch.

Several riders in the race had suffered injuries and two horses had had to be destroyed.

Eric Faversham had broken his neck and died instantly.

Fiona had not pretended to grieve for him.

His numerous love-affairs had humiliated her.

It hurt her to know she could not hold her husband.

Yet her beauty which had improved with age, sent other men into ecstasies.

She had retired to her father's house in the country for the conventional year of mourning.

Queen Victoria would not have approved of it being shortened in any way.

Fiona was sensible enough to return to London only when she had put away the last of her mauve and grey gowns.

Anyway they had not become her half so well as when she had worn black.

Because her hair was red, the deep red of Hungarian women, her skin was dazzlingly white.

Her eyes were not the clear green they should have been with such colouring.

At the same time, once a man had looked deeply into them he felt as if he had fallen into a whirlpool.

There was no chance of being saved.

To say that Fiona caused a sensation in London Society was to describe it mildly.

At twenty-five she was no longer the innocent unsophisticated girl she had been when she first married.

Her husband had taught her about love.

She had also learnt a lot from the women he had likened to "glasses of champagne".

Fiona made up her mind that her second marriage would be very different from her first.

Apart from anything else, she discovered after Eric's death that he had left a mountain of debts and was not nearly as wealthy as both she and her parents had been led to believe.

He had been wildly extravagant in the way he lived, especially in the parties he gave.

Besides this he was unnecessarily generous to the women he favoured and at the same time a compulsive gambler.

There was enough money left for Fiona to be comfortable.

But it was not the fortune she had anticipated.

She knew however, she wanted a position in Society second only to Royalty.

She also desired a husband who was wealthy enough to indulge her every whim.

There was only one man who fulfilled these requirements.

One man who was also attractive enough to make her heart beat faster.

He was the Duke of Moorminster.

When almost by instinct they gravitated towards each other the first time they met, she thought she had won the 'Jackpot'.

The difficulty was to persuade him to say the five magical words –
"Will you be my wife?"

As it happened, the Duke was well aware of Fiona's intentions from the first.

He had been angled for, pursued and seduced by every woman he met from the moment he left Eton.

He would have been very stupid not to be aware he was the biggest matrimonial catch in the country.

He had learned to recognise the danger-signals even before he was forced to confront them.

He had grown adept at managing to avoid the more obvious traps set for him by ambitious mothers.

He found Fiona amusing, witty, and very sure of herself in a way he appreciated.

They were in fact two of a kind.

When he became her lover he found he had to exert himself – which was unusual – in order to dominate the situation as he was accustomed to do.

She was compliant and, as somebody had said, they "talked the same language".

He therefore found it easy to enjoy a situation which he felt confident he could control.

He allowed Fiona to become part of his life.

In London they saw each other almost every day.

They were invited to the same parties, and if he gave one himself she played hostess.

When he went to the country the same thing happened.

Having helped him choose the guests, Fiona came with him.

She made everything during the week or week-end pass smoothly and most enjoyably.

He hardly noticed when she moved her bedroom next to his because it was "more convenient".

He had taken it for granted that they would dine together the following night when he had expected to return from Holland.

It was actually an oversight – or perhaps for once he was being a little more cautious.

But he had neglected to instruct his Secretary in his cablegram to inform Lady Faversham that he was to return earlier than expected.

He went down to dinner.

He thought with a large Dining-Room it would have been pleasant to have her sitting beside him.

She would be telling all that had happened while he had been away.

He knew she would be amusing, and he knew too there would be a lot to hear.

Who the Prince of Wales was courting, who had quarrelled with women.

And of course what new *affaires de coeur* were taking place amongst their intimate friends.

It was actually very unusual for the Duke to dine alone.

Because the silence was somewhat oppressive he talked to his Butler as he and two footmen served the meal.

Redding, who had been with him for many years, was closely in touch with the servants at Moor Park.

The Duke therefore learnt what were the prospects for a good bag at the shoot he had arranged for Boxing Day.

He also learnt how good the hunting had been since he had been away.

"They'd an excellent run on Saturday, Your Grace," Redding

was saying, "an' a kill in Bluebell Wood just afore they reached th' pool."

The Duke knew exactly where that was, and wished he had been there.

Redding put a small glass of brandy beside him because he never drank port.

"Is there anything more, Your Grace?" Redding enquired respectfully.

"See that I am called early tomorrow morning," the Duke ordered. "I will have a lot of correspondence to see to."

"Very good, Your Grace."

Redding bowed and went from the Dining-Room.

The Duke sat back in his chair and sipped his brandy.

As he did so he wished again that Fiona was with him.

"I will see her tomorrow," he told himself.

He had had enough time in Rotterdam to buy her a very attractive and expensive present.

He had intended to give it to her for Christmas, but now he thought she might as well have it at once.

There was only a little over a week to Christmas.

The thought made him remember that he had something to do at Moor Park besides hunting.

He had long ago made up his mind to rebuild the private Theatre.

It had originally been built in the 18th century only to be burnt down in the reign of William IV.

His ancestors had possessed many talents and outstanding qualities.

But none of them had any desire to express themselves either in music or in writing.

Quite unexpectedly the Duke had found himself proficient in both.

While his contemporaries appraised the women on the stage of the theatre, he criticised the Play itself.

Often he felt he could have done better.

To the astonishment of his relations he had started to rebuild the small Theatre at Moor Park.

He intended to restore it as it had been originally.

He had been lucky in this because to his delight he had found the original plans.

They had been drawn up by superlative Architects who had also been responsible for redesigning the house itself.

They had made what had been a "hotch-potch" of many preceding generations into a magnificent building. It was acclaimed as being architecturally perfect.

The facade they created was Georgian, but they had been clever enough to preserve behind it many of the rooms, exactly as they had been originally.

This included the Chapel.

The site where the Theatre had stood had fortunately remained unbuilt-upon.

Having found the original plans, the Duke proceeded to follow them exactly.

The Theatre was almost finished the last time he had been to Moor Park.

If he went home at the end of the week, he would see it completed.

Because he had been so pleased with its reconstruction he had told the Prince of Wales about it, who had said:

"You must certainly invite me to your Opening Performance, Sheldon."

He had paused to think, adding:

"We will spend Christmas at Sandringham, and if you remember, Christmas Day is on a Wednesday this year. The Princess and I will come to Moor Park the following Friday, and you can have your Opening Performance on Saturday night."

"There is nothing, Sir, that will give me greater pleasure," the Duke replied, "and I will try to produce something unique."

"And of course beautiful!" the Prince had added.

That, the Duke thought, went without saying, knowing the Prince had an eye for any pretty woman.

He also enjoyed the Theatre and had shown that when he had courted Lily Langtry.

When this affair was over he had bestowed on her a fame she would never have had without him.

The Duke thought now that he had only two weeks in which to arrange, as he had promised the Prince, "something unique".

The "beautiful" would not be so difficult, were it not that Princess Alexandra would be present.

That meant that the cast on the stage could not include the

Ballet Dancers from Covent Garden, or the undoubted Beauties of Drury Lane.

In a bachelor party it would have been quite easy for them to stay in the house.

After their performance they would amuse the audience in the way which would be expected.

The Duke had been intent primarily on the restoration of the building.

After this conversation with the Prince, he had had no time to consider who should appear on his Opening Night.

Now, he told himself, he had to get busy, and of course Fiona would help him.

He recalled that when he had mentioned it to her before, she had claimed surprisingly that she had a very good voice.

He must, she added, think up some scene in which she could sing for him.

When he questioned her she had explained.

"When I was at home we always used to act a Play of some sort for Papa at Christmas and on his birthday."

"Did you have a Theatre of your own?" the Duke asked.

"No, we used to do them in the Ball-Room, and the Estate carpenter fixed up a curtain for us and provided a backdrop."

She smiled before she went on:

"It would be very exciting to sing in a real Theatre with footlights!"

She looked up at him archly and added:

"I have always thought that if I had not been who I am, I could have had great success on the 'boards'."

"I am sure you would have, seeing how beautiful you are!" the Duke replied because it was expected of him.

"I am sure I would have been another Mrs. Siddons," Fiona had gone on, "and instead of acting a part just for you, my dearest Sheldon, I might have been performing to a full house at Drury Lane!"

"I think you would have found it somewhat arduous," the Duke remarked dryly.

He had had various brief affairs with actresses and dancers.

He was well aware that backstage was very different from the glamour that was seen from the front.

Now he knew he had no time to write anything for Fiona.

Instead he would engage Professionals.

They would include Musicians and famous Singers whom Princess Alexandra would appreciate.

The Duke knew exactly what the Prince's taste was.

But that would be impossible to cater for at what would be a family party.

There was no question of his grandmother who was over seventy, not being there.

If the Christmas house-party stayed on for the Performance as they would insist on doing there would be innumerable other relatives who would all be extremely critical.

They would also be shocked at anything that might be considered vulgar.

The Duke began to realise the whole idea was much more difficult than he had expected,

"I must talk to Fiona about it," he told himself.

He was quite certain she would find a solution.

If not, she would know exactly the people to whom they could turn for assistance.

He was not aware himself how much he had grown to depend on her.

When he thought about it, however, he knew she was making herself indispensable for her own ends.

As he rose from the table having finished his brandy, another idea occurred to him.

Perhaps after all he might as well marry Fiona and get it over with.

She could be ready to take over all the running of the house.

He could concentrate on the estate.

The horses, the pheasants, the farms, the livestock.

Also the great number of people whose lives he controlled because their families had served his for generations.

He walked from the Dining-Room.

Then as he was moving towards his Study he had a sudden thought.

His present for Fiona was upstairs, and there was no reason why he should not take it to her now.

She would be astonished to see him, but she would be very thrilled.

She had made that clear in the letter he had read before he had had his bath.

She had written:

"I am counting the hours until Thursday. Last night I spent a very dreary dinner with the Burchingtons who were quarrelling as usual. I have no plans for tomorrow night, but will just sit counting the hours until I can see you again.

The joy and excitement of it will be overwhelming as it seems like a century since you went to Holland.

I want to be close to you, I want you to tell me that you have missed me, and I want, my most handsome, adorable man, things which it would be a mistake for me to write down."

She signed her name with a flourish and the Duke knew exactly what she wanted.

He wondered if in fact he was too tired.

Then he asked himself how he could even think such a thing at his age.

Half the men in London would give their right arm to be Fiona's lover.

He went up the stairs to collect the bracelet he had bought for her in Amsterdam.

An Equerry to the Queen had been only too willing to tell him the name of the most reliable Jeweller in the City.

The Merchant had produced a bracelet, which the Duke saw was set with extremely fine blue-white diamonds.

He had also shown him a ring which he said he was selling for a Client.

It had a single diamond cut in the shape of a heart.

"It is an exceptionally fine stone, Your Grace," the Merchant said, "and it would be very hard to find another comparable to it."

Turning it over and over so that it caught the light the Duke had known this was the truth.

It struck him because it was heart-shaped that it would make a perfect engagement-ring when he did decide to marry.

The family jewels were magnificent.

When his mother appeared at the Opening of Parliament, she had always been more resplendent than any of the other Peeresses.

Now most of the jewels were in the safe awaiting the moment when he had a wife.

There were, he knew, several engagement-rings that had been passed down from generation to generation.

He had always understood however that a fiancée was given a ring to be her own and not part of the family collection.

Finally, the Duke had bought both the bracelet and the ring.

They were expensive, but he felt he had obtained, as the Equerry had promised, his "money's worth".

As he put the bracelet into his pocket he left the ring in the drawer.

If he did propose to Fiona, it would be waiting for her.

But he had not yet fully made up his mind.

He did not know why, except that she had pursued him so ardently.

He felt as if the whole thing was contrived and, at the same time, too obvious.

He did not know exactly what he did want, except of course that his wife must be beautiful.

All the previous Duchesses of Moorminster had been that.

Of course too her blood must be the equal of his.

That condition was certainly satisfied where Fiona was concerned because her father's Dukedom was older than his.

He wanted somebody who excited him physically.

She must also grace the position she would hold in the same way that his own mother had done.

He remembered when he was a small boy peeping from the Minstrels' gallery at a dinner-party taking place in the Banqueting Hall.

He had thought his father at one end of the table looked like a King.

His mother at the other end looked like a Fairy Princess.

She glittered with every move she made and she was the most beautiful woman present.

Fiona would certainly be that.

It crossed his mind that perhaps she would not be loved as his mother had been.

She was still adored by the servants on the estate.

"T'Duchess be a angel come down from 'eaven to be among us!" he remembered one of the old pensioners saying.

He had been only a small boy at the time but it was something he had never forgotten.

Fiona was certainly no angel.

In fact in the fiery encounters of their love she might be more appropriately described as coming from the fires of Hell.

That sounded somewhat derogatory, but the Duke was smiling.

There was a glint in his eyes that had not been there before.

He wanted Fiona, he wanted her now, and she lived only just around the corner.

Her house was in Carlos Place.

To reach her he had only to brave the elements for a few minutes.

When he reached the hall a footman had his sable-lined coat ready for him.

It had an astrakhan collar to keep his neck warm.

Another footman handed him his tall hat and his gloves.

A third supplied him with a cane.

"You are quite certain, Your Grace, you do not require a carriage?" the Butler asked respectfully.

"No, thank you, Redding, I am not going far," the Duke replied.

There was a knowing look in the man's eyes which the Duke did not see.

The front door was opened, and the Duke walked rather carefully down the steps in case they were slippery with frost.

There was certainly going to be a sharp one tonight, he thought.

Outside it was extremely cold.

The Duke walked quickly and was glad there was no wind.

Carriages were moving through the Square.

In the house next door to his there had obviously been a dinner-party, and the guests were now leaving.

The Duke moved quickly past them in case he should be recognised.

Then he turned into Carlos Place.

Fiona had an attractive house on the left-hand side.

The Duke knew it so well that he thought he could have found his way there blindfold.

As he went up the steps he felt for the key which had been in the drawer in his bedroom.

On one thing he had been very particular.

He had never allowed Fiona to come to his house in Grosvenor Square alone at night.

She did not dine there without a chaperon, nor would he make love to her after his other guests had departed.

"How can you be so pompous?" she teased him.

"I am protecting your reputation," the Duke had replied, "for, as you well know, servants talk."

She shrugged her shoulders, and it was a very pretty gesture.

"Does that really matter to us?"

"I think it does," he said quietly.

She had been slightly petulant about it.

Because he raised no objections about coming to her, she had given him the latch-key.

"I have no footman sitting up and watching who comes and goes," she said.

Therefore, when they were in London the Duke had gone to her house.

It was sometimes very late, if he had been on duty at the Palace or had dined with the Prince of Wales.

She had always been waiting for him in her bedroom.

She looked exquisitely lovely with her red hair falling over her shoulders and her skin translucent as a pearl.

She usually had a surprise for him in one way or another.

Once she had greeted him wearing a necklace of black pearls and nothing else.

Another time it was one of emeralds and a narrow belt of the same stones round her small waist.

Tonight, the Duke was thinking, she would not be expecting him.

Therefore he would have the pleasure of hearing her cry of joy.

He expected she would jump out of bed and throw herself into his arms.

He inserted the key in the lock and found the hall was in darkness.

It was nearly midnight, and he was sure that Fiona would have gone to bed early.

She would be saving herself for tomorrow night.

Only when the stars were fading would he hurry back to be in his own bedroom.

At six o'clock the housemaids in their mob-caps and the footmen in their shirt-sleeves would start cleaning the house.

He took off his coat and put it down on a chair.

He knew it was there without even having to look for it.

His hat and his gloves followed.

In the faint light which came from the fanlight above the front door he could make out the banisters.

Holding onto them he moved quietly up the thick carpet.

He passed the Drawing-Room which extended over the whole of the First Floor.

He climbed the next flight to where her bedroom was situated.

He paused for a moment before he put out his hand towards the handle of the door.

As he did so he stiffened.

There was the sound of somebody speaking inside and the voice was that of a man.

For a moment the Duke thought he could not be hearing correctly.

Or that he must have come to the wrong house.

Then, as he knew to whom the voice belonged, he felt as if he had been turned to stone.

Chapter Two

The Duke was aware that it was his First Cousin Joscelyn Moore who was in bed with Fiona.

Joscelyn was one of his relatives for whom he had no liking.

He had learnt that as his Heir Presumptive he had tried to borrow money from the Usurers.

But because it was only on the chance of his becoming the 3rd Duke of Moorminster they had sent him away ignominiously.

The story had somehow reached the gossips and had been related to the Duke.

It told him that Joscelyn Moor once again was deeply in debt.

He would soon be trying to put pressure on him again to save the family and the heir from disgrace.

The Duke was not mistaken.

This time he had spoken to his Cousin very severely, saying he had been given already more than his fair share of what money was available.

Joscelyn had been furious at being lectured.

The Duke thought now that perhaps he was taking his revenge by seducing Fiona.

As it happened, Joscelyn was very much like Eric Faversham in that he could not resist a pretty face.

His love affairs were so numerous that they had long since ceased to shock his relatives.

Tall, good-looking like all the Moores, he had that strange charisma which men disliked but women found irresistible.

The Duke's first impulse was to go into the room and confront them.

Then his brain told him that this would be undignified.

Moreover he had no right to make any claims on Fiona when he had not asked her to marry him.

To have thought about it was very different from saying the words she longed to hear.

She had professed her love for him so ardently that he had foolishly imagined that she was faithful to him.

At least for as long as he remained her lover.

He now thought cynically that perhaps Joscelyn was not the first man she had taken to her bed when he was not available.

As he stood there unable to make up his mind what to do, he heard Joscelyn speak again.

"You are very lovely, Fiona," he said in a caressing tone, "and you will doubtless be the most beautiful Duchess of Moorminster whose portrait has ever hung in the Picture Gallery!"

"It is what I intend to be," Fiona replied. "At the same time, as you well know, it is not easy to make Sheldon talk of matrimony."

"Dammit!" Joscelyn swore. "He has to make an honest woman of you after getting you talked about by the whole of London."

"Perhaps you would like to tell him so?" Fiona replied mockingly.

"You know damned well he would not listen to me!" Joscelyn said, "and I will have to crawl on my stomach to make him pay my debts!"

"Oh, Joscelyn, are things as bad as that all over again?"

"Worse!" Joscelyn replied. "But Sheldon will have to pay up. Otherwise there will be an almighty scandal, and he will not like that!"

"You know, dearest Joscelyn, that I would help you if only I could, and when I marry Sheldon I will certainly make him more generous than he is at the moment."

The Duke clenched his fists.

He thought of the large amount of money he had given his Cousin.

It had all been thrown away on Actresses, prostitutes and his riotous friends.

To accuse him of not being generous was unforgivable.

He had already been forced to make economies on the Estate.

It was simply because Joscelyn had obtained large sums from him which could have provided wages and pensions for more workers.

Then he heard Fiona say:

"Do not let us talk of anything so depressing as money when we are close like this!"

"You are right," Joscelyn agreed, "and no one could be as soft, adorable and wildly exciting as you!"

There was silence, and the Duke knew that he was kissing her.

Slowly, carefully, so as not to make the slightest sound, he descended the stairs and reached the hall.

He put on his coat, picked up his hat and gloves and let himself out into the night.

As he walked home he was consumed with a fury that made him feel as if his whole body was on fire.

He knew if he was honest it was not only because Fiona had been unfaithful.

But that she should choose Joscelyn, of all men, with whom to do it was unforgivable.

He had talked to her, of course he had, of how abominably Joscelyn was behaving.

She had commiserated with him.

He knew however that as she did so, she was thinking that the answer to his problem was quite simple.

If he married and had an heir Joscelyn would no longer be able virtually to blackmail him.

That was what he was doing in making him pay his debts.

As Joscelyn had said, he could not allow his Heir Presumptive to go bankrupt.

The Duke entered his front door.

As he did so he knew decisively, without there being any further question about it, that he would never marry Fiona.

The Night-Footman, who was obviously surprised to see him back so soon, took his coat.

The Duke walked up the stairs to his bedroom.

He rang for his Valet, undressed without speaking, and got into bed.

When he was alone he lay in the darkness.

He felt that when he least expected it, the ceiling had fallen down on his head.

It was not that he minded so deeply that Fiona had taken a lover.

After all, as he told himself logically, she had every right to do so.

They were not tied to each other in any way.

At the same time, he had believed her continual protestations of love.

She had assured him over and over again that he was the only man in her life.

She had re-iterated a thousand times that she had never known such ecstasy as he had given her.

He had believed her, of course he had, because he wanted to.

And in fact, it was what a number of other women had told him.

Now he knew he had been a fool to think that such a thing was possible.

Fiona's husband had been a rake and a womaniser, and Joscelyn was the same.

Was it likely therefore that she could possibly be the innocent pupil she pretended to be?

The Duke had always prided himself on his intelligence.

He was indispensable to the Queen not merely because of his title and the fact that he was so handsome.

Granted it was well known that Queen Victoria liked handsome men.

She certainly had a "soft spot" in her heart for him.

But she also appreciated his brain.

She had often praised the way he could, when it was required, manipulate a Foreign Diplomat into agreeing to what she wanted.

When Lord Beaconsfield was Prime Minister he had said much the same thing.

"I can always trust Your Grace," he had said on one occasion, "to get your own way, which is my way, and I am very grateful."

The Duke had also believed in his infallibility when it came to ferreting out the truth.

He made sure he was not deceived in any way.

Yet Fiona had managed to deceive him.

He thought now he had been as stupid as a country yokel.

The question was, what did he intend to do about it?

For a start he had no intention of letting either Fiona or Joscelyn be aware that he had crept into her house and listened outside her bedroom door.

That would savour too much of the Servants' Hall.

It would make him appear undignified and even more foolish than he felt already.

Several hours of the night had passed before he finally made up his mind.

First, that neither Fiona nor Joscelyn should have the slightest idea that their behaviour had been discovered.

Secondy, that he would slowly manoeuvre Fiona out of his life. He would do it subtly.

She would not be able to complain of his cruelty or give the clacking tongues of Mayfair anything to talk about.

He was not yet certain of how it should be done.

It was however, something he was determined to do.

At least he knew that he could not bear to see her the next evening as they had arranged.

If they dined together, she would inevitably want to console him for the nights he had spent without her.

He would find himself in the same bed which at the moment was occupied by Joscelyn.

The mere idea revolted him.

It was something which must be avoided at all costs.

Finally, before he fell asleep, he remembered he had told his Valet to call him at seven o'clock.

The Duke's Valet came into the room.

As he did so the Duke told him to inform Mr. Watson, his Secretary, that he was going to the country.

"To Moor Park, Y'Grace?" the man exclaimed in astonishment.

"Pack everything I shall need," the Duke ordered. "We will leave at ten o'clock."

By the time he was dressed and downstairs Mr. Watson was waiting for him.

"Good-morning, Your Grace!" he said. "I have been informed that you intend to leave for the country."

"That is what I have decided to do," the Duke replied as he walked towards the Breakfast-Room. "I have already sent my Assistant ahead to alert Moor Park to Your Grace's arrival," Mr. Watson said, "but I have of course no idea whether Your Grace is taking a party."

"I am going alone," the Duke said firmly.

Because he thought that Mr. Watson looked surprised he added as an afterthought:

"I want to see my Theatre. As you know, we have not yet decided who shall be the performers when their Royal Highnesses are present for the Opening."

"May I inform Your Grace that I have made out a list of the most distinguished singers available and there is also a Conjurer at one of the Music Halls who I am told is remarkable."

The Duke did not answer.

He was now sitting at the breakfast-table.

The Butler and two footmen were presenting him with the dishes that were kept hot on the sideboard.

Mr. Watson moved towards the door.

"I will join you in the Study," the Duke said, "when I have finished breakfast. Meanwhile, Watson, I shall want you to come with me to Moor Park."

What he said surprised Mr. Watson who seldom went with him to the country when the Duke had a party there.

He did not usually require his Secretary there.

He was he said, attempting to escape from the responsibilities which filled his life in London.

There were his duties at Buckingham Palace and Windsor Castle.

Heavy demands also were made on him by the Prince of Wales, sometimes officially and often as a friend.

His presence was often required by the Prime Minister.

He was requested by Ministers to attend innumerable Conferences and functions.

Especially those in which the Secretary of State for Foreign Affairs was concerned.

The Duke had spent a great deal of time in the last few years travelling to other countries.

Not only to countries in Europe, including Russia, but he had also been to America and Africa.

He had been of inestimable value to Ministers who had to rely on reports rather than see a situation for themselves.

The Duke went to his Study where Mr. Watson was waiting.

Apart from one pile of invitations which were undoubtedly social, there was another, that were of a Diplomatic nature.

He suspected there would be a third that were Political.

He seated himself at his desk and with a sweep of his hand said:

"You can bring all those with you. Is there anything urgent to which I should reply before we go?"

"There is a letter from His Royal Highness the Prince of Wales," Mr. Watson replied, "asking Your Grace to dine at Marlborough House tomorrow night, and saying that he would like to see you alone, if possible, tomorrow morning."

"You can send a note to the Prince," the Duke replied, "and everybody else saying that I have gone to the country on urgent matters concerning my Estate."

He paused a moment and then he continued:

"I will of course, contact His Royal Highness on my return."

Mr. Watson noted down what the Duke had said.

Then as there was silence he remarked somewhat tentatively:

"I think Your Grace is expected to dine with Lady Faversham this evening."

"Yes – of course!" the Duke said as if he had just thought of it. "Send Her Ladyship the same message, and all of them are to be delivered late this afternoon, which is when I was expected to return from Holland."

"Very good, Your Grace."

Mr. Watson hurried from the room.

The Duke sat back in his chair with a somewhat twisted smile at the corner of his mouth.

He knew that Fiona would be astonished and perhaps slightly perturbed.

Not only had he left for the country without seeing her first.

More significantly he had not written to her himself.

He had, he thought, struck the first blow in the campaign which would inevitably develop between them.

He knew she would fight like a tiger to keep him.

She would gradually become frantic when she discovered he was being elusive.

He expected there would be the usual tears and recriminations.

Such as had happened at the end of several of his *affaires de coeur*.

But they had never involved the possibility of marriage.

Fiona's position was therefore somewhat different.

He also expected she would inform Joscelyn who would call on him tomorrow.

He knew the tactics only too well.

As Joscelyn had said last night, he would beg him with heard-rending apologies for money.

If he was refused he would begin the familiar semi-blackmail, pointing out how much the family name would suffer.

He would emphasise how deeply distressed their relatives would be if his desperate situation should be reported in the newspapers.

Here he had a point.

The Press would not hesitate, as the Duke knew, to contrast the pitiable state of the Heir Presumptive with that of one of the wealthiest Dukes in the country.

The Duke's face was contorted as he brought his clenched fist down on the desk so violently that it made the ink-pots rattle.

"Curse him!" he exclaimed. "I shall have to pay up, and he knows it!"

He tried to tell himself that while there was nothing else he could do, he should not allow Joscelyn's behaviour to upset him.

Yet when he left the Study there was a frown between his eyes.

There was no time to arrange for his Private Coach to be attached to the train on which he was to travel.

There was however, a Courier to escort him to the Station.

He would see that he was given a Reserved Carriage, and that the door was locked when he entered it.

Mr. Watson would be in the next coach and the luggage deposited in the Guard's Van.

There would be in fact, very little in the way of trunks.

The Duke had insisted on having a duplicate of everything he wished to wear in both of the houses in which he stayed most frequently.

He also had a house in Newmarket and another in Leicestershire.

There were therefore usually very few things to be conveyed from Grosvenor Square to Moor Park.

The most important this time were the letters which travelled beside Mr. Watson in a despatch-case.

The Courier acquired all the daily newspapers and put them in the Duke's carriage.

It was not a long journey as Moor Park was situated North of London in the most beautiful part of Oxfordshire.

It could be reached by road in under three hours.

The Duke however, in the Winter, found it much quicker and on the whole more comfortable to travel by train.

This would stop by request at his Private Halt.

He then had only a two-mile drive to his home.

As he stepped out of the train at The Halt there was a red carpet across the platform.

Three members of his staff were waiting for him.

Outside was a Chaise he liked to drive himself.

There was also a Brake in which to convey everybody else from the Station to the house.

He greeted those who were waiting for him in a somewhat frigid manner, which made them suspect that something was wrong.

Then he got into his Chaise, picked up the reins and drove off.

The Groom travelled in the seat at the back.

Therefore the Duke was not bothered by having the man beside him.

He drove his horses skilfully round the twisting lanes.

As he did, he thought that this was the first time for years that he had come home without a party to amuse him.

At the moment to be alone was all he wanted.

The austerity of it pleased him, just as he enjoyed the cold and frosty air on his cheeks and the greyness of the sky above.

He was not in the mood for sunshine or for the laughter and chatter of flirtatious women.

He wanted to be by himself, to "lick his wounds" before he moved up into the firing-line.

Moor Park was looking magnificent.

It did not matter whether it was Spring, Summer, Autumn or Winter.

The great house always looked the same.

The centre block with its wings reaching out on either side was breath-taking.

To the Duke it was everything that was stable in his life – the foundation of his very existence.

He drove down the long drive.

As he did so he asked himself how he could have thought that Fiona Faversham could take the place of his mother, as the Duchess of Moorminster.

It was not only that she had deceived him.

He knew now that however beautiful she might be, both her character and her personality were wrong.

"If I married her and afterwards discovered her perfidy, it would have not only humiliated me, but smirched the whole history of the family," the Duke thought.

He crossed the ancient bridge over the lake that was as old as the house itself and drew up at the front door.

The red carpet was already down.

Footmen were waiting to open the door of the Chaise for him to alight.

The Butler was standing at the top of the steps.

It was all so familiar.

But the Duke had the feeling that he was seeing it for the first time.

Only now did he realise how much it meant to him.

He walked into the house and because he wanted to distract his mind he went immediately to where the Theatre was being rebuilt.

As he expected, the Architect and the Designer were waiting.

He went in through the door which connected the Theatre with the house.

When the Duke had found the plans drawn up by the Adam brothers he had also found a letter of instructions.

It had been written to them by his ancestor, then the 7th Earl of Moore.

It was his grandson, the 9th Earl who had distinguished himself so gallantly under Wellington that he had been made a Marquis.

It was the Duke's father who had been raised to the Dukedom by Queen Victoria.

The Earl's instructions to the Adam brothers had been made after he had returned from a visit to Russia.

He had been there as a guest of the Tsar.

He told them that he had been exceedingly impressed by the Royal Theatre in the Winter Palace.

And even more so by Prince Ysvolsov's Private Theatre which was exceptional.

The Earl had managed to obtain sketches of the interior of the latter.

The Adam brothers had therefore been able to model their design on it exceedingly cleverly.

The Duke had last seen the Theatre a month before he left England to go to Holland.

He had been sure that his Architect and Designer could recreate the charm of the original Theatre at Moor Park.

He was however, a little apprehensive that he was expecting too much.

They were both waiting for him and led him through the door into the Theatre.

Because the house was on slightly higher ground than the foundations of the Theatre, the Duke found himself on a level with the boxes.

A flight of stairs in front of him went down into what in a Public Theatre would be known as the "Stalls".

The building was quite small, in fact it could hold few more than a hundred people.

It was, the Duke thought, like a child's doll's house.

Yet it had all the charm and beauty of what might have been a Royal Theatre.

In the Stalls were white and gold carved chairs.

The "Circle" was furnished with seats upholstered in crimson velvet.

The two boxes, one of which was intended for Royalty, had the same.

The whole effect was quite beautiful, as was the backdrop on the stage.

Curtains of rich red velvet were drawn back in front of the footlights.

There was a small 'Pit' for the Orchestra and a huge crystal chandelier hung from the ceiling.

The Architect and the Designer were watching the Duke's face.

He looked all round him in silence before he said:

"I congratulate you both! It is exactly what I wanted, and far better than I dared to expect!"

He knew by their looks before they spoke how gratified they were.

When he left them he walked back into the house to have a late luncheon.

For the first time since last night when he had stood outside Fiona's bedroom door, he could think of something else.

He knew he had to work quickly to decide which Prima Donna he should engage for the night the Prince of Wales would be in the audience.

More important, who should take part in the sketch he had half-written and which included a part for Fiona.

He had not realised until she insisted on singing for him, that she had a pleasant voice.

It was nothing exceptional.

But he knew that with her beauty it would not be difficult for her to have an appreciative audience.

Although it would in general be a critical one.

A great number of his relatives, including his grandmother, came to Moor Park every Christmas.

They would have arrived without even receiving an invitation.

It was traditional that they should be there.

A tradition they had every intention of maintaining.

The idea had come to him that he would compose a song for Fiona in which she would appear as an angel.

But now he knew that to introduce Fiona as an angel would be a crime against God.

Then another idea came to him, and there was a melody in his mind that kept recurring.

He knew it would be with him until he had played it on the piano and transcribed it as a score.

He hoped that Fiona would not be staying with him at Christmas.

If she was, she would sit in the Stalls and watch somebody else play her part.

"You will not forget about the song I am to sing in your new Theatre?" she had asked the day before he was leaving for Holland. "I shall need time to practise it, and I know, darling, Sheldon, how you expect perfection."

"How could you be anything else?" he had said automatically because it was expected of him.

Now he told himself furiously that there was nothing perfect about Fiona.

"I will find somebody else for the part," he thought. "It should not be difficult."

After luncheon he ordered a horse from the stables.

As the Head Groom brought the horse to the front door, he predicted there would be snow before long.

"I doubt it!" the Duke replied curtly.

"We loiks t'have a white Christmas," the man remarked. "Las' year, if Y'Grace Remember, it never snowed 'til Boxin' Day!"

The Duke wondered what that proved.

He knew the staff at Moor Park, like his nieces and nephews, looked forward to snow at Christmas.

They were disappointed if they were denied it.

Because the Duke felt he must escape from his thoughts, he rode away over the fields.

He went Northwards passing through the woods he had not visited for a long time.

He knew that sometime he must talk to his game-keepers.

But for the moment he just wanted to be alone to be free of everything.

Most of all of his own feelings.

He rode on and on until he realised it was very cold and that soon it would be growing dark.

It was then he saw just ahead of him a small village that he had not visited for some years.

He remembered it was called "Little Bedlington".

It consisted of a few thatched cottages, an ancient black-and-white Inn, and what looked like a Norman Church.

There was still some left in the County.

The Duke thought dryly that most of the Churches on his estate were ceaselessly in need of urgent repairs.

He rode through the village looking at the thatch on the cottages which seemed to be in good repair.

The fences and gates were the same.

The few children he saw looked rosy-cheeked and well-fed.

He was just about to turn round and hurry home when he heard music coming from the Church.

For one moment he wondered why on a week-day anyone should be playing the organ.

Then as he drew his horse nearer he realised the playing was surprisingly skilful.

He knew only too well how heavy-handed some organists could be.

What he was listening to was an exceptionally beautiful rendering of a Carol "It Came Upon the Midnight Clear", and it brought back many memories.

As a Musician, which was what the Duke believed himself to be, he was impressed.

He could only commend the Organist for having a touch that

was brilliant, and for knowing the way the Carol should be played.

He drew his horse up outside the Church door and sat listening.

As a child he had learnt that Carol and sung it to his mother.

The Organist finished it and stopped.

The Duke was curious as to who was playing.

He also felt that, as one Musician to another, he should congratulate the man.

He dismounted.

He tied the reins of his horse to an ancient post outside the porch and walked into the Church.

He found, as he had expected, that the Church was small.

The nave at any rate, was definitely Norman with its rounded arches and barrel roof.

His eye was caught by a particularly fine stained-glass window above the altar.

Then he became aware that seated in the carved stalls in the Chancel were a number of small children.

As he looked at them a young woman came from the organ behind them to stand in the centre of the aisle.

She was slight, and as he could see, very young.

She had an almost childlike face which was dominated by two large blue eyes.

Her hair which he could see from under her small bonnet, was fair.

It struck him that she had the appearance of an angel.

She stood still for a moment with her back to the altar.

Then she said to the children:

"Now that you have listened to the tune of that beautiful Carol, I want you to try to sing the words. I will sing them to you first, then you must follow me."

There was a little murmur from the children.

Lifting her head the girl, in a sweet, clear, very young voice began to sing.

As she did so the Duke realised that her voice was exactly what he might have expected from an angel.

There was something not human about it.

Something which seemed to have no connection with the world.

It could only come from Heaven where there was no sin, no unpleasantness, no horror, no fear.

He could not imagine why he should find himself thinking this.

Yet as the girl sang, and went on singing the thought came insistently into his mind.

It was almost as if somebody was saying the words to him.

She finished the first verse of the Carol.

The Duke was listening intently.

So, he was aware, were the children.

It was as if she had mesmerised them into silence.

As she finished she smiled and the Duke thought it was as if the sun had come out.

"Now we will do it to the music," she said.

She went back to the organ and the children, without being told, got to their feet.

Playing with the same exquisite touch which had drawn the Duke into the Church, she started the Carol once again.

This time her voice, as if she was "Star of Bethlehem" led the children.

They sang as only children can – with the freshness of youth, which was very moving in itself.

The Duke knew her voice was exceptional.

It was so true and pure that it could only be described as "angelic".

Chapter Three

When the children stopped singing the girl came from the organ and said:

"That was very good! Come tomorrow at the same time."

The children jumped up, eager to leave the Church.

They trooped past the Duke standing just inside the door, barely noticing him.

When they had gone he walked slowly up the aisle to where the girl was tidying away the Hymn Books.

As he reached her she looked up in surprise.

He thought that close to, she was even lovelier than she had appeared from a distance.

"Good-afternoon!" he said in his deep voice.

She smiled and replied:

"I thought I saw somebody at the back of the Church while we were singing."

"I heard you first playing the organ," he said, "and thought you had a professional touch."

She laughed and it was a very pretty sound.

"That is very complimentary, but I only started to play in the Church when the Organist died. My father, who is the Vicar, could not find a suitable replacement."

"I am sure nobody could play better than you do!" the Duke said.

She looked up at him with a shy little glance which told him she was not used to receiving compliments.

Then as she thought it was strange he was there she asked:

"Is there anything I can do for you?"

"I think there is," the Duke replied, "and I would like to discuss it with your father, who I imagine I met when he was first appointed to this Parish."

The girl was still, as if an idea had suddenly struck her.

Then she asked a little tentatively:

"You are not . . you cannot be . . ?"

"I am the Duke of Moorminster," he said, "and I was riding through the village when I heard you playing the organ."

The girl dropped him a curtsy.

"I am . . sorry," she said, "I . . I did not recognise you."

"There is no reason why you should," the Duke said, "and perhaps you would tell me your name?"

"It is Lavela Ashley, and my father has been the Vicar of Little Bedlington for nineteen years."

"In which case," the Duke said, "he was appointed by my father, so I would not know him."

"I am afraid Papa is not at home at the moment, but visiting a parishioner who is ill and lives some distance away."

The Duke thought for a moment. Then he said:

"I suggest that you and your father come to Moor Park tomorrow where I will discuss with you both something I would like you to do for me."

"Come to . . Moor Park?" Lavela Ashley asked in a low voice.

"At about eleven o'clock in the morning," the Duke said. "Have you some means of getting there?"

"Yes . . yes of course . . Your Grace."

"Then I shall be looking forward to seeing you, Miss Ashley, and may I say once again how much I enjoyed your playing."

Lavela curtsied and the Duke turned and walked down the aisle.

As he went he thought with satisfaction that at least he had found somebody to take the part of the angel in his Play.

She would certainly look like one.

He mounted his horse and rode off swiftly to get home before it was dark.

Riding fast because he knew the way, he was just able to manage it.

He rode up to the front door and saw there were servants looking out anxiously as if they wondered what had happened to him.

A groom was waiting at the bottom of the steps.

He went to his Study and took out the manuscript of the short Play he had not yet finished.

It had been copied out for him by Mr. Watson's assistant in excellent writing.

As the Duke read what he had written he knew he had had Fiona in his mind as he wrote it.

Slowly he tore it into pieces.

On one thing he was determined: Fiona should not act or sing in front of the Prince and Princess of Wales.

It occurred to him that she was anxious not only to do so because she liked showing off.

She might, if she found an opportunity, inveigle the Prince into helping her where their marriage was concerned.

It was well-known that the Prince, who was always in love with somebody, enjoyed assisting his friends with their love-affairs.

In fact on several occasions he had married off a hesitant Bridegroom.

He managed this simply by saying firmly to the man in question that he had already got the girl talked about.

"I did not intend to get married for at least another five years!" the Duke's friend had complained to him. "But what could I do with His Royal Highness hinting broadly that I would ruin Alice's reputation unless I proposed to her?"

The Duke thought his friend had been very foolish to have allowed himself to be trapped in such a manner.

He knew only too well that the Prince could never resist helping a pretty woman if she cried.

Too late he thought he should not have told Fiona that the Prince had invited himself to Moor Park.

It was not only a question of the Royal Couple.

All his family would be there, and there was no doubt that she would try to inveigle them into supporting her.

He had never thought of it before for the simple reason that he was determined that he would not be rushed into marriage.

He had forgotten how devious a woman could be when she wished to get her own way.

He decided he must somehow prevent Fiona from coming to stay.

It was going to be difficult because they had already discussed the party.

He knew that as usual, Fiona would more or less act as hostess, even if his grandmother was there.

"What shall I do?" he asked himself helplessly.

There was very little time before Christmas to hope that things might have changed before the party arrived.

If he dropped Fiona gradually, as he meant to do, sooner or later she would demand an explanation.

Then he would undoubtedly have to tell the truth.

"I shall just have to wait," he thought, "and see how things work out."

At the same time he was worried.

Having dined alone, he stayed up very late rewriting his Play.

A new idea had come to him.

It was Christmas and so many of his relatives were growing old.

He would write something which would make them feel that whatever their age, they were not forgotten.

They would be told there was still ways for them to help others and that they were needed.

He therefore envisaged the central figure as an elderly woman, regretting her lost youth.

He had already composed a song which she could sing.

She would regret the excitements, the joys, and the ambitions of youth.

Then because it was Christmas, a small child would bring her a present.

An older girl, also with a gift, would ask her help over a problem which concerned love.

At first the older woman would feel she did not know the answer.

Then she would give the girl the right one.

As the girl goes away happy to find the man she loves, the elderly woman would fall asleep.

While she was sleeping, she would dream.

An Angel appearing with two small cherubs would tell her there was no such thing as death.

Her good deeds would live on after she had left the world.

And even when she was in Heaven, she would still be helping and guiding those she loved.

When the idea had come to the Duke he had thought at first it was too sentimental.

Then he knew his grandmother and his aunts would love it.

It was in fact, something in which he genuinely believed, although he never talked about it.

The women in his life, including Fiona, he knew would have mocked at him if they thought he was religious.

They paid "lip-service" to the Church in that sometimes they attended a Service on Sunday.

They certainly appeared at every fashionable Wedding and Funeral.

The truth was that while they did so they were breaking the vows they had made when they married.

Besides most of the Commandments in one way or another.

He remembered one party at which Fiona was present when somebody had said jokingly to the woman with whom he was flirting:

"I am certainly breaking the Tenth Commandment in coveting my neighbour's wife!"

There was laughter at this and another wit had retorted:

"There is only one Commandment that matters, the eleventh: 'Thou shalt not be found out!' "

The Duke had laughed, and so had Fiona.

He thought now that she would have been shockingly miscast as an Angel.

He could not think of anyone who would really look angelic except the girl he had found today.

He wondered why he had never seen her before.

But there was no reason why he should have unless she had attended a Meet on this part of the Estate.

"Perhaps there is some more hidden talent amongst my tenants!" he thought with a smile.

He rose from his desk realising it was long after midnight.

He had written not a play but a very short episode with more music than words.

There still remained the music.

He thought he might incorporate part of the Carol which Lavela Ashley had sung so beautifully with the children in the Church.

Even as he thought of it he could see how it fitted in.

The music he had been composing himself would make a background for the Angel when she spoke to the old woman.

Perhaps he should write another song she could sing.

Because a tune was ringing in his brain he wanted to go to the Music Room and try it out on the piano immediately.

Then he knew that, in fact, he was very tired.

He had not slept much the night before, had risen early and ridden a long way during the afternoon.

He therefore went to bed.

Before he fell asleep he was again hearing Lavela's voice soaring up to the roof of the Norman Church.

He thought the pureness and clarity of it was different from any sound he had ever heard before.

The Duke awoke early and was humming to himself as he dressed.

After breakfast a horse was waiting for him outside the door and he rode for an hour.

He took all the jumps he had erected on his private race-course with such ease that he decided he should have them heightened a little.

He was back at the house at a quarter to eleven.

He had told the servants that he was expecting the Vicar of Little Bedlington and his daughter.

When they arrived they were to be shown into the Music Room.

This room, which was his favourite, was considered one of the most beautiful in the whole house.

White and gold, it had a painted ceiling of cupids with small harps while Venus in the centre of them was obviously singing an aria.

It had originally been painted by an Italian artist, but was in a bad state of repair when the Duke inherited.

His father who was not in the least musical never went into it.

The Duke as a boy had a piano in the School-Room.

When he grew older, there was one in the Sitting-Room which opened out of his bedroom.

One of the first things he had done when he became the reigning Duke was to open the Music Room.

He had it painted, gilded and the ceiling restored.

It now looked just as it had when the Adam brothers first designed it.

When he reached the Music Room he sat down at the piano.

He played, if not as well as a professional, very much better than the average amateur.

He had taken lessons from a great Concert Pianist when he was in Italy as a young man.

It was something he had never told anybody, thinking they would laugh at him.

In fact, very few people, even the women to whom he made love realised how much music meant to him.

Fiona had become aware of it simply because she was so often with him.

But he knew when he was playing to her one of his own compositions she was really thinking it would be much more enjoyable if she was in his arms.

The words with which she praised him were, he knew, spoken only to make him happy.

Not because she was convinced in her own mind that he was a good performer.

Now he propped a music score in front of him.

He began to note on it the tune which had come into his mind last night.

He had completed quite a lot when the door opened and a servant announced:

"The Reverend Andrew Ashley, Your Grace, and Miss Ashley!"

The Duke rose from the piano-stool.

He had been half-afraid this morning that he had been imagining things yesterday afternoon.

He had been convinced then that Lavela Ashley looked exactly like an Angel.

Perhaps he had been bemused by the music.

Perhaps because it was getting on in the afternoon and the light was fading, his eyes had deceived him.

Now he took a quick glance at her before he looked at her father.

He saw that she was just as angelic in the pale sunshine coming through the window as he had thought her to be.

First he greeted the Vicar, an extremely handsome man as tall as the Duke himself.

He had clear-cut features and his hair was going grey at the temples.

There was moreover something distinguished about him which told the Duke he was a gentleman.

"I am delighted to meet you, Vicar," he said. "It is certainly very remiss of me that I have not done so before."

The Vicar smiled.

"We are at the far end of your Estate, Your Grace, and we live very quietly. I often think that Little Bedlington is forgotten."

"That is something which must be rectified in the future," the Duke replied.

He held out his hand to Lavela saying:

"I am so glad you have accepted my invitation and now I want to tell you what I have in mind."

The Duke walked towards one end of the room where he indicated a comfortable arm-chair for the Vicar.

He seated himself on the one opposite it while Lavela sat on the sofa.

"I expect your daughter has told you," the Duke began, "that quite by chance I was passing your Church yesterday afternoon. I heard her playing the organ and was extremely impressed at how well she did so."

"That is what I have always thought myself," the Vicar replied, "and my wife is also very musical."

"Your daughter sang a Carol with the children," the Duke went on, "and I was aware she has a very unusual and lovely voice!"

He thought Lavela looked shy as he spoke and the colour came into her cheeks.

The bonnet she was wearing was the same one she had worn in Church.

She was also plainly dressed.

Yet it seemed somehow the right frame for her face with its huge eyes and child-like expression.

Once again the Duke could only describe her as "angelic".

In a few words he went on to explain to the Vicar and Lavela what he was planning for the Saturday after Christmas.

"I want to show you my Theatre," he said, "but first I would like your daughter to sing for me as I heard her yesterday in the Church."

"Of course, Your Grace," the Vicar said, "but we did not think of bringing any music with us."

"Never mind," the Duke said. "First I would like her to play and sing part of the Carol she was teaching her choir. Then I will tell her what else I would like her to do."

Without any mock humility or making any protestations, Lavela walked to the piano.

It was obvious she knew the Carol by heart.

In order to accustom herself to the keys, Lavela played a few bars of the tune alone.

Then she began to sing.

If the Duke had been moved by her voice yesterday, in the Music Room, where the acoustics were perfect, he was spellbound.

She finished the last two lines:

> *"The World in solemn stillness lay*
> *To hear the angels sing."*

He thought as she did so that anyone listening to her would be in "solemn stillness" as he was himself.

Lavela took her hands from the keyboard.

"I am sure, Your Grace," she said, "you do not want any more."

"I would like to hear the whole Carol," the Duke said, "but instead if you can read music, I want you to sing a few bars of something I have composed myself."

He handed her the score and sat down at the piano.

He ran his fingers over the keys, playing the melody so that she could hear it without the words.

Then he said:

"Now you try!"

He struck a chord.

Then as he waited, Lavela's voice exactly as he had envisaged it, turned his words into a sound that seemed to soar into the sky.

Once she hesitated, but otherwise she was able to read what he had written almost perfectly.

As she finished the Vicar clapped his hands.

"That was delightful, Your Grace!" he exclaimed. "I had no idea that you were a Musician!"

"It is something that most people do not expect of me," the Duke answered, "and when I was a boy I was too embarrassed to admit it."

"I think you should be very proud that you are able to compose anything so beautiful," Lavela said.

She was studying the music score as she spoke.

The Duke knew she was speaking in all sincerity and he smiled as he said:

"Perhaps one day, when we have time, I will show you some other pieces I have composed and the words I have put to them."

"That would be wonderful," Lavela said, "and very satisfying!"

The Duke was sure that any other woman would have said:

"And you could make a fortune selling them."

Instead he realised Lavela was thinking of how he would feel himself and what in fact, he did feel.

"Come and look at the Theatre," he suggested.

They went from the Music Room to the part of the great house where the Theatre was situated.

When he took them in through the door they stood at the top of the steps with the Royally furnished boxes on each side.

"It is magnificent!" the Vicar exclaimed. "I have often thought it was sad that the original Theatre was burnt down."

"You know about it?" the Duke asked.

"I have always been extremely interested in the history of the house, Your Grace, and your father was gracious enough to show me round himself, explaining the alterations that had been made in 1780 and the parts of the building that were left intact."

"That was a long time ago," the Duke said, "and I would like you to see what alterations have been made since."

"I would enjoy that more than I can say," the Vicar replied.

The Duke took Lavela up onto the stage.

She was as thrilled as Fiona would have been if he had given her a diamond bracelet.

"It is so small," the Duke said, "that I do not think you will feel nervous."

She smiled.

"I never feel nervous when we are acting a Nativity Play, which is what we give every Christmas in the School Hall."

She smiled at him before continuing:

"Of course here the audience will be different, but I expect I will be able to forget them."

"That is the right attitude," the Vicar said before the Duke could speak. "I always tell the children to try to think themselves into their parts, and really believe they are the Three Wise Men, the Shepherds, or the Virgin Mary Herself."

"I can see, Vicar, you have a flair for acting," the Duke remarked.

The Vicar laughed.

"I must admit that I enjoyed performing in a number of Plays when I was at Oxford."

"Papa is a very good actor," Lavela said, "One year, when we were very adventurous and put on *King Lear*, everybody said Papa was wasted as Vicar of Little Bedlington!"

"You are both making me feel that I have neglected my duties in not discovering all this hidden talent on my doorstep before now!" the Duke declared.

"Be careful!" Lavela warned him unexpectedly. "Once you start encouraging people to become actors and actresses there will be a great number who think they are brilliant performers but who are in fact lamentably bad, and it is very hard to get rid of them."

"That is very true," the Vicar agreed. "There are some elderly spinsters in my Parish who either wish to recite endless poems they have written themselves, or to sing, usually out of tune, on every possible occasion."

The Duke laughed.

"Thank you for warning me."

"When they hear about this beautiful Theatre," Lavela said. "You will have the greatest difficulty in discouraging them."

"Then I can only beg you not to talk about it," the Duke smiled.

"To be truthful that would be impossible," Lavela answered, "for even if we do not talk, everybody else will!"

"Everybody?" the Duke questions.

"There is nothing that happens at Moor Park which is not known and discussed simply because it is so exciting."

Lavela thought the Duke looked sceptical and explained;

"You, Your Grace, are our Landlord and also the most thrilling person in the whole Country."

"I suppose I should be flattered," the Duke said ruefully.

"When you give a party," Lavela went on, "every voice seems to rise in a crescendo!"

Her eyes were twinkling as she spoke and the Duke thought it made her look very pretty.

"Now you are definitely frightening me!" he objected. "I had no idea I was the chief topic of conversation!"

167

"But of course you are!" Lavela said. "Actually there is very little else to talk about except when a fox carries off a prize hen, or an otter is sighted in the river!"

"You paint a sad picture," the Duke laughed. "So I suppose I must not complain if my Theatre gives everyone a new topic."

"Which it certainly will!" Lavela said. "And of course, Your Grace, I am very .. very honoured to be .. allowed to .. sing in .. it."

She thought as she spoke that it was something she should have said before.

She glanced at her father as if she expected him to reprove her for having been so remiss.

"I can only say that I am delighted you have promised to play the part I wish you to do," the Duke assured her.

"I feel we should leave now, Your Grace," the Vicar said. "We have imposed for long enough on your time. If you will tell Lavela when you want her again, we will go home."

"As I am alone," the Duke said, "I would like you to have luncheon with me, and afterwards Vicar, I know my Curator will be delighted to show you round the house while I can run through with your daughter what she has to sing."

As he spoke he thought he would certainly enlarge Lavela's part.

Her voice was exceptional.

She must sing a solo either at the beginning of the Play or else at the end.

It was just an idea.

He wondered whether he was making her too important in a Show for which he had intended to engage a professional performer.

"If you are quite certain we are not imposing on Your Grace," the Vicar was saying, "Lavela and I will find that you suggest most enjoyable."

After luncheon the Vicar went off with the Curator to explore the house.

The Duke took Lavela into the Drawing-Room.

He had always thought himself that it was a very attractive room.

He knew by the way Lavela's eyes lit up and the way she gazed around her that to her it was a revelation.

The Duke was used to people who came to Moor Park for the first time being overwhelmed.

First by the sheer size of it, then by the way it was furnished and the treasures it contained.

It was, he thought, only his very sophisticated friends who took it all for granted.

The ladies were more concerned with the gowns their rivals were wearing.

The men were only interested in his horses.

When the Duke showed Lavela his priceless collection of snuff-boxes she looked at them in silence.

Then she said in a low voice as if speaking to herself:

"This is just like being in Aladdin's cave!"

Because she was so young and ingenuous the Duke exerted himself to show her several other rooms on the way to the Music Room.

He liked the way she admired everything without being over-effusive or gushing.

There was a light in her eyes that was more expressive than words.

When they reached the Music Room she said:

"Thank you . . thank you so very much for being so kind. Your house is exactly as I pictured it. I have often driven up the drive just to look at its beautiful façade and the statues on the roof."

It made the Duke think that it was many years since he had gone up onto the roof to look at the statues.

Because he had taken them for granted he had almost forgotten who they represented.

"Until Christmas," he said, "You will not only look at the house from the outside, but come in, and I am sure you will find a lot of things that will interest you."

"So many that I only wish Christmas was further away!" Lavela laughed.

"As it is quite near," the Duke answered, "you will have to work very hard, because I want my first production to be outstanding."

"I will try . . I will really try to be . . good," Lavela promised.

"I am sure you will be," the Duke smiled.

He sat down at the piano and taking off her bonnet as if without it she felt more free Lavela picked up the music.

She sang it through once.

"Please let us do it again," she pleaded.

The Duke was accompanying her softly on the piano when the door was suddenly flung open and Fiona walked in.

The Duke stopped playing.

Fiona was looking even more spectacular than usual.

The gown she wore under a long fur cape was of emerald green which was one of her favourite colours.

There were ostrich feathers to match in her hat, and emeralds glittered in her ears.

She walked across the room to where the piano stood on a low platform.

As the Duke rose slowly to his feet she said:

"Sheldon! How could you leave London without telling me? I could not believe that you had gone home – alone!"

There was a pause before the last word and she looked at Lavela enquiringly.

"I sent you a note informing you that I had many things to see to here," the Duke answered coldly, "and wished for the moment to be alone!"

"Alone!" Fiona exclaimed. "I have never heard of such nonsense! And, darling, you must be aware that I have been counting the days, the hours, the minutes until your return!"

"I shall soon be returning to London," the Duke said. "So your journey here was quite unnecessary."

Before Fiona could reply he went on:

"Let me introduce you to Miss Lavela Ashley, who has a delightful soprano voice and will take part in the Play I have written for the opening of my Theatre, Miss Ashley – Lady Faversham!"

Lavela held out her hand, but Fiona did not move.

She only regarded her with an expression which the Duke was well aware was both contemptuous and disagreeable.

"Why have I never met you before?" Fiona enquired.

"Because I have never been here until today," Lavela replied.

"That is true," the Duke said. "In fact, I discovered Miss Ashley only yesterday, and her father, who is the Vicar of Little Bedlington, is at the moment on a tour of the house."

He thought as he spoke that Fiona relaxed.

He was well aware of what she was thinking.

He would have been quite ready for her to go on doing so if he had not wished to protect Lavela.

He was certain the angel-like girl from the Vicarage had never in her life met anyone like Fiona.

It was obvious from the way she was looking at the older

woman that she was surprised, if nothing else, by her appearance.

"Of course, dearest, I could not bear to think of you being here and lonely with no one intelligent to talk to," Fiona said to the Duke in a very different tone of voice. "So I collected just a few friends and we came down as quickly as we could."

"Who is with you?" the Duke asked in an uncompromising voice.

"As I had so little time, I just invited Isobel Henley since her husband is away and Joscelyn, who is very anxious to see you, accompanied us."

"Joscelyn!"

The Duke with difficulty, prevented his voice from ringing out angrily.

The last person he wanted here at this moment was his Cousin.

Then he remembered that Joscelyn might have insisted on coming anyway.

His interest in seeing him had nothing to do with Fiona.

At the same time, he could feel his anger rising.

Then he told himself he would have to tread very carefully.

In the past there would have been nothing unusual and in fact it was expected, in Fiona being with him at Moor Park.

As she had no idea that he had discovered about her, she had considered it almost her duty to follow him.

To see that everything ran smoothly and he was not lonely.

It suddenly struck him that it would be horrifying for anyone so young and unspoilt as Lavela to discover his association with Fiona.

With a note of authority in his voice he said:

"Order tea for you and your guests in the Blue Room. Miss Ashley and I will join you when we have finished rehearsing."

He spoke so positively that Fiona was wise enough not to argue.

"Of course, Sheldon dear," she replied. "I will do whatever you want. But you have not yet said how pleased you are to see me."

She spoke in her usual flirtatious manner, looking at him with a seductive expression in her eyes.

"It is certainly a surprise," the Duke replied abruptly.

He turned away as he spoke and sat down again at the piano.

Fiona hesitated.

Then as there was nothing else she could do but leave, she swept from the room, shutting the door noisily behind her.

The Duke did not speak.

He merely started to play one of his own compositions which had given him more pleasure than anything else he had ever done.

As he played the music seemed to sweep away his anger.

For a moment he forgot the three people who had come uninvited to his house and was conscious only of Lavela.

He felt her move a little nearer so that she could watch his fingers.

Then as he brought his composition to an end she was completely silent.

He appreciated her silence.

He knew it meant far more than the gushing but superficial praise he would have received from Fiona.

Then Lavela said:

"That was lovely . . absolutely lovely! I am sure you composed it yourself."

"How do you know that?" the Duke asked.

"Because I knew what you were feeling while you played, and the music was . . a part of you."

He was astonished that she should be so perceptive.

After a moment he said:

"I think you understand perhaps better than most people that when there is a melody in your mind, it does not come entirely from the brain."

"No, of course it does not," Lavela agreed. "It comes from one's heart and one's soul. That is what I feel when I am singing."

"I think," the Duke said as if he had just discovered it for himself, "that is what music is all about!"

Chapter Four

As the Duke finished speaking, the door opened and the Vicar came in.

"I have seen a great deal of the house, Your Grace," he said, "and I hear your guests have arrived. I think therefore Lavela and I should now return home."

"There is no hurry," the Duke said quickly. "In fact, I wanted to ask you, now I realise how interested you are in music, if you know anybody who would take the part in my play of an elderly woman?"

He did not wait for the Vicar to reply, but went on:

"Your daughter will be the angel who comes to tell her that, however old she may be, she is still needed, and when finally she dies she will still go on helping those she loves from Heaven."

The Duke became aware that the Vicar was staring at him in astonishment.

Then as if he felt he was being rude he said quickly:

"That sounds exactly what is needed as a Christmas message, Your Grace!"

"Do you think, Papa," Lavela interposed, "that *Madame* would play the part of the old lady?"

The Vicar hesitated and the Duke looking from one to the other asked:

"Are you telling me there is another genius in Little Bedlington?"

"There is, Your Grace, and it would not be hard, if you approached her personally, to persuade Mrs. Grantham to take the part."

"You mean she has a good voice?" the Duke asked.

"She was, before she married an Englishman, Maria Colzaio."

The Duke was still.

"But – do you mean – you cannot mean –!"

"Yes, the famous Maria Colzaio!"

"And she lives in Little Bedlington? I do not believe it! Why was I not told?"

The Vicar smiled.

"Maria Calzaio, who was, as you know, one of the most famous Italian Opera singers in Europe, retired when she was sixty and married James Grantham, an Englishman."

He paused a moment before he went on:

"They were very happy and she was content to know nobody and forget that she had ever been a *Prima Donna*. Then he died."

"When was that?" the Duke enquired.

"Nearly two years ago," the Vicar replied, "and now we have just been able to coax *Madame* into coming to see us occasionally. Six months ago she started to teach Lavela to sing."

"So that accounts for her having such superb intonation," the Duke said, "apart from the fact that her voice is unique."

"That is what I thought myself," the Vicar said simply, "and I am sure, now that *Madame* is interested in life again, that if Your Grace asked her to perform with Lavela she would do so."

"I will come to see her tomorrow," the Duke said. "And as I also want to talk over what Lavela has to do, may I come to you tomorrow morning?"

He thought as he spoke that for him to go to the Vicarage would be far better than for Lavela to come again to Moor Park.

If she did Fiona might try to make trouble.

"We shall be delighted to see you!" the Vicar answered. "And of course we hope Your Grace will stay to luncheon."

"Thank you very much," the Duke said, "that is just what I would like to do."

He picked up his music score. Then he said:

"I suppose you have no more talent in Little Bedlington with which to astound me?"

Lavela looked at her father.

"Papa has taught eight men in the Parish to be Bell-Ringers and I promise you, they are very, very good!"

The Duke knew that bell-ringing went back into Mediaeval times.

Then bells, held by the ringers one in each hand, were tuned to the Tonic Sol-Fa.

When they rang them rhythmically they could produce music as well as a piano could.

"Then that completes my programme for the evening!" he said with satisfaction. "It will be unique in that there will be no professionals! An evening when I introduce Little Bedlington to the Social World."

The Vicar laughed.

"I hope we shall not fail you," Lavela said. "You must remember that no one outside the village knows anything about us, except of course 'Madame', as we always call her."

"I doubt if she will want anybody in the audience to know who she is," the Vicar said, "but of course we must leave that to His Grace."

"And you will arrange for me to see her tomorrow?" the Duke asked.

"Of course," the Vicar said, "and we shall be awaiting with pleasure your arrival at eleven o'clock."

The Duke saw them to the door.

As the Vicar drove away in the old-fashioned gig which had a hood over the two front seats he thought he must be dreaming.

How was it possible for all this musical talent to dwell on his Estate and he had never had the slightest idea of it?

The truth was he knew, that he had always been very reticent about how musical he was.

While in London he attended Concerts and Operas when they were performed by well-known artistes, but he usually went alone.

He was now extremely excited that the opening of his Theatre would take exactly the form he wanted.

He would not need professionals who would want to sing what they considered their best pieces and give a performance which might not please his special audience.

He knew that his relations, if nobody else, would be touched by the idea of the village children singing to them.

He knew too that they would be thrilled to learn that Maria Colzaio was there in person.

Then as he turned from the front door to go back into the hall he remembered something he had been able to forget for the moment.

It was that Fiona had to be coped with and also his Cousin Joscelyn.

"Lady Faversham and the Countess of Henley, Your Grace, are in the Blue Drawing-Room," Norton the Butler told him.

As he spoke the Duke knew exactly what he must do.

He walked quickly in the opposite direction down a passage which led him to the Estate Office.

It also provided a Secretary's Room and he was sure he would find Mr. Watson there.

He was not mistaken.

Mr. Watson was sitting at one desk and his assistant was at another.

As the Duke entered they both stood up.

"I wish to speak to you alone, Watson," the Duke said.

The assistant immediately left the room.

The Duke sat down at the desk he had vacated and started to write a note on a piece of his crested writing-paper.

"Now listen, Watson," he said as he did so, "I want you to send this immediately to Colonel and Mrs. Robertson. It tells them I have arrived unexpectedly with a party from London, and should be delighted if they would dine with me this evening and stay for the next two nights."

He paused before he added:

"I have suggested it might be dangerous with such a heavy frost for them to drive home late."

Mr. Watson took the note after the Duke had put it into an envelope.

As he did so he asked:

"Who is at the Dower House?"

"You remember, Your Grace, you loaned it to Lord and Lady Bredon while they are having their own house repaired after it was damaged by fire."

"Yes, of course!" the Duke exclaimed.

He started to write another note and Mr. Watson waited.

"I have asked Lady Bredon, who is of course my Cousin, if they will come here for the weekend," the Duke said, "and if she would act as hostess to my party."

He thought as he spoke that Mr. Watson looked surprised, though he made no comment.

Enid Bredon was a rather bossy, overwhelming woman of fifty whom the Duke usually avoided whenever possible.

He had found it difficult to refuse what was almost a demand on her part to be allowed to use the Dower House.

He had however, made no effort until now to include her in any of his house-parties.

He thought now with a slight twist of his lips that if anyone could prevent Fiona from playing hostess it would be Enid Bredon.

He put the note he had finished into Mr. Watson's hands, then said:

"I want a large luncheon-party tomorrow, an even larger dinner-party, and the same applies every day until my present guests leave."

His voice was sharp, but Mr. Watson, with his usual tact, only said quietly:

"I suppose, Your Grace, you wish me to ask all the nearest neighbours?"

"Invite those who live further away, and ask them to stay," the Duke replied. "There is plenty of room in the house, and I am sure you can always get extra help from the village."

"Yes, of course, Your Grace."

Mr. Watson hesitated, then asked somewhat tentatively:

"Are you leaving the choice of Your Grace's guests to me?"

"You know better than I do, Watson, who is available, and I want the house full – do you understand? Until, as I say, Lady Faversham and Mr. Joscelyn leave."

Mr. Watson was well aware there was a reason for this very unusual request.

As the Duke left the office he rang for his assistant and started to put the wheels in motion which nobody could do more efficiently than he could.

There was a cynical smile on the Duke's lips as he walked towards the Blue Room.

He was determined to make things as difficult as possible for Joscelyn to approach him.

He knew he was determined to do so and to plead for money with which to pay his debts.

The Duke also wanted, in what he thought was a very subtle manner, to show Fiona that her reign had ended.

As he entered the Blue Drawing-Room she gave a little cry of delight and ran towards him eagerly.

"Oh, here you are at last, dearest Sheldon!" she exclaimed. "We wondered how you could have immersed yourself so quickly in Parochial matters!"

What she said told the Duke that she had made enquiries as to who Lavela was.

She would have been informed by the servants that the Vicar was also in the house.

The Duke did not answer Fiona, but walked towards the Countess of Henley and kissed her on the cheek.

"I am surprised to see you here, Isobel," he said. "I always believed you hated the country at this time of the year!"

"Moor Park is not the country!" Isobel Henley replied. "It is a Palace of luxury, and that is different!"

It was the sort of remark that always made people laugh and Joscelyn obliged.

"How are you, Sheldon?" he asked the Duke. "You will understand that as these two lovely ladies wished to follow you, I could only oblige by being their escort."

"Of course!" the Duke replied. "And I hope you will not find your visit too boring."

He then sat down beside Lady Henley and started to talk to her about their mutual friends in London.

She was an acknowledged Beauty.

At the same time she had a sharp tongue which could at times, be venomous.

She was more or less separated from her husband.

He preferred being on his Estate in the North of England, while she enjoyed the endless round of social events in Mayfair.

To the Duke's knowledge she had taken lover after lover.

He knew now as he flirted with her she was considering whether it would be possible to wean him away from Fiona.

He was aware that both Fiona and Joscelyn were watching him.

It was with a sense of relief that as they finished tea the Butler came to his side to say:

"Mr. Watson would like a word with you, Your Grace!"

"Forgive me," the Duke said.

He rose to his feet. Then looking down at Isobel he remarked:

"You are more amusing than ever, Isobel, and I am looking forward to dinner tonight!"

The Countess gave him a provocative glance.

He was aware as he walked across the room that Fiona was looking after him angrily.

In the hall Mr. Watson was waiting for him.

"I have a reply from Colonel and Mrs. Robertson, Your Grace, who will be arriving in time for dinner. And Lord and Lady Bredon have asked for a carriage to be sent for them immediately!"

"Thank you, Watson!" the Duke said, "and I want the Countess of Henley on my right at dinner and Mrs. Robertson on my left."

Mr. Watson made a note on the pad he was carrying.

"Lady Bredon will sit at the other end of the table tonight and for the rest of her visit," the Duke ordered.

He then walked quickly in the direction of his Study.

When he got there he locked himself in and started to work on the Programme for his Opening Night.

It was incredible to think that he had Maria Colzaio living on his doorstep.

As he thought of it, he realised that Little Bedlington was actually by road nearly six miles from Moor Park.

It would be dangerous for the Robertsons to drive home at night when they lived on the other side of the Park.

It would certainly be very dangerous for the children to return to the village on Saturday after the performance.

"They too must stay the night," he decided.

He thought it would be amusing and would certainly give everybody something to talk about.

He imagined that many of the children were quite small.

This would mean he would have to accommodate at least some of their mothers to look after them.

He made notes of everything he decided upon.

He would give them to Mr. Watson after he had finished arranging the house-party.

The Duke felt he was almost like a General, working out a campaign against the enemy which, in this case, consisted of just two people.

However, both in their own way were extremely formidable.

Fiona and Joscelyn joined the Duke in the Drawing-Room where they assembled before dinner.

It was obvious that they were astounded to find Lord and Lady Bredon there.

Colonel and Mrs. Robertson were announced a few minutes later.

The newcomers were obviously delighted to have been invited, even at such short notice.

"Surely you have come home very unexpectedly?" Lady Bredon said questioningly.

"When I came back from Holland," the Duke replied, "I was so tired of pompous speeches and long-winded Statesmen that I ran away!"

Everybody laughed at this, and Lord Bredon said:

"I know exactly what you mean, Sheldon, and if the frost ceases you will be much happier hunting."

"It is such a pity you were not here last week," Mrs. Robertson said as they sat down to dinner.

She was delighted to find herself on the Duke's left.

She went into a long and graphic description of last week's runs and a fox they lost.

She added a few criticisms of the huntsmen which the Duke expected.

He usually found her rather a bore.

But tonight he was determined to make a fuss of everyone with the exception of Fiona.

The Countess certainly made the most of her opportunity of sitting on the Duke's right.

She flirted with him and made him laugh.

She managed at the same time to hold Lord Bredon who was on her right, spellbound.

The dinner was excellent.

The Duke thought that with the exception of Fiona, who was looking sulky, everybody enjoyed themselves. When they moved into the Drawing-Room there were two card-tables set out for Whist.

As they were exactly the right number the Duke seated everyone, making sure that his table included neither Fiona nor Joscelyn.

Fiona made every possible attempt to get close to him.

Somehow he managed to be so evasive that she failed.

Finally, while the rest of the party were saying goodnight, she went upstairs to bed.

She gave a lingering look in the Duke's direction which told him exactly what she expected.

The rest of the party stayed talking until Mrs. Robertson said:

"I feel we are being selfish, for I am sure dear Duke, that having come all that way from Holland, you are very tired."

"I am rather," the Duke admitted.

His eyes focused on Joscelyn who was moving towards the door.

Rather reluctantly the Countess was following.

Mrs. Robertson finished the lemonade that remained in her glass.

As she did so she said to the Duke:

"What a lovely party! It was so kind of you to have us."

"I was delighted to have you," the Duke replied.

"I have always admired Lady Faversham," Mrs. Robertson went on, "and she is more beautiful than ever."

"I agree with you!" the Duke murmured.

"It is, of course, very sad that she is unable to have a child."

The Duke was still.

"Why do you say that?" he enquired.

"I thought you knew!" Mrs. Robertson said. "My family were near neighbours to the Duke of Cumbria's Estate and I remember Fiona as a child."

"I had no idea of that," the Duke remarked.

"She was fifteen," Mrs. Robertson continued, "when she had an accident out hunting, and it was a very bad one!"

The Duke was listening intently as Mrs. Robertson went on:

"She eventually recovered, but the doctors said she could never have a child, and I have often thought that was why her marriage to Eric Faversham broke up."

She gave a short laugh.

"I know of course that he was a 'naughty boy' in many ways, but I feel if there had been a son it might have made all the difference to their marriage."

She finished speaking and started to walk towards the door.

The Duke followed her, feeling as if he had been shocked into silence.

It had never struck him for one moment when he had considered marrying Fiona that she might be unable to provide him with an heir.

He knew now it would have been disastrous if he had asked her to marry him, and found this out later.

He thought he must have been very stupid.

Why had he not asked why during the years she was married to Eric Faversham, who was, if nothing else, an ardent lover, they had never had any children.

He said goodnight to Mrs. Robertson at the door of her bedroom and moved on to his own.

It was at the far end of the corridor.

As he did so he thought that by the grace of God he had been saved.

It was from something so disastrous that it did not bear thinking about.

Of course Fiona in her desire to be the Duchess of Moorminster would not have told him.

He had a suspicion however, that Joscelyn knew the truth.

It would certainly be greatly to his advantage in his desire to be the next Duke if the Duchess was unable to produce an heir.

As the Duke went to his room he felt as if Lavela was telling him that he must say a prayer of gratitude.

He had been saved from asking Fiona to be his wife as he had seriously considered doing when he came back from Holland.

His Valet was waiting for him, and when the man left him he knew he had another problem in front of him.

One which he had little time to solve.

Fiona would be waiting for him.

She would find it very strange and would undoubtedly be suspicious if he did not join her.

He had no intention of doing this.

At the same time, he knew she would not hesitate to come to his room when she realised he was not coming to hers.

The obvious answer was to lock his door.

But it struck him that she might knock on it, and there was always the chance that she might be heard doing so.

It was certainly something the Robertsons would talk about, and so would the Bredons.

With a swiftness of thought which had got him out of many political difficulties, the Duke made up his mind.

He disliked his house to be cold.

He had therefore given orders that in the Winter a fire was to be lit in every room, whether they were in use or not.

There were two men whose duty it was to go round the great house making up the fires.

This occupied them from first thing in the morning until last thing at night.

The Duke therefore merely moved a little further down the corridor to a room that was not occupied.

The fire there was nevertheless burning brightly.

Once inside he locked the door and got into the bed.

In the morning he would tell his Valet that the fire in his room was smoking, and he had therefore moved into another room.

Before he fell asleep he had forgotten about Fiona.

He was once again thinking of his theatre and Lavela's voice.

He also had another idea about how the whole Programme should start which he wanted to discuss with the Vicar.

As he fell asleep another tune came to his mind.

This time for the Overture which would be played as soon as the audience was seated.

The following morning the Duke had left the house before Fiona and Isobel Henley came downstairs.

The Robertsons and the Bredons had breakfast at nine o'clock.

Mr. Watson in the Duke's absence asked them what they wished to do.

They replied they would like to go riding.

Only Lady Bredon said she had some letters to write.

Later, perhaps this afternoon, she added, she would like a carriage in which she could call on some of her friends.

When the rest of the party had set out on their ride, Mr. Watson on the Duke's orders showed her his list.

It contained the names of those who were arriving for luncheon and also for dinner.

Most of them had accepted the Duke's invitation to stay in the house.

"Whatever made the Duke suddenly decide to entertain in this wholesale fashion?" Lady Bredon asked with her usual blunt frankness.

"I gather His Grace was very bored while he was in Holland, My Lady," Watson replied, "and a number of these guests have in fact, not been invited to Moor Park for a long time."

"If I have told Sheldon once, I have told him a thousand times," Lady Bredon said, "that he should give a Garden Party in the Summer as his father did, and get all the bores off at the same time!"

"I am sure that is a good idea, My Lady," Mr. Watson agreed.

"What is more," Lady Bredon went on, "he should have a series of evening parties such as we will have tonight."

She paused a moment to smile as she said;

"I know the 'Locals' will greatly enjoy mixing with my Cousin's smart London friends."

Mr. Watson declined tactfully to say the obvious.

Which was that the Duke's London friends would not much care for the "Locals".

Instead he informed Lady Bredon that he would bring her all the other acceptances as they arrived.

He also gave her the task of placing the guests at meals.

It was the Duke of course who had told him exactly what to do.

He had then ridden away towards Little Bedlington, like a boy playing truant from School.

He actually arrived at the Vicarage before eleven o'clock, but Lavela was there ready to greet him.

"You have really come!" she said. "When I told Mama what you were planning, she thought we were joking."

"I must assure your mother that I am very serious," the Duke replied, as he walked into the Vicarage.

He was surprised, although of course he did not say so, at how well-furnished it was.

It was obvious that the Vicar had extremely good taste.

The curtains and carpets were attractive and there were some pictures which the Duke would have liked to own himself.

He knew who was responsible however.

After he had worked with the Vicar and Lavela on the Programme he met Mrs. Ashley.

First, however, they had to concentrate on his determination to produce the whole Programme entirely from Little Bedlington.

Of course a great deal depended on whether Maria Colzaio would consent to perform.

The Vicar was optimistic, and he had arranged to take the Duke to meet her after luncheon.

The Duke sat down at the very good grand-piano which stood in the Drawing-Room of the Vicarage and started to play.

"What is that?" the Vicar asked.

"It is the Overture," he explained. "I intend it shall be played on two pianos – one played by Lavela and one by myself."

"That is wonderful!" Lavela exclaimed. "But . . supposing I am not . . good enough?"

"That is a question I should be asking of myself!" the Duke replied.

She laughed.

"Now I think you are being modest! You play exceptionally well, while I am only a beginner!"

"I am not listening to that nonsense!" the Duke asserted. "You will play with me, and I already have an idea for a new composition which will delight everybody!"

"I must have time to practise it," Lavela said breathlessly.

"I promise I will finish it tonight," the Duke answered.

"Then what happens?" the Vicar enquired.

"You appear before the curtains," the Duke explained, "to wish the audience a happy evening and tell them in verse what they are going to see."

He smiled before he added;

"I imagine, after what you have told me of your performances in the past, you have a Fancy-Dress somewhere which might be appropriate."

"I can either be a Harlequin or a Courtier at the time of Charles II," the Vicar replied, "complete with wig and moustache!"

The Duke laughed.

"I leave the choice to you!"

"What happens then?" Lavela asked excitedly.

"The curtain will go up," the Duke answered, "and your choir will sing exactly as I heard them in the Church."

"Just the choir?"

"You will conduct them from the pit so that no one sees you clearly. On the stage it will just be the children."

Lavela nodded and the Duke went on;

"I think you will have to include some of my nephews and nieces who will be with me at Christmas. They will be disappointed if they are not allowed to play some small part in the performance."

"Of course," Lavela agreed, "and if I can, I would like to have at least one rehearsal with them."

"I may send them here to you," the Duke said, "but I have a new plan for the actual night of the performance."

He then explained how he thought it would be a good idea for the children and their mothers to stay the night at Moor Park.

Lavela clapped her hands together.

"It is the most wonderful idea I have ever heard!" she said. "They will be so thrilled, so excited! But are you sure there will be enough room for them?"

The Duke laughed.

"They will have the whole of the East Wing, which has over twenty bedrooms in it!"

"I apologise," Lavela said. "I had forgotten how enormous your house is!"

"I can imagine nothing that would please the Parish more," the Vicar said, "and it is very generous of you, Your Grace!"

"I am being entirely selfish," the Duke replied. "You know as well as I do that it is Lavela and Maria Colzaio, if she accepts, who will make it the most sensational evening that has ever been known in my house!"

"I shall feel .. terrible if .. you are .. disappointed," Lavela answered.

She looked so worried as she spoke that the Duke said quickly;

"I have a feeling none of us will be disappointed, and we will enjoy the evening as much as the children will."

"I hope you are .. right," Lavela said in a low voice.

"After that," the Duke went on, "there will be the Bell-Ringers. I only ask you, Vicar, to make quite certain that they play happy, really 'Christmassy' tunes that even the most tone-deaf member of the audience can recognise."

The Vicar laughed.

"What you are saying, Your Grace, is that they are not to be too 'high-brow'."

"Exactly!"

"They will certainly do their best," the Vicar smiled. "And I need not tell you how thrilled the performers will be!"

"What comes after that?" Lavela asked as if she could not prevent herself from hurrying on to her entrance.

"Then it is your time," he answered, "and I just need two girls, one to give the flowers to Maria Colzaio, the other to beg from her advice regarding her love-affair."

"I think I have the right one for that," Lavela said. "The Doctor's daughter is seventeen and a very intelligent girl. Papa and I both think she will play the part to perfection."

"I am sure she will," the Vicar said. "She has already been a 'shining light' in our Nativity Play that takes place every Christmas, and was a very successful Juliet when our School put on *Romeo and Juliet* a few months ago."

The Duke did not say anything.

He could think of no other village on his Estate which would have its children performing Shakespeare.

"What happens after that?" the Vicar enquired.

"I was going to ask Lavela if the children knew any other Carols which they can sing as well as they sing *It Came Upon the Midnight Clear*."

"Yes of course they know several," Lavela replied. "But I think the best is *O Little Town of Bethlehem*."

"Splendid!" the Duke exclaimed. "They can sing that and again you can conduct them from the Pit. Then 'Father Christmas' which is me, will arrive on a sleigh which will be pulled into place by four of my footmen."

He paused before he went on;

"The sleigh will be loaded with presents for everybody in the audience. I will hand the presents to the children who will run down from the stage and present them to everybody in the Stalls."

He looked at the Vicar as he went on;

"While they are doing that, I want a Male Voice Choir, which I have a feeling you have somewhere in Little Bedlington, to sing the Carols which everybody knows."

Lavela laughed.

"How did you know Papa had a Male Voice Choir?" she asked.

"You told me your father had a good voice," the Duke answered, "and I could not believe that he would be the only man singing in his Church."

The Vicar laughed.

"Your Grace's quite right! We have six men who really sing extremely well. We entertain not only those who come to Church, but also go to the local Inn to herald in the New Year."

The Duke threw up his hands.

"I only find it extraordinary that you have 'hidden your light under a bushel' for so long! But now the whole Estate will be aware that Little Bedlington is an example to every other village."

"I shall be very unpopular," the Vicar said ruefully.

"Does it matter?" the Duke asked. "And perhaps I will set an example and a challenge to other Landlords to encourage musical talent on their estates."

"That is certainly a very good idea," the Vicar answered, "and it may result in more people going to Church."

The Duke had no wish to discuss this.

His Church was just inside the Park.

Yet when he had a sophisticated week-end house-party he often missed attending Matins on Sunday.

"One thing is quite certain," Lavela said. "We must start work at once and I will tell the children when they come to Church after School this afternoon that they are going to perform at Moor Park and stay the night there."

"I do not think you will have any absentees after that!" the Vicar smiled.

The Duke then sat down at the piano to play to Lavela his Overture.

When he had done so she took his seat at the piano and played it with just one hesitation, brilliantly.

"We shall have to practise this with two pianos," the Duke said. "I do not suppose you have another one here?"

"I am afraid not," Lavela replied.

The Vicar had left the room.

The Duke knew that she hoped he would ask her to Moor Park, so that she could play there in his beautiful Music Room.

He was, however, still uncertain, as to how much trouble Fiona might make and was determined to be out of the house as much as possible.

"I will send a piano over tomorrow," he said, "which will be an upright one. I will have to arrange for the two Grand Pianos we shall require for our duet to be fitted somehow on the stage."

"There is not room for them in the Pit?" Lavela asked.

He shook his head.

"No, we have an upright one there."

"I understand," Lavela said.

"I would like to come here while we are rehearsing," the Duke went on, "for the simple reason that my house is now full of guests. I do not want them to hear any of the music until the Opening Night of the Theatre."

"No, of course not," Lavela agreed, "and I know Mama and Papa will be delighted for you to come here whenever you wish."

Both the Vicar and his wife echoed this.

Mrs. Ashley had appeared just before luncheon and it was no surprise to the Duke to find that she was very beautiful.

But, he thought, she was not English.

She spoke perfect English, but there was just something about her which made him sure she had some other nationality.

However, he realised that, if she was not shy, she was very retiring.

While she was extremely pleasant and hospitable during luncheon she disappeared immediately afterwards.

Because she was so beautiful and the Vicar was so handsome, it was not surprising that their only child was lovely.

But it did not account for Lavela's angelic looks.

Except, the Duke thought, that the Vicar and his wife were very much in love with each other.

He was too experienced not to be aware of the softness in their voices when they spoke to each other and the expression in their eyes.

It seemed to him almost extraordinary after they had been married for so many years.

But he knew it was very much the same as the love that had existed between his father and mother.

Unless they were together they had always appeared unhappy and restless.

When they were together the way they looked at each other and the way they spoke made it clear to the most obtuse outsider that they were still in love.

"That is what I want too," the Duke thought.

He knew however, that because he was a Duke he was very unlikely to be married for himself alone.

He would be deceived, as he had been by Fiona, over and over again.

It was a depressing thought.

He pushed it aside, concentrating instead on the surprisingly intelligent conversation.

The food was delicious.

He found he was eating dishes that were so imaginative that they might have been provided by his very expensive Chef.

When luncheon was over he said to Mrs. Ashley;

"I hope you will not think me impertinent when I say how very much I have enjoyed your delicious and unusual meal!"

He smiled beguilingly as he said;

"As a traveller, I have always known that the French have the best *cuisine* in the world, and the English are perfectly content with what is simple and obvious."

The Vicar laughed.

"That is certainly true, Your Grace, but I should explain that I have travelled a great deal abroad and have become a *gourmet*. I believe that my wife could, if she wished, open a Restaurant and make an outstanding success of it!"

The Duke raised his eye-brows.

"Is your husband telling me that you cooked this meal?" he asked Mrs. Ashley.

"Some of it," Mrs. Ashley replied. "But I have also taught two women from the village who look after us extremely well how to produce the dishes which are my husband's favourites, and to be prepared to try those I appreciate."

"I really cannot bear it!" the Duke exclaimed. "If you astound me with any more of your brilliant talents in Little Bedlington I shall leave Moor Park and come to live here amongst you!"

"You are very welcome to do so," the Vicar replied, "although I think you would find it rather cramped!"

"But how romantic it would be," Lavela exclaimed, "to have a Duke living in one of our cottages!"

"I am afraid what would happen then is that hundreds of people would follow me, and it would change from being a charming village into an ugly Town," the Duke replied.

They were all thinking this was an amusing idea and laughing about it when Mrs. Ashley disappeared.

It was then the Vicar said it was time to go and visit Maria Colzaio.

As they drove away in the Duke's carriage he was thinking he had never enjoyed a meal more.

He felt certain his collection of guests at Moor Park would not have found their luncheon so stimulating and entertaining.

As the horses increased their pace the Duke sitting beside the Vicar said;

"You must be aware, Vicar, that I am extremely curious as to why, seeing how beautiful your wife and daughter are, you bury yourselves in the country!"

There was a perceptible pause.

The Duke realised he had intruded on something intimate.

After what seemed a long silence the Vicar replied;

"There are reasons why we should do so, Your Grace, and I am sure you will understand that they are very personal ones. We are extremely happy just as we are, and it is something I do not wish to discuss."

"Of course, and I apologise if I have intruded," the Duke said quickly.

"There is no need," the Vicar said, "and I am in fact delighted that Lavela has found something as exciting as your Theatre to occupy her and where her voice will be heard by discriminating people."

He paused before he went on;

"What is perfect for my wife and myself might become in time frustrating for a young girl."

"I understand," the Duke said, "and I promise you, Vicar, I will make sure that Lavela enjoys herself; at any rate this Christmas."

"Thank you," the Vicar said.

They drove on.

The Duke was aware there was nothing more he could say.

He was however, no less intensely curious.

He was determined to try somehow to discover, without causing any embarrassment, the truth.

Chapter Five

In the next few days the Duke thought he had been very clever.

He left the house early each morning to go riding.

Then he either rode to Little Bedlington or else drove there in his Chaise.

He had of course persuaded Maria Colzaio to sing for him.

She had offered him her Drawing-Room in which to rehearse with her and Lavela undisturbed and in comfort.

It was a beautiful room containing a magnificent grand-piano which the Duke enjoyed playing.

As the Vicar had said, Maria Colzaio's voice was not as high as it had been.

But it still had the beautiful warm quality that had made her so famous.

After the first day when she was obviously a little nervous, she said to the Duke;

"I am really enjoying myself, and may I say, Your Grace, it is wonderful to have an accompanist who plays as well as you."

"I think this is one of the most exciting things I have ever done," the Duke replied, "and to hear you sing one of my own compositions is beyond my wildest dreams!"

In contrast, Lavela's young, clear voice, was, he thought, very moving.

He knew that when she performed before the audience including the Prince and Princess of Wales, they would be astonished.

He had deliberately not told the Ashleys, nor Maria Colzaio who his principal guests would be.

He thought it would make Lavela nervous.

He was afraid too it might upset Maria Colzaio who still wished to be incognito.

He therefore merely told her they were performing for his Christmas Party guests.

Also for the mothers of the children who were perform ing who could be squeezed into the back of the Stalls.

There were in fact only five who were going to stay the night at Moor Park.

The rest could not leave their other children, who were still small.

"You have no idea what excitement you have caused!" Lavela told him. "If you had thrown a bomb into the centre of the village it could not have been more sensational!"

When she was not rehearsing, Lavela was finding the right clothes for the children to wear.

While they sang their Carols they would wear their own best dresses.

But she decided they should wear also a small wreath of mistletoe which they made themselves.

It would be tied at the back of their heads with red ribbons.

They would also hold a little bouquet of mistletoe and holly.

"I wish I had not thought of that," she complained to the Duke. "I have been removing the thorns from the holly and my fingers are very sore!"

"I have always believed that angels fear no pain!" he teased.

"Then I must have come from somewhere very different from Heaven!" Lavela retorted.

They found so many things to laugh about at the rehearsals with Maria Colzaio.

It sent the Duke away so cheerful that he began to forget the difficulties at Moor Park.

The first night he knew from the condition of his bed when he returned to his room that Fiona had waited for him.

After that he locked his door.

He had also moved Fiona and Isobel Henley from the corridor in which his own room was situated.

He told Mr. Watson what he was to do.

When they returned from a drive the second afternoon of their visit, Mr. Watson informed them very apologetically that he had been obliged to change their rooms.

"What do you mean by that?" Fiona asked sharply.

"Two of His Grace's relatives are arriving tomorrow, My Lady," Mr. Watson replied.

"What has that to do with me and *my* room?" Fiona demanded.

"*Your* room, as you call it, My Lady," Mr. Watson replied, "has always been used by His Grace's grand-mother the Dowager Duchess, and Lady Henley's by His Grace's Aunt the Marchioness of Seaford."

There was nothing either of the uninvited visitors could say to this.

Fiona, of course, was furious.

She was already very angry because she had found it impossible ever to speak to the Duke alone.

He had always left the house before she came downstairs in the morning.

To her astonishment, he never returned for luncheon, although a number of other guests had arrived.

Lady Bredon was the hostess, and there was nothing Fiona could do to assert her authority.

When the Duke came down to dinner on his return from Little Bedlington he made certain that the Drawing-Room was half-full before he appeared.

He apologised profusely for being late, explaining that he was working on his plans for Christmas.

He did not wish too many outsiders to be present at the Opening of the Theatre.

He was therefore careful not to mention what was to happen.

"I have to see you alone," Fiona hissed at him, as the gentlemen joined the ladies and the party was bigger than ever.

"Of course!" the Duke agreed pleasantly. "But I cannot think when."

Fiona drew in her breath.

She was just about to give him the obvious answer when the Duke moved away.

He was busy arranging his guests at the card-tables.

The younger members of the party were dancing to an Orchestra in what was known as the "Small Ball-Room".

The Duke watched them swinging round to a spirited Waltz.

He suddenly thought it was something Lavela would have enjoyed.

"I should have invited her," he thought.

He had not done so simply because he did not want to spoil the impact she would make when she appeared as an angel in the Theatre.

Now he thought he had been very selfish.

He remembered he had promised her father that she should be entertained.

On Christmas Day the Duke knew that Lavela would be busy playing the organ in her father's Church.

It was traditional for him to sit in the family pew in his own Church.

He read one of the lessons, and listened to a Sermon from the Vicar who was also his Private Chaplain.

This he had requested to be short and to last no longer than ten minutes.

When the party returned to Moor Park they filled the great table in the centre of the Banqueting Hall.

There were also two smaller tables at which Lady Bredon had placed the younger members of the family.

There was turkey and Christmas pudding which was carried in by the Chef having first had brandy poured over it and lit.

And of course there were crackers and plenty of champagne with which to drink the Duke's health.

He made a short speech, paying a tribute to his grandmother.

He spoke too of some of his older relatives who were delighted by the attention.

Afterwards the gentlemen sat for a long time drinking port or brandy and exchanging jokes.

As was traditional, in the evening the Duke received his tenants and employees in the huge Servants' Hall.

His grandmother received them, and his nieces and nephews handed out Christmas presents to everybody present.

It was a custom that had been started by the Duke's Great-Grandfather and had been a tradition in the family ever since.

Then the local Carol Singers from the village sang in the Servants' Hall.

In the Duke's opinion they did not even begin to sing as well as the children of Little Bedlington.

After that most people were tired.

So there were no further festivities on Christmas night.

He also had had a rehearsal with the Male Choir which had been trained by Mr. Ashley.

They were to be appropriately dressed when they appeared in the *Finale* on Saturday.

A number of costumes had been found in Little Bedlington, but the Duke also scoured his attics.

He went to the house Seamstress with Mr. Watson to see what else was required.

Early on the morning of Boxing Day he arrived at the Vicarage bringing with him his Christmas Presents.

He had chosen a very special one for Lavela.

He was sure it was something she would appreciate.

It was a snuff-box which he had seen in one of the shops in Bond Street.

He wondered at the time to whom he should give it.

Fiona would not appreciate anything that was not jewellery with which to bedeck herself.

The snuff-box was enamelled with a painting in the centre of small cupids holding a wreath of roses.

It was exquisitely done and round the picture were small diamonds interspersed with pearls.

When Lavela opened the Duke's present she stared as if she could not believe what she was seeing.

Then she asked;

"This is . . for . . me?"

"I thought when you admired my collection that you might like to start your own 'Aladdin's Cave," the Duke replied.

For a moment she was silent.

Then she said in a rapt little voice which told him how thrilled she was:

"How can I thank you . . or find the . . words to tell you that this is the most beautiful thing I have ever seen, let alone possessed!"

"I hoped it would please you," the Duke answered, "and it is also to thank you for singing my compositions so beautifully!"

Because he had had so many meals at the Vicarage he had brought the Vicar a pâté made by his own Chef.

There was also a jar of caviar and a case of champagne.

"I have not enjoyed caviar since I was in Russia!" the Vicar exclaimed.

"You have been to Russia?" the Duke asked in surprise.

"I visited it many years ago," the Vicar replied, "and came back via the Scandinavian countries."

As he spoke he exchanged a glance with his wife which the Duke did not miss.

It was, he thought, obviously part of the puzzle he was hoping to solve.

He had not questioned the Vicar since the first time.

Nevertheless he was still intensely curious.

He longed to know why anyone so intelligent and in Mrs. Ashley's case, so beautiful, should bury themselves in Little Bedlington.

There was no doubt they were happy.

In fact, he had never seen two people so happy just to be together.

He was determined to bring Lavela in contact with more exciting society than the villagers and the children she taught to sing.

They had all enthused over their presents.

Mrs. Ashley was delighted with the very elegant sunshade he had given her.

Then the Duke said;

"Now that your main Christmas festivities are over, I would like you all to come to Moor Park this evening and stay until next Sunday."

The Vicar looked at him in surprise and the Duke went on:

"I have many young relatives staying with me whom I would like Lavela to meet. Also I think it important now to rehearse in the Theatre itself. As you know, Vicar, a Drawing-Room however large is not the same as a stage."

"You are quite right," the Vicar agreed, "and I see Your Grace's point. At the same time . . "

"Oh, please, Papa," Lavela broke in, "do let us go! I have been wondering how I could suggest that we should have a rehearsal on the stage before the performance. It would be awful if we made a mess of it on the night."

"That is true," the Vicar agreed.

He looked questioningly at his wife who said:

"Of course it is a good idea, Andrew, and I think you and Lavela should go. But I will stay here and only come to Moor Park on Saturday night."

"Is that what you really want?" the Vicar asked in a low voice.

His wife nodded and he said:

"Very well, I will go with Lavela, but I shall have to return on Friday for my service."

"My horses, Vicar, are at your disposal," the Duke said hastily, "and I will of course, send a carriage for Mrs. Ashley early on Saturday evening."

It was all arranged.

When Maria Colzaio – it was impossible to think of her by any other name – said she would come with Mrs. Ashley, the Duke did not make any objections.

He knew they could rehearse quite well without her.

She undoubtedly would be more at home on the stage than anybody else.

So he hurried back to Moor Park to join the Boxing-Day Shoot which was another long-standing family tradition.

His friends were astonished that he should have missed the first two drives, but he was there now for the third.

After luncheon there were two more drives at which the Duke shot brilliantly.

It annoyed him that he had had to alter the position of the guns.

Joscelyn had made no offer to leave Moor Park and had insisted that he should join the Shoot.

The Duke knew in a way it was his own fault that Joscelyn was still there.

His cousin had tried to get him alone, but he had always managed to avoid him at the last moment.

The Duke had the feeling that Joscelyn and Fiona were plotting something, although he had no idea what it might be.

Without appearing to do so, he had noticed that on several occasions they were whispering together in a conspiratorial manner.

He was quite certain that anything they were saying about him would be derogatory.

At the same time, they were both frantic to succeed in getting him to themselves.

Christmas Day had been difficult when he had been in the house all day.

Now that everybody was thinking about the Shoot, it was easier for him to avoid them.

He had hoped against hope that Fiona would lose her temper and leave before the Prince and Princess of Wales arrived.

But she was made of sterner stuff than to give in so easily.

One moment on Christmas Day had been very revealing.

After luncheon the Duke had joined the ladies in the Drawing-Room for a short time.

He had gone first to his grandmother who was seated by the fireside.

"I hope you are enjoying yourself, Grandmama," he said.

He bent to kiss her.

"It is the best Christmas I have ever known!" the Dowager Duchess replied. "But there is one toast I would have liked to add to those we have just drunk in the Dining-Room."

"What is that?" the Duke answered.

"One to your son and heir, dearest boy," the Duchess replied.

The Duke was wondering what he should answer when he realised that Fiona was standing beside him.

For a moment he met her eyes.

As he did so he suddenly was sure she knew he was aware that she was unable to have a child.

Because they had been so close to each other for so long he knew what she was thinking.

She also could read his thoughts.

For a moment they just stared at each other.

Then the Duke bent and kissed his grandmother's cheek and walked out of the room.

When the day's shooting was over, the Duke was congratulated by everybody taking part.

It had been an excellent day's sport.

After tea most of the party retired to rest before dinner.

The Duke however went to the Music Room with Lavela who had just arrived.

Without her being aware of it he locked the door so that they would not be disturbed.

They went over the alterations he had made to the score while they had been rehearsing with Maria Colzaio.

"It is perfect," Lavela exclaimed when they had finished, "completely perfect! If you do any more it will be like over-painting a picture."

"I suppose like all Composers," the Duke said, "I want to achieve perfection."

"And that is what you have done!" Lavela answered.

"Now we must go to dress for dinner," the Duke said. "We are having a dance tonight as I do not want you to be tired tomorrow before the Christening of my Theatre."

"That is what it is going to be?" Lavela asked. "Have you thought of a special name for it?"

"To name it had not occurred to me until this moment," the Duke said, "but of course we must choose one!"

They walked up the stairs side by side.

Lavela thought of one name, the Duke another, but they neither of them seemed right.

The Duke escorted her to the room she was to occupy, with her father next door.

There were two people at the end of the corridor talking together.

He realised they were Fiona and Joscelyn.

It flashed through his mind that perhaps, as she had done before, Fiona was consoling herself with Joscelyn.

Then because he was with Lavela and she had an aura of purity about her, he did not want to think of Fiona.

Besides the young people staying in the house, Mr. Watson on the Duke's instructions had invited a number of others in the County to the dance

An Orchestra had been engaged from London.

The Big Ball-Room was opened and decorated with flowers from the hot-houses.

It was something which had often happened before at Moor Park.

But the Duke knew it was the first time for Lavela, and that she had never been to a real Ball.

She was very simply dressed.

Yet once again he thought the white gown which revealed the curves of her breasts and the smallness of her waist was a perfect frame for her beauty.

"That is how she must look when she is the Angel!" he told himself.

The idea pleased him.

While she was far down the table from where he was sitting at dinner, he found himself watching her.

Her eyes were shining.

She was continually laughing at what the two young men on either side of her were saying.

Fiona, he noticed, was also animated but in a very different way.

He was certain that every remark she made had a double meaning.

Every look she gave the men next to her and every movement she made had something seductive about it.

It struck him for the first time that apart from everything else that he now knew about her, she did not really fit in at Moor Park.

He told himself it was something he should have been aware of before.

The men did not linger over their port as they had the previous evening.

The Duke knew the girls, and especially Lavela, were waiting excitedly for partners.

She certainly did not lack them.

The Duke asked her to dance after he had done his duty with the older members of the party.

He thought as he did so that nobody could look more radiant.

"I can see you are enjoying yourself," he remarked.

"I have wings on my feet!" Lavela answered. "This is not an 'Aladdin's Cave' but the Prince's Palace and I am only afraid that when midnight strikes it will all vanish!"

"I shall be very upset if it does!" the Duke smiled. "And I hope if you are handing out roles in your Fairy Story I am Prince Charming!"

"But of course," she answered, "except that you are a Magician at the same time!"

The Duke laughed.

"As long as I am not the Demon King I am quite content."

As he spoke Joscelyn passed by.

He thought that if ever there was a candidate suitable for that role, it was his Cousin.

He only hoped that Lavela would never come in contact with anyone so evil.

At the same time, he realised she was being a great success.

The other men in the party were begging her for dances.

When her card was full they insisted that she added a number of extras to it.

The Duke was also aware that the Vicar was enjoying himself.

He was talking to his grandmother and a number of his older relations.

Several of them told the Duke what a delightful man he was and asked why they had not met him before.

"I was very remiss in not knowing he existed," the Duke explained, "and it is something I assure you will be rectified in the future."

"His daughter is lovely!" one of his Aunts said. "I am sure she would be a huge sensation in London."

"It might spoil her," the Duke replied quickly.

When the evening came to an end and the Orchestra played "*God Save The Queen*" everyone regretted it was over.

Those who were going back to their own houses in the County begged the Duke to give another Ball as soon as possible.

"I will certainly think about it," he promised.

When Lavela said goodnight to him she said;

"Thank you for the most exciting evening I have ever had! There is no words by which to describe it except wonderful! I seem to be saying that over and over again ever since I met you."

"All you and I have to concentrate on now," the Duke replied, "is to ensure that everyone will be saying the same on Saturday evening."

"I am quite certain they will say it a thousand times!" Lavela replied.

She walked up the stairs with her father.

The Duke said goodnight to some of his relations, many of the older ones having retired earlier.

Fiona was not to be seen.

That, he thought, was a relief.

Having told Newman the Butler that everything had gone exactly as he had wished he too went up to bed.

He thought as he reached his room where his Valet was waiting that he was not really tired.

It had been a very satisfactory day.

Nothing the Duke thought, could have given him more pleasure than to see Lavela's eyes shining like stars.

He pulled back the curtains to look up at the sky.

As he did so his Valet said;

"Goodnight, Your Grace! Shall I call Your Grace at your usual time?"

"Yes, of course," the Duke answered.

He did not turn round but stayed looking up at the stars.

Then the door opened again and he thought it was irritating that Jenkins had forgotten something.

But when the voice behind him spoke he turned round sharply.

It was not Jenkins who was standing inside his bedroom but his Cousin Joscelyn.

Like the Duke, Lavela when she reached her room was not tired.

Although it was two o'clock in the morning she felt she could have gone on dancing until it was dawn.

She had never danced with a young man before, but she had danced with her father.

Her mother had insisted when she was a child that twice a week she had dancing lessons.

When she had danced with the Duke, it was something, she thought, she would always remember.

It had been easy to follow his steps.

She thought when he held her hand it was as if he transferred some of his strength and brilliance to her.

"He is so wonderful!" she thought, "so very, very wonderful! I cannot believe there is another man like him in the whole world!"

She wanted to thank God for the evening.

In fact, for all the exciting things that had happened to her since the Duke had heard her playing the Church organ.

At home, whenever she wanted to say a special prayer, she could go into the Church by an underground passage.

It had been built many years ago by a Vicar who suffered from a weak chest.

He had not dared to go outside on a cold or windy day.

Now Lavela wished that she could go into the Church and pray in front of the altar.

Then she remembered there was a Chapel at Moor Park.

Her father had told her how beautiful it was.

She had in fact, found out that it was at the back of the house, not far from where she was sleeping.

She enquired about it from the maid who had prepared her bath for her.

"We 'as a Service there sometimes, Miss," the maid said, "but t'Vicar likes us to go t'the Church in the Park."

"I would like to see the old Chapel," Lavela replied.

"It's easy enough, Miss," the maid told her. "If you slip down that staircase on t'other side o'the corridor there's a passage straight ahead o'you, an' the Chapel's at the end o'it."

"Thank you," Lavela said.

Now she thought that late though it was, she would like to pray in the Chapel.

It seemed appropriate that she should thank God there for all the Duke had done for her.

Her father had told her the Chapel had been built a hundred years before Moor Park was redesigned.

Opening her door she found the lights were still lit in the corridor and it was easy to find her way to the staircase.

There were also candles in silver sconces to show her the way down to the passage below.

She moved softly along the passage until she saw the Chapel door ahead of her.

There was a light shining through it.

She thought it strange that the Chapel should be lit at night.

At the same time, it was in keeping with the huge fires burning in every room.

As she reached the door of the Chapel she realised there was somebody inside.

Fearing she might be intruding, she stood still.

Then she heard a man's voice say harshly;

"You have to marry her, Sheldon, and there is nothing you can do about it!"

"I absolutely refuse!"

It was the Duke who spoke.

Surprised and at the same time frightened that something very strange was happening, Lavela moved a little nearer.

Now she could see that standing in front of the altar were three people.

One was the Duke, wearing a long robe like one her father wore over his nightshirt.

Then there was Lady Faversham looking, Lavela thought, exceedingly beautiful, and sparkling with jewels.

On the other side of the Duke was Joscelyn Moore, to whom she had been introduced earlier.

She had thought there was something unpleasant about him although he was good-looking.

When he had touched her hand she had known that he was evil.

Now she saw there was a revolver in his hand and he was pointing it at the Duke.

With an effort she prevented herself from screaming.

Then she saw that facing the three people was another man.

She had not noticed him at first because he was short and somehow insignificant.

He was wearing a surplice and she knew he was a Parson.

"You are in no position, Sheldon, to refuse to marry Fiona," Joscelyn Moore was saying in the same harsh voice he had used before.

"You brought me down here by telling me there had been an accident to one of my staff," the Duke answered. "Now I intend to go back to bed, and if you have not left my house by breakfast-time tomorrow, I shall have you thrown out!"

Joscelyn Moore laughed, and it was a very unpleasant sound.

"Do you really believe, Sheldon, that you can defy me?" he asked. "I am pointing a fully loaded revolver at you."

"If you kill me you will hang," the Duke retorted, "and I cannot believe that is what you want."

"What I want," Joscelyn snarled, "is that you marry Fiona, whom you have most certainly compromised. That will ensure that I shall become the third Duke of Moorminster!"

"What makes you so sure of that?" the Duke enquired.

"Fiona tells me you know already that she cannot have a child," Joscelyn replied, "and although you are a young man, an accident might befall you which would save me from having to wait too long to attend your Funeral!"

"Do you really believe I am willing to go through the rest of my life expecting any moment that you will contrive somehow to cause my death?" the Duke said scornfully.

"I have already said you have no choice, and we are wasting time. If you do not marry Fiona, and the Clergyman is here ready to unite you two in Holy Matrimony, I will not hesitate to use this revolver!"

"And kill me?" the Duke asked mockingly.

Joscelyn shook his head.

"Oh, no!" he replied. "But I will maim you so that you can never make love to a woman again, nor be capable of producing a child."

He almost spat the words at the Duke.

Lavela listening, shocked and horrified, wondered frantically what she could do to save the Duke.

Chapter Six

Lavela was hesitant.

She wondered if she should run to fetch somebody to rescue the Duke.

She was however, afraid that while she was gone he would be already married.

If only she could reach her father, she felt sure he would do something.

Even while she hesitated, Joscelyn Moore said to the Parson:

"Get on with it, and the quicker the better!"

The Parson opened his Prayer Book and Lavela knew there was no longer any time.

Hardly realising what she was doing she moved farther into the Chapel.

On either side of the door there was a pillar and standing on each an angel complete with wings.

The Duke had bought them in Bavaria.

They had been carved a hundred years earlier with that country's unique skill.

Then they had been painted in the soft colours which made every Bavarian Church a delight to the eye.

Lavela moved behind one of the pillars.

The Parson was beginning the Service.

"Dearly beloved . . "

"Cut out all that nonsense!" Joscelyn Moore ordered. "Get on to the Marriage Service itself."

"If the man knows what is best for him he will refuse to perform a Service which is illegal," the Duke warned, "and I shall not hesitate to take the matter to the Courts!"

Joscelyn laughed.

"And create a scandal? My dear Cousin, you know as well as I do that the one thing you have always been afraid of is anything that would shame our Noble Family!"

He spoke the last words mockingly and Fiona said:

"Be quiet, Joscelyn! There is no point in upsetting Sheldon more than he is already. All I want is to be his wife!"

"And that is what you will be," Joscelyn replied.

He looked again at the Parson.

"Do what you have been paid to do," he said, "otherwise I will have you defrocked, or whatever they do to punish creatures like you."

"I'm doing my best, Mr. Moore," the Parson said in a trembling voice.

He turned over two pages of his Prayer Book.

It was then that Lavela, who had been praying for help, knew what she must do.

She could feel the agony the Duke was going through in his mind.

She knew, almost as if he was telling her so, that he was trying to think of some way that he could knock his Cousin down and disarm him.

Anything to prevent this mockery of a marriage from taking place.

At the same time, the Duke was aware that Joscelyn was pointing his revolver straight at him below the waist.

His finger was on the trigger.

"Oh, my God, what can I do?" she asked silently.

"Help .. me! Please .. God .. help .. me!" Lavela prayed.

As she spoke she put up her hands and pushed at the angel in front of her.

For a moment she thought it was firmly attached to its stone pillar.

Then as she felt it move a little, she raised her hands higher and pushed with all the strength she could muster.

The angel moved, hovered, then toppled onto the stone floor with a loud crash.

It echoed round the Chapel walls.

Involuntarily Joscelyn turned to see what had happened.

It was the opportunity the Duke had been waiting for.

With his left hand he seized the revolver, thrusting it upwards.

At the same time, with the whole force of his very athletic body he struck Joscelyn a blow on the chin.

It was a punch that would have won the admiration of any Pugilist.

Joscelyn staggered, then fell backwards.

As he did so he pulled the trigger and a bullet shot upwards into the ceiling.

The explosion made even more noise than the falling angel.

It was added to by a shrill scream from Fiona.

Joscelyn's head had hit the stone floor as he fell, and he now lay still.

The Duke bent down and picked up the revolver.

It was lying a little way from his Cousin's body.

As he straightened himself the Parson cringed back against the altar saying in a quavering voice:

"He made me do it! He made me do it!"

The Duke gave him a contemptuous look and turned to Fiona.

As he did so the Night-watchman and the footman on duty in the hall came running into the Chapel.

They passed Lavela without seeing her.

She slid silently into the shadows at the side of the Chapel.

The Night-watchman reached the Duke first.

"Be ye all right, Yer Grace? Us 'eard a shot."

He looked as he spoke at the revolver in the Duke's hand.

"Nobody is injured," the Duke answered curtly.

Then as the footman came up beside the Night-watchman he asked:

"How did this Parson get here?"

" 'E come in a Post-Chaise, Yer Grace. It be waitin' fer 'im outside."

"Then take him to it," the Duke ordered, "and put Mr. Joscelyn in the carriage with him!"

The footman and the Night-watchman looked surprised.

Then obediently they walked to where Joscelyn was lying unconscious.

They picked him up, one taking his shoulders the other his legs.

The Duke watched them as they moved down the aisle.

With a gesture of his hand he indicated to the Parson to follow them.

He did so hurriedly passing the Duke as if he was afraid of being struck.

As he scuttled down the aisle the Duke said to Fiona:

"Because you are a woman, and it is late, I will not make you go with them. But you will leave this house first thing tomorrow morning!"

She moved towards him.

"How can you do this to me, Sheldon?" she pleaded. "I love you! I have always wanted to be your wife!"

"I am being merciful in not making you go with your lover," the Duke said sharply, "and I hope never to see you again!"

For a moment Fiona just stared at him.

Then as she realised what he said and that he knew about her and Joscelyn, her eyes flickered.

Defeated, she moved away holding her head high.

Only when she was out of sight did the Duke call softly;

"Lavela!"

He looked towards the dark corner where she had hidden herself.

Because she could not help it she ran towards him.

When she reached him she said breathlessly;

"I prayed . . I prayed . . desperately that I could . . help you!"

"You saved me," the Duke said quietly, "and I am more grateful than I can possibly say!"

He gave a deep sigh.

"I can hardly believe it all happened, and that you were there at exactly the right moment."

"I . . came down . . stairs to . . the Chapel because I . . wanted to say a . . prayer of gratitude for the . . wonderful evening," Lavela explained, "but I think . . God must have sent me to . . help you."

"I am quite sure of it," the Duke replied.

He put the revolver he still held in his hand down on the nearest pew.

Then he said;

"I think we should offer our thanks together."

Lavela gave him a smile which made her look even more like an angel.

Then as if she understood what he wanted she knelt down on the altar steps.

The Duke joined her and they both closed their eyes.

Then as the Duke finished the most fervent prayer he had ever said in his whole life, he put out his hand.

He drew Lavela to her feet.

"You saved me!" he said again, as if he could hardly believe himself it had actually happened.

"You do not .. think he will .. try to .. hurt you again?" she whispered.

"I expect he will," the Duke replied, "and I can only hope that when he does you, as my Guardian Angel, will somehow manage to protect me."

"I will .. try .. you know I will .. try," Lavela said, "but .. I am frightened."

She looked so lovely as she looked up at him with a worried expression in her eyes that the Duke said;

"I have thanked God, but I think also, Lavela, I should thank you!"

He put his arms round her as he spoke and bending his head he kissed her.

It was a very gentle kiss, for he was not at the moment thinking of her as an attractive woman.

She was an angel who had saved him from a fate that was too humiliating to contemplate.

Then as he felt the soft sweetness of Lavela's lips his kiss became more demanding, more possessive.

At the same time there was still a reverence about it.

To Lavela it was as if the Gates of Heaven had opened and she had been swept inside.

She had never been kissed, and she was astonished at the touch of the Duke's lips on hers.

She thought it was very wonderful that somebody so magnificent and marvellous as the Duke should actually kiss her.

Then she felt a strange sensation she had never known before.

It was as if the light from the stars was twinkling inside her.

She knew that the same light enveloped both the Duke and herself, and it was the light of God.

Without being conscious of doing so, she moved her body closer to his.

His arms tightened and the sensations within her increased.

They were so intense, so perfect, and at the same time so Divine that she knew this was Love.

This was a love unbelievable, amazing and overwhelming.

As the Duke's lips became more possessive she felt she was no longer herself, but his.

When he raised his head to look down at her the Duke thought he had never seen anyone look so radiant.

At the same time so beautiful.

As she looked up at him he knew she was not thinking of him as a man, but as someone she worshipped.

"My Darling, how can you make me feel like this?" he asked.

Then he was kissing her again.

Kissing her now as if she was no longer an angel, but a woman who was utterly and completely desirable.

Because they were in the Chapel and had passed through a gruelling experience, he knew that what he felt for Lavela was very different from what he had felt for any other woman.

He kissed her again, but now more gently.

Then he said:

"I think it would be a great mistake for anyone, to know what has happened here tonight."

"Will not . . the servants . . talk?" Lavela asked hesitatingly.

"I will make sure they do not!" the Duke answered.

He looked at her very tenderly. Then he said:

"I want you to go to bed and forget this happened to spoil your happy evening, which you enjoyed so much."

"How can I forget it . . when you . . are still . . in danger?" Lavela murmured.

"For the moment I am quite safe," the Duke answered, "and my disreputable Cousin will not be in a position to hurt anyone for at least 48 hours!"

"B . . but . . after that . . ?"

"After that I shall rely on you, and of course God, to keep me safe," the Duke said simply.

He spoke with a sincerity which would have surprised him at any other time.

It brought the light back into Lavela's eyes.

"I will do what you say," she said, "but . . promise you will be . . careful."

"We will talk about that tomorrow," the Duke answered.

He took her by the hand and they walked out of the Chapel, leaving the candles burning.

At the bottom of the stairs which led up to the floor on which

Lavela was sleeping the Duke kissed her again and said;

"Goodnight, my Darling, dream happy dreams and forget the nightmare we have just passed through."

"I will . . dream of . . you," Lavela answered.

Then because she knew he was waiting, she walked up the stairs.

He watched her from below until she reached the top.

She waved to him and when she had disappeared from his sight he walked to the hall.

As he expected, the Night-watchman and the footman were waiting.

The front door was still open, letting in the cold night air.

The Duke could see a Post-Chaise drawn by two horses in the distance.

It went over the bridge which spanned the lake.

It vanished from sight under the branches of the ancient oak trees which lined either side of the long drive.

When he could see it no longer he said sharply;

"Shut the door!"

The footman obeyed him and thrust home two bolts besides turning the key in the lock.

The Duke then spoke more quietly.

He told them what had happened tonight was not to be repeated to anyone in the house or outside.

He said that if they disobeyed him they would be instantly dismissed without a reference.

"That is something I have never said before to anyone in my employment," he said, "but as this is a very serious matter, I want you to promise me on your word of honour that you will never speak of it to anyone."

"Oi gives yer me word o' honour, Yer Grace!" the Night-watchman said, and the footman echoed him.

Then when the Duke would have walked away he asked:

"Where did that Post-Chaise come from?"

"From London, Yer Grace, an' th' driver tells Oi it took nigh on four hours in comin' 'ere 'cause th' Reverend Gent kep' stoppin' at every Inn on the way to 'ave a drink!"

The Duke did not say anything, and the footman added:

"The driver, Your Grace, asks fer a mug o' ale when 'e gets 'ere an' Oi give 'im one, an' before he goes orf 'e were singin'!"

The Duke thought such behaviour was what he might have expected of the type of Clergyman that Joscelyn would employ.

He knew it was always possible to find one in London who would marry couples late at night.

They were in regular demand by unscrupulous women who had trapped some rich drunkard into matrimony when he had no idea of what he was doing.

Had he been married to Fiona he might not have been able to prove the ceremony was illegal.

At the same time, as Joscelyn was aware, he would have found it hard to face the distress an attempt to do so would cause to his family.

As he walked upstairs to his bedroom he wondered how he could ever be grateful enough for having escaped.

It was a baited trap which would undoubtedly have ruined his whole life.

As he got into bed he was thinking of Lavela.

Not only of how beautiful she was, but also how clever.

No other woman could have thought of a way of preventing the marriage.

Joscelyn had planned it so craftily.

When his cousin had come into his bedroom he had said in an agitated voice;

"There has been an accident, Sheldon, in the Chapel, of all unlikely places, and I think you had better come quickly!"

Mention of the Chapel immediately brought Lavela to the Duke's mind and he asked;

"Who is it? What has happened?"

"There is no time to talk," Joscelyn replied, "just follow me as fast as you can."

He had gone ahead and the Duke had been unable to ask any more questions.

When he reached the Chapel he had found Fiona there.

Then Joscelyn produced a revolver and he realised that he had been caught.

He thought now it was somehow appropriate that Lavela, who looked so like an angel, had used one to save him.

He was very proud of his two Bavarian angels.

He only hoped the one which now lay on the stone floor could be skilfully repaired.

214

But nothing really mattered except that he was safe, at least for the moment.

And that he loved Lavela.

"I am too old for her to be interested in me!" he told himself.

Then he knew from the way she had responded to his kiss, the way she had moved closer in his arms, that she loved him.

It was as he had wanted to be loved.

Not merely because he was a Duke.

From the moment they had prayed together there had been a close affinity between them, but he had not realised at first it was love.

It was a very different love from what he had ever felt before.

That was why he had not recognised it.

It was not the wild burning fire of passion.

That was something completely physical and what he had felt for Fiona and the women before her.

He knew now that Lavela worshipped him as he worshipped her.

She was everything that was perfect in a woman.

He knew without her telling him that she loved him not only with her heart, but also with her soul.

The Duke had not thought of his soul until now; but if he possessed one, he knew it was hers.

Before he fell asleep he was thinking that no one could be more blessed than he was.

At the same time, he was wondering what his family would say.

They would obviously disapprove when he told them he was going to marry the daughter of the Vicar of Little Bedlington.

The Duke woke early.

His first thought was that he must make sure that Fiona obeyed his instructions.

He hoped she would leave the house before she could come in contact with any of his other guests.

As she had been humiliated he thought it unlikely that she would want to talk.

Yet one could never trust a woman not to be indiscreet.

He therefore rang for his Valet, and when he came sent him to fetch Mr. Watson.

He instructed Mr. Watson that Lady Faversham was to leave on the first available train which could be stopped at the Halt.

The Housekeeper was to see that all her things were packed.

After that the Duke thought he need never again concern himself with Fiona.

Instead he could think of Lavela.

Now in the light of day the difficulties of marrying her seemed to close in on him like vultures.

He was worried not for himself but for her.

He knew only too well that his family would be upset.

They would be horrified that he was not marrying somebody whose blood was the equal of his own.

Someone who would fill the position of Duchess with dignity.

That could hardly be expected from a girl who had seldom been out of the village of Little Bedlington.

They might even be unkind and rude to her.

The Duke knew how women, especially older women, could intimidate and humiliate a young girl.

Especially one for whom they had no respect.

Every instinct in his body made him want to protect Lavela.

Not so much from physical injury as from anything that would hurt her spiritually and mentally.

He hated the thought that her trust in other people might be destroyed.

She had always lived in a house of love.

She had never come up against the envy, hatred and malice of the Social World.

Nor the cruelty a woman could inflict on another woman.

It was not only by what might be said, but the way that they thought about her.

The Duke knew the first thing he must do was to prevent anybody knowing what he and Lavela felt for each other.

It must be an absolute secret until the house-party and the Opening of the Theatre were over.

He wanted the audience to look at Lavela as a beautiful singing angel.

Not as a local girl who had managed by some skilful means of her own, to capture a Duke.

He therefore sent his Valet with a note to tell the maid who

216

was looking after Lavela that he wished to see her in the Theatre immediately.

He knew his request would be taken at its face value and that it concerned Lavela's performance.

He waited for her in one of the boxes.

Five minutes later she came speeding through the door which led from the house.

For a moment she did not see him.

He watched her as she looked round the Theatre.

She had an expression of expectation in her eyes which made his heart turn a somersault.

Then as he spoke her name very softly she saw him in the box beside her.

She gave a little cry of delight.

Spontaneously, without thinking, she flung herself into his arms.

As he held her against him she asked:

"Is it true .. really true .. what you .. said last night .. that you .. love me?"

"I adore you!" the Duke confirmed in a deep voice.

She smiled.

"When I first .. woke up I thought it .. could not be .. true and that I had .. only been dreaming."

"That is what I felt too," he said.

Then he kissed her until they were both breathless.

"Now listen, my precious," he said at last, "I think it would be a great mistake, and I know you will think the same, that anyone should know how much we love each other until after tomorrow evening."

"Yes .. of course .. I understand," Lavela said "I want people to think about your .. music Play and realise how .. clever you are."

"That is what we hope they will think!" the Duke smiled. "And when my family has left and everybody else with them, then we can think about ourselves."

She smiled at him.

She was even lovelier than he had thought her to be yesterday.

"I love you!" he said. "All I want is to keep telling you so, but we both know we have a lot of work to do."

Lavela nodded.

Then in a different tone of voice she asked:

"You have . . made sure that . . no one will talk about . . what happened . . last night?"

"Absolutely sure," the Duke affirmed, "so do not think about it today. You just have to concentrate on rehearsing the children."

"Yes, of course," she agreed.

The Duke kissed her again.

Then he said:

"Now we will both be very, very careful that no one guesses our precious secret. But if you look at me as you are doing now, we shall be unable to hide it!"

"Then I will . . try not to look at you," Lavela answered seriously, "but it will be difficult because I keep thinking you are . . too wonderful to be . . real."

"I am very real, and I love you, just as you love me," the Duke said. "But now we must get back to reality, and that is – breakfast!"

Lavela laughed.

"I feel we should be eating nothing but Ambrosia which is far more romantic than eggs and bacon!"

The Duke kissed her again.

Then he took her from the Theatre back into the house.

As Lavela made her way to the Breakfast-Room he went to his Study.

Mr. Watson was there waiting to see him which he thought was unusual as he did not normally send for him so early.

"I am afraid I bring you bad news," Mr. Watson said.

"What is it?" the Duke enquired.

"I have just been informed, Your Grace, that there was an accident last night at the cross-roads outside the village."

The Duke was still.

"What happened?" he enquired.

"A Post-Chaise containing Mr. Joscelyn and a Clergyman came into collision with the Carrier's cart!"

The Duke waited.

"According to the Carrier, Your Grace, the driver of the Post-Chaise was drunk and whipping up his horses in the most reckless manner."

"Go on," the Duke prompted.

"The Post-Chaise was overturned," Mr. Watson continued. "The Clergyman had a broken leg, but I regret to tell Your

Grace that Mr. Joscelyn was very badly injured and is in a coma."

"He is alive?" the Duke questioned thinking his voice sounded strange as he did so.

"The Doctor says there is no chance of saving him, but he and the Clergyman have been taken to a Hospital."

The Duke sat down at his desk.

He could not be so hypocritical as to pretend that if Joscelyn died it would be anything but a relief.

At the same time, it was something of a shock to realise that in sending him away as he had done, he was partly responsible.

"I was wondering," Mr. Watson said, "if as their Royal Highnesses are arriving today, it would be best for nothing to be said about Mr. Joscelyn's condition until after the Performance tomorrow evening?"

"Yes, of course – you are right," the Duke agreed.

"Doctor Graham is awaiting Your Grace's instructions. He recognised Mr. Joscelyn, but as he was in evening clothes no one else knew he was staying, and the Doctor did not enlighten them."

The Duke knew Dr. Graham.

He was an elderly man who had attended his father and himself and any members of his family who needed his services when they stayed at Moor Park.

He realised the Doctor was being very tactful and understanding.

He knew it would ruin the Christmas house-party and be uncomfortable when they were entertaining the Prince and Princess of Wales anticipating Joscelyn's death.

Dr. Graham being so closely associated with the Moores, was doubtless aware of Joscelyn's disreputable behaviour.

Of course the village was talking about the way he threw money away on riotous living.

"I will call on Dr. Graham myself as soon as I have had breakfast," the Duke said aloud.

"That is what I thought Your Grace would say," Mr. Watson replied.

"He is right, of course," the Duke went on. "It would be extremely awkward and would certainly spoil the party and our Show tomorrow night if anyone knew what has happened."

Dr. Graham said that only a few of the villagers knew there had been an accident, and they had no idea the Post-Chaise had anything to do with him.

"I am extremely grateful for Dr. Graham's discretion," the Duke said, "and thank goodness, Watson, I can rely on yours."

Mr. Watson smiled and the Duke left the Study to go to the Breakfast-Room.

As he did so he was thinking that Lavela would not need to tell him again that he had to be grateful.

He was very, very grateful that Fate or God, had been so generous to him.

Chapter Seven

Their Royal Highnesses arrived on Friday evening.

They were extremely courteous to all the members of the Duke's family.

The Duke, however, was watching Lavela's reaction.

He thought the excitement in her eyes was like that of a child at a Pantomime.

Almost immediately the party went up to dress for dinner.

The Chef, as excited as everybody else, excelled himself. Each course was a poem in itself.

It was not the first time the Prince had stayed at Moor Park.

It was however, the first time he had done so with the Princess.

"I am so looking forward to the opening of your Theatre," Princess Alexandra said in her sweet voice to the Duke, "and I am sure you have something delightful in store for us."

"I only hope you will like it, Ma'am," the Duke said. "It is certainly unusual."

As he spoke he remembered that the Princess was very musical.

Being very poor before her father came to the throne of Denmark, she had been taught by her mother.

The Queen was a member of the Hesse-Cassel family, and all her six children were extremely talented.

The Duke was sure that Princess Alexandra would be impressed that at the Opening of the Theatre all the performers came from one small village.

When the gentlemen joined the ladies after dinner the Duke heaved a sigh of relief that Fiona was no longer there.

There was no need for him now to be afraid that she would enlist the Prince's help in forcing him to marry her.

Nor need he be worried that Joscelyn would do anything to offend the rest of the family.

As he came into the Drawing-Room he saw, to his surprise, that Lavela was sitting beside Princess Alexandra.

They were talking animatedly.

He could not help thinking it extraordinary that someone as young and unsophisticated as Lavela should not seem nervous or in any way shy at being in the presence of Royalty.

In fact as he watched her she appeared to be completely at ease.

Both she and the Princess were laughing when he walked across the room to join them.

"I am curious, Your Royal Highness," he said, "as to what Lavela is saying to make you laugh."

"We were actually talking about Musicians and their strange idiosyncracies when they are performing," the Princess replied.

The Duke raised his eyebrows and Lavela explained:

"I was telling Her Royal Highness about one of Papa's friends who was a most distinguished violinist. He had a strange habit of kissing the handkerchief he put under his chin on which to rest his instrument, because he thought it would bring him luck!"

"And I was telling Miss Ashley," the Princess chimed in, "about one of our most distinguished pianists in Denmark who carries a spider in a box in his pocket, which he always uses when he is gambling."

The Duke laughed and said:

"Now I think about it, a great number of famous people have strange ideas like that. Perhaps we should collect them and publish them in a book."

The Princess laughed, but Lavela said;

"If they read it, it would only make them nervous, and then perhaps they would not be able to play as well in the future."

The Duke thought it was a nice thing to say and he smiled at her.

Then as she smiled back he remembered that they were supposed to appear indifferent towards each other.

Everybody went to bed early.

The Duke was sure a great number of his guests were lying awake thinking of what they would do tomorrow.

He wanted to be with Lavela and help her to rehearse the children who were sleeping in the East Wing.

He had arranged that the Princess should have a guided tour of the house.

Also that the Prince should visit the stables and be shown the horses.

Because both of the Royal Couple had been very busy the previous week and over Christmas he guessed they would not wish to exert themselves unnecessarily.

He had in fact asked if the Prince would like a Shoot.

The reply was that His Royal Highness had a sore arm after a very arduous day's shooting at Sandringham.

The Prince would therefore rather have a quiet day.

This suited the Duke, who had no wish to shoot when he had so much to do in the Theatre.

He knew he must be present as host if His Royal Highness was one of the guns.

The next morning he left his relations to look after themselves.

He found Lavela in the Theatre conducting the children from the Orchestra Pit while they sang their Carol on the stage.

She had improvised something since he had last been present.

In between the verses they joined hands and danced around in a circle.

Because the children were so small it looked very attractive.

It was too in keeping with the stage itself where the Duke had arranged flowers at the back and on each side.

Big pots of lilies concealed much of the grand pianos.

He had always thought they were not particularly attractive instruments.

They had been pushed to each side so that the audience would only just see the two pianists.

The Duke also arranged that when they had finished the Overture the pianos could be pulled back still further by unseen hands off-stage.

He walked down the centre aisle to stand behind Lavela.

She was very conscious of him.

Finally the last verse of the Carol came to an end and the children walked forward to curtsy gracefully.

The Duke clapped his hands.

"Bravo!" he said. "I know tonight you will receive tremendous applause. In that case, you must curtsy for a second time before the curtains are pulled to."

The children understood, and as they went from the stage he put his hand on Lavela's shoulder.

"I love you!" he said very softly.

She looked up at him.

There was no need for her to speak or tell him what she felt about him.

"You are not nervous?" he asked.

"Only in case . . you are . . disappointed," she answered.

That, he was certain, would not happen.

The Duke had arranged because the children were so young that the performance would take place before dinner.

At six o'clock the audience were taking their places in the Theatre.

The Prince and Princess entered when everybody else was seated and they all stood for *God Save The Queen*.

The lights were then extinguished in the auditorium and the Duke and Lavela began the Overture.

The applause they received at the end of it was very gratifying.

Then the Vicar, well disguised as Harlequin recited his welcoming and very amusing poem.

The curtains drew back to show the children grouped to resemble a bouquet of flowers, which caused a murmur of delight.

After that the Programme was as professional as anything that might have been seen on the London stage.

The Duke's episode was outstanding, and he felt it was a pity there was to be only the one performance of it.

He knew that Maria Colzaio was singing as brilliantly as she had done in all the great Opera Houses in Europe.

She did not however, outshine Lavela.

She looked so lovely as the Angel that it was difficult for him to think of anybody else.

The words of her song were very moving:

"One thing I know, life can never die,
  Translucent, splendid, flaming like the sun.
Only our bodies wither and deny
  The life force when our strength is done."

The song went on to tell the listeners that her good deeds and the love she had given while she was on earth would live for ever.

When finally the curtain closed on the play there was that appreciative silence for which every artist longs.

It is the greatest accolade they can receive.

Then the applause rang out and the Prince of Wales was heard to cry;

"Bravo! Bravo!"

As the Duke thought, after that everything went on well-oiled wheels.

Finally he appeared as Father Christmas.

The children ran down from the stage to distribute the presents, which was a surprise to everyone.

He had given Mr. Watson *carte blanche* to buy what presents he thought suitable.

Nobody was disappointed with what they received.

The Male Voice Choir singing behind him sang *God Rest Ye Merry Gentlemen.*

Then finally the children went back onto the stage and the curtain fell, there was another burst of applause.

Then the Prince and Princess told the Duke they would like to meet the Performers.

The red curtains were therefore drawn back again and Their Royal Highnesses walked down from the box and onto the stage.

They congratulated everyone in their usual charming manner.

The Duke took off his Father Christmas robes and escorted them from the stage and up the aisle which led to the house.

They had almost reached the steps which would take them there when Princess Alexandra stopped suddenly.

Sitting with the five mothers of the performing children in the last row of the Stalls was Mrs. Ashley.

The Princess was staring at her.

The Duke wondered if he should introduce her when the Princess exclaimed:

"Louise! It *is* Louise?"

Mrs. Ashley with a little sob held out her arms.

To the Duke's amazement the next minute the two women were kissing each other, and there were tears in their eyes.

"Louise! I have found you! I have found you! I have missed you so terribly all these years!"

"As I missed you, Alex," Mrs. Ashley said.

The Prince and the Duke were looking in astonishment at what was occurring.

The rest of the audience had turned round to stare too.

As if she was suddenly aware of it, Princess Alexandra said to the Prince:

"Darling, this is my Cousin Louise Hesse-Cassel, who ran away years ago and we had no idea where she had gone!"

"I can imagine your surprise at finding her here!" the Prince said. "You must tell us the whole story."

The Duke took charge.

"I think we would be more comfortable, if we went into the house," he said, "and, as Your Highness is aware, dinner is waiting."

"Louise must come with us," Princess Alexandra said quickly.

"Of course," the Duke replied, "and Your Royal Highness has already met Mrs. Ashley's charming husband and her beautiful daughter Lavela."

The Princess took Mrs. Ashley by the hand.

"How could you have gone away like that, Louise? I cried and cried for nights after you left?"

"Oh, dearest Alex, I did not want to hurt you," Mrs. Ashley answered, "but I was so very much in love!"

The Princess laughed.

"Then that means, of course, that I shall have to forgive you!"

They went up the steps together followed by the Prince and the Duke who could hardly believe what he had just heard.

If Mrs. Ashley was, as the Princess had said, her Cousin, it would make it easy for him to marry Lavela with the full approval of the Moore family.

The Duke could not tell Lavela what he had planned until after the Royal Couple had left Moor Park on Sunday.

It had been snowing all the previous evening but now the sun had come out.

It made the park and gardens and the great house look even more beautiful than they did usually.

Mrs. Ashley spent the night with them but not only because the Princess wished her to do so.

It was snowing hard by the time dinner came to an end.

The Duke was informed that his coachman considered it too dangerous to take the horses out and almost impossible to reach Little Bedlington.

Maria Colzaio was therefore another guest.

As she was fêted and congratulated by everyone in the house-party the Duke was sure she would, in the future, no longer wish to remain incognito.

What interested him most was that he had found the answer to what had been puzzling him about the Ashleys.

For the first time he learned that Andrew Ashley was the younger son of Lord Ashbrook.

He had been ordained after leaving Oxford.

He had insisted however, before he accepted one of the Livings on his father's estate, that he would explore the world first.

He had therefore left England for nearly three years.

He had travelled all over Europe, visited the East and on his way home, went to St. Petersburg.

From there he journeyed to Denmark.

"The moment I saw Louise," the Vicar said, "I knew she was the one person I had been looking for all my life."

"And I felt the same about Andrew," Mrs. Ashley said softly.

"It was very cruel of you to steal her away from us!" Princess Alexandra said accusingly.

"It was impossible, Ma'am, for me to leave her behind," the Vicar replied.

Mrs. Ashley put up her hand.

"You must not be unkind to Andrew. He tried to save me from himself, but we both knew how utterly miserable we would be for the rest of our lives."

"You have been happy?" Princess Alexandra asked.

"So blissfully, over-whelmingly happy," Mrs. Ashley answered, "that I never for one moment regretted running away, except, dearest Alex, that I missed you."

The Duke listening could hardly believe that this was all happening.

He realised however, that what he felt for Lavela was exactly the same as her father and mother had felt for each other.

They had run away and he knew it was something he too had to do.

When Joscelyn died it would be impossible for there to be a wedding in the family for at least six months.

Queen Victoria would expect it to be longer.

He moved from the Blue Drawing-Room where the Royal Couple

and the Ashleys were talking intimately and went to find Mr. Watson.

Having given him a list of instructions he went into the Salon where all his family were gathered.

They were all immensely curious to discover what was happening.

When he told them who the Vicar they admired so much actually was, they said they were not in the least surprised.

"He is such a good-looking man and so charming!" one of the Duke's Aunts said. "I felt he could not just be an ordinary Vicar of Little Bedlington."

The Duke knew that was exactly what they would have said if he had married Lavela without her Royal connections.

"It has been one of the best parties you have ever given!" the Prince of Wales declared when he said goodbye.

"It has been a great honour to have you here, Sir!" the Duke responded.

Princess Alexandra was kissing Mrs. Ashley.

"You must promise me, Louise," she said, "that you will come and see us at Marlborough House. And the next time we go to Sandringham all three of you must be our guests."

"Of course we will come, dearest Alex," Mrs. Ashley said, "and you know I want to see your children."

"We will give a special Ball for Lavela later in the Season," the Princess promised.

When the Royal Couple had departed the Duke took Lavela's hand in his and said to the Vicar and Mrs. Ashley:

"I would like you to come to my Study, as there is something important I want to tell you."

The Vicar and his wife were surprised.

But they followed the Duke, who still kept Lavela's hand in his, down the passage to the Study.

Newton opened the door and as the Duke entered he said:

"Stay outside the door, Newton. I do not wish to be disturbed."

"Very good, Your Grace."

The door shut and the Duke walked to the fireplace and stood with his back to the fire.

The Ashleys sat down, but Lavela stayed beside him.

He released her hand and she sat down on a chair looking up at him, he thought a little apprehensively.

"Lavela and I," the Duke announced, "wish to be married immediately!"

"Married?" Mrs. Ashley exclaimed looking at her daughter. "Oh, Darling, why did you not tell me?"

Lavela jumped up kneeling beside her mother's chair, and Mrs. Ashley kissed her.

"It is everything I could wish for you," she said, "as long as it will make you happy."

"It is the most . . wonderful thing that could ever . . happen," Lavela murmured.

The Vicar rose, put out his hand and said:

"There is no man to whom I would rather entrust my daughter than yourself!"

"Thank you," the Duke replied. "At the same time, there is some difficulty about it, and I need your help."

He then told them very briefly what had happened last night.

He also was truthful about the part Fiona had played in his life.

At the same time he made it clear that, while she had wanted to marry him, he had had no intention of marrying anyone until he met Lavela.

"That is exactly what I felt about Louise," the Vicar murmured.

"Then you will understand that I was only waiting to tell her how much she meant to me until this evening was over."

The Vicar nodded.

"However, this morning," the Duke went on, "I learnt something which could prevent us from being married for a long time."

Lavela, who was still kneeling beside her mother's chair, gave a little cry.

"But . . why? What has . . happened?"

"Last night after Joscelyn left here," the Duke explained, "he and that disreputable Parson of his were involved in an accident."

"An accident?" the Vicar exclaimed.

The Duke repeated what Mr. Watson had told him.

The Parson had a broken leg, but there was no hope of saving Joscelyn's life and he would die within a few days.

The three people listening were silent and the Duke went on quietly;

"You will understand that if he dies I shall be in mourning for my Cousin."

He paused a moment and then went on:

"It will be impossible for me to marry in the near future without arousing a great deal of criticism and certainly the disapproval of the Moore family."

"Yes, of course, I understand that," Mrs. Ashley said. "So you and Lavela will have to wait."

"On the contrary," the Duke said, "like you and your husband, we are going to run away!"

He smiled before he added:

"You set a precedent, so you can hardly blame us if we do the same!"

"What are . . we going . . to do?" Lavela asked.

"Your father is going to marry us first thing tomorrow morning," the Duke said, "and we shall leave here immediately."

Lavela's face was radiant as she rose to her feet.

"Can we . . do that? Can we really do . . that?" she gasped.

The Duke put his arms around her when she was standing beside him.

"It is what we are going to do," he said, "and we are going on a very long honeymoon. There are so many places in the world I want to show you, and so many things we can do together."

She was smiling up at him as he looked down at her.

They were both obviously so happy that tears came into Mrs. Ashley's eyes.

She put out her hand towards her husband.

"You are quite right," the Vicar said quietly.

"It is what I intended to do anyway," the Duke went on. "A long engagement would only allow my relatives to frighten Lavela by telling her what a bad husband I will be!"

He spoke teasingly, but Lavela replied seriously:

"You do not imagine I would . . listen to . . them?"

"Now you are going to find out for yourself whether I am good or bad!" the Duke smiled.

Lavela gave a little cry of happiness and put her cheek against his arm.

"I will see that everything is ready for you," the Vicar said, "and as you do not wish anyone to know about the ceremony I suggest we meet at your Chapel at eight o'clock."

"That is what I thought myself," the Duke replied. "Some of my relations are leaving this afternoon and the rest intend to depart tomorrow morning."

"It must be . . kept a secret . . until we have . . actually left . . the house," Lavela said.

"Of course," the Duke agreed, "and I know your father and mother understand that. Luckily my relatives have quite enough to talk about already!"

He smiled at Mrs. Ashley as he spoke and said:

"I felt there was some mystery about you and your husband, and wondered why you buried yourselves in Little Bedlington. I was curious – but I never expected to find the answer in such a dramatic fashion!"

"I thought Alex would not recognise me after so many years," Mrs. Ashley answered.

"If anyone had once seen you it would be impossible for them ever to forget you, my Darling!" the Vicar said.

His wife slipped her hand into his.

"I think, Dearest, you are prejudiced," she smiled. "At the same time, I am very happy to have found Alex again, and she says she is sure her father and mother will forgive me. Then we will be able to go and stay in Denmark and of course with my family in Germany."

"And what is going to happen to Little Bedlington," the Duke asked, "if you are going to be travelling abroad and becoming a part of London Society?"

The Vicar laughed and replied:

"That is quite easy. You and Lavela will have to keep up the high musical standards we have set in the village, and perhaps you could extend it over your whole Estate."

"That is a challenge," Lavela said before the Duke could speak.

"I will certainly think about it," the Duke replied, "but quite frankly at the moment all I want is to have Lavela to myself."

. . . . .

The Duke and Duchess of Moorminster drove away from Moor Park at eight-thirty the following morning.

There was no one to see them off except the servants, the Vicar and Mrs. Ashley.

"God bless you, my Darling," the Vicar said as he kissed Lavela goodbye.

"He has done that already by giving me such a wonderful husband," Lavela replied.

She looked very lovely as she seated herself beside the Duke in his Travelling-Carriage.

It was drawn by four perfectly matched horses.

There were two out-riders to accompany them.

The pale sun was just rising in the sky.

It made Lavela, the Duke thought, look like an angel who had come down from Heaven to be with him.

He knew while they were being married that he was starting a new chapter in his life.

It would be very different in every way from anything he had done before.

The Chapel on his instructions had been transformed from what it had been the night when Joscelyn had tried to force him to marry Fiona.

It had now looked like a bower of love.

There were lilies on the altar and flowers of every colour and description arranged round the walls.

There was no one else present except Mrs. Ashley.

But the Duke knew that for Lavela the angels were singing overhead, and he thought he himself recognised the tune.

When they knelt for the Blessing he was saying in his heart words of gratitude which he knew Lavela was also saying in hers.

"How can we have been so fortunate as to have found each other?" he asked. "And for the future to be as golden as the sunlight?"

Fortunately the snow had stopped falling before dawn and there was no frost.

The roads therefore were not dangerous.

As they sped through a white world the Duke thought it looked as pure as Lavela herself.

"I love you, my Darling!" he said.

"As I love you."

She spoke in the same rapt little voice with which she had made her responses in the Marriage Service.

Very gently the Duke took off the small hat she was wearing and put it down on the seat beside them.

Then he pulled her close against him and said:

"We have run away – we have escaped! Now nobody can prevent us from being together and I no longer have to be careful how I look at you."

Lavela laughed.

"I was so afraid that people would see me looking at you and know I was longing to be close as we are now."

"We are not yet close enough," the Duke said.

He saw his wife blush and added:

"Tonight we are staying in a house on the Dover Road which is my own but which I have only used when I have been going abroad."

"Do you realise," Lavela asked, "that I have not asked you where we are going? There has never been time."

"I have planned everything," the Duke said, "but I want it to be a surprise. You just have to shut your eyes until I tell you to open them."

She laughed.

"I am quite happy to do that as long as when I do .. open my eyes .. you will be .. there."

"You can be quite certain of that," the Duke answered.

The house which they reached late in the afternoon was small, but very comfortable.

The Duke had bought it from a friend because he disliked staying at Hotels.

It was too far for his horses to reach Dover in one day.

He liked to think he could slip across the Channel whenever he grew bored.

But what usually happened was that he went on a special Mission to Europe for either the Queen or the Prime Minister.

It was then he found his house convenient.

It pleased him to think he had never taken any other woman there.

Lavela was enchanted.

"It is like a doll's-house!" she exclaimed.

"I wanted you to think it was a Palace and I was 'Prince Charming'!" the Duke teased.

"You know you are that," she said, "and always will be, whether we are at Moor Park or in a cave! You will be you, and that is .. all that .. matters!"

It was what the Duke had always wanted and thought he would never find.

A woman who loved him for himself and not because of his title or possessions.

When later in the evening the Duke had undressed and went into Lavela's room he thought she would be in bed.

Instead she was standing at the window.

The curtains were drawn back so that she could look out.

The snow was quite thick on the ground, but the stars had come out in the sky.

A nearly full moon was rising over the trees.

Its light gave the world beneath it a magical ethereal look.

It was difficult to believe it was the Earth and not some spiritual Paradise in which they were the only living creatures.

The Duke walked across the room and put his arms round Lavela.

"When you look away from me like that," he said, "I am half-afraid you will vanish back to where you came from and I shall never be able to find you again."

"You will never lose me now," Lavela said. "I knew when we were being married that we became not two people, but one, and now I am . . a part of you as . . you are a part of . . me."

The Duke kissed her forehead and lifting her up in his arms he carried her to the big silk-canopied bed.

He put her down against the pillows.

She looked across the room to where through the window she could still see the stars.

The Duke joined her and as he took her in his arms she asked:

"Is . . it true . . really true that we . . are here . . together . . and the moon and the . . stars are giving . . us their . . blessing?"

"It is really true," the Duke said, "and I will love you, my Darling, until the stars fall from the sky and the seas run dry!"

Then he was kissing her; kissing her very gently, so as not to frighten her.

Then as he felt her lips respond to his and her body quiver against him, his kisses became more passionate, possessive and demanding.

It was then he knew that the blood was pulsating in his temples.

A fire arose within him because he wanted Lavela to be his.

Yet at the same time his love was different from anything he had ever known before.

He knew, because Lavela was so young and innocent, that he must be very gentle with her and not hurt or frighten her.

He knew too because their love was so perfect that everything he did would be a part of the Divine.

"I love you! Oh God, how I love you!" he exclaimed.

"I feel .. when .. you are .. kissing me," Lavela whispered, "as if the .. stars are .. shining in my .. heart."

"That is what I want them to do."

Then as the Duke kissed her again he felt that he had awoken a response within her.

It was turning the shining stars into little flames of fire.

There was a great deal he had to teach her.

It would make them even happier than they were at this moment.

This he thought was like their Overture in the Theatre.

It heralded a wonder and beauty of something which came from Heaven itself.

"I love you .. oh .. Sheldon .. I love you!" Lavela was saying. "When you .. kiss me .. I feel as if I am .. flying in the .. sky!"

Something broke within the Duke and his kisses became more passionate.

He kissed her eyes, her lips, the softness of her neck and the little valley between her breasts.

Then, as he made Lavela his, he knew that together they touched the stars.

The light from them enveloped them both.

They were no longer human but with God in a Heaven which would be theirs for all Eternity.

Too Precious to Lose

AUTHOR'S NOTE

The discover of the South of France as a resort for the British and which made it eventually the Playground of Europe in the Spring began at Cannes.

It was also said if Cannes was the creation of Lord Brougham then Nice was the discovery of Smollett.

The Author of 'Humphrey Clinker' found there was no English Colony there in 1763 and no English comforts.

But when he had written about it in his travels the great humorist brought it to the notice of the sightseers.

Invalids also thought the mild weather of the Mediterranean would do them good.

That was the beginning, then gradually, year by year, royal personages like the Duke of York spent the Winter there.

A few years later his brother the Duke of Gloucester stayed a few months at a Villa on the other side of the Paglione.

The Royal Dukes having led the way, English aristocrats began to make their own discoveries along the coast.

Beautiful Villas enclosing their own little Eden of semi-tropical vegetation began to appear on the hills.

Numberless paths led into lovely dells bright with wild flowers.

Beyond Villefranche the beautiful village of Beautlieu situated on one of the most sheltered rocks in the Riviera drew visitors like a magnet.

The Marquess of Salisbury built a large pink Villa up above it with magnificent views of the Mediterranean.

To-day, it is difficult to find a place that has not been built on.

But the Villa I describe at Cap d'Estel was actually built at the beginning of the century as a private house.

It has a small 'Cap' of its own with the road high above it and it is on the sea side of the railway.

it has a charm and a mystique all its own.

Although it is now an Hotel what I describe in this novel could easily have happened from the Villa in the past.

Nowadays it is more fashionable to go to the South of France in the Summer where there are sun-bathers and sea-bathers on every rock.

But they cannot spoil the beauty and charm it had at the end of the century.

Then the wealthy aristocrats from all countries including Russia flocked either to Monte Carlo, Nice or Cannes for the sun, and of course the irresistible excitement of gambling.

Chapter One

Norina turned round when she heard a knock on the door.

"Come in," she said.

The door opened and a footman appeared carrying a tray.

He did not say anything, but thumped it down on the table and walked out of the room.

She gave a little sigh. Her mother would never have allowed anyone to be served in such a manner or by so surly a servant.

Her Stepmother chose footmen by their appearance and had filled the house with servants Norina had never seen before. They were obviously not impressed that she was Lord Sedgewyn's daughter.

It would have been unheard of in the past for her to eat in her bed-room instead of one of the other rooms downstairs, even if she had not been allowed into the Dining-Room.

It was her Stepmother who, whenever she could, barred her now from attending the dinner-parties she frequently gave.

Norina knew it was because of her appearance.

"There is nothing I can do about it," she said to herself when she looked at her reflection in the mirror.

It was because she was so lovely that, from the moment her Stepmother set eyes on her, she hated her. It was with a ferociousness which vibrated, Norina thought, across a room.

She was even conscious of it behind locked doors.

When her mother had died two years ago her father had been distraught.

Lord Sedgewyn had adored his wife. She was a sweet, gentle, loving person who wanted everybody around her to be happy.

At sixteen it was very difficult for Norina to know what to do about her father or how to comfort him.

They lived in the country and he therefore went off by himself on long rides, – only to return more despondent and depressed than he had been when he left.

Finally, as if he could bear the house no longer without his wife, he decided he would go to London.

He actually also had an appointment with his Solicitors to discuss the money his wife had left. He told Norina he would be back in two days.

To her surprise, the two days had lengthened into two months, and she had been getting very worried about him when finally he reappeared.

He certainly seemed more cheerful than he had before.

At the same time, she knew that he shuddered every time he passed his wife's bed-room.

But it was less than a week before he said he had once more to go to London.

She realised later that, because she was so young, she had never anticipated for one moment that her father would marry again.

But, five months after her mother's Funeral, he told her that he had asked a very attractive woman to take her mother's place.

Norina could hardly believe what she was hearing.

Yet because her father seemed happier, or rather, less miserable, she said as little as possible.

She hoped that he would find some happiness with his new wife.

Violet Meredith, for that was her name, had been married before.

Her husband, Norina gathered, had left her very little money. She had appealed to her father in a bewildered fashion to help her understand her finances.

When Lord Sedgewyn's six months of mourning was over he married Violet Meredith. It was then Norina realised for the first time that a disaster had happened to her.

Her father was married very quietly.

He went on honeymoon with his new wife, then brought her down to Sedgewyn Hall to meet her Stepdaughter.

Norina thought it would be impossible for her ever to forget the expression she saw in her Stepmother's eyes.

Nor to misunderstand the vibrations of loathing which came towards her.

The new Lady Sedgewyn was, however, too clever to be anything but charming. She told her husband how delightful she found his daughter.

"What a pretty child!" she said in a cooing voice, "but of course, dearest, how could you, being so handsome, have a child who was not in a small way a mirror of yourself?"

It was obvious to Norina that her father was delighted at the compliments his new wife paid him. He was also obsessed by her.

She was perceptive enough to realise that what he felt for Violet was not the love he had given her mother.

She attracted him physically.

She made him feel strong and masculine by her flattery and the caressing manner in which she always spoke to him.

"How can you be so wonderful!" she would exclaim twenty times a day.

She never spoke to Norina without saying:

"Of course, as your clever and brilliant father said . ."

Or:

"Are you not a lucky girl to have such a splendid and understanding father! I only wish mine had been the same."

Norina realised this was a clever act.

She always made herself out to have had a sad, deprived and often cruel life until Lord Sedgewyn rescued her.

She soon learnt to doubt the truth of everything that Violet said. She was therefore quite certain that this was just an act.

What however was not was Violet's determination to isolate Norina as much as possible from her father.

She suggested she should be sent to a Finishing School but Lord Sedgewyn would not hear of it.

"I do not approve of these Schools where they teach girls a lot of new-fangled ideas, and I want Norina with me."

Because he was adamant Violet gave in.

She arranged, however, that Norina had so many Governesses, Tutors and extra lessons of every sort that there was little time for her to be with her father.

Actually, in a way, Norina thought that she benefited by this. Her education was far more comprehensive than any other girl of her age was likely to have.

It was the tradition among the nobility that, while the sons went to Eton, then on to Oxford, the daughters were taught at home,

241

usually it was by a Governess who often knew little more than they knew themselves.

Violet determined that Norina should always be occupied and therefore not an encumbrance to her.

She hardly had a moment to herself except when she was riding.

Fortunately, Violet was not a skilful horsewoman. The only opportunity Norina had of being alone with her father was to ride with him before breakfast.

It was then he talked to her as he had in the old days when her mother was alive.

She knew, although he did not admit it in actual words, he still yearned for the woman he had loved so devotedly.

They had spent some months in the country when Violet had the clever idea that she wished to go to London.

She persuaded Lord Sedgewyn that he should open his house in Park Street. It had been closed for years for the simple reason that he preferred the country and so did his first wife.

Norina was left at Sedgewyn Hall with Tutors and Music Teachers coming every day to give her lessons. She also had an attendant Governess.

She had, too, a French Teacher and an Italian one, a Dancing master and a retired Professor who taught her Literature.

Of all her lessons, Norina enjoyed the Literature lessons most.

The Professor was a very intelligent man, and she found him not only an expert in English Literature but also that of a great number of other countries. He had visited the majority of these at one time or another.

She was in a way happy even though she missed her father. She also found it difficult to adjust to her life without her mother.

A dozen times a day she found herself wishing she had asked her advice on one thing or another. She wanted too to tell her something that she found exciting.

It was actually her Governess who brought her education to an end.

Lord Sedgewyn came down to the country to discuss the Estate with his Manager. Also, to Norina's delight, to be with her.

It was then Miss Graham, who had been with her since before her mother died, said to Lord Sedgewyn:

"I would like to speak to you, My Lord, about Norina."

He smiled.

"You are not going to tell me, Miss Graham, that she has done something reprehensible or that she is not showing the promise that you expected of her?"

"On the contrary, My Lord," Miss Graham said, "I think I should tell you that Norina is now too old and too clever to require a Governess."

Lord Sedgewyn just stared at her while Miss Graham went on:

"I have enjoyed being with her, and in fact she is the most brilliant pupil I have ever had or ever imagined having, but quite frankly, it is time she grew up."

"What do you mean by that?" Lord Sedgewyn asked in a puzzled tone.

"Norina is eighteen years and seven months old but mentally very much in advance of any girl of her age."

Miss Graham lowered her voice before she said softly:

"I think if Norina's mother was alive she would want her to appear in London as a débutante and meet young people of her own age, rather than spend her time with 'old fogies' like me and her other Instructors."

Lord Sedgewyn looked at Miss Graham in consternation.

"I see I have been very remiss," he said. "I had actually forgotten Norina is growing up, and you are quite right, Miss Graham. She must come to London for the Season."

"I hoped that was what Your Lordship would say," Miss Graham answered.

Lord Sedgewyn had been very generous to her. She announced that she was going to take a long holiday before she considered taking another post.

When she left, all the other Tutors were dismissed. Lord Sedgewyn said firmly that Norina was to come to London.

At first she was excited by the idea.

But when she arrived at the house in Park Street she realised how furious her Stepmother was at what had happened.

She had not seen her father and Violet together for a long time, therefore she had not realised how completely his life had altered.

The house in London had been redecorated from top to toe and very extravagantly.

There was a mass of servants Norina had never seen before. Her Stepmother entertained every day and every evening.

It was obvious however that Violet was determined to exclude Norina from any entertainment which took place in the house.

Lord Sedgewyn had arranged that his sister should present her at Court. She was married to the Earl of Winterton.

Through her Aunt, Norina was invited to a number of Balls at which there were other débutantes like herself.

She could not help feeling rather old compared to the other girls. She therefore, did not enjoy the parties as much as she had expected to do.

She also realised that her Stepmother grudged every penny that was spent on her clothes. It did not take Norina long to become suspicious.

She was finally convinced that Violet was not only spending her father's money in an extremely extravagant manner, but also collecting from him every penny she could.

Violet expostulated angrily about what was being spent on Norina. It was then she learnt that the money with which she had been so prodigal had mostly belonged to the first Lady Sedgewyn.

She came to Norina's bed-room where she was reading. One look at her face told Norina that something was wrong.

She had not been given a Sitting-Room, but a fairly large bed-room. There were two arm-chairs and a table on which she could have her meals if she did not go down to the Dining-Room.

Violet crossed the room and, sitting down in one of the arm-chairs, she said:

"I want to talk to you, Norina."

"What about?" Norina asked.

"I have learnt from your father," Violet said in a hard voice, "that your mother was a wealthy woman. Is that true?"

Norina hesitated for a moment.

She wanted to say that she had no wish to discuss her mother or her affairs with Violet.

Then she thought it would be a mistake to be rude.

"If that is what Papa told you," she said, "then of course, it is true."

"Are you telling me that when your father dies the money he has use of now will be yours?"

Norina had read her mother's Will and she knew this was so.

She hesitated before she replied:

"I am not quite certain what the arrangements are, but I am sure Papa will tell you if you ask him."

"Your father has told me, though in a somewhat garbled fashion," Violet said. "I just wanted it confirmed."

"Then there is really nothing I can say," Norina answered.

"I thought when I married your father," Violet said angrily, "that he was a very wealthy man."

"We have always been able to have anything we wanted, Stepmama," Norina said, "but perhaps you want different things from those papa enjoyed before he married you."

"What I want," Violet replied, "is to make sure that I am not left penniless, as I was by my first husband, and I consider it right that your father should, when he dies, settle on me everything he possesses."

She looked at Norina in a hostile way before she added:

"But apparently at least three-quarters of what I thought he possessed belongs to you!"

Norina stiffened before she said:

"Papa is not yet fifty. I cannot imagine, Stepmama, why you should be worried about what happens when he dies."

"That is the kind of idiotic thing a young girl would say!" Violet replied. "But when you are older you will realise that you have to look after yourself and make sure that you are not left desolate, having given somebody the best years of your life!"

She snapped the words at Norina. Then she went from the room slamming the door behind her.

Norina sighed and thought it was very much what she expected.

From the very first moment she had felt that Violet's protestations of love for her father were merely a way of getting what she wanted.

"Why, oh, why," she asked herself, "did Papa marry anyone who was so very different from Mama?"

There was no answer to this. She began to think it might be wise if she suggested going back to the country.

At the same time she knew that her father wanted her to meet the people to whom her Aunt introduced her.

The first two months of the Season passed quickly.

Norina then began to think they might all go back to the country.

245

At least she would then be able to ride with her father early in the morning, as she had before.

"I must suggest this to him," she told herself, "without Stepmama realising the idea comes from me."

She was however finding it very difficult to be alone with her father. Somehow Violet always prevented it.

What was more, Norina realised to her consternation that in the evening he was drinking a great deal more than he had ever done before.

She was quite sure, although she could not prove it, that this was part of Violet's doing.

When dinner was over she knew it would be difficult to have a coherent conversation with him. She would often hear him stumbling along the passage when he went up to bed.

She knew how horrified her mother would have been. She began to pray that somehow she could rescue him from Violet's clutches.

However, she knew despondently it was something Violet would never allow her to do.

She put down her book and walked towards the table on which her dinner-tray was waiting. She thought if her father asked where she was, he would undoubtedly be told 'with friends'.

Even if she tried to see him later it would be impossible. Violet's friends were mostly middle-aged men who drank heavily and would stay until the early hours of the morning.

Then, also, it was unlikely her father would even be aware that she was in the house.

Violet had made it quite clear that she did not want her downstairs to-night.

"Have you not an invitation for this evening?" she asked. She spoke in the harsh voice she always used to Norina unless her father was there.

"No, it is Monday, Stepmama, and there are seldom Balls on Monday."

"Well, I am having a dinner-party and if you are present there will be more women than men."

"Then of course I will have my food upstairs," Norina said.

It was easy to acquiesce politely. Far worse to be told rudely that that was what she would have, whether she liked it or not.

Actually, she had no wish to be with Violet's friends. They either paid her extravagant compliments which infuriated her Stepmother, or else ignored her completely.

She thought they were the sort of men that her father in the old days would have called 'Bounders'.

But he obviously accepted them now because his wife demanded it.

She looked at the tray which had been set down without the footman troubling to put a cloth on the table. Nor had he arranged the dishes that were on it.

There was a small soup tureen, a china plate which had a silver cover and a glass bowl containing fruit salad.

There was a jug of water, a glass and a piece of bread on a plate. It had a pat of butter beside it because there was no room for a butter-dish.

It was not the way anything would have been served, Norina thought, if the new servants had not taken a lead from her Stepmother. They considered her of no importance.

She sat down at the table and as she did so heard a plaintive 'meow'. She realised to her surprise that the kitchen cat must have followed the footman upstairs.

It was a rather ugly ginger cat. It was kept below stairs to catch the mice which always frightened the house-maids.

Now it meowed again, and Norina wondered if it was hungry.

She would not be surprised. The servants were so different from those her mother had employed. They would not be particularly interested in animals of any sort.

In the country there were dogs and cats at home and the servants had been as conscientious in looking after them as they were for themselves.

The cat rubbed itself against her leg and she asked:

"Are you hungry?"

She took the lid off the small tureen of soup as she spoke. She poured it into the plate on which it stood.

It smelt quite edible, if not particularly exciting. She wondered what they were having downstairs in the Dining- Room.

She knew her Stepmother took a great deal of trouble over the dinners she gave to her friends. She insisted on the best and most expensive food.

She also served superb wines which she coaxed her husband into buying.

The cat was meowing again plaintively. Norina lifted the silver cover from the plate and saw the reason.

Fish of some sort had been sent up to her. She thought as she looked at it that it did not look very appetising.

It also had a distinct smell which had attracted the cat.

She wondered whether she should give it a few spoonfuls on another plate.

Then she decided she was not hungry.

"I think your need is greater than mine!" she said with a smile. She put the plate down on the floor.

She then returned to the soup, finishing what was in the pot.

The fruit salad which contained peaches and straw- berries was delicious.

She was sure it was not being served in the Dining-Room. If it was, there would be cream to go with it, and doubtless another pudding as well.

Norina ate the fruit with delight. At the same time she thought that if she was at Sedgewyn she would be able to pick the peaches herself in the greenhouse.

There would be figs ripening on the trees, as well as plums and nectarines.

When she put down her spoon she looked down to see if the cat had eaten the fish.

The plate was half-empty but for the moment she could not see the cat.

Then she realised he was lying in front of the door as if he was trying to get out.

"Do you want to go back to the kitchen?" she asked.

Rising from the table Norina walked towards him.

Only as she reached the animal did she think it was strange he should be lying on his side. As she looked at him she saw his eyes were shut.

A sudden thought struck her and she bent down to touch him. Then she knew without doubt that he was dead.

For a moment she could hardly believe it.

Yet as she made an effort to revive him she knew it was hopeless.

The cat was dead and half what he had eaten was still on the plate by the table.

She picked it up, looked at it and put it down on the tray.

She then faced the answer clearly and calmly – her Stepmother was trying to kill her.

In fact she would have died if she had not given the fish that had been sent up for her dinner to the cat.

At that moment Norina was not hysterical or even agitated.

She felt calm and rather cold. If the cat had not come up to her room she herself would be lying either dead or dying on the floor.

When she was discovered, her Stepmother would have some very reasonable explanation.

Also doubtless she would have a Doctor who obligingly would certify that she had died of a heart-attack.

It was how her mother had died. It would be quite easy to pretend that it was something she had inherited.

Norina went to the window. She stood looking out over the garden at the back of the house.

It was a garden shared by a number of houses in Park and South Street, yet there was seldom anyone in it.

As a child, when she was troubled or unhappy, she would run into the woods for comfort. She thought now even by looking at the trees, the flowers and the green lawn, they would give her the answer to her question.

"What shall I do?"

Everything looked very quiet and serene. Yet the houses on each side of the garden, like sentinels, were imprisoning what lay inside.

It was then Norina started to pray to her mother.

"Help me, .. Mama, .. help me! I do not want to die. If she .. fails this time, .. Stepmama will .. try again. She .. hates me and .. more than .. anything .. else she wants .. your money!"

Norina had been told by the Solicitor that her father had the handling of her mother's money for his lifetime.

If she was not there to inherit it, then it would belong to him, and Violet would be able to obtain it.

"Help me, Mama, help me! I cannot die in such a futile manner!"

She wondered who she could tell.

If she went to her Aunt her story might not be believed. If she went to her father Violet would make quite certain he would believe she was having hallucinations.

She could imagine all too clearly Violet saying in her plaintive voice:

"How can she believe anything so cruel and wicked of poor little me?"

It was the sort of act she could do so well. Naturally her father would have to comfort her.

It was then, almost like a light in the darkness, she remembered there was one person in the house she could confide in.

He was a servant who had been with her father and mother for over thirty years. Dawes was now her father's Valet.

Coolly, not allowing herself to panic, she moved the ginger cat very carefully from the door. She placed him in a corner where he could not be seen.

She carried her tray outside so the footman could collect it from the corridor without having to enter her room.

She wondered how she could speak to Dawes. It might be a mistake to send for him.

Glancing at the clock she realised that, because she had eaten quickly, the guests would still be in the Dining-Room.

She tried to think calmly of what she should do.

Dawes would therefore not have gone to the House-keeper's Room for the meal the servants had when they had finished serving dinner.

She hurried to her father's room praying she was right and Dawes would be there.

She opened the door, and to her relief, he was.

He was a man of over forty who had come to Sedgewyn House first as a knife boy. He had raised himself year by year until he eventually became Valet to her father.

He travelled with Lord Sedgewyn wherever he went.

Norina had therefore seen very little of Dawes since her Stepmother had insisted on going to London.

But she had known him when she was a child and her mother had trusted him. He had always been a very good servant in every way.

As she entered the room he was collecting the clothes her father had worn during the day.

He looked up as she entered and said:

"Good-evening, Miss Norina! It is nice to see you lookin' so well!"

"I want your help," Norina said.

Dawes put down the coat he had over his arm.

"Just like old times, Miss Norina, you comin' to me with one request or another! I misses th' country, an' I knows 'is Lordship does, when 'e thinks about it."

"Please, Dawes, will you come with me? I have something to show you," Norina said.

Dawes put down the things he carried on his arm and walked towards her.

She hurried ahead of him and when they reached her bedroom she opened the door.

Dawes followed her in.

She shut the door behind him and to his surprise locked it.

Then she said:

"I said that I had something to show you."

She walked to where she had put the ginger cat in the corner. Dawes looked down at it in surprise.

"Why, it be Ginger!" he exclaimed. "What's 'e doin' up 'ere?"

"He followed the footman who came up with my dinner," Norina said, "and because I thought he was hungry I gave him the fish to eat and when he had eaten it . . he died."

She spoke quietly. But she felt suddenly as she said the words that she might burst into tears.

Dawes stared at her in astonishment. Then he bent down to touch the Ginger cat.

There was no doubt that the animal was stiffening.

"He ate th' fish, you say, Miss?" he asked as if he was getting it straight in his mind, "which was intended for you?"

"It was . . my dinner," Norina said, "and it was . . poisoned!"

Dawes stood up. She knew by the expression on his face that he understood what she was telling him.

"You have to save me!" Norina said in a voice hardly above a whisper, "otherwise, if I stay here I too will be dead!"

For a moment Dawes did not reply. Then he said:

"Do yer really mean that, Miss? I can't believe Her Ladyship would go so far!"

"She hates me, Dawes."

Dawes scratched his head.

"Her's jealous o' you, right enough. Women be all the same,

an' yer've grown as pretty as yer mother, an' I can't say fairer
than that!"

"It is not only my looks," Norina said. "It is the money Mama
left me. She has only just learnt that, if anything happened to Papa,
it becomes mine."

Dawes' lips tightened. Norina guessed he was not going to
contradict that statement.

"Yer'll 'ave to go to Her Ladyship yer Aunt," he said.

"She will never believe me! You know she will never believe me,
and my Stepmother will insist that I come back. Next time, there
will not be a cat to save me."

"Then what do yer suggest, Miss Norina?" Dawes asked.

She could not bear to stand looking down at the ginger cat that
lay at their feet. She walked towards the window.

After a moment's hesitation Dawes came and stood behind her.

"I shall have to disappear," Norina said finally as if she was
speaking to herself.

"Yer can't go alone, Miss, not without a chaperon."

Norina had already thought of this, and she was silent until
she said:

"Perhaps I could find something to do. I could be a Governess
to small children."

There was silence while Dawes thought this over.

Then he said:

"Yer be too young for that sort of job, Miss Norina, an' too pretty.
Yer'd get into trouble, one way or another, then yer'd just have to
come back."

"There must be something I can do!" Norina said. "I have been
well-educated, as you well know. And I cannot stay here and wait
for my Stepmother to try again."

Dawes was scratching his head, then after a moment he said:

"P'raps, Miss, while yer thinks it over, yer could be a companion to an old lady. Some of 'em likes to have a reader 'cause
their eyes aren't strong enough for them to read for themselves.
And at least yer'd be safe until we can think o' somewhere
better."

Norina clasped her hands together.

"You are right, Dawes! That is just the sort of thing. I could
keep in touch with you and you could tell me what is happening
to Papa. I am frightened for him too!"

"Yer don't suppose His Lordship would believe yer if yer tells him th' truth?"

Norina made a helpless little gesture with her hand.

"Would you have believed me if you had not seen the cat?"

Dawes shook his head.

"I'd 'ave thought yer were a-dreamin', Miss Norina."

"That is why you have to find me somewhere to go .. and quickly!"

She gave a little shudder before she said:

"I will not eat anything in this house unless somebody else has tasted it first."

"Yer'll not go 'ungry as long as I'm alive," Dawes said. "But I agrees with yer, Miss Norina, yer can't stay here, but Gawd knows where we'll find anywhere else."

"Surely there is a place where one engages companions and anyone else who is employed?"

"Course there be," Dawes agreed, "and this lot, 'though some of 'em are a bit queer, all comes from Hunt's in Mount Street."

"Then that is where I will go," Norina said.

"I thinks that'd be a mistake," Dawes said. "I'll go for yer, Miss Norina, an' all yer 'ave to think of is a new name an' produce some references."

"I can write those," Norina said, "and sign Papa's name."

"Then yer do that, Miss," Dawes said, "an' I'll go to Hunt's first thing in t'mornin'."

He paused before he added:

"Yer understands, Miss Norina, it might not be easy to find somethin' suitable right away. Yer might have t'wait, an' while yer're waitin', yer'll just 'ave to be careful."

"I will not eat the food in this house," Norina said, "unless you bring it to me."

She looked at Dawes piteously before she asked:

"You do not imagine she will try to kill Papa too?"

"Not as long as yer're alive, Miss!" Dawes answered.

Norina gave a sigh of relief.

"No, of course .. I had forgotten that. I have to die first so that Papa gets my money. Then she will get it from him! Oh, Dawes, what would Mama say if she was alive?"

Now the tears ran down her cheeks.

"Now, don't yer fret yerself," Dawes said. "Yer've been saved by the mercy of God from a woman as oughta hang by her neck until her's dead! Yer're alive, an' that's the way we're goin' t'keep yer, one way or another."

He spoke in such a determined tone that Norina smiled through her tears.

"Thank you, Dawes, thank you! I knew I could rely on you," she said, "and you know there is nobody else!"

Chapter Two

Norina went down to breakfast when she heard her father passing her door.

She knew her Stepmother would not be called until at least ten o'clock.

As she entered the Breakfast-Room her father looked round.

"Good-morning my dearest," he said. "I missed you last night."

"And I missed you, Papa," Norina replied.

"Your Stepmother said you had a headache," he went on.

Norina did not reply.

She had no wish at the moment to make any trouble. She thought it was the sort of thing Violet would say.

If she had told her father that she had been sent upstairs out of the way he would have insisted that she came to the party.

Lord Sedgewyn was helping himself from the silver entree dishes on the sideboard.

Norina watched him carefully, determined to eat nothing he had not sampled first.

During the night she had thought over what Dawes had said. At least her father would be alive for as long as she was.

"I am not really being selfish in running away," she said, "I am saving Papa's life as well as my own."

She was quite certain now that once Violet had got her money safely into her father's hands he would have a mysterious accident. Alternatively an illness from which he would never recover.

The whole idea made her shudder. But she was determined not to be frightened to the point where she could not think clearly.

She helped herself from the dishes which her father had already sampled. Then she sat down at the table next to him.

As she did so she thought he was not looking as well as he used to.

There were dark lines under his eyes which she suspected were also slightly bloodshot. His voice was thicker and sounded older than it had been in the past.

She wondered if she told him the truth and begged him to go away with her whether he would do so.

Then she knew the whole story would sound to him far-fetched, over-dramatic and theatrical. Her father, who was a very logical man, would not believe her.

He might, however, challenge his wife with the story.

"Then there would be an unpleasant row and I am sure that eventually she would kill me," Norina thought, "perhaps in an even more painful way than she planned last night."

The poison must have been very strong. The ginger cat had died quickly and without making a sound.

Norina wondered from where her Stepmother had obtained the poison.

Then deliberately she forced herself to think of something else.

She talked to her father who said he was going out for the rest of the day and would be in at dinner-time.

"I hope it will not be a late one," he said, "I find it very tiring when people stay until the early hours of the morning."

"It would be nice if we could have dinner together, Papa," Norina said.

He did not reply. She was sure it was because he did not wish to appear unappreciative of his wife.

Lord Sedgewyn ate his breakfast quickly then looked at the clock on the mantelpiece.

"I must be going!" he said. "I have a meeting in half-an-hour with the Prime Minister."

"How exciting, Papa! I am sure you will enjoy it."

"I doubt it," her father replied. "Politicians invariably talk too much and for too long!"

They both laughed. As he rose from the table Norina rose too and kissed him.

"I love you, Papa!" she said, "always remember that I love you very much!"

"You are a good girl, Norina," he said, "and very like your mother."

He left the room hastily and Norina sat down at the table to finish her coffee.

She usually drank tea.

Because her father had this morning poured himself a cup of coffee she had done the same.

When she knew he had left the house she went upstairs.

She looked into his bed-room, but Dawes was not there as she expected. She guessed that as soon as his Master had gone he had hurried to Hunt's Agency in Mount Street.

She went to her own room which had already been tidied, if somewhat perfunctorily, by the housemaids.

Sitting at the small desk which stood in a corner she wrote herself a reference. She thought it would be exactly what was wanted if Dawes found her a position as a Companion.

It was however difficult to say what she could do until she knew what situations were vacant.

All they had really decided last night was the name she would use.

"It be no use yer 'avin' a reference as being good wi' old people," Dawes had said, "if I finds ye somethin' in a Nursery with children."

"No, of course not," Norina agreed.

"I thinks for the moment," Dawes went on, "yer'll have t' take what's available. But yer can't stay here, an' that's a fact!"

"I agree with you," Norina said, "but, please, wherever I go to, make sure they take me at once."

"I'll do me best," Dawes had said. "Now then, what are yer goin' to call yerself?"

Norina hesitated and he said:

"It oughta be somethin' yer can't forget. I've always thought if yer're asked yer name sudden like, yer tells the truth."

"Yes, I understand that," Norina said.

She hesitated, then she said:

"I know! Do you remember that Governess I had for a very short time who married the Under-Manager of Papa's Stables?"

"Aye, of course I does," Dawes replied. "A pretty thing, her was. I never imagined she'd settle down in t'country!"

"Well, her name was Wyndham," Norina said, "and I used to laugh and say we must be half-related to each other, and that is easy for me to remember."

"All right," Dawes said.

He stayed talking to her until he was sure all the staff would be having supper.

Then he wrapped the body of the ginger cat in some old dusters. He carried it downstairs to put it in the dustbin.

He also emptied away what was left of the fish on the plate. The footman had forgotten to collect the tray from outside Norina's bed-room door.

"Careless b'aint the word for these young men," Dawes said, "but 'Er Ladyship likes 'em to be tall an' 'andsome, and yer can't expect 'em t' have brains as well!"

Sitting at her desk Norina tried to remember the references she had read in the past so far as her Governesses were concerned.

She knew however that both her father and her mother believed it was better to use their intuition than to rely on what her father scornfully called "bits of paper".

When Violet had first married her father and they had gone to London, she had heard that they were continually changing the staff.

Butlers had succeeded each other so frequently that in the end her father had said:

"You had better leave the senior servants to me, Violet."

"Of course, if you want it," Violet had agreed sweetly, "you are so clever and so very perceptive. I am sure you will never make a mistake."

Her father had therefore chosen the Butler who was with them now. He had proved to be considerably better than his predecessors.

Norina had the idea that it was Dawes her father had sent to Hunt's to make the preliminary enquiries.

She put down her pen and looked out of the window.

'Please, Mama, let him find me somewhere I can go,' she prayed. "How can I stay here not daring to eat anything in case it is poisoned and wonder all the time what other means she will use to try and dispose of me?'

It was a prayer which came from her heart.

Then because she was frightened she walked across the room. She picked up the miniature of her mother which she always had with her.

She prayed that, wherever she was, her mother would be thinking of her and loving her.

Then like a child she repeated over and over:
"Help . . me Mama . . help me."

Norina had been right in thinking that Dawes had left the house.

He had gone out of the back door at the same time as his Master was leaving by the front.

It was only a short walk to Mount Street. He walked there so quickly that he was breathless when he arrived.

Hunt's Bureau was on the First Floor and he climbed up the stairs followed by a frightened-looking girl. She had obviously just come to London from the country to try and 'better herself'.

The Domestic Bureau consisted of a long room. Prospective servants sat on hard benches just inside the door.

At the far end there was a high desk which was occupied by Mrs. Hunt.

Beyond that was a small room where a would-be employer could interview a servant without being overheard.

Beside Mrs. Hunt's desk, which was large and awe-inspiring, was a smaller one. This was occupied by her friend, who acted as her Secretary.

Mrs. Hunt did not look up as Dawes walked directly across the room to the desk.

Only as he stopped in front of her did she close the ledger in which she was writing.

"Why, it's you, Mr. Dawes!" she exclaimed in surprise.

Dawes politely removed his bowler hat as he said:

"Nice t'see you, Mrs. Hunt, and lookin' as bloomin' as ever!"

Mrs. Hunt, who was approaching sixty, simpered girlishly at him.

"Now, what can I do for you?" she asked. "Don't tell me that last Butler's got the sack, "cause I won't believe it!"

"No, he be all right," Dawes replied.

"Well, that's a relief, at any rate!" Mrs. Hunt said. "I managed to place the last man Her Ladyship said was no good and the Duke of Hastings ain't found nothin' wrong with him!"

She spoke aggressively.

She disliked the senior servants she placed in good positions having to return, especially if they were told they were "not up in their duties."

"Now, what I've come to see ye about," Dawes said, coming to the point, "is a young lady who be a distant relative of His Lordship, an' has asked me to help her find a position as a Companion."

"What would she want with that kind of job if she's a Lady in th' real sense of the word?" Mrs. Hunt asked.

"She's certainly that!" Dawes replied, "I gives you me word on it!"

"The only difficulty is," Mrs. Hunt said, considering it slowly, "that we've no one on our books at the moment looking for a Companion, but there's sure to be one in a week or so's time."

Dawes was disappointed.

"It's like this, Mrs. Hunt," he said confidentially, "the young Lady, an' ever so nice she be, is in straitened circumstances an' can't wait."

Mrs. Hunt put up her hands.

"What can I do?"

"What else you got?" Dawes asked.

At that moment Miss Ackroyd, Mrs. Hunt's assistant, rose to her feet and whispered in her friend's ear.

"I think I might be able to help," Mrs. Hunt said to Dawes.

She looked at him for a moment before she went on:

"Edith has just reminded me that we've got one applicant on our books who wants a Secretary as speaks fluent French, but he's asked for a man."

"Fluent French?" Dawes exclaimed, "Well, the Lady as I'm speaking of speaks several o' them foreign languages, 'though I could never get the hang of them meself."

"I have had only one man apply for the post," Mrs. Hunt said, "and he came back within the hour saying as how his French weren't good enough."

She hesitated before she went on:

"The Gentleman as requires a Secretary is, as I understand it, elderly and blind and therefore the young woman would not care for a place like that, even if he would consider her."

Dawes was thinking quickly and he said:

"P'raps I've misled you. I said as 'ow the lady in question were young, which was somewhat of a figure of speech."

"You mean she's much older?" Mrs. Hunt enquired sharply.

"She be young in heart, Mrs. Hunt," Dawes said, "just like yourself. No one would call you old!"

"Oh, go on with you, Mr. Dawes! You're a flatterer – that's what you are!"

"As it 'appens," Dawes said, "I think the Lady what I'm concerned with be just the right person for an old gentleman as can't see, but is acute of hearing when it comes to French."

"The servant as come here and is French, was very insistent that he required a man."

"Well, give him a chance to say 'no'," Dawes pleaded.

"He'll say it sharp enough," Mrs. Hunt retorted. "The man I sent him yesterday come back like a dog with his tail between his legs!"

"Well, I promise you," Dawes said, "and I swears as I'm speakin' the truth, that the Lady speaks French like a 'Froggy'!"

Mrs. Hunt laughed.

"All right, Mr. Dawes, you win, but if she comes back in tears, don't blame me!"

"I won't," Dawes promised.

"Just give me her name," Mrs. Hunt said, "and I'll make out a card for her to present at the door, an' if the gentleman won't see her, you can only blame yourself!"

"I've taken some hard knocks in my life," Dawes said jovially.

"I'll bet you have!" Mrs. Hunt said meaningfully, "and softer ones too!"

They both laughed.

Mrs. Hunt picked up her white quill pen.

"Now what's this lady's name?"

"I thinks I forgot to tell you," Dawes said, "but she be a widow."

"A widow!" Mrs. Hunt exclaimed. "I thought you was talking about a young girl."

"Her were a widow unexpected like," Dawes explained. "Her 'usband had a nasty accident. Broke 'is neck out ridin', and left her without a penny to 'er name!"

"Poor woman, it must have been a shock!" Mrs. Hunt remarked.

"That it were," Dawes agreed, "and when her turns to me for 'elp, what could I do but try an' 'elp her?"

"You're too kind-hearted, Mr. Dawes – that's wot you are – always takin' other people's troubles on your shoulders!"

"I does what I can," Dawes said with a sigh.

"Well, what's her name?" Mrs. Hunt enquired.

"It's Mrs. Wyndham," Dawes answered, "spelt with a 'Y'."

Mrs. Hunt wrote it down in a somewhat uneducated hand on a card. On it was already printed the name and address of the Bureau.

"My fee," she said, "is 15% of the first three months' wages, which she might remind that Frenchie chap as came here in case he forgets."

"I'll ask Mrs. Wyndham to do that," Dawes said.

He put the card into his pocket and stretched out his hand across the desk.

"Thank yer for all yer help," he said. "I knew I could rely on yer."

"Don't you go 'counting your chickens before they're hatched'!" Mrs. Hunt admonished him, "and if Mrs. Wyndham doesn't get the job, I'll try and find her something else, but it's not easy at this time of the year."

Dawes shook her warmly by the hand and also shook hands with Miss Ackroyd.

Then he walked jauntily back down the room. While they had been talking a number of servants, young and old, had occupied the benches.

Outside in the street Dawes hurried as quickly as he could back to Sedgewyn House.

He wanted to see Norina before Lady Sedgewyn was up and about. She would be doubtless expecting to hear that her Step-daughter had died during the night.

He slipped in by the door in the basement and hurried up the back stairs.

Knocking on Norina's door he entered. She jumped up from the chair in which she was sitting.

"Oh, Dawes, you are back!" she cried. "Have you found a position for me?"

"I have, Miss Norina, but it's not quite what yer expected."

"I will go anywhere .. do anything," Norina said, "even if it means scrubbing floors – rather than stay here."

"I understands 'ow yer feels, Miss Norina," Dawes said in a low voice.

He walked across to the window as he spoke. Norina, after one glance of surprise realised why. He was moving as far away from the door as he could in case they were over-heard.

As she joined him he drew the card from his pocket and handed it to her.

"You *have* found me a place, Dawes!" she exclaimed.

Then she looked at the card and before he could speak said: "*Mrs.* Wyndham?"

"You're a widow, Miss Norina, for the simple reason you're goin' to be interviewed by an old gentleman who wants a Secretary as can speak good French."

"I can do that!" Norina exclaimed.

"He asked for a man!"

"A man!" Norina repeated in a different tone of voice. "Then . . why should he take me?"

"There's no other person for the position at the moment," Dawes said, "an' the old gentleman refused to employ the man they sent him yesterday 'cause his French weren't no good."

"Well, at least I can speak fluent French!" Norina said. "*Mademoiselle*", if you remember, always said I spoke perfect Parisien French."

"I remembers that," Dawes agreed. "But, Miss Norina, you shouldn't stay alone with a gentleman!"

"What harm can it do if he is old and blind?" Norina laughed.

"It's something I can't allow," Dawes said firmly, "so that's why yer has to be a widow."

"But . . what has happened to . . my husband?"

"I tells Mrs. Hunt 'e had an accident out riding an' broke 'is neck.'

Norina gave a little laugh.

"Oh, Dawes," she said admiringly, "how can you have thought of that on the spur of the moment?"

"Well, Miss Norina, it's like this," Dawes replied, "I knows it's goin' to be difficult to find yer anywhere to go 'cause yer're too young an' too pretty, an' even a blind old man'l 'ave friends as will talk."

Norina looked at him with wide eyes.

"Do you mean they would think it improper of him to have a young unmarried girl as his Secretary?"

"It's not exactly – improper for 'im, Miss!" Dawes said, "but they might treat yer in a way yer'd find – embarrassing."

Dawes was thinking slowly. He was obviously finding it difficult to answer Norina's question.

After a moment she said:

"I never thought a Companion would need a chaperon."

"There's Companions an' Companions!" Dawes said enigmatically. "As I tells yer from the beginning, Miss Norina, the only chance yer've got of being employed is if yer be an older woman."

"Then let us hope that the old gentleman will not object to a young widow," Norina said.

Then, as she looked up and saw the expression in Dawes' eyes, she said:

"You are thinking I must pretend to be old."

"Not *old*, Miss Norina," Dawes corrected, "but not so young or so beautiful."

Norina made a helpless little gesture with her hands.

"Then . . what can I do?"

"Well – I were a-thinkin' as I were comin' back to t'house," Dawes said, "that yer used to act them Plays with Miss Graham an' very good yer were in them!"

Norina stared at him.

"Dawes, you are right!" she exclaimed. "If I have to be a Companion who is unhappy because she has lost her husband, then of course I can act the part. I can – of course I can!"

"That's wot I 'oped yer'd say."

Norina's eyes were shining as she looked at him.

She remembered how Miss Graham, who was a very good Teacher, had made her read all the Shakespearean Plays so that they could act out the parts.

At Christmas, to amuse her father and mother they had staged a short play, and it was sometimes written by Miss Graham herself.

Norina would be the lead. Some of the children in the neighbourhood would play the minor roles.

They would enact little comedies, sing and dance, while the servants in the house and on the Estate would be the audience.

Norina had loved every moment of it.

She thought now that she could easily play the part of a widow. No one would ever guess her real age or that she looked very different from how she appeared.

Dawes was watching her with his shrewd eyes.

"I shall need a black gown," Norina said aloud, "and of course a widow's hat with a veil, which is very concealing."

"I thinks too," Dawes added, "yer could wear some spectacles when there's anyone about."

"That is a sensible idea," Norina agreed. "But the first thing is to get my black gown and my widow's hat."

"If we goes out," Dawes said in a whisper, "before 'er Ladyship finds you be alive, yer can say yer wanted something for your father, and I went with you to show you the shop he always patronises."

"Dawes, you are a genius!" Norina exclaimed.

She went hastily to the wardrobe. She picked up her hat and the little jacket that went over the gown she had on.

Her hand-bag was in a drawer as were her gloves.

She started to leave the room. Then she remembered she had been writing her references at the desk in the corner.

She hurried to pick up the piece of paper on which she had scrawled a few words. She would have put it in the waste-paper basket but Dawes took it from her.

"Yer don't want t'leave anythin' incriminating about the place, Miss Norina!"

"No, you are right, Dawes," Norina agreed. "It was stupid of me not to think that anyone who was suspicious might look in the waste-paper basket."

"Yer've got to be watching every move yer make in the future," he warned.

He did not wait for Norina to reply, but opened the bed-room door cautiously.

There was nobody about and they hurried down a side staircase.

As they reached the bottom of it Dawes said in a whisper:

"Wait 'ere a moment, Miss Norina, I've got an idea!"

He left her. She wondered what he was planning until a few seconds later he returned.

She saw then that in his hand he carried a key.

She knew it was the key which opened the door leading into the garden.

"Now, just yer walk across th' lawn," Dawes said, "open the gates at th' far end which'll lead yer into the Mews. Go slow an' I'll be waiting for yer there."

Norina did not argue, but took the key from him and let herself out of the house.

Walking slowly under the trees she stopped occasionally apparently to admire the flowers in one of the beds.

If by any chance somebody was looking out of one of the windows they would assume that she was just enjoying the morning air.

She reached the end of the garden. Quickly she let herself out by the door in the wall which led into the Mews.

She was half-afraid she had arrived there before Dawes. To her relief he was already there and had a Hackney Carriage waiting.

As Norina got into it he told the Cabby to take them to a large Emporium in Oxford Street.

Norina had never been there herself. But she had seen it advertised in some of the Ladies' Magazines.

Only as they drove off did Dawes say:

"I've just thought, Miss Norina – I didn't remind you to bring any money with yer – so how will yer pay for anythin' yer buys?"

"I can write a cheque for the gown," Norina said, "and I have enough money in my purse to pay for the hat. It might seem a strange purchase if I paid for it by cheque."

Dawes looked relieved. Norina guessed that he had felt upset because he thought he had slipped up in his arrangements.

It made her realise that she would need a great deal of money if she was going to disappear for any length of time.

Fortunately on her eighteenth birthday her father had given her a cheque-book.

"One day, my darling," he had said, "your husband will handle your money, but I think it is a good idea, as it is yours, that you should be able to spend some of it without having always to ask someone's permission."

"Yes, of course . . . thank you, Papa," Norina had said.

"You should know how to write a cheque," Lord Sedgewyn went on, "and feel for the moment, at any rate, that you are independent even of me."

Norina had thought that what he was really saying was that her Stepmother would not be able to interfere in anything she spent.

To please him however she merely answered:

"I love having you to look after me, Papa. At the same time, I shall now be able to keep what presents I buy you at Christmas and birthdays a secret!"

Her father had laughed. Norina found he had put a thousand pounds in her name into the Bank.

In fact she had spent very little of the money. When she had come to London her father had insisted that he should pay for the clothes she was to wear as a débutante.

"It is a present to my beautiful daughter," he said.

Norina had been aware that her Stepmother's lips had tightened. There was a flash of hatred in her eyes.

Violet had however praised her husband for his generosity.

"And I am very lucky to have such a lovely Stepdaughter to present to the Social World," she cooed.

Now Norina said beneath her breath:

"If she can act, so can I."

The Emporium boasted it could provide everything a woman might ever want.

It produced a pretty black gown when Norina said she needed one for a Funeral.

She also bought a black coat to wear over it in case it was cold.

At the same time, she realised that black accentuated the whiteness of her skin.

Her hair which was 'gold flecked with fire.' This was how her father had once described her mother's.

When Norina went to the Hat Department she explained that she was buying a hat for a friend who had been bereaved.

She tried on several.

The one she bought had a touch of white on the fore-head. When the fine crepe veil was thrown back off her face she looked a very young and very attractive widow.

Norina did not speak to Dawes while they were in the Department.

He kept very much in the background, and she heard him explaining to anybody who was interested that he was escorting the young Lady because her personal maid was indisposed.

Without him prompting her, Norina was wise enough to realise that she would need black stockings, black shoes and gloves.

On an impulse she also bought a black evening-gown which she saw hanging up as they passed through the Department.

Although it seemed unlikely, she thought it might be useful to have one.

She paid for everything by cheque with the exception of the hat.

Having left the shop she said to Dawes once everything had been placed in the carriage beside her:

"I knew what you were thinking when I was trying on the black hats, and, while I can cover my hair in the day-time, I am wondering what I should do about it in the evening."

"I were a-wonderin' the same thing meself," Dawes admitted, "an' I thinks if yer're accepted for the job I'll 'ave to get yer a wig."

Norina gave a little cry and clapped her hands.

"Dawes, you are brilliant! I never thought of it, but of course a wig is the perfect solution, and as I bought a lot of black ribbon I can tie it where the wig joins my forehead."

"Yer'll still look young, Miss Norina," Dawes said, "so just yer remember to keep them spectacles on yer nose if there be anyone about, man or woman."

He sounded so worried that Norina answered:

"I will do everything you tell me, but I was thinking that one thing is very important. Once I have run away from home I must be able to contact you."

Her voice trembled before she finished:

"I .. I might be in .. difficulties .. and not .. know what to do."

"I was a-thinkin' the same thing meself, miss," Dawes said, "and it'll be quite easy. Yer can write to me care o' Mrs. Rolo who be a relative of mine an' who I've just caught up with, so to speak, since I comed to London."

"Oh, Dawes, that sounds an excellent idea! She need not know who I am, but you must make sure, if she did, she would not betray me."

"I'll tell her nothing," Dawes said, "at the same time, her be discretion itself – I promise yer that!"

Norina gave a little sigh.

"All I have to do now is to get the position, and you have to get me there."

"I was a-thinkin' about that while yer was tryin' on the clothes," Dawes said, "an' if it's all right, I'll take yer straight to Mrs. Rolo, now. It's only round the corner in Shepherd Market where hers got a little shop."

Norina stared at him.

"You mean I can change there into the clothes I have just bought?"

"That's the idea," Dawes agreed, "then I can drive with yer to th' gentleman's house an' wait 'til yer comes out."

"Dawes, you are wonderful" Norina exclaimed.

Mrs. Rolo lived in a small house in Shepherd Market.

She was a large rosy-cheeked woman who Norina thought should be in the country and not in London.

She greeted Dawes with enthusiasm and was very polite to Norina.

"Nice to meet you, Miss," she said. "I've been hearing about you from Andrew, and he tells me how pretty you are, but it were only half the truth!"

"Thank you," Norina smiled, "and 'Andrew,' as you call him, has been very kind to me ever since I was a baby, so I think of him as one of the family."

"I've been telling him he should have a family of his own," Mrs. Rolo laughed, "but, there – he always was one for the girls and won't settle down as he should!"

"What I says," Dawes retorted, "is 'there's safety in numbers,' an' Miss Norina knows as I always speaks t'truth."

When he explained that Norina wished to change her clothes Mrs. Rolo took her upstairs.

The staircase was small and narrow. The bed-room, which Mrs. Rolo explained was there in case any of her relatives wished to stay, was tiny.

At the same time, it was spotlessly clean. Even the windows shone as if they were made of diamonds instead of glass.

Norina changed quickly. When she put on the widow's hat she thought, as she had in the shop, that she looked too young to be a widow.

Perhaps, too, the Frenchman would think her too young to be a Secretary.

She looked at her reflection in the mirror.

Because he was blind the gentleman would not realise that, if she had been married, it could not have been for very long.

When she went downstairs Dawes was waiting for her in the Parlour.

The front room was the shop which contained a large amount of mysterious substances. Some of which were herbs and elixirs which apparently Mrs. Rolo obtained from the country.

"Do I . . look all right?" Norina asked anxiously.

"I thinks this be what yer need," Dawes answered.

He held out a pair of spectacles as he spoke and Norina gave a little cry.

"How have you managed to buy these?"

"I found 'em in one o' the shops in the Market," he said. "They enlarge the sight a bit, but I thinks they'll make yer look older."

Norina placed them on her nose. When she looked at herself in the mirror she laughed.

"Now I look like an owl," she said, "but certainly older."

Dawes was regarding her critically.

"Some of yer hair be showing," he said. "It'd be wiser if yer could tuck it away an' I'll get yer a wig in a different colour from yer own."

"Yes, of course," Norina agreed.

Obediently she pulled her hat lower and tucked her hair underneath it.

Then she drew the veil forward so that it hung over the side of her cheeks.

"That's better!" Dawes approved. "Now I'll get a carriage to set yer down at the corner of Hill Street so that yer'll be able ter walk up to th' house."

Norina understood. Anyone who was poor enough to need a job would hardly be so extravagant as to hire a Hackney Carriage.

Dawes was far more sensible in these matters than she was.

When they reached Hill Street the carriage drew up at the corner where it joined Berkeley Square. Dawes paid off the Cabby.

Then he said:

"It be No. 42, on this side of th' road, Miss Norina. I'll be waiting for yer when yer comes out."

Norina flashed him a smile, then hurried away.

She had no idea that Dawes, watching her as she went, thought how elegant she looked in her black gown.

Her waist was very small. She walked with a grace and an eagerness which made her seem very young.

"I ought not ter be lettin' her do this," Dawes muttered beneath his breath, "but Gawd knows I can't think of any other way her'll be safe from that Devil!"

Norina walked up the steps to No. 42 and raised the silver knocker.

It made a rat-tat that was quite audible in the almost empty street.

Norina waited, feeling it was a long time before she heard footsteps inside.

Then the door opened.

Chapter Three

The door was opened by an elderly man with white hair.

He looked at Norina questioningly. She took from her pocket the card which Dawes had given her and held it out to him.

"I have come from Hunt's Domestic Bureau," she said.

The man took the card and looked at it. Then, leaving Norina standing just inside the door, he walked across the hall.

He disappeared under the stairs and Norina heard him shout: "Mr. Blanc! Mr. Blanc!"

She waited. The house appeared to be well-furnished and obviously belonged to somebody who had money.

A few seconds later a middle-aged man whom she guessed must be a senior Servant or Secretary came hurrying towards her.

He held the card from the Agency in his hand.

As he looked at her Norina thought he seemed somewhat surprised at her appearance.

Then he said:

"I tell . . Agency . . place . . for man!"

His English was halting and he mis-pronounced some of the words.

On an impulse Norina replied in fluent French:

"It is impossible for the moment for them to find a Secretary and a man who is fluent in French. I have therefore come because, as you can hear, *Monsieur*, I speak French and I am an experienced Secretary."

The man stared at her in astonishment.

Then he said:

"You . . wait – I speak – Master."

The servant closed the front door. Although he did not ask her to do so Norina sat down on a hall chair that was against the wall.

She sat upright, holding her hand-bag in her lap. She was praying in her heart that she would be accepted.

If not, Dawes would have to go back to the Bureau and she would be forced to return home. She would not dare to eat anything until Dawes found her somewhere to stay.

She had the feeling that it would be a mistake to ask Mrs. Rolo if she could occupy her spare bed-room.

Norina was sure she would agree.

At the same time, Shepherd Market was too near to her Stepmother, and the servants would obviously shop there.

If she was seen, even her disguise might not be sufficient to prevent them from recognising her.

The Frenchman seemed to be away for a long time.

Then he came back to say:

"You . . come!"

Norina felt her heart leap.

At least she had a chance if the old gentleman was prepared to see her.

The Frenchman walked ahead down a narrow passage and opened a door.

When Norina walked inside she thought he had made a mistake. The room was dark, the curtains drawn over the windows and the only light came from a fire burning in the grate.

Then she saw the man beckoning to her, indicating a chair just inside the door. She guessed it had been put there specially for her.

It was a hard upright chair and she sat down on it.

As her eyes accustomed themselves to the gloom she realised there was a man in the room. He was sitting in an arm-chair directly in front of the fire.

It meant that he had his back to her and she could see only the top of his head.

The Frenchman walked to his side.

"*Madame est ici, Monsieur,*" he said in a low voice.

There was no reply and he walked out of the room, shutting the door behind him.

Norina waited.

At last the man, who spoke in a deep voice, asked:

"*Vous parlez Français?*"

This she knew was her opportunity.

In her very best Parisien French she answered:

"*Mais oui, Monsieur*, I speak fluent French and can write as easily as I speak. I am a proficient Secretary and am used to writing letters on behalf of whoever employs me."

She paused for breath.

There was a silence until the man whom she could not see suddenly started to reply. He spoke with a rapidity which was quicker than anything Norina had ever heard before.

Her Teacher had warned her that the French spoke at a great speed. It was with a sense of relief that Norina realised she could understand every word.

The man in the arm-chair was asking her if she could translate political articles from a newspaper, if she understood the value of French money, and if she had travelled at all in France.

He used difficult phrases and ones that were not used in everyday conversation.

When finally he had finished Norina answered him almost as quickly as he had spoken.

She told him once again how proficient she was and how easy it was for her to translate English into French, or French into English which-ever was required.

When she stopped speaking there was silence.

Then the man sitting in front of the fire said:

"Your French is excellent, *Madame*, but I require a man."

Norina gave a little gasp of sheer disappointment.

Then because it was so important she said pleadingly in a very different tone of voice:

"Please, *Monsieur*, please give . . me a chance . . I promise you I will try to do . . everything that is . . required of me, and it is very . . important that I . . obtain a position . . immediately."

There was a pause before the man asked:

"Why are you in such a hurry?"

"I have . . nowhere to go and I have to . . earn my . . living."

"You mean – you have no money?"

"Very little, *Monsieur*, but what is more important is that I should find . . somewhere to . . stay."

She almost said 'to hide', then checked herself at the last minute.

There was what seemed to her to be a long silence.

Then he said:

"I must explain that I am asking for a Secretary who is completely trustworthy and will not betray anything that I say or do to anybody else."

"Of course, *Monsieur*, that is understood!"

"But – women talk and you are a woman!"

"That is . . something I cannot help, but I . . swear to . . you that if you . . employ me I will be . . completely loyal and would never . . do anything that might . . hurt or . . harm you in . . any way."

She did not quite know why she used those words. She felt perceptively that they were somehow appropriate.

Again there was a long pause before the man said:

"How can I be sure that I can trust you? Because I am blind you will have to read my letters, however private and personal they may be."

"That of course I understand, and if you . . employed a man you would . . expect him to behave . . like a Gentleman. I can only . . promise you, *Monsieur*, that I will . . behave like . . a Lady."

"That is what I am afraid of!"

There was, however, a hint of laughter in the man's voice. It struck Norina that he did not sound as old as she had been led to believe.

Because she felt that she was losing rather than gaining ground she said:

"I do not know . . how I can promise you that . . everything I do for you will remain . . a secret, except if I say that I vow it on . . everything I hold . . sacred."

"Are you a Catholic?" the man asked.

Norina hesitated, then she told the truth.

"I was baptised a Catholic because my mother was one, but because she adored my father and wanted always to be with him they worshipped together in the village Church, and I with them."

"But she had you baptised in her own faith!"

"Yes, *Monsieur*, but I believe God hears our prayers whatever . . label is put on us . . so it is not . . important."

"That is a very interesting explanation!"

Again there was a hint of laughter in the man's voice.

"Please . . please, *Monsieur*, give me . . a chance!" Norina pleaded.

She had a sudden fear that after all they had said he would tell

275

her to go away. She would then have to face the horror of what was awaiting her in her father's house.

It seemed as if a century passed before the man in front of the fire said slowly:

"If I answer that question in the affirmative, how soon could you come to me?"

"Do you .. mean that .. do you .. really mean .. it?" Norina asked.

Now there was a lilt in her voice that had not been there before.

Then as she realised she had not answered his question she replied:

"I can come .. this afternoon, I just have to .. collect my luggage."

"Very well, *Madame*, I will expect you in two or three hours' time."

"Thank you, oh, thank you, *Monsieur*, you are very kind! I can only say .. again that I will never let .. you down and I am grateful .. more grateful than I can put .. into words."

She rose to her feet as she spoke. Before she could step forward to shake his hand he must have pressed a bell.

The door opened and Jean came quickly into the room.

"*Madame* is fetching her luggage, Jean," the man in the chair said, "and will join us in a few hours."

Jean opened the door wider and waited for Norina to leave the room.

She looked back at the top of the head she could just see above the arm-chair.

"*Merci, Monsieur, merci beaucoup*" she said and walked out into the hall.

She followed Jean and he opened the front door for her.

"I am very glad that I am coming back here!" she said in French.

"*Moi aussi, Madame*," he replied.

He bowed as she went down the steps. Then she heard the door shut behind her.

She hurried down the street knowing that Dawes would join her.

It would, however, be a mistake for Jean to realise a man had been outside waiting for her.

Dawes did not come to her side until she was almost in Berkeley Square.

"Yer've got the position, Miss Norina?" he asked.

"I have got it, Dawes! It was difficult and I thought at first he would send me away because I was a woman."

"That's good news, very good news!" Dawes exclaimed, "and when do you start?"

"As soon as I can collect my luggage."

As she spoke Norina realised that that in itself was another problem.

"I've been thinkin' about that, Miss Norina," Dawes said. "I'll go back an' pack yer things an' bring 'em to yer at Mrs. Rolo's."

"But . . supposing my Stepmother sees you and asks questions?"

Dawes drew a watch from his breast-pocket and looked at it.

"It be after a quarter past noon," he said, "an' 'Er Ladyship's attendin' a large luncheon party. She'll be leavin' the house in a quarter-of-an-hour."

Norina gave a sigh of relief.

"Then you can pack everything for me, Dawes, and it had better be everything I possess. It would be a mistake to spend money unnecessarily."

Even as she spoke she gave a little cry.

"Money!" she exclaimed. "I must have some money with me! I have very little in my purse, having paid cash for my hat."

"I thinks o' that, Miss Norina," Dawes said, "and I suggests we go to th' Bank so's yer can cash a cheque. Yer've got yer cheque-book with yer?"

"It is in my hand-bag," Norina replied.

Dawes hailed a Hackney Carriage and they got into it.

He gave the name of Lord Sedgewyn's Bank to the cab-driver and told him it was in Mount Street.

As they drove along Norina drew her cheque-book from her hand-bag.

"Perhaps," she said as she looked at it, "it would be a mistake for me to go inside the Bank. I have been there with Papa."

"I'll fetch out an ink-pot and pen for you, Miss Norina," Dawes said, "and say you've 'urt your foot an' it's painful to walk on."

Norina gave a little laugh.

"So many lies! I am sure you remember, as Nanny always said, one lie leads to another and all lies lead to Hell!"

"That's one place yer're ain't goin', not if I have anythin' t'do with it!" Dawes said stoutly.

When they reached the Bank there was no difficulty.

Dawes, as he said he would, fetched her pen and ink. Norina wrote out a cheque for £300.

"It seems such a lot of money," she said, "but you never know, my Stepmother might instruct the Bank to alert her if I go in for any more."

"Yer keep it well hidden," Dawes warned, "No one will suspect a person who's earning her living to 'ave much money."

As an afterthought he asked:

"Did th' Gentleman say 'ow much he was a-payin' yer?"

"No, and I did not think to ask him," Norina replied.

"I should 'ave reminded yer," Dawes said. "To them as 'as to work money's important."

"I realise that," Norina said, "but I have the feeling he will be generous."

She did not say any more. Yet she felt Dawes was somewhat sceptical, as if he thought she was going to be cheated.

The Hackney Carriage took them back to Shepherd Market. Norina slipped quickly into Mrs. Rolo's house hoping nobody noticed her.

Dawes kept the carriage and drove back to Park Street.

He was too sensible to drive up to the house, and got out at the corner.

Norina had given him the money with which to pay the cab-driver. When she had tried to give him something for himself he refused.

"Yer'll need every penny yerself, Miss Norina," he said, 'an' don't go bein' too generous with it either. They'll expect a woman as is 'ard-up to count th' coppers."

"Then that is what I will do, Dawes," Norina promised. "But do not forget – if you ever need anything – you only have to ask me."

She thought as she spoke that she would much rather Dawes had her money than her evil Stepmother.

At the same time, it seemed horrible that any woman, or man for that matter, would be prepared to kill her just because they wanted her money.

She was touched to find that Mrs. Rolo had prepared an elaborate meal for her.

"How kind of you to take so much trouble!" she exclaimed.

She sat down in the small kitchen which shone as cleanly as the rest of the house.

"I enjoys having someone to cook for," Mrs. Rolo said, "and to tell the truth, Miss, I loves company. I misses me old man more'n I can possibly say!"

"When did he die?" Norina asked.

"Nigh on four year ago! I wept me eyes out every night 'til Andrew come along to cheer me up."

"It is good for him, now that he is in London so much with my father, to have you," Norina said.

"That's what he says," Mrs. Rolo agreed. "But he spends too much time with me, which is kind. I tells him there's plenty of young girls only too willing to 'step into my shoes'."

"I am sure he would rather be with you," Norina said.

She enjoyed her luncheon.

When it was finished Mrs. Rolo hurried into the shop. Norina sat waiting for Dawes to return.

When he did she peeped out of the window. She saw that the Hackney Carriage in which he had arrived was filled with her luggage.

He must, she thought, have remembered everything she had brought with her from the country. This included two or three mauve gowns she had worn as half-mourning for her mother.

They at least might come in useful when she was working for the blind man. He would not be able to see what she was wearing.

"At the same time, I must be careful," she told herself.

As Dawes had said to her – servants talk.

He came into the kitchen and she exclaimed:

"I can see you must have remembered everything! How clever you are!"

"Just as I thinks, Miss Norina," Dawes said, "'Er Ladyship had gone out but it seems she's asked a lot of questions about yer and where yer was."

"What did she say?" Norina asked nervously.

"I thinks," Dawes answered, "although no one else realises it, her was very surprised to find yer weren't lyin' as dead as poor Ginger this mornin'!"

Norina shivered.

"Did she ask where I had gone?"

"Mr. Bolton tells her yer must 'ave slipped out after breakfast as he didn't see yer leave the house. Then he says t'her:

"I 'spects as 'ow Miss Norina's gone to Her Ladyship. I knowed as how she were lunching with 'er to-day."

Norina put her fingers up to her lips.

"Oh Dawes, I forgot! I was supposed to be lunching with my Aunt, and of course I should have let her know."

"Yer leave things as they be," Dawes said. "Yer've got away, an' that's all that matters for the moment."

"Did they not think it strange that you were packing my luggage and taking it away with you?"

"I tells 'em yer was goin' to the country for a few days with some friends, an' yer asked me to pack yer clothes and convey them to Victoria Station."

"Oh, Dawes, did they believe that?"

"'Course they does!" Dawes replied with a grin, "an' when I gets back I'll say as a servant I've never set me eyes on afore comes for yer luggage and I leaves it with 'im'.

Norina laughed.

Dawes' tale was so evasive that it would be a long time before anybody realised she was nowhere to be found.

Yet he could not possibly be held responsible for her disappearance.

"You are very clever!" she enthused, "and you know how grateful I am."

"I don't know what yer'll think of this," Dawes said holding out a paper bag as he spoke.

Before she opened it Norina guessed what it contained.

It was quite a pretty wig of dark brown hair. It was obviously made to be worn on the stage and was curled and elegantly arranged with a chignon at the back.

Norina had taken off her widow's hat while she was having luncheon. Now lifting up the wig she ran to the mirror which hung on a wall.

It was a little tight but it fitted her quite neatly.

If she arranged the black ribbon where the wig joined her forehead, no one would suspect for a moment that it was not her own hair.

It certainly made her look very different. She was sure that even her father would not recognise her if he saw her unexpectedly.

"It ain't bad!" Dawes said with satisfaction.

"It is beautiful, and I look different without being too ugly."

"Yer could never be that, Miss Norina," Dawes said loyally. "But yer don't look like yerself, an' that's a fact!"

Norina arranged her widow's hat on top of the wig, then put on the spectacles.

"The only thing I am afraid of," she said, "is being seen unexpectedly. If I suddenly appear looking like myself I might be turned out of the house for being an impostor."

"Yer be very careful, Miss Norina!" Dawes warned in a serious voice. "And if yer in any trouble yer come right back 'ere to me – d'yer understand?"

"Of course I understand, Dawes, and I will do exactly as you say, but I cannot see myself getting into any trouble of the sort of which you are so afraid."

Dawes shook his head.

"Yer can't trust them there Frenchies," he said. "If the old gentleman 'as a lot o' friends yer keep outa sight. Remember, 'Er Ladyship will be lookin' for yer, an' careless words can cost a man 'is life!"

"Or a woman's," Norina said beneath her breath.

Then with an effort she forced a smile to her lips.

"You have been so wonderful over this, Dawes," she said, "and one day I will be able to tell Papa how kind you have been to me. Promise you will tell me if anything happens to him? And of course warn me if my Stepmother appears to be on my track?"

"Just yer let me know if yer 'as to move on, Miss Norina. That French gentleman might wish to go 'ome."

"I hope he does!" Norina replied. "I shall feel safe if I am far away in France."

"Wherever yer goes yer write t'me 'ere," Dawes ordered. "I'll call round every day t'see if there's a word from yer."

"Thank you for that, Dawes," Norina said. "There is nothing else I can say except 'Thank you' again and again!"

She put out her hand and Dawes shook it solemnly.

He opened the door for her. Quickly, so as not to draw attention to herself she hurried into the carriage.

Dawes gave the Cabby the address and they drove off.

It took them only a very short time to reach the house in Hill Street.

Norina found she had quite a large sum to pay the cab-driver, but she knew, because Jean was listening as he carried in her luggage, it would appear that she had come a long distance.

"I am afraid I have quite a number of trunks with me," she said apologetically, "but I have come up from the country and brought everything I possess."

Jean did not reply.

She thought he looked rather grumpy at having to take so many things upstairs. It involved a number of journeys for both him and the man-servant.

Her bed-room was large and comfortable.

Her trunks had been piled against one wall. She sat down in front of the mirror and very carefully removed her hat.

She also took off the small jacket which went with her gown.

Very neatly she arranged the black ribbon so that it concealed the edge of the wig at the hairline.

She felt she was looking at a stranger, but at the same time she looked older.

Just as she was wondering what she should do next, there was a knock on the door.

Quickly she put on her spectacles before she crossed the room to open it.

Jean was standing outside.

"The Master wishes to see you, *Madame*," he said in French.

It was an improvement on his very bad English and Norina replied:

"I will come at once. If he requires me to write any letters for him I am afraid I shall need ink and a pen which I do not have with me."

"I will see to it, *Madame*," Jean replied.

She followed him down the stairs.

When he opened the door of the room she had been in before she saw to her relief that the curtains were drawn back. The sunshine was shining through the windows.

The arm-chair in which the blind man had been sitting had now been moved from the front of the fireplace to the side.

For a moment Norina stood just inside the door taking in her surroundings.

Now for the first time she was able to see the man who had employed her.

One quick glance told her that he was quite different from what she had expected.

His eyes were heavily bandaged and she could not see above the end of his nose.

She realised however now that she could see his mouth and chin that he was not, as she had understood, an old man.

She had seen the top of his head, but now she realised he had thick dark hair. It was brushed back from what, when it was not bandaged, should be a high forehead.

He was tall and certainly more broad-shouldered than she would have expected of a Frenchman.

He sat in his chair with his legs crossed. She had the impression that he was in fact slim and athletic.

Jean went out of the room shutting the door. Feeling unexpectedly a little shy, Norina moved forward.

"So you have come back!" the Frenchman said, "and bringing, I understand, a mountain of luggage with you."

"I must apologise for having so much," Norina replied, "but you will understand, *Monsieur*, that I am at the moment travelling with everything I possess, until I find somewhere permanent to settle down."

"And you really think that will be with me?"

"I . . I am hoping . . so," she answered.

"I was thinking when you left," the Frenchman said, "that I had been somewhat remiss in not making it clear that if I find the right type of man to take your place I shall ask you to leave."

Norina drew in her breath.

Then she said:

"I can only hope, and perhaps pray, that it will be a long . . time before . . he turns up like the proverbial 'bad penny'."

She said the last words in English and the Frenchman laughed.

There was a silence and Norina wondered if she could sit down.

Then he said:

"I have some work for you to do. Look on the desk. You will find some letters there".

Norina walked to the desk which stood in front of the window.

There was a pile of letters which she realised must have accumulated while he had been blind.

She picked them up and went back to the fireplace.

"I have found them, *Monsieur*, and there are quite a number."

"You will have to read them to me," the Frenchman said, "but do not bother with the bills, just the invitations and the private letters."

Norina sat down in the chair opposite him where there was a small table beside her.

She quickly sorted out the bills and put them down on it.

There were a number of envelopes she knew immediately contained invitations.

They looked like the ones she had opened for her Aunt. She even thought she recognised the hand-writing on some of them.

She went back to the desk for a letter-opener. She found it had a gold handle and was engraved with a monogram.

Norina realised she did not yet know her employer's name. She wondered if she should ask him what it was.

Then she told herself she need only open one of the invitations to find it inside.

She slit open an envelope then saw what she knew must be his name on top of the card:

Le Marquis de Charlamont

For a moment her eyes widened.

She had not expected her employer, who had taken her on in such an unusual manner, to be so distinguished or of such importance.

"There is an invitation here, *Monsieur*," she said aloud, "from Lady Heatherton for dinner the day after tomorrow."

There was silence before the *Marquis* said:

"See what other invitations there are. I will tell you how to answer them."

Norina opened four more invitations.

Two were for dinner-parties, two were for Balls to which he was invited and asked to dine first.

She put them in a neat pile also on the side-table.

Then she said:

"There are two letters here, *Monsieur*, and both appear to be in the same hand-writing."

She saw the *Marquis's* lips tighten before he replied:

"Then of course as I cannot read them myself, you will have to read them for me."

The tone of his voice told Norina that he very much disliked anybody reading what had been written personally to him. There was however no alternative.

Norina opened the first letter, realising as she did so that it was scented with an exotic fragrance.

She started to read the first line, then paused to say a little nervously:

"This is a very private letter, *Monsieur*. It is written in English. Would you like me to read it in that language, or would you prefer it in French?"

For a moment the *Marquis* did not reply.

Then he said harshly:

"Read it as it was written to me!"

Norina felt she would have rather translated it into French. But she could only obey his orders and she read aloud:

"My Dearest Adorable Alexus.

I cannot tell you how deeply distressed I am at what occurred last night. How could I have guessed for one moment that Hugo would come home unexpectedly and find you here?

He was very angry and told me he had taught you a lesson. I do not know what he meant but if he has hurt you, I shall be very upset.

I love you – I love you, Alexus, and how could I have guessed when Hugo said he would not be back until the early hours that he would return so quickly?

I know it was wrong of me to deceive you into thinking he would be away all night, but I longed to see you. I wanted your kisses, your arms around me, and to know that you love me as I love you.

Oh, Alexus. I must see you again! I cannot live without you and I cannot bear to think that you might be angry with me.

Write to me and send the letter care of my maid as you have done before, and remember, I shall be waiting . . waiting and counting the hours until once again I can be in your arms.

Yours Adoringly.

Patsy."

Norina finished reading the letter and looked across at the *Marquis*.

She had been aware while she was reading that he was very angry.

She could feel the vibrations coming from him were those of fury.

Because she felt embarrassed she remained silent as she replaced the letter in its envelope. Then she opened the other one that had lain on her lap.

When she unfolded the letter she knew she had been right in thinking it came from the same person.

As the *Marquis* still did not speak she said:

"Here is the . . second of the . . two letters."

She read aloud:

> *Beloved Alexus,*
> *Fantastic. Wonderful news! Hugo is going to the Doncaster Races to-morrow!*
> *I have questioned the friends with whom he is staying to make certain there is no mistake.*
> *Oh. My Darling. This is my chance to see you again! Come to me! Come to me!*
> *I shall be waiting at the garden-door at ten o'clock. I love you and I know I shall die if you disappoint me!*
> *Patsy."*

Norina's voice died away and she put the letter back in its envelope.

"That is all, *Monsieur*," she said.

I can feel your condemnation without you expressing it!" the Marquis remarked

"I . . I am sorry, *Monsieur*, if . . that is the . . impression I have given . . you," Norina replied.

"You sounded shocked and very disapproving," the *Marquis* remarked accusingly.

"But not . . particularly of you," Norina said impulsively.

"Then of whom?"

Norina thought it would be a mistake to answer the question. Yet just as she might have discussed the subject with her father she said:

"I suppose I am . . shocked that any woman who is married . . should be so . . blatantly unfaithful to . . her husband."

There was a twist to the *Marquis's* lips as he said, and his voice was bitter:

"Then you must have been living in the country, for you obviously have little knowledge of London."

"It is not .. the sort of .. knowledge I wish to .. acquire," Norina answered.

"I suppose by now you can understand what happened?" the *Marquis* said.

It was a question and Norina replied:

"Did the .. husband of the .. Lady who has .. written to you .. hurt your eyes?"

She thought as she spoke she was being rather brave in asking such a question.

"He fired at me with a shot-gun." the *Marquis* replied. "I was fortunate in that I was wearing an over-coat and hat, which received the majority of the pellets. However a number embedded themselves around my eyes and to save my sight the Doctors have insisted that I keep them bandaged for quite a long time."

Norina stared at him.

This was something she had never anticipated might be the reason for his blindness. In a voice he could hardly hear she said:

"He .. shot at you .. even though .. you were .. unarmed? I cannot believe .. anyone who was .. a Gentleman could .. do such a thing!"

"The man in question will tell you he is a Nobleman and therefore does not have to behave like a Gentleman!"

"I think it is .. utterly disgraceful!" Norina said, "and if it was .. known he would be .. turned out of his Club .. and no .. decent man would .. speak to .. him."

"I can see, *Madame*, you have an idealistic view of how English Gentlemen behave but I am afraid when it comes to jealousy they are as *gauche* as any *gamin* in the back-streets of Paris!"

Now the bitterness in the *Marquis's* voice was unmistakable.

Norina clasped her hands together.

But if the Oculist .. says you will .. get well – surely it is .. only a .. question of .. time?"

"Yes – time," the *Marquis* said. "but I have no intention of being laughed at and sneered at for trusting a woman who was quite obviously untrustworthy!"

"Then .. what can you do?" Norina asked.

"I will leave to-morrow for Paris," the Marquis said. "Are you prepared to come with me?"

"Yes .. yes, of course," Norina agreed.

"Then answer the invitations formally by saying:

287

"*Le Marquis de Charlamont* thanks you for your kind invitation, but has had unexpectedly to return to France owing to the illness of one of his relatives.'

"A . . and the . . letters?" Norina asked.

"Tear them up throw them in the fire and let her wait!" the *Marquis* answered.

Now the venom in his voice was unmistakable.

As Norina did as he told her she thought she could understand exactly what he was feeling.

A woman had treated him as treacherously as she had been treated by Violet.

The flames devoured the two letters she had flung into the fire. As they did so. Norina wished she could destroy in the same way the ties which bound her to her Stepmother.

"They are . . both utterly . . despicable!" she told herself.

Chapter Four

Despite the *Marquis's* resolution to escape from London, they were not able to leave until the next day.

The Courier who was engaged to arrange the journey explained that it would be impossible, at such short notice, to obtain cabins on the Cross-Channel Steamer.

Nor, he pointed out, for the French to attach the *Marquis's* private coach to the Express train to Paris.

Grudgingly the *Marquis* conceded that he would wait another day.

He gave strict instructions to Jean that nobody was to know that he was still in residence.

Norina, by this time, had learnt that the house belonged to Lord Winterburn, who was a friend of the *Marquis*.

He was abroad and had lent him the house while he wished to remain in London.

The man-servant was also the Caretaker and his wife the Cook.

Surprisingly Norina found the food delicious. She discovered that most of it had been prepared by Jean.

She had expected to eat alone, but when it was time to dress for dinner the *Marquis* said:

"If you dine with me I can go on discussing any further business there is to be done."

He said it sharply almost as if he resented the fact that she would be with him.

However, Norina only answered quietly:

"*Merci, Monsieur.*"

She thought with a smile of amusement that the black evening-gown she had bought would come in useful after all. Although of course the *Marquis* would not be able to see her in it.

It was in fact very becoming. More so, she thought, than the white gowns she had worn as a débutante.

She wondered a little wistfully if she would ever wear those again.

It was depressing to think of the large amount of money her father had expended on her.

It reminded her again that she must be very careful with what she possessed. It had to last for a long time.

She was already afraid that when they arrived in Paris the *Marquis* would dispense with her services.

Then she would have to look around for other employment as well as a place to stay.

As if she was talking to her father she said to herself:

"It is always a mistake to be frightened by a fence before one has to jump it. I shall just have to wait and see what turns up."

It was a relief, at any rate, to know she could eat everything that was served at the table instead of being afraid she was being poisoned.

It was difficult to think of what had happened last night without feeling a sense of panic sweep over her.

Then she told herself that she had to behave calmly and coolly. It was what her mother would have expected.

Lady Sedgewyn had often said to her:

"Royalty always behaves with dignity in public. They do not cry at Funerals or at any other time, and they keep themselves strictly under control, even if they are shot at or bombs are dropped near their carriages."

Norina was aware that Queen Victoria had behaved with great bravery when a young man had shot at her in the Park. She told herself that one could not be certain of anything.

Even the *Marquis*, who she was sure was a most unlikely person, had been shot by a jealous husband.

It was impossible to think of a worse punishment than to be blinded for life.

At dinner the *Marquis* talked quickly and dispassionately on a number of subjects. None of them were in the least personal.

Fortunately, Norina was used to discussing Political and International Affairs with her father. She did not therefore feel at a loss with the conversation.

In fact she surprised the *Marquis* with her knowledge of recent events in France.

She thought with a little smile that he was unlikely to suspect her of being as young as she actually was.

Dinner was not a long meal. The *Marquis* had everything cut into small pieces by Jean.

He ate elegantly. She knew he was determined to appear as natural as possible.

When dinner was finished she retired to bed because she was in fact very tired.

When she took off her wig she brushed her hair, said her prayers, got into bed and fell asleep almost immediately.

Norina was woken by the woman who was married to the man-servant pulling back the curtains.

"Breakfast 'll be ready in 'alf-an-'our, Ma'am," she said.

She left a can of hot water on the wash-stand and went from the room.

Norina wondered if she had noticed her hair. Then she remembered that she had not seen her before and would therefore not be surprised.

She however fixed her wig very carefully. It would be disastrous if the *Marquis* was told she was disguising herself in any way.

At breakfast he said very little until they had finished.

Then the Courier who had been given instructions the previous day came into the room.

"I thought I should tell you, *Monsieur le Marquis*," he said very politely, "that I have managed to engage the two best cabins aboard the Cross-Channel Steamer, and have received this morning a telegram from France to say that your private coach will be attached to the afternoon train."

"Thank you," the *Marquis* replied. "You made sure that no one was aware of my identity?"

"I booked the accommodation at Victoria and in the Steamer in the name of *le Comte de Soisson*."

"Very good," the *Marquis* replied.

The man bowed and left the room and the *Marquis* said as if he was speaking to himself:

"The difficulty now will be for me to board the Steamer without anybody noticing me."

Norina thought, then she asked:

"Might I make a suggestion?"

"What is it?" the *Marquis* asked.

"Because you are tall people are bound to notice your bandage, but, if you were in a wheel-chair, people will merely think you are an old man."

"That is a very intelligent suggestion," the *Marquis* remarked. "I cannot imagine why I did not think of it myself."

He sent Norina quickly to find out if the Courier had left the house. Fortunately he was still there.

The *Marquis* explained to him what he needed. The Courier said he would arrange for a wheel-chair both at Dover and Calais.

The *Marquis* then allowed Norina to lead him to the Study where a large number of letters had arrived by the morning post.

There were invitations, which the *Marquis* ordered to be answered in the same way as those of yesterday, and circulars.

Norina had been given a small room off the hall as an office.

She was about to go there when Jean came into the Study with a note on a silver salver.

"What is it?" the *Marquis* asked.

"A note, *Monsieur*," Jean replied, "delivered by a groom."

The *Marquis* stiffened.

Jean, without being told, passed the silver salver to Norina.

She saw at once that the note was written in the same hand and on the same writing-paper as the two letters she had burned yesterday.

She waited until Jean had left the room before she said:

"I think *Monsieur*, this letter comes from the Lady who waited for you last night. Do you wish me to read it?"

To her surprise the *Marquis* asked:

"What do you suggest?"

She looked at him wondering if he really wanted to know her opinion.

Realising he was waiting, she said after a moment:

"Let me . . throw it on . . the fire. It will only . . hurt you to think of . . what happened, and the . . sooner you . . forget it the better!"

"Do you really think I can forget that I am blind?" the *Marquis* asked.

"You are not *permanently* blind," Norina insisted, "you are only inconvenienced by not being able to see as clearly as you would wish to do."

She spoke impulsively and the *Marquis* said:

"Why should you be so sure that my sight will not be impaired?"

"It is something I feel so strongly that I know I am correct in saying that within a few weeks you will be able to forget that this ever happened and just be yourself again."

The *Marquis* smiled.

For the first time it was not the bitter, cynical smile that had twisted his lips yesterday.

"You certainly think in an original way, *Madame*," he said, "and you are encouraging me to be optimistic."

"You would be very stupid to be anything else," Norina replied. "If your eyes really were badly damaged with no hope of recovery the Oculists would have told you so when they first examined them. It is therefore only a question of patience, which is irksome but not soul-destroying!"

The *Marquis* gave a short laugh.

"Thank you, Mrs. Wyndham. You are very wise!"

It was an hour later that the Oculist called. When Norina knew he was in the house she prayed that she had not been over-confident.

When she learned that the *Marquis* was alone she went to his Study. She could not wait to know the verdict.

He was sitting in the window in the sunshine and as she crossed the room he said:

"Have you come to ask whether you were right or wrong?"

"Of course I have," Norina replied. "You did not send for me and I could not bear to sit worrying until I knew the truth."

"I am flattered that you should be so interested," the *Marquis* said, "and I am delighted to tell you that you were right. But the Oculist insisted that I continue to wear the bandage."

Norina clasped her hands together.

"That is good news . . very good . . news!" she cried, "and I am thrilled to know that you will soon be well."

"Then, of course, I will be able to read my own letters," the *Marquis* said.

Norina was suddenly still.

"Are you . . saying," she asked in a very small voice, "that it is . . unnecessary for me to . . come with you . . to France?"

"Would it upset you to be left behind?" the *Marquis* enquired.

"Please, take me . . with you . . oh . . please do! I cannot explain . . but it is very . . important that I . . leave London!"

As soon as she spoke she realised she had made a mistake, for the *Marquis* said:

"Tell me why. I thought yesterday that your desire to stay with me was rather strange, but now I find it even stranger that you should wish to leave your own country."

There was silence. Then Norina answered:

"Please . . do not think me rude . . but I . . cannot answer . . that question."

"You are in trouble," the *Marquis* said. "But I thought your husband was dead."

"He is . . I am a widow . . I am wearing mourning . . for him."

"Then if you are not hiding from your husband – who is it that has frightened you?"

Norina made no reply and the *Marquis* said:

"I know you are frightened! I can hear it in your voice and although I am not touching you I could swear that you are trembling!"

Norina walked a little nearer to the window so that she could look out at the sunshine.

She did not speak and after some seconds the *Marquis* said:

"I think you owe me an explanation."

"It is . . something I . . cannot explain," Norina answered, "please . . be understanding and just . . accept me as a competent Secretary and . . Reader."

She looked hastily round the Study. The morning newspapers were lying on a stool in front of the fireplace.

"I am sure," she said desperately, "that you would like me to read the newspapers. If I read you the headlines you can tell me which stories you would like me to read further."

"You are running away," the *Marquis* said, "but you have made me curious and of course, as I cannot see I shall have to use my perception, or what you might call my 'Inner Eye' to find out what is worrying you."

"Perhaps that is something which will keep you occupied,"

Norina said, "and when you do learn the answer you may find it disappointing."

"I feel that is unlikely," the *Marquis* replied.

Norina picked up the newspapers and started to read some of the headlines.

At the same time, she was no longer trembling. It was obvious that the *Marquis* was taking her with him to France.

The *Marquis* and Norina left early in the morning.

In case there was anyone on the platform who might have seen her at a party or a Ball, Norina covered her face with her black veil.

She did the same when they arrived at Dover.

The *Marquis* in his wheel-chair was lifted on board the steamer with Jean pushing and the Courier pulling the chair.

The *Marquis* was wearing an overcoat, the collar of which he pulled up over his chin. His hat came down to cover his face.

Norina followed discreetly behind. She thought that none of the passengers there were in the least curious about an elderly man in a wheel-chair.

All they were concerned with was hurrying aboard and taking the best seats.

She was delighted to find that she had a small, quite comfortable cabin to herself.

The *Marquis* was next door and there was only one other private cabin on the Steamer.

There was a strong wind and the sea was choppy even before they left the harbour.

Norina was not certain whether or not she would be a good sailor. She decided not to take any chances.

She therefore took off her hat and lay down on the bunk.

When they left the harbour the sea was very rough.

She found her wig which, as she had told Dawes when he brought it to her, was tight. It was so restricting that it gave her a headache.

She therefore took it off to lie down with her eyes closed.

The Steamer pitched and rolled. While at first she was afraid she would be sea-sick, she unexpectedly fell asleep.

*   *   *

Norina was awakened by the Courier knocking on the door of the cabin and calling:

"We are in harbour, Mrs. Wyndham, and will be going ashore in a few minutes!"

Norina jumped up hastily.

She had been dreaming that she was on the swing which her father had tied between two trees when she was a little girl.

Quickly she put on her hat and coat. She was just ready when Jean came in to collect her hand-luggage.

"I am taking *Monsieur* ashore first," he said.

Norina thought it a good idea that they should board the train before the other passengers disembarked.

This was obviously the *Marquis's* idea.

He was pushed at a tremendous pace along the Quay and on to where the train to Paris was waiting.

His private coach was at the very end of the train. Norina following him thought there would be no prying eyes to recognise them.

She had never seen a private coach before.

The *Marquis's* was obviously very comfortable. It had deep arm-chairs and small tables in front of them on which a meal could be served.

There was a Pantry and, as she was to discover later, two bed-rooms. Besides a convenient amount of room for the luggage.

Once they had seated themselves Jean produced a bottle of champagne.

"I feel this is something we both need," the *Marquis* remarked, "after that very unpleasant crossing."

"I luckily missed it," Norina said, "because I fell asleep!"

"Then you are certainly a better sailor than most women!" the *Marquis* remarked dryly.

Norina had drawn the veil back from her face.

As she lifted the glass of champagne to her lips she thought she might as well take off her hat. She wanted to be comfortable for the long journey to Paris.

It was then, to her consternation, she realised she had forgotten to replace her wig.

Having taken it off she had put it down on the berth on which she was lying.

When she got up so hastily she must have thrown the rug which covered her over it, forgetting it was there.

There was nothing she could do.

She hoped that Jean would not mention to the *Marquis* that she had suddenly changed the colour of her hair.

"Perhaps he will not be aware of it," she consoled herself.

At the same time, it was extremely annoying after Dawes had gone to so much trouble in procuring the wig.

It was however impossible not to be excited when the train moved out of the station. She was seeing France for the first time.

At first there were the well-cultivated fields which looked very similar to their English counterparts.

Then there was the wide open land.

The broad hedges and the great forests seemed enormous enough to contain the dragons which as a child she had believed lurked in them.

She thought the *Marquis* might be interested to know what they were passing. She therefore detailed to him what she was seeing.

"There is a very unusual Church," she exclaimed "with two spires, and I am sure it must be very old. There is what looks like a Convent or a Monastery on one side of it."

There were picturesque little hamlets that delighted her. Also the long roads with their sentinel-like trees on either side.

She described everything she was seeing quite naturally to the *Marquis*. She thought it was a mistake for him to sit brooding over his blindness.

Finally, when darkness fell, Jean brought them their supper from the Pantry. It must have been ordered by the Courier before they started on their journey.

It seemed to Norina to be delightful. But the *Marquis* complained about the soup and was not as enthusiastic as she was over the pâté.

"I believe the best cheeses come from Normandy," she said after they had finished a main dish of chicken.

"Who told you that?" the *Marquis* enquired.

"I expect it was my father," Norina replied, "but I have read a great deal about France, and I cannot tell you how exciting it is for me to be here!"

"I am sorry I cannot show you Paris," the *Marquis* said, "and of course, you will not be able to wander about by yourself."

"Why not?" Norina asked in surprise.

"Because, Mrs. Wyndham, you are a woman, and I gather, even with your spectacles, a very presentable one!"

"Did Jean . . tell you . . that?" Norina asked. "I am . . flattered!"

"How old are you?" The *Marquis* asked unexpectedly.

Norina drew in her breath.

This was an important question which she knew she would have to answer intelligently.

After a moment she said:

"As a woman you will understand that I do not willingly reveal such personal information about myself, but shall I say we are perhaps, *Monsieur*, somewhat of the same age."

"I shall be thirty next birthday," the *Marquis* said, "which I am sure you will think very old."

"I have always been told," Norina said, "that forty is the youth of old age and the old age of youth!"

The *Marquis* laughed.

"Was it a Frenchman or an Englishman who said that?"

"I am not certain, but I think that a Frenchman would be too polite to probe deeply."

"I stand corrected!" the *Marquis* said, "but as we have nothing else to talk about, tell me a little about yourself. To begin with, what is your Christian name?"

Norina had already thought of the answer to this. She had decided it might be dangerous to call herself Norina.

At the same time, she did not wish in an unguarded moment to forget what she had decided her name would be.

She therefore replied "Rina", knowing that was a name that would not slip her mind.

"Rina!" the *Marquis* repeated pensively. "And now tell me about your husband. Did you love him very much?"

"Of course," Norina said quickly, "but I do not want to talk . . about him . . or about . . myself."

"Now you are being difficult again," the *Marquis* said. "I am trying to create a composite picture of you in the darkness of my mind, and I think the least you could do would be to give me some clues. Even in a Paper Chase the runners can look for the paper!"

"That makes it too easy!" Norina objected, "and you will just have to find out for yourself."

She bent forward as she spoke to draw back the curtains over the windows. She looked out into the darkness.

"The stars are coming out," she said, "and the little hamlet we are passing has lights in practically every window. It is very romantic!"

"Is that what you are looking for?" the *Marquis* asked, "another romance?"

He did not wait for her answer, but went on:

"Of course you are! Love is what every woman wants, and they feel if they do not find it there is something wrong with them."

"I think the love you are talking about, *Monsieur*," Norina said coldly, "is different from the love that I have known in my life."

"Tell me about it," the *Marquis* said.

Norina was thinking of her father and mother as she said:

"Real love, which as you say, is what all women want – is the companionship of the mind, the heart and the soul."

"And what about the body?" the *Marquis* enquired.

"It is everything, and that of course is important, but what really matters is that a man and a woman look for the other half of themselves, and if they find it then they are blissfully happy for ever."

"It cannot be for ever," the *Marquis* said, "but only until one dies."

Norina shook her head.

"I am quite certain," she said, "that if two people really love each other then they will be together for eternity. When they are born again they will not be apart, but will find each other as they did in this life."

"That is the Buddhist theory rather than the Christian," the *Marquis* observed.

"I do not think it matters what it is called," Norina said, "but in Life there cannot be Death."

There was silence for a moment.

Then the *Marquis* said:

"So you are quite certain that is the truth and you will find your husband again?"

Again there was silence.

Norina had not been thinking of herself, but of ideas of love she had read about. It was the way her mother had loved her father.

Yet she was wondering as she had a million times before how

her father could possibly have married Violet and put her in her mother's place.

It hurt her agonisingly to think of it, so that for a moment she forgot that the *Marquis* was waiting for an answer to his question.

Suddenly he said:

"What is hurting you? Why are you so unhappy? I can feel it as if it was a wave sweeping over me."

Norina was startled.

"You are reading my .. thoughts!" she said, "and that is something you must .. not do, and I am .. sure you would not do .. if your eyes were not .. bandaged."

"I thought you approved of me using my 'Inner Eye'," the *Marquis* said.

"But not where I am concerned!"

"Then for what else?" he enquired. "We are alone together and it would be very boring if we could not talk about fundamental interests rather than stocks and shares!"

Norina laughed.

"I have no wish to talk about them!"

"Surely you are interested in money?" the *Marquis* asked. "And do you realise that you have never asked me what salary I intend to pay you?"

Norina remembered how Dawes had told her that was what she should do.

"It was foolish of me," she admitted, "but it did not seem to .. matter, apart from the fact that you were taking .. me .. away from England."

"I am still waiting to hear what 'Big, Bad Wolf' is frightening you!" the *Marquis* remarked.

Norina thought that Violet was hardly a "Big, Bad Wolf". She was more like a poisonous snake slithering along the ground and making it difficult for her victim to escape.

"But you have escaped!" the *Marquis* said.

Norina gave a little cry.

"Now you are reading my thoughts again and it is not fair! I shall shut my eyes and see if I can read yours!"

"I am delighted for you to do so," the *Marquis* said, "and shall I tell you that I am finding this journey far more interesting and definitely more amusing than I expected?"

"Thank you," Norina said, "and it is only fair that you should enjoy it when I am thrilled with every mile as we draw nearer and nearer to Paris."

The *Marquis* did not speak for a little while.

Then he said:

"I am wondering if I am making a mistake."

"About what?" Norina enquired.

"In going to Paris," he said, "I wanted to escape from London because I could not bear to have anybody knowing what happened to me. But the same applies to Paris. It would be a good story to know that 'The Wicked *Marquis*' has got his 'just deserts' at last!"

"The Wicked *Marquis*?" Norina repeated. 'Is that your reputation?"

"It is," the *Marquis* admitted. "I am well aware of what people say about me, and as I find beautiful women irresistible, there are always jealous husbands and other men who quite naturally feel they must defend their honour."

He put up his hands to his bandaged eyes as he spoke, and the bitterness was back in his voice.

"What you have to do in the future," Norina said, "is to ask yourself if it is worth the risk."

"I am already asking myself that."

"I think the answer is that you should settle down and have a large family," Norina said. "That should keep you occupied when you are in the country."

She paused before she added:

"I expect you have a magnificent *Château* somewhere in France?"

"I have one in the Loire Valley," the *Marquis* replied, "but I have no intention of going there."

"Why not?"

"Because I have a great number of relatives who would exclaim over my wounds and at the same time wag their heads and say they always knew something like this would happen sooner or later!"

Because the way he spoke sounded so funny Norina laughed.

Then she said quickly:

"Forgive me . . I am not really laughing at you but . . you must admit it is going to be difficult to keep yourself hidden and for anyone to know what has occurred."

"It cannot be impossible," the *Marquis* said, "and of course you must help me."

She looked at him enquiringly and realising he was waiting for her reply she said:

"I will help you in any way I can."

"That is what I wanted to hear," the *Marquis* said, "and of course you understand that my friends and my enemies will accept it as being quite natural if I disappear from Social life provided they believe I have somebody with me who must not be seen."

Norina stared at him.

"Do you . . mean . . ?" she began,

"Exactly what you are thinking," the *Marquis* said. "Now, tell me what you look like."

Chapter Five

Norina could not think how to answer.

She stared ahead looking at the wall of the coach as the wheels rumbled on to Paris.

The *Marquis* waited. Then he said:

"Turn your face towards me, Rina."

Because Norina was so bemused she obeyed him and realised he was sitting sideways to face her.

She had taken off her spectacles because they blurred her vision. She wanted to see the stars and the land through which they were passing.

She would have put them on again, but the *Marquis* reached out and cupped her face with his hands.

A little shiver went through her at his touch and he said quietly:

"I will not hurt you. I am only trying to find out whether Jean was right in saying you are *tres jolie*."

It was impossible for Norina to move.

Still with one hand on her left cheek, the *Marquis* slowly outlined her face with a finger of his right hand.

First he moved it gently over her forehead. She was glad she was not wearing a wig.

Then he outlined her eye-brows and, very slowly so that she was not nervous, slid his finger down to touch the lids of her eyes.

Because she was shy she shut them. His finger-tip lingered for a second on the length of her eye-lashes.

Then his finger moved down her straight little nose. It paused beneath it before he touched the curves of her lips. First left – right, then her underlip.

She did not understand, but it gave her a strange sensation she had never felt before.

She made a little murmur in her throat. Yet she did not move as he outlined the contour of her chin, rising up finally to her ear.

He touched it. Again she felt something strange streak through her breast. She thought it must be because she was nervous of what he was doing.

Then, so quickly that she was surprised, he released her.

Sitting back again in his seat he said:

"Jean is right, and I am prepared to wager a large sum that you are in fact very lovely."

Because Norina felt strangely shaken by what he had just done she turned her head away. She looked out of the window from which the curtains were drawn back.

Her hands still lay in her lap holding her spectacles. Again unexpectedly the *Marquis* put out his left hand and covered them. She thought he was going to refer to the fact that she wore spectacles.

Instead his fingers crept a little lower. Then he said in the tone of some-one who has made a discovery:

"No wedding-ring. It is what I suspected!"

Too late Norina remembered, when Dawes had suggested she should be a widow, that she should have taken her mother's wedding-ring from her jewel-box.

Now she thought about it, having packed everything she possessed he would not have forgotten her mother's jewellery. It had been in the safe while her own was kept in a special drawer in her bed-room.

Because she felt she must make some explanation she said a little lamely:

"I . . I left it for . . safety with my other . . jewellery and forgot to . . put it on when we . . left this morning."

"That sounds very plausible," the *Marquis* said taking his hand away. "At the same time, I am suspicious of that mythical husband about whom you say you do not wish to talk."

'I . . cannot think . . why," Norina replied.

She meant to speak defiantly. Instead her voice was soft, very young and frightened.

"Would it not be best," the *Marquis* asked, "if we had no secrets from each other? After all, you have learned mine."

He spoke in the beguiling voice which most women found irresistible.

Norina had a sudden vision of her Stepmother stalking her, waiting to pounce and murder her wherever she might be.

She was sure it would be a mistake to speak of it to anybody, even the *Marquis*.

"I . . think," she said hesitatingly, "that . . it would be safer for . . me . . and for you . . if we . . left things . . as they are."

"You are determined to make me curious," the *Marquis* said.

"When we reach . . Paris I am sure . . there will be a . . great number of . . other things for . . you to think . . about."

"Not if I am to isolate myself alone with you. I shall feel it rather tiresome to be eternally with a Sphinx who is more enigmatic than any Sphinx has ever been before!"

"Once you know . . my secrets," Norina argued, "you will find them very . . dull and then there will be . . nothing to . . think about, but . . yourself."

The *Marquis* laughed.

"You always say the unexpected," he said, "and while I find it infuriating, I am still intrigued. Now tell me, beautiful little Rina, what you are going to do about us."

Norina glanced at him and glanced away.

She had a feeling that in some subtle manner he was flirting with her.

It was what she had been told Frenchmen did with any woman with whom they came in contact.

There was a smile on his lips and she thought that when his eyes were not bandaged he would in fact be exceedingly handsome.

She felt a sudden panic in case she should become too closely involved with him.

Supposing, as apparently a great number of other women had, she fell in love with him? Then she would write him a desperate despairing letter when he no longer had any use for her.

"I must be sensible about this," she told herself, "and I must remember his reputation. To him I am just a Secretary who can never be of any importance in his life."

Because she was so vividly conscious of him sitting next to her she rose a little unsteadily to her feet.

"I think I would . . like to go and . . lie down," she said. "We have a long way to go and the movement of the train is making me sleepy."

"I am sure that is sensible," the *Marquis* agreed. "It will be nearly midnight when we arrive in Paris. We could stay in a siding until

305

the morning, but I would rather move out of the train when it is dark so that we will not be noticed."

"I am . . sure that is a . . good idea," Norina agreed.

She walked across the coach and found her way into one of the small bed-rooms attached to it.

She had left her widow's hat on the bed. Now she put it on a chair and stretched herself out.

She intended to go to sleep.

Instead she kept feeling the *Marquis's* fingers moving over her skin.

She could still feel the strange sensation he had evoked in her breast when he touched her lips.

"Please . . God . . do not let . . me fall . . in love with . . him," she prayed, "but let me . . stay working for . . him. I like being with him. I like talking to him . . but whatever . . happens, I must . . not think of . . him as a . . man, but . . just as . . my employer."

It was, as the *Marquis* had warned Norina, very late when they arrived in Paris.

He insisted that they waited in the coach until practically all the passengers had left the train.

Then they walked slowly down the platform to where, outside the *Gare du Nord*, a carriage was waiting.

Norina only had time to notice before they stepped into it that the horses were very well bred. The uniforms of the servants were exceedingly smart.

Jean jumped up on the box beside the footman. The Courier stayed behind to see to the luggage.

Although it was late there were still lights in a great many windows.

People were moving about in the street and every so often there was the sound of music.

There was also a considerable amount of traffic.

To Norina it was all very exciting.

She sat forward looking out of the window, thinking that Paris was all she had expected it to be. There was some irresistible magic in the air.

They passed the Opera House and she recognised it from the pictures she had seen.

Then they went down what she was sure was the *Rue de la Paix* before they reached the *Place Vendome*.

Two minutes later she gave a little cry of excitement because they were in the *Place de la Concorde*.

The fountains were playing and the lights made the water thrown up into the air iridescent and luminous.

"It is lovely . . perfectly lovely!" she exclaimed. "Oh, thank you, thank you for bringing me here!"

"I thought that was what you would feel," the *Marquis* said in a deep voice.

"How could anyone not be thrilled by the *Place de la Concorde*?" Norina asked.

The *Marquis* did not answer. The light from one of the street lamps illuminated his face and she saw he was smiling.

They only had a short distance to go before the horses turned off the *Champs Élysèes*. A moment later they passed through some iron gates and up a short drive.

"Is this where you live?" Norina asked. "I have read that the houses in the *Champs Élysèes* are the most distinguished in the whole of Paris."

"That is what I like to think," the *Marquis* replied.

The horses came to a standstill and a number of servants appeared.

There were footmen in white wigs and very elaborate uniforms.

Norina got out first.

Then Jean assisted the *Marquis* to alight, and led him by the arm into the house.

A *Majordomo* more resplendent than the other servants, greeted him respectfully.

Norina was aware that he was looking at his Master's bandaged eyes in consternation.

"We are tired," the *Marquis* said, "and will go straight upstairs to bed."

"There is food and wine in the *Salon, Monsieur le Marquis*," the *Majordomo* replied.

"I want nothing," the *Marquis* said firmly, "but perhaps *Madame* Wyndham would like . . ?"

"No, No," Norina interrupted. "Thank you very much, but I too would like to go to bed."

The Housekeeper was waiting at the top of the stairs to show

307

her to a bed-room. It was on the First Floor and exceedingly luxurious.

Norina wondered if the Courier had been told she was to be treated more as a guest than a Secretary.

A maid unpacked her nightgown and what she needed, and helped her out of her clothes.

As soon as she was in the big bed, which was very comfortable, Norina fell asleep.

But her last thought was that she must not become too involved with the *Marquis*.

When Norina awoke it was morning. Her breakfast was brought in and set beside her bed.

It was, she thought a delight and exactly what she expected.

There were deliciously light hot *croissants* with a variety of different *confitures* or honey to spread on them.

The coffee tasted better than any she had ever tasted before.

When she sat back against her pillows she could see the sunshine shimmering on the trees outside. The sky above them was very blue.

Because it was so exciting she jumped out of bed and ran to the window.

"Whatever the *Marquis* might say," she told herself. "I have to explore Paris and if there is no one to go with me. I shall go alone!"

She then remembered she had duties to perform. She rang for a maid who brought her hot water and helped her dress.

She went downstairs wondering if her relationship with the *Marquis* would be in any way different from how it had been before.

He was waiting for her in a magnificent *Salon*.

It was decorated with what she was sure was Louis XIV furniture and pictures which she longed to inspect.

She was however determined to be businesslike and when she entered the room she said:

"*Bonjour, Monsieur*! I am sure in your absence there must be a large amount of correspondence awaiting your attention, and I am wondering where I might find it."

"I have already thought of that," the *Marquis* replied, "and my permanent Secretary has dealt with all but those of an obviously personal nature."

Norina started.

"Y .. your .. permanent .. Secretary?" she repeated. "Then .. you do not .. need me?"

She felt as she spoke as if the ceiling had suddenly crashed down on her head. The sunshine had vanished.

"My permanent Secretary," the *Marquis* explained, "also runs my house, but he does not deal with my private correspondence."

"Then you do .. still need .. me?"

"I will tell you when you are no longer necessary," the *Marquis* replied.

The relief made Norina for a moment feel weak. Without waiting to be told she could do so she sat down on a chair.

"You .. frightened .. me!" she said accusingly.

"You frightened yourself," the *Marquis* replied. "You might not have noticed, but my eyes are still bandaged!"

"I can .. hardly say that I am .. glad," Norina said in a voice that shook.

"Then suppose you do your duty," the *Marquis* suggested, "and open the letters that are standing on that *Secretaire* by the window?"

Norina rose and walked to where she could now see a large pile of letters.

It was obvious that they were private and personal. She thought some of the envelopes were scented as .. Patsy's had been.

She picked them up with a letter-opener that lay beside them and turned round.

The *Marquis* was now sitting in a high-backed arm-chair. With his legs crossed and very elegantly dressed he looked like a *Grand Seigneur*.

She walked nearer to him. Sitting down in a chair she slit open the first envelope.

As she did so the *Marquis* asked:

"What are you wearing?"

"My black gown."

"I think that is a mistake."

She looked at him in surprise.

"Why?"

He thought before he spoke that she looked very lovely. Then he said:

309

"I have already told you that you are my excuse for not receiving my friends, and therefore you must look the part."

Norina stared and he went on:

"Servants talk and nothing can prevent them from doing so. By to-night a great number of people in Paris will know that I have returned home. They will also learn that I wish to receive no visitors. The question they will inevitably ask themselves is – why? Do you understand?"

"Y . yes . . yes . . of course," Norina said hesitatingly.

"Then I suggest," the *Marquis* said, "that either you put on a gown that is not black, or if you do not have one with you, then I will provide it."

"No . . no . . of course . . not!" Norina protested. "I could not allow you to . . pay for . . my clothes. It would be most . . improper! As it happens . . I have some very . . pretty gowns . . with me."

"And who paid for those?" the *Marquis* enquired.

"My father," Norina said automatically.

Because suddenly she guessed what he suspected she said:

"I do not . . want to take . . part in this . . Masquerade. It is very . . embarrassing."

"You would prefer to find someone else?" the *Marquis* asked coldly.

Norina drew in her breath.

She knew he was saying that if she did not do what he wanted she could leave.

But how could she do that with nowhere to go?

Quickly because she was frightened she said:

"I will . . do what . . you want, but I am . . afraid of making a mistake which would . . hurt you."

"I think really," the *Marquis* answered, "you are worrying about your own reputation."

"No, that is . . not true," Norina said. "My reputation is of . . no importance, and I can say . . that in all honesty."

She was thinking as she spoke that it was true because what she was doing was saving her life.

If she was gossiped about or unkind things were said it would hardly be of any consequence if she was dead.

As if he was reading her thoughts again the *Marquis* said:

"Now, suppose we go back to the beginning and let me ask you, because you promised to help me, to make yourself look as pretty and attractive as possible."

He paused then went on:

"As you are married, your husband has gone Big Game Hunting or is visiting America and is not aware you are here with me in Paris."

Norina stared at him, then she laughed.

"Why are you laughing?" the *Marquis* asked.

"Because everything is becoming . . more and more complicated," Norina replied, "and I am going to find it difficult remembering which is . . really me, or just . . part of a . . Fairy Tale."

"In which case, I am obviously the 'Bold, Bad Villain"! the *Marquis* said.

"I have not . . said so, and I think if you are honest you . . are . . fishing for . . compliments!"

"I can hardly be 'Prince Charming'," the *Marquis* answered, "with my eyes bandaged, unable to see how beautiful the Princess is, who is also in hiding."

"It is . . your story," Norina answered, "so of course, you can . . play any part in it . . you choose. I am quite willing to be '*Cinderella*' after the Fairy Godmother waved her . . magic wand and changed . . her rags into a . . beautiful gown."

"You shall go and change it as soon as you have opened my letters," the *Marquis* said. "There will be no one to see you in the house, but descriptions of you will be carried on the wind as they inevitably are."

It all sounded so ridiculous that Norina laughed again.

"I am sure I am . . dreaming!" she said. "This . . cannot be . . true!"

"Then let us hope you do not wake up to anything unpleasant," the *Marquis* said somewhat mockingly.

"I do not . . believe there is anything . . unpleasant in . . Paris!"

She opened the *Marquis's* letters and read them aloud.

Quite a number of them were from Ladies begging him to let them know as soon as he returned. They all told him how miserable they had been in his absence.

There was a repetition about them.

It made Norina think that intelligent and witty as Frenchwomen were reputed to be, there was a lamentable sameness in the way they expressed themselves when they were in love.

The *Marquis* made no comment as she went from one letter to another.

Finally when she had read the last one he said:

"Put them on the fire!"

"You .. you do not .. wish me to .. answer any of .. them?"

"There is nothing to say."

She rose to her feet and put the letters one by one into the fire. The flames flared up and the pages of passion curled beneath them.

When the last one had burned to ashes she turned away.

"What are you thinking?" the *Marquis* asked.

"I am .. feeling sorry for .. those women," Norina answered.

"And for me?"

"There is no reason why I should feel sorry for you, but they are tributes at your feet, or incense, if you prefer, from worshippers before your shrine."

She spoke lightly, and only as she finished speaking did she think she had been rude.

"I am .. sorry," she said quickly, "that is .. something I should .. not have .. said."

"Always the unexpected!" the *Marquis* remarked. "Go and change."

Norina ran upstairs.

She found that, without instructions, the maid had unpacked several of her trunks.

The gowns which her father had bought for her in London were hanging in the wardrobe.

She felt it embarrassing to have to explain why she was changing so soon. She therefore managed to undo her gown herself.

She put on a pretty summer gown which she also managed to button up at the back.

She thought it was suitable for a young girl and not for the married woman she was supposed to be.

As she expected, Dawes had packed her jewellery as well as her mother's.

The cases were standing on a beautifully inlaid commode.

She looked into her mother's box and found, as she should have done before, her wedding-ring.

She put it on her finger. Because it was a little large she made sure it would stay on by adding one of her mother's smaller diamond rings.

Also, to make herself look older, she put on a pair of pearl and diamond ear-rings. They had also belonged to her mother.

Shutting the jewel-box she went back downstairs.

The *Marquis* was still in the room where she had left him, but standing at the open window.

She felt that he was longing to be out. Perhaps driving in the *Bois* or riding one of his horses.

When he heard her approach he turned round slowly and as she went towards him he asked:

"You have changed?"

"I am wearing white with a skirt that is decorated with broderie anglais, and there is a blue sash round my waist."

The *Marquis* did not speak and she added:

"I am also wearing the wedding-ring which I told you was in my jewel-box."

She spoke defiantly because she still had no wish for him to know how young she was. She was not, whatever he said, prepared to admit that she was not married.

The *Marquis* took her hand in both of his and felt her rings.

"Diamonds?" he questioned. "If your husband was a rich man why are you forced to work for your living?"

There was no answer to this and Norina did not reply.

He put up his hand again as if towards her cheek, but instead he touched her ear.

"Ear-rings!" he exclaimed, "and of course you could have sold them rather than become a Secretary."

"Now you are questioning the old 'me'," Norina said reluctantly. "I thought we had moved into another world in which I am a rich, important social figure who has eloped with you to the Continent."

"Yes, of course," the *Marquis* agreed. "Forgive me. We must of course act out our parts and be careful not to forget them."

He put his arm around Norina as he spoke. Before she could realise what was happening he pulled her against him.

She looked up at him in amazement, then realised he was about to kiss her.

His lips had almost touched hers when she cried:

"*Non! non!*"

She fought herself free and moved away from the *Marquis* to the other side of the window. She held onto the window-sill to support herself.

313

He was standing where she had left him. She thought although she was not certain he was astonished by her reaction to his advances.

She was breathing quickly and was not certain what she should do.

Then the *Marquis* said quietly:

"I thought you had agreed to play the part I have assigned to you."

"But . . we were only . . pretending!" Norina managed to gasp.

"Then of course I must apologise," the *Marquis* said, "and may I suggest in my own defence, Rina, that if any other woman had been in your position she would have thought it very remiss if I had not kissed her in gratitude for her help."

"But . . you must not kiss me!"

"Why not?"

"Because . . it would be . . wrong."

"Why wrong?"

It was a question that was difficult to answer and Norina said:

"I think one . . should only . . kiss somebody with whom . . they are very much . . in love."

The *Marquis* smiled.

"Surely it would not be difficult for us to pretend to be in love, at least while we are acting a play in which it is actually a necessity?"

"I . . I do not think . . that is . . true!" Norina said, "and . . please . . I do not . . want you to . . kiss me."

She thought if the *Marquis* kissed her it would give her the same feelings as when he had touched her lips with his fingers.

Then she might easily fall in love with him.

That would mean nothing but misery in the future.

She might find herself writing the sort of letters which "Patsy" and the other women wrote when he was no longer interested in them.

"That is a plea which of course I cannot refuse," the *Marquis* said quietly.

He put out a hand to find the back of a chair. He guided himself back to where he had been sitting before.

Then he paused.

"Do not be so frightened, Rina," he said. "I will not hurt you. I assure you, I have never forced myself on any woman who is unwilling."

"H . . how do you . . know I am . . frightened?" Norina asked in a childlike little voice.

"I can feel it," the *Marquis* answered.

As he spoke he moved not in the direction of his chair, but towards her.

He stood in front of her before he said:

"Give me your hand."

She held out her hand and his fingers closed over hers.

"I have no wish to cause you any distress," he said gently. "Just trust me and we can, I am sure, be happy together."

As he finished speaking he raised her hand to his lips.

It was the perfunctory gesture for a Frenchman but for a second she felt his mouth against her skin.

Instantly there was that same strange sensation within her breast she had felt before.

It made her quiver.

As if the *Marquis* was aware of it he released her hand and turned awkwardly in the direction of the fireplace.

She knew he was groping to find something to support him. Automatically she moved forward to take his arm and guide him to his chair.

As he seated himself he said:

"Thank you, Rina, I am very grateful to you."

"That is . . really what I . . should be . . saying to . . you," Norina replied.

The *Marquis* smiled.

"Then at least we have one thing in common!"

Luncheon was delicious and served in the most attractive small Dining-Room Norina had ever imagined.

As they moved back to the *Salon* with Jean assisting the *Marquis*, he said:

"We can hardly stay cooped up in the house all day. Where shall we go, Jean?"

Jean shook his head.

"There is nowhere, *Monsieur*, where you would not be seen."

"I need some air."

"If *Monsieur* sat in the garden behind the bushes he would be invisible except perhaps for two windows on that side of the house."

"Then that is where I shall go," the *Marquis* said. "Are you coming too, Rina?"

"I would like to join you," Norina said, "but may I first write a letter which I want posted at once?"

"Of course!" the *Marquis* agreed.

She went to the *Secretaire* and wrote a short note to Dawes. She told him where she was staying and with whom, adding:

"Thank you so very much for all you have done for me. It is very exciting being in Paris and please, let me know if there is any news."

She signed it just with her initials and addressed the envelope to Mr. Dawes, c/o Mrs. Rolo.

The *Marquis* had gone out into the garden, but Jean had come back to wait for her letter.

"Will you please post it immediately," she asked, "and send it to London by the quickest route possible?"

"I'll see to it, *Madame*."

He took the letter from her and added:

"It's good for *Monsieur* to have someone to talk to."

"I am afraid he will find it very restricting after a little while," Norina said.

"*Monsieur's* eyes grow better every day," Jean replied, "but he must do as he is told and keep them bandaged."

He spoke as if he almost suspected Norina of trying to encourage the *Marquis* to remove it.

Then she guessed that Jean was used to women who wanted his master to admire them, and they would resent the fact that he could not see them.

"*Monsieur* must certainly try to obey the Oculist's orders," she said aloud and Jean smiled at her.

He walked away. She was just tidying away the writing-paper and putting the pen back on the tray when the door opened.

She thought Jean must have returned to say there was something wrong with her letter.

But when she looked round it was not Jean who had come into the room.

Instead there was a smartly dressed man who she knew was French even before he spoke.

He looked around the *Salon* before he asked:

"I thought Alexus would be here. Who, may I ask, *Madame*, are you?"

Norina rose from the chair.

"The *Marquis* is not receiving people at the moment, *Monsieur*."

The Frenchman laughed.

"He will receive me. I am one of his oldest friends. I thought he must be up to some mischief when I heard he was in Paris and had not notified me of his return."

"He has notified no one, *Monsieur*," Norina replied, "because, as I have already said, he is entertaining no one and wishes to be alone."

The Frenchman smiled again.

"Except, *Madame*, for you! You, of course, are the exception."

"*Oui, Monsieur*, that is correct," Norina said, "and so, may I ask you to leave. I will however inform *Monsieur le Marquis* that you have called, if you would be so kind as to give me your name."

The Frenchman was obviously astounded at what she said and just stared at her before he said:

"I am *le Vicomte Leporte* and as I have already told you, *Madame*, Alexus's oldest friend. I have no intention of being turned away as if I was an intruder!"

"But that, *Monsieur*, is exactly what you are!" Norina retorted, "so I can only beg you to accept my assurance that the *Marquis* has no wish to see anyone for the moment."

She spoke very politely, at the same time firmly.

The *Vicomte* stood looking indecisive.

She knew he was wondering whether he should defy her or not and she held out her hand.

"*Au revoir, Monsieur le Vicomte!*" she said. "I hope we shall meet again in more congenial circumstances."

Slowly and with obvious reluctance the *Vicomte* took her hand and bowed over it.

Then he walked to the door. As he reached it he said:

"Tell Alexus I do not forgive him for this, but having seen you, *Madame*, I understand the reason for his seclusion."

He walked out of the room as he spoke and Norina heard him going down the passage.

She waited until she was certain he must have left the house.

Then quickly she ran out into the garden to where she knew the *Marquis* was sitting behind some bushes.

The sunshine was warm on her face as she sped out and across the lawn.

It was not difficult to guess where the *Marquis* would be sitting.

She turned to where in the distance she could see a yew hedge behind which she was certain he had isolated himself.

She ran and when she reached him she found he was sitting on a wooden seat on which there were satin cushions.

He was holding his head up into the sunshine which was percolating through the trees.

She was almost breathless as she sat down beside him, saying:

"There is . . trouble, and . . I have come to . . tell you what . . I have . . done!"

"Trouble?" the *Marquis* questioned. "What has happened?"

Her breath was still coming in gasps as Norina related exactly what had occurred since he had left the *Salon*.

When she mentioned the *Vicomte's* name the *Marquis* gave an exclamation.

"Ramon Leporte! A very old friend, but one of the biggest gossips in the whole of Paris! How the devil did he find out I was here?"

"You said . . the word would be 'carried on the wind'!" Norina replied.

"I knew I had made a mistake in coming to Paris," he said. "The servants are so damned silly and whatever I say they will allow my friends, if they are important enough, to enter the house."

"Then . . what will you do?" Norina asked.

"We will leave!" the *Marquis* said, "and the sooner the better!"

"L . . leave? But we have only just arrived. Where can we go?"

"Where I should have gone in the first place," the *Marquis* answered, "to my new Villa in the South of France!"

Norina's eyes widened.

"Can we really go there?"

"That is what we are doing," the *Marquis* said firmly, "so go back to the house and tell the *Majordomo* to send for a Courier – not the one we have just used – but a man who is called Breste."

The *Marquis* gave the order sharply and Norina rose from the seat.

"I will do as you say," she said, "although I am sad that I shall not see Paris."

"If you are very good," the *Marquis* said, "and do not make a fuss, I will tell you what we will do. When it is dark, we will drive along the Seine, see Notre Dame and come back along the Rue de l'Opera, when everything will be lit up and be far more glamorous than it looks in the daytime."

Norina clasped her hands together.

"Can we do that?"

"I never break my promises," the *Marquis* said, "and I hope one day I will be able to show you Paris properly when I can see it myself."

"That will be . . wonderful!" Norina exclaimed.

At the same time she thought it would be something that was very unlikely to happen.

When the *Marquis* could see again she would have to leave him.

She felt a sudden depression at the thought.

Then she told herself it was no use looking ahead.

She would have a glimpse of Paris, then she would go on to see what she had always longed to see – the South of France.

"I am lucky . . very . . very . . lucky!" she was saying as she ran back towards the house to carry out the *Marquis's* orders.

Chapter Six

Dawes came out of his Master's room and paused at the top of the stairs. He saw Bolton letting two men into the house.

He thought they looked strange, especially one of them. He watched them as they moved across the hall and were shown into the Drawing-Room.

Bolton came up the stairs to inform Lady Sedgewyn, who had not yet left her bed-room, that she had visitors.

As he reached the top of the stairs Dawes said to him:

"Who are those two men calling in the morning?"

"One of them's a queer-looking Monk," Bolton answered, "and the other looks to me like a ferret."

He walked past Dawes to knock on Her Ladyship's door.

The word "ferret" made Dawes think as he had last week, Lady Sedgewyn was employing a Detective to search for Norina.

She and Lord Sedgewyn had at first not been particularly perturbed that Norina was staying with friends.

But when they heard nothing from her Lord Sedgewyn began to grow anxious about her disappearance.

"Where the devil is my daughter?" he asked Dawes. "It is not like her to upset me or to leave London when she has a number of engagements. The Countess tells me she has been expecting every evening to take her to some Ball or other."

Dawes was wise and said nothing.

He thought, however, that Lady Sedgewyn seemed even more perturbed than her husband. He guessed the reason for it.

Now he slipped along the passage and entered an Ante-Room next to the Drawing-Room. It was rarely used except as a card-room when there was a large party.

He shut the door by which he had entered and tip-toed across the room.

Very gently he eased open the communicating door of the Drawing-Room.

As soon as he had done so he could hear the two men talking.

He heard the one he thought looked like a ferret say:

"Now this is just up your street and I expects you to remember me when you gets the girl in your hands".

"You'll not be forgotten," the Monk-like man replied.

He spoke English but with a definite foreign accent.

They then whispered together in such low voices that Dawes could not hear what they said.

A few minutes later the door opened and Lady Sedgewyn came in.

"Good-morning, Mr. Wentover," she said. "I have been wondering when you would call on me."

"I was waiting," the man called Wentover replied, "until I had some news for Your Ladyship, an' now I you'll be very pleased."

"That is what I am hoping!" Lady Sedgewyn replied.

She must have glanced at the other man present because Wentover said:

"May I introduce Father Jacques of the Convent of St. Francis."

"It's a pleasure to meet Your Ladyship," the Monk said slowly.

"Will you sit down," Lady Sedgewyn suggested, "and then, Mr. Wentover, you can tell me what I am waiting to hear."

Dawes put an ear to the crack in the door as the Detective began:

"Following your Ladyship's instructions we made every possible enquiry as to the whereabouts of Miss Sedgewyn. We found that she bought a widow's hat at an Emporium in Oxford Street, and wore it the next morning to travel with the *Marquis* de Charlamont to Paris."

"With the *Marquis*?" Lady Sedgewyn exclaimed.

"That's right, Ma'am. He has, as we understand it, suffered an accident to his eyes. They was bandaged and he travelled incognito on the Steamer."

"And my Stepdaughter Norina was with him? But, why?"

"That we have not yet ascertained," Mr. Wentover replied, "except that as he's blind he might have needed somebody to guide him."

"I do not understand," Lady Sedgewyn murmured.

"They arrived in Paris, but after two days," Mr. Wentover

321

continued, "they left for the South of France where the *Marquis* has a Villa he's recently built on a small promontory called Cap d'Estelle."

"You are quite sure that my Stepdaughter is with him?" Lady Sedgewyn asked.

"There's no possibility of my being mistaken," Mr. Wentover answered, "but this, my Lady, is where Father Jacques can be of great help."

Lady Sedgewyn looked at the Monk.

He was rather dissolute-looking, she thought, with bags under his eyes. It made her suspect he was a heavy drinker.

At the same time, she was obviously anxious to know what part he was to play.

"It's very fortunate," Mr. Wentover was saying, "that Father Jacques happened to be in England, on a mission which he'll not mind telling you concerns the death of the Earl of Kingswood's daughter."

"The young lady entered my Convent as a postulant," Father Jacques explained, "but she unfortunately succumbed to a fever, which often occurs in the South of France, and died."

Lady Sedgewyn was thinking quickly.

She remembered hearing that the Earl was an avid gambler and ran up enormous debts at the green baize tables.

She also recalled that his daughter had been an heiress.

"You say the Earl's daughter died while in your Convent," she said to the Monk. "What happened to her money?"

There was a little pause before Father Jacques replied:

"It is usual for the Postulants to make over all their worldly goods to the Convent, but in that instance, because of a previous arrangement, half of what the Lady Imogen owned will go to her father."

There was a pregnant pause.

Then Lady Sedgewyn said:

"If my Stepdaughter is taken to your Convent, I am prepared to give you two thousand pounds now for your expenses in finding her, and ten thousand pounds on her death as well as another ten thousand pounds when my husband leaves this life."

Father Jacques nodded his head.

"I understand, My Lady, and I will immediately, on my return to France - and I leave to-morrow morning – get in touch with Your Ladyship's Stepdaughter."

There was a short pause before he added:

"I am sure she can be – *persuaded* to worship in our Convent which is very near to the Cap d'Estelle."

He accentuated the word 'persuaded'.

Dawes did not wait to hear any more.

He slipped out of the Ante-room and left the house by the back door.

He hurried all the way to the Post Office which was in Mount Street.

When he reached it he said to the man behind the counter:

"I want to send a telegram to France."

"To France?" the man repeated rather stupidly.

"Yes, France, and don't let there be any mistake about it!" Dawes said.

He was handed the proper form and very laboriously, because he was not a fluent writer, completed it.

He was surprised at the charge, but fortunately he had enough money with him.

Then, wiping his forehead, he left the Post Office and walked slowly back to the house.

Norina finished dinner and said to the *Marquis*.

"That was the most delicious meal I have ever tasted, but then I say that every night."

"The new Chef is certainly worth his wages," the *Marquis* replied, "and we must thank Jean for finding him."

Norina looked round the small Dining-Room. The windows opened onto a wide balcony which overlooked the garden.

She had never imagined that anything could be so lovely as the Villa the *Marquis* had just finished building.

Cap d'Estelle was a small promontory between Eze and Cap Ferrat on which there was just room for a Villa and a small garden.

It was usual for Noblemen who built their Villas in the South of France to set them high up above the sea between Nice and Monte Carlo.

But the *Marquis* five years ago had seen the promontory. He realised it was for sale and started building.

The Villa, Norina thought when she first saw it, owed something to the Greek Temples. Also to an imagination which incorporated the natural landscape.

To reach the Villa one descended from the main road down a twisting drive.

Then the house itself started half-way towards the rock which protruded out into the sea, and on this the *Marquis* was now forming a garden.

When they reached the Villa there was what appeared to be the Ground Floor yet there was another below it, and two floors above.

It was far too large for a single man alone. But as the *Marquis* pointed out, he had innumerable relatives who would, when it was completed, continually wish to borrow it from him.

"It is so lovely and so quiet that I feel people chattering and of course gossiping would spoil it," Norina said.

"I am certainly thankful that we have it to ourselves at the moment," the *Marquis* remarked, "and in fact at this time of the year there are few people to gossip or chatter because this part of France is only fashionable in the Spring."

"Well, I would rather be here now!" Norina said.

"It certainly suits our purpose," the *Marquis* agreed.

He rose from the table and walked out onto the balcony which surrounded the Villa.

There was a long flight of marble steps which led from the centre of it down into the garden.

There, surprisingly, there were large trees and flower-beds which had just been planted between the rocks.

What entranced Norina when she arrived was that there were climbing geraniums everywhere. Also a great number of clematis of every sort, flowering over the rocks and even encircling some of the trees.

"It is a Fairyland!" she declared.

The *Marquis* smiled at the rapture in her voice.

Now the sun had just set and the sky was still crimson. The first evening stars were twinkling directly overhead.

"Tell me what you are seeing," the *Marquis* said quietly. "I am looking to where the crimson fingers of the sun touch the sea. That is the horizon and I know there are other horizons beyond that."

"And you want to reach them all?" the *Marquis* asked.

"Of course!" Norina answered, "and you have brought me to the first one, but perhaps I will find the others only in my imagination."

The *Marquis* moved beside her. They stood in silence until Norina said:

"The newspapers have come and I know you are longing to hear what is happening in England, so we had better go inside and I will read them to you."

She took him by the arm as she spoke and assisted him along the balcony. They passed through another window into the *Salon*.

It was a room she found exquisite. All in white with French furniture, and pink curtains which were the colour of the geraniums outside.

She picked up the newspaper and read the headlines, then the Editorial.

The *Marquis* appeared to be listening.

Yet when she asked what he would like read next he hesitated. It was as if he had been listening to her voice rather than what she said.

She read him a rather dull description of Queen Victoria's visit to Kew Gardens and an even duller speech made by the Prime Minister which had been severely criticised by the Opposition.

Then the door of the *Salon* opened and Jean came in.

He had in his hand a telegram.

"This has come from the Villa that is on the road above us, *Madame*," he said. "They regret it has been delayed, but they were away from home and the postman pushed it through the door."

"Is it for me?" Norina asked in surprise.

"Yes, *Madame*," Jean replied, "but the name of the Villa was incorrectly spelled and the Postman made a mistake."

Norina took it from him.

She looked at it and saw that not only was the name of the Villa mis-spelt, but so was the *Marquis's*.

"Who is it from?" the *Marquis* asked. "I thought no one knew you were here!"

It was then Norina guessed who had sent it and tore open the envelope.

For a moment the writing on the form seemed to swim before her eyes. Then she read:

*HIDE QUICK FROM MONK STOP SHE KNOWS WHERE YOU
ARE STOP – DAWES."*

She read it again, then gave a shrill cry of horror.

"What is it? What has happened?" the *Marquis* asked.

"I have . . to hide! They will . . kill me! Please . . help me . .
where . . can I . . go?"

Norina got to her feet with the telegram in her hand. Now she
flung herself down on her knees beside the *Marquis's* chair.

"My Stepmother has . . found out where I . . am! I have to . .
go away . . at . . once!"

"Your *Stepmother*!" the *Marquis* repeated quietly. "So it is she who
has made you so frightened!"

"Sh . . she tried to . . kill me!" Norina said. "I . . I was only . .
saved because . . I was not . . hungry and gave . . my dinner to the
. . cat . . and he . . d . . died at . . once!"

She gave a little gasp and cried:

"Now that . . she knows . . where I am . . she will come . . here!
She will . . kill me . . one way or . . another! Hide me . . please . .
hide me . . !"

She put out her hands and the *Marquis* took them in his.

The strength and pressure of his fingers was comforting.

"Suppose you start from the beginning," he said quietly, "and
tell me your secret and what all this is about."

She would have moved away, but he held her hands. She put her
head down against his knee.

"My . . Stepmother," she murmured, "is . . wicked . . evil . . and
she . . wants my money . . the money my mother . . left me . . when
she d . . died."

"But your father is alive?"

"My father is . . Lord Sedgewyn."

"I have heard of him," the *Marquis* remarked. "I believe he has
some race-horses."

"A few," Norina admitted, "but he prefers hunters, and was . .
very happy in the . . country when . . my mother was . . alive. Then
. . he married . . again,"

"And you say your stepmother wants to kill you?"

"She thought my father was . . very rich . . but then she discovered
that . . the money he spends . . is mine and it only . . becomes really
his if I . . die before him."

"And she has actually attempted to kill you? I can hardly believe it!"

"It is .. true! It is .. true! And I .. ran away .. because I .. knew no one would .. believe me .. and if I told .. any of my relatives .. they would .. only say I was being .. hysterical and .. laugh at me!"

"I believe you," the *Marquis* said.

"Then .. please .. help me! I do .. not want to die! .. I want to live .. and .. and I have been .. so .. so happy here."

The *Marquis's* fingers tightened on hers.

"You are not going to die!" he said. "Do you really think I would allow anyone to kill you?"

"But .. how can you .. prevent it? She will put poison .. in my food again .. or she might get .. somebody to .. shoot at me .. while I am in the .. garden. There are a .. thousand ways by .. which I could lose .. my life .. and no one .. would ever .. guess that she had .. murdered me!"

"Who told you this was what she intended?" the *Marquis* enquired.

"It was Dawes. He is Papa's Valet, and he has been with us ever since I was a baby .. and he is the .. only person I can .. trust."

"So it was he who sent you the telegram!"

"Yes, and it was Dawes who went to Hunt's Domestic Bureau in Mount Street to find me .. somewhere to go, but they .. said the only vacancy was .. yours. That was .. why I was so .. frightened you would .. refuse to .. employ me."

"But I have employed you," the *Marquis* said, "and now we have to make certain this wicked woman does not succeed in her desire to do away with you and gain your money."

"Can we .. do that? Where .. can I .. go?"

"It is quite easy," the *Marquis* replied.

"Easy?" Norina asked.

"My yacht is in Nice Harbour. I sent for it as soon as I arrived."

"Your yacht!" Norina breathed. "That means we would be at sea and she could .. not approach .. me."

"Not unless she can swim or fly!" the *Marquis* answered.

Norina gave a sigh of utter relief and shut her eyes.

The *Marquis* put his hand on her hair.

"You will be quite safe," he said, "until I am well enough to contact your father or someone who will make sure that your Stepmother never tries to kill you again!"

"I have . . been . . so afraid," Norina said.

"Of course you have," the *Marquis* answered. "And now that you have told me what has been frightening you, everything will be far easier."

"You are sure of . . that? But . . there is no . . reason why . . you should become . . mixed up in this horrible . . situation."

"I think, Rina," the *Marquis* said, "we have been together long enough to know that we both have an obligation towards each other."

"Now that I have . . told you what is . . frightening me . . you will not . . send me . . away?"

"I will tell Jean now that we will join the yacht tomorrow morning. He will send somebody to alert the Captain and we will be aboard before your Stepmother or anybody else can be aware of it."

"That will be . . wonderful!" Norina said, "and thank you . . thank . . you for . . being so . . kind to . . me."

The *Marquis* stroked her hair and she felt as if the crimson light of the sun was moving through her.

It was such an unexpected relief to know that she was no longer alone in her fight against her Stepmother.

The *Marquis* was beside her, defending her, helping her.

Quite suddenly, because there was no need for her to go on fighting she felt limp and as if she might collapse.

"You are tired," the *Marquis* said quietly. "Go to bed now and sleep without dreaming. To-morrow we will leave here and only return when it is safe to do so."

"How can I ever be safe?"

"I am not certain," the *Marquis* said quietly, "but somehow we will find a way."

"I will pray . . I will pray very hard that you will do so," Norina said, "and when I say my prayers to-night I will thank God because you are so understanding."

The *Marquis's* lips opened and she thought he was about to say something.

Then as if he changed his mind he said:

"Go to bed, Rina – if that is really your name."

"Actually, it is 'Norina'," she said, "Norina Wyn. I called myself 'Wyndham' because it was easy to remember."

The *Marquis* laughed.

"You are always practical, even in a storm," he said. "One of the things I most enjoy about you is the way your brain works."

Norina looked at him.

Then because she felt there was no other way to thank him she bent forward and kissed his hand.

She rose to her feet.

"Good-night, *Monsieur*," she said, "and thank you .. thank you!"

The *Marquis* did not answer. As she suddenly felt shy she ran from the room.

Only as she went upstairs to the next floor did she think of a thousand ways in which she might have expressed her gratitude better.

"He understands .. I am sure he .. understands." she thought.

She reached the top of the stairs.

She knew Jean had seen her leave the *Salon* and now he would have gone to his Master to guide him to his room.

To make it easier while his eyes were bandaged the *Marquis* slept in a bed-room on the same floor as the *Salon* and the Dining-Room.

It was not as impressive as his usual bed-room which he had designed himself. This was on the same floor as the one occupied by Norina and had a fine view of the sea.

But as he could not see it was not for the moment important.

What was important was that Jean's room was beside his in case he needed any attention during the night.

Norina went into her own room.

There were a number of servants in the Villa, but they had a separate house of their own.

It was at the back, so once they had retired, there was no noise to disturb the *Marquis* or anybody else.

"It is so peaceful," Norina thought as she undressed.

How was it possible that her Stepmother's evil hands could reach out to her? Therefore she had to lie and pretend to be somebody other than herself?

She would be safe in the yacht with the *Marquis*.

If anybody knew she was alone with him and that she was her father's daughter, her reputation would be ruined for ever.

"What .. does it .. matter?" Norina asked.

329

At the same time, she knew it would distress her father and also her mother if she was alive.

"There is . . nothing . . else I . . can do," she said, "but how can this . . go on for . . ever?"

As she asked the question she was afraid of the answer.

Because she wanted to sleep rather than to think she got into bed.

She was just slipping away when suddenly something was placed over her mouth.

She awoke with a start.

Before she could realise it was not just a frightening dream her mouth had been forced open and a gag tied tightly behind her head.

She could not utter a sound.

A rope then encircled her body and something dark and heavy covered her completely.

She tried to struggle and attempted to scream but it was useless.

Strong arms were carrying her from the bed.

Then she realised in horror that she was supported on ropes, she was let down over the balcony outside her room to the floor below.

Her feet were bare and she could feel the night air on them.

What covered her face and most of her body made it almost impossible for her to breathe.

She only knew that she was being taken away on her Stepmother's orders.

Long before the *Marquis* was even aware that she was no longer in the Villa she would have been killed.

Everything that was happening was done so precisely and so cleverly. The men, and she was sure there were a number of them, made not a sound.

As she reached the balcony below two men lifted her in their arms. She knew they were carrying her down the flight of steps which led into the garden.

They were walking across the lawn to the end of the garden. There were rocks which ended in the sea.

She thought despairingly that the *Marquis* would not know where she had been taken. There was no way of telling him.

Then as she struggled against the ropes that pinioned her arms

330

to her sides she was aware that she still wore her mother's wedding-ring.

Pushing her third finger with her thumb she managed to loosen it.

Just at that moment the men came to a stop. She guessed they were above the rocks that led into the sea.

Although there was still very little sound she could hear the lap of the waves. She guessed there must be a boat waiting.

She pushed the ring until it slipped from her finger.

Another moment and it would have been too late. The men moved forward and now she knew they were standing on the rocks. They passed her to two other men who were standing lower down.

Then she was handed over to two men who were in the boat.

She could feel it rocking beneath them and they put her down in it.

The men involved in her kidnap climbed in and started to row.

The sea was calm as they moved swiftly and without speaking.

"I am lost .. I am lost!" Norina thought. "They will throw .. me into the .. sea and when I am .. washed up on the .. shore I will be .. dead!"

She felt her whole body tense with fear as she waited for the moment when the men lifted her up. Perhaps they would remove the ropes before they pushed her into the water.

But the oarsmen rowed on and on. Suddenly there was the sound of the bow of the boat being embedded in sand.

She heard two men spring ashore and start to pull the boat further from the water.

When they had done so they were lifting Norina again.

Then she knew she was not going to die – at any rate – not by being drowned.

At the same time, she had no idea where she had been taken, and she could only cry in her heart:

"Save me .. save me!"

She was praying to God, but it was a plea that also went out to the *Marquis*.

How would he know, how could he guess that she had been carried away in this frightening manner?

Where would he begin to look for her?

"Help me .. oh .. help me!" she cried.

Then she thought that perhaps because she loved him he would even if he was asleep, hear her voice calling him.

She was picked up again.

Then one man spoke in French saying to the other:

"We've done that job well! No one heard us, and Father Jacques'll be pleased!"

"That he will," another replied, "and if this one's anything like the last, we'll all get a good 'Rake-off'!"

"Which is no more than we deserve!" the other man said.

Father Jacques!

That must be the Monk about whom Dawes had warned her against.

How could she have been so stupid? With the telegram coming so late she should have left the Villa to-night and not waited!

She should not have listened to the *Marquis's* idea that they should join the yacht to-morrow.

"Dawes warned . . me! He . . warned me!" Norina thought miserably, "only I was too . . foolish to . . understand!"

Then she was praying again. Sending up a cry that came from the very depths of her being to the *Marquis*.

"Save me . . I love you! No one else will . . hear me save . . me! Save me!"

It came to her mind as she prayed and cried that she should have let him kiss her once as he had intended.

Then she would have something to remember as she died.

Chapter Seven

"Bring me a brandy and soda!" Lord Sedgewyn said as he finished his bath.

When Dawes had one waiting for him he said:

"I am tired, Dawes."

"Yer're doin' too much, M'Lord!" Dawes replied.

"I know that," Lord Sedgewyn answered, "but I am also worried about Miss Norina. I wonder where she can be?"

Dawes did not answer.

He only helped his Master into his evening-coat.

He was thinking as he did so that His Lordship was much thinner and more lined than he had been even a few weeks ago.

Lord Sedgewyn finished his brandy and walked towards the door.

"Do not wait up for me, Dawes," he said. "I do not expect to be back until the early hours."

Dawes watched him as he walked down the passage and thought to himself:

"She's killin' 'im, that's wot she's doin' with 'er parties and suchlike!"

He drew in his breath.

An idea had come to him and he knew it was something he had to do.

He tidied the bed-room and waiting until he knew Lord and Lady Sedgewyn would have left the house.

Then he walked down the corridor.

As he did so Miss Jones, Her Ladyship's maid, came out of the bed-room almost bumping into Dawes in her hurry.

"Yer're in a rush!" Dawes said accusingly.

"I know," Jones replied, "I'm goin' out, an' it's about time! Toodle-oo!"

She ran down the corridor as she spoke and Dawes watched her until she was out of sight.

Then he went into Lady Sedgewyn's bed-room.

He locked the door behind him. He started to look for the key of the cabinet which was attached to the wall over her wash-hand-stand.

During the years he had been in service Dawes had grown used to finding keys of safes, of despatch-boxes, of jewellery-cases and a number of other things.

He located the key he wanted under the lining-paper in the centre drawer of the dressing-table.

Going to the small cupboard over the wash-stand he found what he sought. It was behind some bottles, hair-tonics and throat-sprays.

It was a very small bottle, dark and rather sinister-looking.

Dawes was certain it was what he was seeking.

He pulled out the cork and sniffed it, and knew he was not mistaken.

Then he walked to the side of the bed where he knew Jones would have left Her Ladyship's *tisane*. She drank it every night to make her sleep.

It was a mixture of honey and herbs besides, Dawes suspected, a little luminal if she had been very late.

He poured into it a teaspoonful of the poison.

He was sure that was all that would be required and he put the bottle back in the cupboard. He locked it and replaced the key from where he had taken it.

He walked down the corridor to have his supper.

He was thinking he had not only saved his Master to whom he was deeply devoted, but also Miss Norina.

Norina felt herself deposited roughly on what she thought was a bed.

Then the heavy material over her head was removed and for a moment she thought she had gone blind.

Then she realised the room into which she had been taken was in darkness.

She could not even see the men who were removing the ropes that were wound round her body and the ones that tied her ankles together.

She could only feel their hands touching her. She was too frightened even to breathe.

One of them pushed her head sideways and undid the gag which was knotted at the back.

It had hurt her mouth and her throat was dry. Although she wanted to scream, no sound would come.

Then a rough voice said in French:

"*Voila!* You stay here quietly or we'll gag you up again. The Prior'll speak to you in the morning."

There was the sound of their footsteps walking on a bare floor towards the door.

Then as it shut behind them the key turned in the lock.

Norina was unable to move.

She could only lie stiff and terrified thinking for the moment, at any rate, they had not killed her.

She was startled by a voice saying in English:

"Who are you? Do you speak English – or – *parlez vous le francais?*"

In a voice that did not sound like her own Norina replied:

"I . . I am English."

"Oh, good! Now I can talk to someone! But, why did you come here?"

"I . . I have been . . kidnapped."

"That is what they did to me."

"Where are we?" Norina asked. "Please . . tell me where we are."

"We are in the Convent of St. Francis which is on a small island off the mainland and I believe once the Monks who lived here were good and holy men, but now they are evil and wicked!"

"I . . I think they are . . going to . . kill me!" Norina said and now there was a break in her voice.

"They will do that later," the English girl answered.

"They . . will? H . . how do you . . know?"

The girl lowered her voice as if she was afraid she might be overheard.

"Every girl who comes here or is kidnapped is rich and they make us sign documents handing over everything we possess to God and the Convent, which is really them!"

Norina made a little murmur.

Now she understood why Dawes had warned her against the

335

Monk. It was her Stepmother who had arranged for her to be brought here.

When they had killed her, her money would be Violet's.

"I suppose you are rich," the girl said.

"I have . . some money," Norina admitted, "but my Stepmother . . wants it . . all so I cannot quite . . understand what will happen if I make it . . over to . . the Monks."

"I expect she will give them half, or something like that," the girl said. "I know that is what will happen where I am concerned."

"You have . . signed away your . . money?" Norina asked.

"They made me sign the papers, as they will make you."

"How will they do that?"

There was silence before the girl said:

"You will learn that tomorrow from the Prior, but I do not want to frighten you."

"I . . I would . . rather . . know what to . . expect," Norina said.

"They ask you to sign the documents and if you refuse they say you must do penance for your sins and they flog you!"

Norina gave a little cry.

"I do . . not . . believe . . it!"

"That is what they did to Imogen who was another English girl who was brought here. When finally she gave in and signed the papers, the next day she was drowned!"

Norina bit her lip so as not to scream.

She was afraid that if she did so the men who had warned her not to make a noise would come back.

Now she could see the whole plot quite clearly. She knew that, unless by some Miracle the *Marquis* could save her, she too would be drowned.

"How can they get away with this?" she asked when she could speak. "Surely somebody will be anxious about the disappearance of these girls?"

"If they are they obviously do not complain," the girl answered, "and my Mother's lover who has arranged that I shall die will certainly celebrate my death by drinking more than he usually does!"

She spoke bitterly, but somehow calmly, which was more upsetting than if she had cried.

"Surely we can do something?" Norina cried. "I do not . . want to . . d . . die."

"Nor do I," the girl who was talking to her said. "But the man who has arranged for me to be murdered is giving my Mother drugs and, when the money has been shared out by the Monks, I am quite sure he will kill her too."

Norina felt she could hardly believe what she was hearing.

Lying in the darkness it was like living in some terrible nightmare from which she could not wake up.

"What is your name?" the girl beside her asked.

"Norina. What is . . yours?"

"Claire, and my father, when he was alive, was Sir Richard Bredon. He was such a kind and wonderful man."

"You can only . . pray that your father will . . help you now," Norina said, "as I am . . praying to my . . mother."

"Do you really think our prayers will be heard in a place that has been desecrated by thieves and murderers?"

Norina did not answer.

She was praying frantically . . praying that she would not scream and draw attention to herself. Praying that she might yet be . . saved.

But only God would know how that was possible.

Claire did not speak to her any more and Norina knew she had gone to sleep.

She herself dozed a little before she was awakened by the light showing through the rough curtains over a window.

Her first thought was that it might be a way of escape.

She jumped up to run to it, but when she looked out she knew why it was not barred as she might have expected.

There was a sheer drop down into the sea.

The waves were moving gently against the rocks on which the Convent had been built.

Only the most powerful swimmer, she thought, would be brave enough to dive into the sea not knowing how deep it it was.

As she stood looking at the mist which hung over the sea as the sun rose a voice behind her said:

"There is no escape that way."

She turned and saw that Claire was sitting up in the bed next to hers.

Now she could see that the only furniture in the room were two iron bedsteads. The walls were of ancient stone without any covering.

Claire was a pretty girl with dark brown hair falling over her shoulders, small features, and long-fingered hands which she held out now to Norina.

"You are lovely!" she exclaimed. "Just as I thought you would be, and I am so glad you are here. It has been frightening with no one to talk to."

Norina went back to sit on her bed.

"Are there any other girls here?" she asked.

"Oh, yes," Claire answered. "There are nearly a dozen. Some of them are older than us, but we are the only ones who are English now that Imogen has gone."

"Are they all rich?"

"I suppose so," Claire said, "but I speak only a little French. There are some who talk Spanish and others who are Italian."

"And you really think the Monks intend to . . drown them all?"

"They may have other ways of disposing of them," Claire replied, "but they certainly drowned Imogen and I suppose . . I am next!"

"Do not speak like that," Norina said quickly. "We have to escape or perhaps if we pray hard enough somebody I know will come and . . rescue us."

"The Monks never allow anybody to come onto the island," Claire said, "and I think they have guards at the front entrance to the Convent at night."

Norina's heart sank.

There was the sound of a key being turned in the lock.

As she was wearing only a thin nightgown she got quickly back into bed.

A man dressed as a Monk, but with a hard, ugly, common face looked round the door.

"Here's a robe for you," he said in French to Norina, throwing it down on the floor, "an' you're both to come down to breakfast immediately."

He spoke the words in French in a surly tone. Then he pulled the door to again and they heard his footsteps walking away.

Norina got out of bed.

"Did you understand what he said?" she asked Claire.

"I understood *petit dejeuner*," Claire replied, "and in a moment or two we will hear the bell. If we do not hurry there will be nothing left to eat."

Norina was putting on the robe which she realised was that worn by a postulant Nun.

It was of a very coarse material and, she thought, none too clean.

There was, however, no use complaining and Claire, who had got out of bed, was putting on her clothes.

They consisted of a few underclothes in which she must have arrived at the Convent, then a robe which was similar to the one the Monk had brought Norina.

Somewhere in the distance there was the loud clang of a bell and Claire said:

"Hurry, or the other girls will eat everything!"

She ran off as she spoke. Norina followed her down some twisting, uncarpeted stairs, then along a narrow corridor.

She had a quick glimpse through a window of a statue surrounded by cloisters on each side.

They reached a long low room in which there was a refectory table where a number of young women were hurrying to sit down.

On the table there were three loaves of bread and a small amount of butter.

There was also a large pot of what smelt like cheap and unpleasant coffee and a number of cups without saucers.

The girls and women, who were a miscellaneous collection, were all grabbing at the loaves of bread. They were pulling rather than slicing pieces of them.

They seemed to Norina like animals.

Then she realised they were hungry. Like animals they had to fight for every crumb to assuage their hunger.

She made no effort to compete, but Claire snatched a piece of bread and divided it.

"Here you are," she said. "It will have to last you until luncheon-time. Let us go and get a cup of coffee while we have the chance."

Norina took the bread and as she was about to put it into her mouth she asked in a whisper:

"You do not think it is poisoned?"

"No, no, they will not kill you until you have signed the documents," Claire answered.

It was cold comfort and Norina ate the bread.

Then she managed with Claire's assistance to obtain a quarter of a cup of coffee which was all that was left.

As she was looking at the girls, wondering if she should speak to those who were French, a man dressed as a Monk came to her side.

"Come with me" he said curtly in French. "The Prior wants to see you."

Norina gave a frightened glance at Claire, but she knew she had to obey the order.

The man walked ahead, his heavy shoes clattering on the stone floor.

As she followed him Norina could see that the Convent had once been a fine building and was undoubtedly ancient.

It was now, however, very dilapidated.

Stones had fallen from the walls and the square which was surrounded by cloisters was thick with weeds around a statue of St. Francis.

It was obvious that nothing was being done to preserve the place or even keep it tidy.

The man ahead of her stopped and opened a door.

As Norina walked into the Prior's room she could see that he, at any rate, lived in comfort.

There were deep arm-chairs, a fine writing-desk, pictures on the walls and heavy rich velvet curtains at the windows.

The Prior was waiting for her with his back to a medieval fireplace.

He looked, Norina thought, exactly as she might have expected.

He was a large portly man and what hair he had, which was very little, was grey.

She thought she would have recognised him anywhere as being a criminal.

His eyes were shrewd and his lips were set in a hard line.

She could feel every instinct in her body shrinking from any contact with him.

The man who had brought her there did not speak, but merely withdrew shutting the door behind him.

Norina stood looking at the Prior.

"Good-morning, Norina!" he said, speaking in good English. "Welcome to our Convent! I know you are waiting to discover why you are here."

"I have some idea of that already," Norina replied.

"That makes things easier," the Prior answered. "I have some documents for you to sign on my desk, and I expect you have already been told the penalty for disobeying my orders."

Norina felt a little tremor of terror run through her, but she lifted her head proudly.

"I can hardly believe," she replied, "that as you pretend to be a Man of God you would really do anything so appalling, so unmerciful and wicked!"

The Prior laughed, and it was a very unpleasant sound.

"As you knew before you ran away, your Stepmother requires your money, and of course this Convent is a very expensive place to keep up."

Norina did not answer and he said in a jeering tone:

"Come along, my dear, give up your worldly goods to God, and you will, of course, get your reward in Heaven!"

He looked towards the desk as he spoke. Norina saw on it were some official-looking papers.

She knew he would force her to sign them.

If she did so, she reasoned, then undoubtedly she would die as quickly as it could be arranged. Then he would not have the expense of keeping her.

Somehow she knew she had to play for time.

Then, almost as if a voice, and perhaps it was her Mother's, prompted her, she gave a little groan and collapsed slowly onto the floor.

Her eyes were closed and she lay there motionless.

The Prior swore and they were French words that Norina had never heard before, but she knew they were lewd.

Then he went to the door and shouted:

"*Henri! Gustave!*"

Two men came running into the room.

"She has collapsed or fainted," the Prior said in a tone of disgust.

"Shall we slap her back into consciousness?" one of them asked.

"No, take her away," the Prior said. "Put her in her room and give her no food. She will be amenable enough when she is hungry!"

The two men lifted Norina from the floor and she forced herself to be completely limp.

She kept her eyes closed and hardly breathed as they carried her back the way she had come, along the passages and up the staircase which led to the room she had slept in last night.

They threw her down on the bed rather roughly. Yet she managed not to make a sound.

She merely lay where she had been thrown, one arm hanging over the side of the bed.

"We'd better lock her in," one of the men said. "That's what the Prior said."

"What about the other English girl?"

"Oh, she'll have to sleep somewhere else. There's plenty of beds available for them as can pay for them!"

The other man laughed as they went out of the room and locked the door.

Norina waited until she was quite certain they had gone. Then she went to the window.

If only there was someone to whom she could signal!

If she could wave, they might realise she needed help.

But there was only the Madonna blue of the sea, which, now that the sun had risen, reflected the sky overhead.

Once again she knew there was nothing she could do but pray.

The day passed very slowly.

As it grew dark and no one came near her Norina wished that Claire was with her. At least she would have somebody to talk to. She was also growing hungry.

"I suppose I shall have to sign the papers," she thought desperately.

Darkness came and the stars filled the sky. There was a moon, not full but a half-moon which turned the sea to a silver enchantment.

Norina lay on her bed.

She had taken off her robe because she felt it was unclean. Fortunately it was not a cold night, and there was no wind.

She was praying, at the same time thinking of the *Marquis* and how much she loved him.

"He will never .. know when I am .. dead that I have .. given him my .. heart," she thought.

She was so carried away by her thoughts that she did not at first hear a faint sound at the door.

It was now too dark to see it clearly but she thought it opened. She was instantly afraid, but in a different way from before.

Supposing one of those rough men had come not to kill her, but for a very different reason?

Because she was so frightened she could only lie still. She was filled with a sudden terror because somebody was in the room, and coming slowly towards her.

Their feet made no sound, but she knew they were there.

They reached the bed. Then when she would have opened her mouth to scream her lips were captive and two strong arms enfolded her.

She felt a sudden rapture streak through her whole body.

It was the sensation she had felt when he touched her before and she knew who it was.

Then the *Marquis* said very, very softly so that she could hardly hear:

"Do not make a sound. You have to be very brave."

She wanted to tell him she loved him. Instead she could only put out her hands to touch him and make sure he was really there.

He lifted her off the bed and to her astonishment took her to the window.

She wanted to tell him there was no possible escape that way.

Then she realised he was putting a rope round her which in some strange way was attached to him.

Yet she could only think he was beside her. Nothing else in the world mattered.

The rope had come not from inside the room but through the window. Before she could wonder how, the *Marquis* said:

"Now you have to be brave. Shut your eyes and hold onto me. I promise you you will not be hurt."

She looked up at him and for the first time saw in the faint light of the moon that his eyes were unbandaged.

"You . . can . . see!" she whispered.

He put his fingers on her lips and she felt ashamed that she had spoken.

Then he put one leg out of the window. Because she was tied to him she was obliged to do the same.

"Shut your eyes," he whispered again.

She felt a pull on the ropes he had attached to her as they were lifted over the sill.

She knew a moment's panic as she realised they were swinging in air. At the same time being lowered into the sea below.

Then the *Marquis's* arms enfolded her and she could hide her face against his shoulder. She told herself if she died now she would die with him.

They were lowered slowly, clear of the rocks. At last two men were holding first their feet, then their bodies, and guiding them into a boat.

It was quite large and the men removed the rope by which they had descended.

Then the boat was moving away. Norina found herself sitting in the stern with the *Marquis's* arms round her.

He did not speak but they were rowed very swiftly out to sea.

It was a little later that Norina saw the *Marquis's* yacht looming up above them.

She was helped aboard and as the *Marquis* joined her he took her through a door and inside what she guessed was the Saloon.

There were no lights anywhere. Norina knew it was because every-thing had been done in secret so that they would not be seen.

Then, as the Saloon door closed behind them, she was in the *Marquis's* arms.

"You have . . saved . . me!" she whispered, "you have . . saved me . . how . . can you have . . done so? I . . thought . . I was . . going to . . d . . die."

It was then because she could not help herself that she burst into tears.

The *Marquis* picked her up in his arms and sat down on a sofa. He held her across his knees as if she was a child.

"It is all right, my darling," he said gently, "you are safe and this shall never happen to you again."

It was the way he spoke as much as the endearment which made Norina forget her tears. She raised her face to his.

"H . . how you . . could have . . come . . like an Archangel from . . Heaven . . and taken me . . away from that . . e . . evil place?"

Her words were almost incoherent.

At the same time, she was looking up at him as if he was in fact not human, but a Messenger from God.

"I had to save you," the *Marquis* answered, "not only because I could not let you die, but because you are too precious to lose and I love you!"

As he finished speaking his lips found hers.

He kissed her until she thought she must in fact have died and reached Heaven.

His love swept over her like a wave of the sea. Yet there were stars in her breast and the light of the moon or perhaps it was the Light of God which dazzled her eyes.

The *Marquis* kissed her until they were both breathless.

Then she said in a little voice he could hardly hear:

"I .. love you .. but I never .. thought .. you would .. love me!"

"I have loved you for a very long time" the *Marquis* replied "but I wanted to see you with my eyes as well as with my heart before I told you so."

"And now .. you have .. saved me!"

Norina realised that as they had been talking, the engines had started up and the yacht was moving.

"You have .. saved me!" she said again "but there is another .. English girl .. there and a lot of .. others. How can we .. save them?"

"It is all arranged" the *Marquis* replied. "The Police are moving in at dawn and three gendarmes are already on the roof. They let us down. Because I would not have you involved in all that cruelty and wickedness I persuaded them to let me get you away so that you will not have to appear at the Inquiry."

"H .. how .. can you .. have been so .. clever?" Norina asked.

"I was thinking about you, my darling," the *Marquis* said, "and also of course of – myself. Do not forget that we are both in hiding."

She put her hand to his face.

"Your bandage has .. gone and you are .. just as I thought .. very, very .. handsome!"

"I have to wear glasses in the daytime," the *Marquis* replied, "but not for very much longer."

His lips were very near to hers as he said:

"I would be prepared to become completely blind rather than allow anyone to rescue you except myself!"

His arms tightened.

"I was so desperately afraid there would be a mistake at the last moment, or that I would not be in time."

"H .. how .. did you .. know .. how did you .. guess where I had gone?"

345

"I found your ring," the *Marquis* replied. "It was clever of you, my precious, to leave it for me and I also knew what had been in your telegram."

"And you .. thought the Monk from .. whom I was warned to hide .. must have come from the .. island?"

"The Police have been suspicious for some time of the men who have taken over the ruined Convent, but, as no one had made any complaint, there was nothing they could do."

"And you gave them the excuse they needed to enter it."

"*You* did that," the *Marquis* replied, "but I will not have you having to face all that unpleasantness, so we are going away, my darling, on a very long honeymoon."

Norina gave a little cry.

"How can .. you think of .. anything so .. wonderful? But .. please .. are .. you quite .. quite certain that you .. want to m .. marry me?"

"I am certain!" he said, "because I can fulfil what you demanded."

His lips moved against the softness of her cheek as he said:

"I love you with my mind, my heart and my soul – and also, my precious, with my body, and of course, my 'Inner Eye'."

"That is .. how I .. love you," Norina whispered.

The *Marquis* did not answer.

He was kissing her again. Kissing her until she felt little flames rising within her to answer the fire on his lips.

Then she was aware, a little belatedly, that she was wearing only her nightgown.

She made a little murmur and hid her face against his neck.

Her heart was beating tumultuously and she could feel his doing the same.

"You must go to bed," the *Marquis* said, "and now that we are away from the island we can put on the lights, but I feel it will make you shy to be seen as you are now."

Norina slipped off his knees. He put his arm round her to help her to the door and down the companionway.

He took her to the end of the passage and opened a door of what she was sure was the Master cabin. It was so large it filled the whole of the bow.

"I must .. not take .. this cabin .. it is yours," Norina said quickly.

"To-morrow night it will be *ours*," the *Marquis* answered. "We

346

are being married, my darling, on French soil and because I am a Frenchman there will be no difficulties. After that we can go anywhere in the world you like."

"Anywhere . . will be . . Heaven if I am . . with you," Norina answered.

He put his arms around her. Then, instead of kissing her passionately as she expected he was going to do, his lips were very gentle.

"I love and adore you," he said, "but I know, my sweet, that you are very innocent, and I have no wish to shock you."

He lifted her into the big bed and pulled the covers over her.

Norina caught hold of his hand.

"Promise me that . . I am not . . dreaming," she pleaded, "and I will . . wake up to find I am . . still a . . prisoner."

"You are my prisoner now," the *Marquis* answered, "mine – from now until eternity – and I will never, and this is a vow, my Love, lose you or let you go."

"That is . . what I . . want to . . be," Norina said, "but . . will you . . promise me . . something?"

"What is it?"

He sat down on the edge of the bed and bent towards her.

"I am so afraid . . that I will . . bore you," she murmured, "like . . those other . . ladies who . . write to you."

The *Marquis* would have spoken, but she went on:

"Will you . . teach me how to . . keep you happy and content so . . that I do not . . lose you?"

He could hardly hear the words, but he smiled.

"You have already told me how to do that," he answered.

She looked up at him in surprise.

"Have you forgotten," he asked, "my Château in the country and how you said I ought to settle down and produce a large family?"

Norina made a little murmur. His arms were round her as once again his lips were very near to hers.

"I have a great deal to teach you," he said, "and it will be the most exciting thing I have ever done in my whole life! You are mine, my lovely Norina, as I am yours, and nothing will ever divide us."

He gave a deep sigh before he said:

"I suppose all my life I have been searching for love – the real love that you understand – and now, my precious, we have both found it, and this is where the real adventure of life begins – our life together!"

Then his lips were on hers and Norina knew that he was right.

They had found the only thing that mattered, what all men sought, fought and died to find.

It was the love of the mind, the heart and the soul, when two bodies were joined together as one.

They had passed through dangers, wickedness and evil yet by the mercy of God they had survived.

"I love you, *Mon Dieu*, how much I love you," the *Marquis* exclaimed.

And then there was only LOVE and more LOVE going on to Eternity.